Praise for Leslie Meier and her Lucy Stone Mysteries!

Silver Anniversary Murder

"The frenzied pace of the city, effectively contrasted with the more tranquil atmosphere of a small town; the reappearance of familiar characters; and numerous plot twists all contribute to the appeal of this satisfying entry in a long-running series."

—*Booklist*

Turkey Trot Murder

"Timely . . . Meier's focus on racism gives this cozy a serious edge rare for this subgenre."

—*Publishers Weekly*

British Manor Murder

"Counts, countesses, and corpses highlight Lucy Stone's trip across the pond . . . A peek into British country life provides a nice break."

—*Kirkus Reviews*

Candy Corn Murder

"Meier continues to exploit the charm factor in her small-town setting, while keeping the murder plots as realistic as possible in such a cozy world."

—*Booklist*

French Pastry Murder

"A delight from start to finish."

—*Suspense Magazine*

Christmas Carol Murder

"Longtime Lucy Stone series readers will be happy to catch up on life in Tinker's Cover in this cozy Christmas mystery."

—*Library Journal*

Easter Bunny Murder

"A fun and engaging read. It is quick and light and has enough interesting twists and turns to keep you turning the pages. If you like this type of mystery and this is your first meeting with Lucy Stone, it will probably not be your last."

—*The Barnstable Patriot*

Books by Leslie Meier

MISTLETOE MURDER
TIPPY TOE MURDER
TRICK OR TREAT MURDER
BACK TO SCHOOL MURDER
VALENTINE MURDER
CHRISTMAS COOKIE MURDER
TURKEY DAY MURDER
WEDDING DAY MURDER
BIRTHDAY PARTY MURDER
FATHER'S DAY MURDER
STAR SPANGLED MURDER
NEW YEAR'S EVE MURDER
BAKE SALE MURDER
CANDY CANE MURDER
ST. PATRICK'S DAY MURDER
MOTHER'S DAY MURDER
WICKED WITCH MURDER
GINGERBREAD COOKIE MURDER
ENGLISH TEA MURDER
CHOCOLATE COVERED MURDER
EASTER BUNNY MURDER
CHRISTMAS CAROL MURDER
FRENCH PASTRY MURDER
CANDY CORN MURDER
BRITISH MANOR MURDER
EGGNOG MURDER
TURKEY TROT MURDER
SILVER ANNIVERSARY MURDER
YULE LOG MURDER
HAUNTED HOUSE MURDER
INVITATION ONLY MURDER

Published by Kensington Publishing Corporation

BRITISH MURDER

LESLIE MEIER

KENSINGTON BOOKS
www.kensingtonbooks.com

To the extent that the image or images on the cover of this book depict a person or persons, such person or persons are merely models, and are not intended to portray any character or characters featured in the book.

This book is a work of fiction. Names, characters, places, and incidents either are products of the author's imagination or are used fictitiously. Any resemblance to actual persons, living or dead, events, or locales is entirely coincidental.

KENSINGTON BOOKS are published by

Kensington Publishing Corp.
119 West 40th Street
New York, NY 10018

All Kensington titles, imprints, and distributed lines are available at special quantity discounts for bulk purchases for sales promotion, premiums, fund-raising, educational, or institutional use.

Special book excerpts or customized printings can also be created to fit specific needs. For details, write or phone the office of the Kensington Sales Manager: Kensington Publishing Corp., 119 West 40th Street, New York, NY 10018. Attn. Sales Department. Phone: 1-800-221-2647.

ISBN-13: 978-1-4967-2628-5 (ebook)
ISBN-10: 1-4967-2628-6 (ebook)

ISBN-13: 978-1-4967-2627-8
ISBN-10: 1-4967-2627-8
First Kensington Trade Paperback Edition: March 2020

10 9 8 7 6 5 4 3 2 1

Printed in the United States of America

Contents

English Tea Murder
1

British Manor Murder
217

ENGLISH TEA MURDER

Chapter One

Something was wrong. Very wrong.

Lucy Stone tapped the miniature TV screen fastened to the back of the seat in front of her, but it didn't even flicker. The tiny little image of an airplane that represented British Airways Flight 214 was still hugging the coast of the United States, and more than five hours of flight time remained before they would cross the blue patch representing the Atlantic Ocean to land on the dot symbolizing London, or more accurately Heathrow Airport.

Lucy nudged her seatmate, Sue Finch, who was flipping through a copy of British *Vogue* that she'd snagged while passing through the roomy first-class cabin, which was dotted with luxurious armchairs complete with footrests and privacy screens—a far cry from the cramped economy cabin where they were sitting.

"What is it, Lucy?"

"We're going to die."

"I don't think so." Sue turned the page and pointed to a photo with her perfectly polished fingernail. "What do you think of Katie Holmes's new haircut?"

"We're six miles up in the air and the temperature outside is MINUS one hundred and fifty degrees and all you can think about is Katie Holmes's haircut?"

Sue leaned over and peered at Lucy's screen. "Thirty-seven thousand feet, honey. That's not six miles."

"Yes, it is! Do the math! A mile is about five thousand feet."

Sue was now studying a photo of Victoria Beckham in mini-shorts. "Her legs are like sticks."

Lucy was busy recalling her multiplication tables. "Okay, I was wrong and you're right. SEVEN miles. That's absolutely crazy. And who even knew the thermometer goes down to one hundred and fifty degrees below zero. We live in Maine and the coldest it ever gets in Tinker's Cove is minus twenty or so." Lucy frowned. "And that's pretty darn cold."

"I don't know what you're so upset about. The temperature only goes up to ninety on a hot summer day, but the oven can go up to four hundred and fifty. I guess it's the same with cold."

"These planes are not as sturdy as you think," muttered Lucy darkly. "Remember the one that landed in the Hudson River? It was brought down by a *goose*."

"Well we're in luck, then, because it's way too cold up here for any geese." Sue indicated a photo of a top hat decorated with the Union Jack. "Look at this. There's a show of hats at the Victoria and Albert Museum. Maybe we can go."

"If we survive the flight."

"Oh, stop fussing." Sue tucked a wisp of glossy black hair behind her ear. "Flying is safer than driving. You might as well relax and enjoy the flight. That tinkling sound means the drinks trolley is coming."

Lucy might not be an experienced traveler, but she had done her homework. "You're not supposed to drink alcohol when you fly. It causes dehydration."

"Don't be ridiculous. If we're seven miles above the earth in freezing weather, we should drink every drop they'll give us."

Lucy was struggling to reach her carry-on bag, which she'd stowed beneath the seat in front of her. "How much do drinks cost?"

"They're included. And you'll get a nice dinner and breakfast, too."

Lucy fluffed her short mop of curls, which had gotten mussed when she reached for her wallet. "I had to pay for a Coke when Bill and I flew down to Florida for his uncle's funeral."

"That's on domestic flights. They take good care of you on these transatlantic flights. So relax. Watch a movie. This is supposed to be a vacation."

Sue was right, reflected Lucy as she pumped her heels up and down to avoid blood clots in her legs. This was her first trip out of the country, except for a few vacations in Canada, and she'd been looking forward to it for months. She'd always wanted to go to Europe, and now she finally had the chance. A few rows farther down the aisle, she could see her friend Pam Stillings's elbow, recognizable from the colorful sleeve of her tie-dyed shirt. It was due to Pam's job teaching yoga at Winchester College's night school that Lucy and Sue, as well as their friend Rachel Goodman, had learned about the trip. "Only two thousand dollars, and that includes airfare and hotel, admissions, everything except lunch and dinner, for nine whole days," Pam had exclaimed at one of their regular Thursday morning breakfasts at Jake's Donut Shack. "We should all go. This professor, George Temple—he's in my yoga class—is organizing the whole thing. All we have to do is sign up."

"Our kids are grown, and our husbands can manage by themselves for a week," said Sue. "Let's do it."

"I don't know if Ted will let me go for such a long time," said Lucy, who worked as a part-time reporter for the Tinker's Cove *Pennysaver.* Ted Stillings was the owner, publisher, editor, and chief reporter. He was also Pam's husband.

"I'll take care of Ted," promised Pam.

Rachel Goodman smiled sadly, running her finger around the thick rim of her white coffee mug; her big eyes were as dark as the black coffee. "I'd love to go, but I can't leave Miss T for a whole week." Rachel provided home care for the little town's oldest resident, Julia Ward Howe Tilley, and was very fond of her.

"Molly could fill in for you," said Lucy, referring to her daughter-in-law. "Patrick's almost a year old now. I think she'd enjoy getting out of the house, and I know Miss Tilley would enjoy seeing Patrick."

"Then I guess we're agreed," crowed Pam. "We have to put

down a deposit of two hundred and fifty dollars to hold our places, so give me your checks as soon as you can."

It had seemed like a great idea at the time, but Lucy had no sooner written the check than she began to feel guilty. For one thing, unlike her friends, she wasn't an empty nester. Toby, the oldest, was married and settled on nearby Prudence Path with Molly and baby Patrick, and Elizabeth, next in line, was a senior at Chamberlain College in Boston. Sara, however, a high school sophomore, and Zoe, in middle school, were still at home. Bill, her restoration carpenter husband, would have his hands full managing his work and keeping an eye on the two girls. Even worse, she realized, she'd miss Patrick's first birthday on March 17.

"Don't be silly," Bill had argued when she voiced her concerns about leaving home for more than a week. "You've always wanted to go to England, and this is your chance—and you can find a terrific present for Patrick in London."

So Lucy had studied the itinerary and read the guidebooks and packed and repacked her suitcase several times. She'd even gone to the bank and changed five hundred American dollars into three hundred and fifty British pounds, which hadn't seemed like a very good deal at all.

"On the contrary," the bank manager had informed her. "The pound was trading at two dollars just a few months ago. You would have gotten only two hundred and fifty pounds if you bought back then."

"I hadn't realized," said Lucy, tucking the bills with Queen Elizabeth's face on them into her wallet.

"Have a good trip," said the manager, giving her a big smile.

Remembering the transaction, Lucy patted the little bulge her money belt made under her jeans, where she'd stowed her foreign money, emergency credit card, and a photocopy of her passport, just as the guidebook had advised. She checked the progress of the drinks trolley, which was making its slow way down the aisle, and glanced at George Temple, seated across the aisle from her. Temple, the tour leader, had suffered an asthma attack at the airport, and she hoped he was feeling better.

In contrast to the wheezing and coughing he'd exhibited in Terminal E at Logan, Temple now seemed quiet and withdrawn. He was sitting in an odd posture, hunched forward and completely ignoring his seatmates, two Winchester students who were also along on the tour. Pam had pointed them out to Lucy while they waited at the gate. The one next to Temple—a girl with spiky black hair; numerous piercings in her nose, lips, and ears; and a tattoo of a chain around her neck—was Autumn Mackie. "A wild child, a bit of a legend on campus," Pam had said. "But I can't figure out what she's doing with Jennifer Fain. She not only looks like an angel but she also acts like one." Jennifer, who was seated by the window, had long blond hair and was wearing a loose, pink-flowered top that looked almost like a child's dress over her skinny gray jeans. It gave her a sweet, innocent air that contrasted sharply with Autumn's black Goth outfit.

The two made an odd pair, whispering together like the best of friends, but Temple wasn't noticing. He was sitting rigidly, leaning forward with his hands on his thighs, his shoulders rising and falling with each labored breath.

Lucy reached her hand across the aisle and tapped his arm. "Are you all right?"

"Asthma," he said, producing an inhaler. "This should help."

Lucy watched as he placed the inhaler between his lips and took a puff, sucking in the aerosol medication with a short, harsh gulp. When he exhaled, it took a long time and was accompanied by a wheezing sound that caught the attention of the two girls, who giggled. Temple ignored them and took another puff of medicine, and this time it seemed to go better, with less wheezing.

Reassured that he was gaining control of the attack, Lucy pulled the in-flight magazine out of the seat pocket and turned to the entertainment menu, choosing a film she hadn't seen: *Doubt*. The drinks trolley was closer now, and Jennifer was rummaging in her backpack, eventually producing a plastic ziplock bag that appeared to contain trail mix. She ripped it open and tossed it to Autumn, who caught it and began stirring the contents with her fingers, finally producing a raisin, which she popped into her mouth.

Temple's breathing seemed to worsen, but Lucy's view was blocked by a flight attendant, who asked if she'd like something to drink.

"White wine?" Lucy inquired.

"Of course. And would you like another, for your meal?"

Lucy looked at Sue, who nodded sharply.

"Thank you," said Lucy as two little wine bottles were placed on her tray table, along with a plastic glass and a tiny packet of pretzels. Sue opted for the same, but when the trolley moved on, Lucy saw that the girls had refused the refreshments and were sharing the bag of trail mix, passing it back and forth between them. Temple had accepted a glass of water, which was sitting on his tray, and his condition seemed to have improved. He was resting quietly now, leaning back in his seat, and the wheezing had stopped. Lucy felt she could relax, too, and poured herself a glass of white wine. On the tiny screen, Meryl Streep, costumed in the black bonnet and long-skirted habit of a nun in the 1960s, was terrorizing a schoolyard full of boisterous children. Lucy took a sip of wine, then another, and was soon absorbed in the movie.

Meryl Streep wasn't much liking Philip Seymour Hoffman—that was clear from her pursed lips and disapproving expression—when Lucy felt a tap on her upper arm. She turned toward George Temple and was shocked by his appearance. His face was grayish, his lips blue, and he was trying to tell her something but couldn't get the words out.

"Stay calm," she told him, pushing the button with the graphic of a flight attendant. "I'm ringing for help."

The two girls, she saw, were completely oblivious to his condition, listening to their iPods with earbuds and bouncing along to the music.

Temple nodded slowly and again raised his inhaler to his mouth, but before he could take a puff, Autumn Mackie gave an extra big bounce and flung out her hands, knocking the inhaler into the untouched glass of water. Horrified, Lucy watched as Temple turned slowly toward her and passed out.

The flight attendant, not at all the glamorous stereotype but a sturdy, middle-aged woman with thick English legs and a blouse that billowed out of her waistband, took one look and hurried back to the compartment containing medical supplies. As she returned with a small oxygen tank and mask, an announcement came over the PA system.

"We have a medical emergency. If there is a doctor or nurse aboard, please make yourself known to a crew member."

"Gramps!" It was Jennifer, her face pale, rising up by pulling against the back of the seat in front of her. "My grandfather is a doctor!"

An older gentleman, gray-haired in a tweed jacket and bow tie, was already hurrying down the aisle, a small leather case in his hand. He quickly examined Temple, checking his pupils and his pulse. "Anaphylactic shock," he told the flight attendant.

"I'll get the EpiPen." She whirled around, ready to dash down the aisle.

"I have one," said the doctor, producing a small plastic cylinder. Opening it, he extracted a syringe and snapped the cap off, revealing a short needle that he jabbed into Temple's thigh, right through his trousers. He then massaged the site of the injection, watching for signs of recovery.

Lucy couldn't see Temple—her view was blocked by the doctor and the flight attendant—but she could hear sobbing from one of the girls. The plane was quiet, everyone aware that something serious was happening. The drinks trolley was stalled, its return to the galley blocked by the caregivers in the aisle.

"A second shot?" whispered the flight attendant.

There was movement as the doctor felt Temple's pulse, then closed his eyelids. "I'm afraid it's too late."

The attendant quickly crossed herself, then asked Autumn for her blanket.

Autumn drew her dark brows together and scowled. "Blanket? The one that was on my seat?"

"Right. I'll get you another, but I need to cover this gentleman."

"Jennifer, give her your blanket," said the doctor.

"Okay." Jennifer obediently handed over the neatly folded square of blue acrylic, wrapped in plastic, and watched as the flight attendant ripped it open and carefully spread it over Temple's body.

"What are you doing?" Autumn's face was hard, her tone challenging. "You can't leave him here!"

"I'm afraid we have no alternative." A male flight attendant had joined the little group. "The plane is full. There are no empty seats."

"So you're just going to leave him here?" Jennifer had turned paler than ever. The black mascara she was wearing stood out like two rows of exclamation points, dramatizing her huge blue eyes.

Lucy turned and looked at Sue, grabbing her hand. They clung together, stunned by the enormity of the scene they had just witnessed.

"I know this is terribly upsetting and unfortunate, but there's really nothing we can do," said the steward, rubbing his hands together briskly. "So, who'd like another drink before dinner?"

Chapter Two

"Are you crazy?" Autumn Mackie's face had gained some color; red blotches were appearing on her pallid cheeks and tattooed neck. "You can't expect me to sit next to a stinking corpse all the way to London!"

The steward's expression was quite stern. "Miss, please lower your voice."

"I will not lower my voice. This is outrageous! It's probably illegal! There's a health issue here!"

"Once again, I must ask you to lower your voice. I do not wish to have to restrain you, but I am empowered to do so."

The little hoops in Autumn's eyebrows trembled. "Restrain me? For what? What am I doing?"

The steward's expression was impassive. "You are disturbing the other passengers and interfering with the crew's performance of its duty." The scent of cooked food was filling the cabin, and there were sounds from the galley of trolleys being shifted and loaded. Lucy was ashamed of herself but felt quite hungry. It was almost eleven o'clock, hours later than her usual dinnertime.

"I am not the crazy one here," declared Autumn, stabbing at her chest. "This is a dead body. It's unsanitary. I don't want to have anything to do with it. Get it?"

"I understand, miss. This is an unfortunate situation, but we must make the best of it."

"I have a solution," said the doctor before the steward could reply. "I will change seats with the young lady."

"Is that agreeable?" inquired the steward.

"Yes. Anything to get away from this . . . this corpse."

The steward turned to the doctor. "Thank you very much indeed."

"It's nothing, really. I would actually prefer to sit with my granddaughter." He smiled at Jennifer. "I will go and fetch my things."

"All right, miss. If you will just climb over . . ." The steward was holding out his hand to Autumn, offering support so she could clamber over Temple's body.

"Well, move him!" ordered Autumn. "I don't wanna touch him!"

"I'm afraid we must leave him in place for the coroner," said the steward.

At this the two girls exchanged glances; then Autumn quickly scrambled over Temple's still corpse, averting her face as she did so. Jennifer gathered up Autumn's possessions—the iPod, a magazine, a paperback book, the half-empty bag of trail mix—and stuffed them in a backpack, which she passed over. The steward ushered Autumn down the aisle, passing the doctor who was already returning to his granddaughter. He paused in the aisle, extending his hand to Lucy.

"We're going to be neighbors for the duration," he said. "I'm Randall Cope. This is my granddaughter, Jennifer Fain. I recognized you from the airport. You're on the Winchester College tour also, aren't you?"

"Yes, I am." Lucy took his hand, finding it strong and warm and very reassuring. "My name's Lucy Stone. This is my friend Sue Finch."

"Delighted to meet you both. And I am sorry about the, uh, situation."

"You did everything you could," said Lucy.

His expression was a combination of regret and caring, and Lucy understood that he'd faced the same situation many times in his medical career. "Well, yes, but it wasn't enough."

Turning and moving quite easily for a man of his age, he stepped over Temple's body, eased himself into Autumn's vacated seat, and fastened his seat belt. Once settled, he placed his big, comforting hand over Jennifer's tiny white one. She leaned her head against his shoulder, and he reached across his chest with his free hand and smoothed her long, wavy hair.

The motherly flight attendant returned, holding a tray with a number of miniature liquor bottles. "This has been a bit of an upset," she said in a soothing nanny voice. "Would you care for a bit of brandy to soothe your nerves?"

Lucy certainly did, and so did Sue.

"What's going to happen?" Lucy sipped the fiery brandy, feeling its warmth spread through her body. "He was our leader."

Sue had polished off her brandy in a single gulp. "I don't know. I can't think that far ahead. Right now, all I want is something to eat."

Crew members were already working their way down the aisles, distributing dinners, and it wasn't long before their meals were placed in front of them and they tucked into their Tuscan chicken and pasta.

"It's not bad." Lucy stabbed a tiny square of chicken.

"It's horrible, but it beats starving." Sue was polishing off her tiny bowl of salad. "I can't believe I have any appetite at all."

"They say death has that effect." Lucy lowered her voice. "It makes people hungry—and not just for food. Sex, too."

Sue gazed at the blue lump on the other side of the aisle. "Survival instinct, I suppose."

Lucy followed her gaze and saw that while Dr. Cope was eating his dinner, Jennifer had refused her tray and was staring at the blank TV screen in front of her. She remembered how happy the girl had seemed only a short time before, bouncing around to her iPod with Autumn and sharing the trail mix snack. Now, Temple's sudden death had changed everything, and a carefree jaunt had turned tragic.

This was supposed to be the trip of a lifetime, thought Lucy, her first trip abroad, and now it was spoiled. She remembered how excited she'd been when Pam had told them all about the tour and how she'd almost rationalized her way out of going. "It's too expensive; I'll be away too long; I can't leave you all," she'd told Bill. But he had brushed away her objections. "You were an English major in college. You've always wanted to go to England. You should go."

Lucy's friends had backed him up. "You're the mom and grandma. You've been taking care of everybody else for twenty-five years. It's time for you to do something for yourself," Rachel had told her when they had lunch together one day at Miss Tilley's antique Cape-style cottage.

"You don't think it's selfish?"

"They'll be glad to be rid of you," said Miss Tilley with a wave of her blue-veined hand. "That's what I told Rachel. We all need a break from each other once in a while. I'm looking forward to putting real cream in my coffee and eating potato chips." She scowled at Rachel. "My keeper here never lets me have potato chips."

"It's for your own good," said Rachel, placid as ever.

Lucy suddenly felt homesick, thinking of Miss Tilley and her cozy house and her own comfortable old farmhouse on Red Top Road and Bill and the girls and Libby the Labrador and little baby Patrick. She missed them all, she thought, as the flight attendant removed the remains of her meal. She latched the little folding table back in place and leaned back in her seat, letting out a big sigh. It seemed she'd been right: This trip was a big mistake.

She checked the progress of the flight on the little screen, discovering that the tiny plane icon was about a half inch into the blue Atlantic and they had more than three hours of airtime left. The lights were dimmed, and she decided to try and get some sleep, imagining she was back in bed at home, spooning with Bill.

Next thing she knew, the lights were flicked on, the scent of coffee was in the air, and the flight attendants were distributing breakfast packs containing crisp fruit salad and soggy apple pastry.

"Good morning, sunshine," said Sue, looking at her with dark-rimmed eyes.

Lucy yawned. "Didn't you sleep?"

"Not a wink."

"I'm surprised I did." Lucy glanced at the body and the sight depressed her. Dr. Cope was still sound asleep, his head thrown back and his mouth slightly open, and Jennifer was sitting in the same position as before, staring straight ahead and rigid with tension.

Lucy still felt uncomfortably full from dinner, which seemed to have settled like concrete in her tummy, so she only ate a few bits of fruit and sipped her coffee, then made a trip back to the toilet. There she splashed a little lukewarm water on her face and attempted to brush her teeth with the toothbrush and tiny tube of toothpaste provided by British Airways. When she returned to her seat, it seemed that the pace was picking up—the breakfast packs were collected, and the pilot soon announced it was time to prepare for landing. Lucy checked her watch and discovered it was 3:40 a.m. She fastened her seat belt, sniffing the refreshing green tea scent of the moisturizer Sue was applying to her cheeks and hands. The plane gave a shake and a rattle, landing with a big thump, and they were in England.

Once again, the captain's voice came over the PA system. "Welcome to London. It's 7:50 a.m. and the temperature is ten degrees Celsius with clouds and passing showers." He paused. "And now I'm going to turn this over to our head steward, Ron Bitman, who has a special announcement."

"I want to remind you to remain seated with seat belts fastened until the aircraft comes to a complete stop and the fasten-seat-belt light is turned off. And we must ask the following passengers to remain in their seats: Laura Barfield, William Barfield, Randall Cope, Jennifer Fain, Sue Finch . . ."

Lucy's and Sue's eyes met and the voice continued: "Rachel Goodman, Autumn Mackie, Ann Smith, Caroline Smith, Thomas Smith, Pamela Stillings, and Lucy Stone. Thank you."

"It's everyone on the tour," said Sue as the jet taxied to the gate.

"Looks like there's going to be a police investigation," said Lucy, looking past Jennifer through the oval window and glimpsing a cluster of police cars and an ambulance on the ground.

The plane stopped, the fasten-seat-belt light went off with a ding, and people all around them were stretching and getting to their feet and opening the overhead compartments to retrieve bags and coats. The aisles were packed with people, and then suddenly everyone was gone, leaving behind crumpled pillows and blankets and newspapers—and the twelve people whose names had been called. They were all told to please move forward into the first-class cabin.

"I was hoping for an upgrade," quipped Sue. "But I would have appreciated it earlier in the flight."

When they entered the first-class cabin, which was every bit as rumpled and untidy as their own, although much roomier, they found a pair of uniformed police constables with checked caps tucked under their arms blocking the exits, as if the group was composed of dangerous prisoners who must be kept under guard.

"What happened? Why are we being kept on the plane?" asked Rachel as they gathered in a little group.

Pam was looking around. "Where's George? How come they didn't call his name?"

Lucy cast a questioning look at Sue, who delivered the bad news. "He's dead."

Pam was stunned. "What?"

"How on earth?" asked Rachel.

"I knew something was wrong. There was a fuss, but I never imagined. . . ." said Pam.

Rachel was clasping her hands together. "Was it the asthma?"

"He was having trouble breathing at the airport," recalled Pam, stepping aside to let a young woman in a white disposable overall pass. She was snapping on a pair of latex gloves as she hurried to the economy section.

"Probably the medical examiner," said Lucy, whose job as a reporter had given her some familiarity with the procedures surrounding unexpected death. She watched as a tall, rather distinguished-looking man in a gray suit entered the cabin, receiving nods from the two uniformed officers. He was soon followed by a shorter, sturdier man wearing a tweed jacket and a rather stout, red-faced man wearing a beautifully tailored suit.

"If you'll all take a seat, we can begin, and hopefully we won't delay you for very long," said the man in the gray suit. "I am Inspector John Neal of the Metropolitan Police. It is the responsibility of the Met, which you may know better as Scotland Yard, to investigate any unexplained deaths." There was a little stir from several tour members, and he quickly explained. "Due to the configuration of the aircraft, you may not know that the leader of your tour, George Temple, expired in midflight." He paused a moment, waiting for this information to be absorbed, before continuing. "My colleague"—he indicated the sturdy man in the sport coat—"is Sergeant Chester Luddy. Mr. William Bosworth is the coroner." He indicated the man in the expensive suit. "Mr. Bosworth will determine from our investigation here today whether an inquest is required." He paused again, his gaze moving from one person to another. "I need hardly point out to you all that the more helpful and open you are at this time, the sooner we can wrap this up and you can carry on with your travel plans."

Sergeant Luddy passed a sheet of paper to the inspector, and he began reading names. "Laura and William Barfield, please identify yourselves."

A slight woman with wispy, chin-length brown hair raised her hand. She was dressed in a pair of beige wool slacks and a brown leather jacket with a gold paisley scarf tucked into the neckline. "I'm Laura Barfield and this is my son, Will."

Will was a tall kid who needed a haircut, his streaky blond hair flopped over his forehead. He was dressed in jeans, a white Oxford button-down shirt that wasn't tucked into his pants, and a bright blue sweater.

"I understand you are a student?" Neal was looking at Will.

"That's right. I'm a freshman at Winchester College."

Neal nodded and went on to the next name on his list. "Dr. Randall Cope."

The doctor stood up. "I am a medical doctor, and I attended George Temple in his final moments."

"I see." Neal made a tick next to his name. "Jennifer Fain."

"That's me." Jennifer lifted her hand. She looked quite tiny and vulnerable in the roomy club chair.

"And you are also a student at Winchester College?"

She nodded.

Dr. Cope was seated beside her and patted her knee protectively. "Jennifer is my granddaughter."

The inspector was consulting his list. "Sue Finch."

"Here." Sue raised her hand with a decisive motion.

Neal's eyes seemed to flicker briefly as if he found her worth a second look. "Are you connected to Winchester College?"

"No. The tour was open to anyone, so I signed up with three friends. Just a little vacation."

"I see." Neal passed his eyes over the group. "Rachel Goodman."

Rachel spoke up in a low, clear voice. "That's me. I'm one of the friends."

Neal didn't smile but went on to the next name. "Autumn Mackie."

"I saw the whole thing," said Autumn, sounding defensive. "It was disgusting."

The sergeant passed another paper to Neal, indicating something with his finger.

"You were seated next to the deceased gentleman?"

"They were going to make me sit next to a corpse!" declared Autumn, outraged. She pointed to Dr. Cope. "He changed seats with me."

"I see." Neal consulted the list. "Ann, Caroline, and Thomas Smith. Are you all the same family?'

"Yes," said Tom Smith, a fortyish man with a brush cut and a beer belly spilling over his Dockers. He and his daughter were standing behind his wife, who was seated. "My wife, Ann," he said, tapping her on the shoulder. "And my daughter, Caroline."

Ann, Lucy saw, was painfully thin, with a pinched face and unattractively short gray hair. Caroline, on the other hand, was overweight, with a bushy mop of curly orange hair.

"This is the first we even knew about Mr. Temple's, um, death," said Tom.

"Quite so," said Neal. "Pamela Stillings."

Pam gave a little bounce in her chair, half standing. "I'm Pam," she said. "One of the four friends. I didn't know anything about this. I was sitting in the front, you see, in a middle seat. I couldn't see what was going on in the rear of the cabin."

Neal exchanged glances with Luddy, who shrugged. "Lucy Stone."

Lucy raised her hand. "I was sitting across the aisle from Mr. Temple."

"I guess we'll begin with you, then," said Neal. "Come with me."

Me and my big mouth, thought Lucy, following the inspector to the far corner of the cabin. The coroner and Luddy joined them, making a tight little circle around her chair. She felt hemmed in.

"When did you first notice Mr. Temple was having difficulty breathing?" asked Neal after he had taken down Lucy's address and studied her passport.

"At the airport, actually, in Boston."

Neal raised an eyebrow. "Really?"

"Yes. I happened to be behind him when he went through the security screening. For some reason they took him away, and when he returned and joined us at the gate, he was breathing heavily." Lucy was thinking hard, trying to recall any detail that might be important. "His breathing was ragged. With a little wheeze. But when he used his inhaler, he seemed to improve. Then he took a roll call and discovered somebody was missing—that kid Will—and his breathing got worse again. We were all quite concerned, and that lady, Ann Smith, I think, urged him to stay calm and relax. She tried to teach him some relaxation technique and even attempted to cover him with a shawl she had, but he refused it. He was almost angry—*flustered* is maybe a better word. Then we lined up and boarded. I sort of lost track of him until I found my seat and he was on the other side of the aisle. Will made it to the gate in time, obviously, but I didn't see that."

"And who was sitting on the other side of Mr. Temple?"

"Autumn, the dark-haired girl who is so upset, and Jennifer, Dr. Cope's granddaughter, had the window."

"How did Mr. Temple react to takeoff?"

"He seemed fine. He used the inhaler again, and he was sitting forward a bit, quite calm and quiet. I thought he was improving."

"And how long was this?"

"Quite a while. We were well into the flight—they were serving drinks—when he kind of reached over and grabbed me. He was trying to say something. I could see he was in distress and rang for the flight attendant. Then they called for the doctor, and he came and gave him an injection but it was too late." Lucy was exhausted. She felt quite empty as she recalled the horrifying chain of events. "It was so unexpected. The last thing you'd think would happen."

"What about his seatmates? Did they try to help him?"

Lucy hesitated for a moment before answering. "They're only kids. They didn't seem to realize he was in distress. They were listening to music on their iPods and kind of dancing in their seats."

Neal's and Luddy's eyes met.

"In fact," recalled Lucy, "Autumn accidentally knocked his inhaler out of his hand. It fell into his drink."

"Anything else you can remember?"

"Well, they were eating something. They had a bag of nuts and raisins they were sharing."

"What sort of bag?"

"One of those zip bags you're supposed to use for liquids."

Neal nodded. "Thank you. You've been very helpful."

Released from the hot seat, Lucy went back to join the group, feeling oddly guilty, as if she'd ratted on the girls. But they hadn't done anything terrible. They were just young and full of energy, caught up in themselves.

She was just sitting down when the inspector called Dr. Cope. He got to his feet rather stiffly, not quite as nimble as he'd been earlier, and made his way to the other side of the cabin. His granddaughter, Jennifer, watched anxiously, biting her lip.

"What did you tell them?" whispered Sue.

"Just what I saw. What else could I do?"

"You told them about the girls and the inhaler?"

Lucy was a bit defensive. "Yeah. Wouldn't you?"

Sue shrugged and checked her watch. Time, Lucy realized, was crawling by. She was stiff and tired, and she felt grubby and wanted to wash her face properly. Instead, she was virtually a prisoner on this airplane while the inspector systematically questioned each member of the tour. She wouldn't have minded quite so much, if only she could hear what they were saying. But even though she strained her ears, she heard very little. Autumn was the loudest, and Lucy heard her proclaim something about "How was I supposed to know?" but that was all.

The inspector was interviewing Rachel, the last member of the group, when a sharp snap indicated the medical examiner had finished her examination and was removing her gloves. She stood in the rear of the cabin, not far from Lucy, and the coroner went over to her.

"What have you got?" he asked.

"I was only able to do a superficial exam, but my observations are consistent with anaphylactic shock."

Lucy remembered Dr. Cope using the phrase when he examined Temple.

"That accords with the witnesses' reports," said the coroner.

"Of course, I'll know more when I get him back to the morgue."

"Do you really think that's necessary?"

"It is customary."

"That's not what I asked you," snapped the coroner. "Do you have any reason to think it wasn't anaphylactic shock?"

The woman spoke slowly. "Uh, no."

"Well, then I guess we can save the rate payers some money."

"Whatever you say." She proceeded through the cabin, stripping off the overall as she went and shaking her head.

The inspector was now standing at the front of the cabin, addressing the group. "Thank you all for your cooperation. You're free to go, and I hope there will be no further unpleasantness to spoil your visit to the UK."

They were starting to stand up when a rosy-cheeked man with slicked back hair suddenly appeared. "I'm Reg Wilson from British Airways, and I, too, want to thank you for your cooperation. Furthermore, I have arranged transport for your group to your hotel. Now, if you will gather up your things, I will escort you to immigration and on to the baggage area."

Pam was bouncing on the balls of her feet, itching to go. "Let's get this show on the road," she said.

Lucy smiled, resolving not to let Temple's death ruin her vacation. After all, she hadn't really known the man. And she was finally here in England. "Tallyho," she said.

Chapter Three

The group was quiet as the minibus crept along in heavy traffic on the M4, a highway Lucy recognized from those BBC mystery dramas she loved to watch. It was a lot like the Maine Turnpike, except all the cars were driving on the wrong side of the road. Lucy peered out the window at the passing scenery, fascinated by everything she saw. The houses were subtly different from houses in America, she thought. They were mostly built of brick, instead of the shingles or clapboard used in Maine, and they were tightly packed together in rows with tiny, fenced backyards instead of the spacious lawns she was used to. They were passing an old brewery that seemed oddly familiar—had it been a set in a costume drama?—and then the highway ended and they were on a London street, passing shops and museums and more row houses. These were taller and more imposing than the ones they'd seen from the highway and didn't have front yards. Some had flower boxes at the windows or a plant in a tub set on the front steps. The street widened, and there was the giant flickering TV screen at Piccadilly Circus. They continued weaving through narrow streets, past theaters and restaurants, until they suddenly broke into a square with a leafy green park in the center. A few more turns through streets that were now arranged in a series of neat squares and the bus stopped in front of yet another tall brick row house. The gilded letters in the transom above the shiny black front door announced they had arrived at the Desmond Hotel.

"What happens now?" asked Tom Smith, as if only now realizing the group had lost its leader. "Who's in charge?"

"I'll fill in for George, for the time being," said Pam, rising and moving to the front of the bus. "I work at the college part-time, so I know the president. I'll call her and explain the situation." She checked her watch. "It's eleven here. That means it's six in the U.S. That's awfully early for a Saturday morning. I'll wait a bit—I should have some information for you by dinnertime."

"What do we do in the meantime?" asked Laura, looking a bit lost.

"For the time being, I guess we're all on our own," said Pam. "We might as well get settled here at the hotel. I'm sure the hotel staff can suggest some things to do. After all, this is London." She smiled at the bus driver. "You can start unloading the luggage, and I'll go in and see about checking in."

The bus driver had just pulled the last bag from the luggage compartment when Pam reappeared with a piece of paper and a handful of keys. "We're all set. George took very good care of us," she announced, standing on the steps in front of the hotel. "Barfields, you're in room seven," she said, handing over two keys. "The larger one is for the outer door, the smaller for your room."

The bus drove off and the group on the sidewalk gradually dispersed as Pam distributed the keys until only the four friends remained. "Here you go," she said, handing a set of keys to Sue. "You and Lucy are in room twenty-seven and Rachel and I are in twenty-six. I think that means we have a bit of a climb."

Once inside, Lucy found herself in a small hall with a steep flight of carpeted stairs directly opposite the front door. The entry was homelike with a small console table holding a lamp, guestbook, and vase of fresh flowers. A narrow hallway ran alongside the stairs, ending in a small office, where a middle-aged man was talking on the telephone in a Cockney accent. Following Sue, Lucy began climbing, dragging her suitcase behind her up four flights of stairs until they reached the top floor and their rooms.

Room 27 was small, but it had two large windows overlooking

the street, two twin beds with white coverlets, and a very tiny bathroom with a shower. It was also very hot, so Lucy headed straight for one of the windows, which was sealed with an inner storm panel. She'd never seen anything like it before, but it opened easily and soon a cool breeze was lifting the white net panels that hung behind the wildly flowered drapes.

Sue emerged from the bathroom. "Good thing we're both slender," she said. "Otherwise we couldn't fit between the sink and shower to get to the toilet."

Lucy poked her head inside the bathroom and discovered Sue wasn't exaggerating. "It's a tight squeeze but very clean."

"And we each get a whole towel to ourselves," said Sue, pointing out the neatly folded bath towels resting on the foot of each bed. Extremely small, thin towels, judging from their flatness.

"And we share the soap." Lucy was holding up the tiny pink rectangle she'd found on the tiny white sink.

"It's not exactly the Four Seasons," said Sue.

"It's not even a Holiday Inn," said Lucy, sitting on the end of a bed.

"Well, sweetie, when the going gets tough, the tough get going. Shopping, that is. And since it's Saturday, we can go to Portobello Market!"

"But I want to take a nap," said Lucy, falling backward onto the bed.

"Worst thing you can do. Come on, up you go! We're in London! You can sleep tonight."

Slowly, very slowly, Lucy dragged herself to her feet. From the street outside, she could hear the roar of traffic, the voices of passersby. It was true. She wasn't in quiet little Tinker's Cove anymore.

Downstairs, they met Pam and Rachel. In response to Pam's inquiry, the proprietor, a short and stocky fellow in a worn olive-green sweater vest, gave them directions to Portobello Market. "Just walk up the street to the Euston Square tube station, take the Circle Line to Notting Hill Gate, and follow the Pembridge Road to Portobello Road. You can't miss it."

"I'm so excited," declared Sue as they headed up Gower Street. "I'm so glad you're not going to miss Portobello."

"What is it exactly?" asked Pam.

"A giant street fair. There's antiques and junk and all sorts of stuff. Kind of like a giant flea market."

Rachel was consulting her guidebook as they walked along. "It says here you shouldn't be afraid to bargain. The dealers expect to come down at least ten percent."

"Sounds like my kind of place," said Lucy as they descended the stairs to the Euston Square station.

There they gathered in front of the machines that sold tickets and tried to figure out the system for payment.

"In Boston you have to buy a CharlieCard," said Pam, who often returned to her hometown to visit her mother.

"This Oyster card is new—they didn't have it last time I was here," said Sue.

Looking around, they found a cashier sitting in a booth behind a thick Plexiglas window who sold them the cards, collecting twenty-three pounds from each of them.

"Seems expensive," complained Lucy.

"No, no," said Sue, repeatedly tapping the card on the yellow disk that was supposed to operate the entry gate, but to no effect. "The Tube is fantastic, you'll see. It will take us everywhere."

"If we can get in," said Rachel.

"May I?" A tall gentleman togged out in a suit and tie took the card from Sue. "You just touch the back of the card to the disk, like so," he said, demonstrating. The gates opened.

A train could be heard arriving at the platform below, so they hurriedly thanked him and dashed for the stairs—a very long flight of stairs. "It's hopeless. We'll have to wait for the next one," said Pam in a resigned tone. But when they reached the platform, an illuminated sign informed them that the next train would arrive in two minutes. "Could that possibly be right?" asked Pam, pointing at the sign.

When the train pulled in, exactly on schedule, Rachel was impressed. "This is amazing," she said.

The train ground to a halt, the doors slid open, and a mellifluous female voice reminded them to "Mind the gap" as they boarded. They were seating themselves on upholstered benches and noting the clean carriage when the voice continued. "This is a Circle Line train. The next stop will be Great Portland Street."

Stunned by British efficiency, they rode in silence to Notting Hill Gate, where they were once again urged to mind the gap.

"Why can't we have trains that run on schedule in America?" asked Rachel as they emerged from the dim station into the sunny street.

"And actually let you know where you're going in clearly understood announcements. The last time I was in Boston, I got the last train of the evening, which I thought was lucky, but unfortunately it didn't go where I thought. I ended up at the end of the line on some deserted street trying to get a taxi at one in the morning." Pam's expression was dark. "Not much fun at all."

They were walking past neat white row houses with tiny front gardens behind black-painted iron railings in what seemed to be a very nice neighborhood. Lucy wondered what it would be like to live in one of these houses.

"Up and down stairs all day," said Sue, reading her mind.

It was true, she realized. The houses seemed to be one room wide but were three or four stories tall. You'd get plenty of exercise just getting out of the house in the morning, especially if you forgot something in an upstairs bedroom.

When they turned the corner onto Portobello Road, they were confronted by a colorful riot of activity. The narrow street was packed with people who jostled their way along the sidewalks and squeezed between the shops and the temporary stalls that filled the street. Most of the shops sold antiques, but there were also restaurants and clothing boutiques, even a Tesco supermarket. The stallholders sold everything from crafts and cheap imports to all sorts of fruits and vegetables, baked goods, meats, and even fish. One enterprising man had set up three enormous paella pans and was browning chicken pieces in sizzling oil; on the ground beneath the huge braziers, plastic bins full of shellfish were ready to hand. The air was full of scents: cooking chicken, fish, fragrant flowers, incense. Suddenly, Lucy felt quite dizzy and stumbled against a T-shirt stall.

"Whoa, there," exclaimed Sue, reaching out to steady her.

Rachel took one look at Lucy's white face and made an executive decision. "We need lunch."

Fortunately there was a nearby café, and they took an outside table. Pam kept Lucy company, basking in the warm March sunshine, while Rachel and Sue placed orders for tea and sandwiches.

"I feel so foolish," said Lucy, who was still a bit dizzy.

"Don't be silly." Pam sounded tired. "We've all had a terrible shock, but you were right next to George. You saw the whole thing. It's no wonder you're a bit fragile."

"It's probably just low blood sugar." Lucy felt a surge of sympathy for Pam, who had assumed responsibility for the group. "Were you able to reach the college president?"

"My cell phone doesn't work here, so I sent an e-mail from the hotel—they have a computer for guests."

"You shouldn't feel as if you have to take charge. We're all adults. . . ." Lucy remembered the four students: Caroline, Will, Autumn, and Jennifer. "Well, almost adults."

"I still can't believe it happened." Pam looked up as Rachel and Sue arrived with their food, distributing ploughman's lunches and cardboard cups of tea. "Poor George."

"What was he like?" asked Lucy, taking a sip of tea. She wasn't quite ready for the sandwich, which consisted of cheese, pickle, and lettuce on whole wheat bread.

"I only knew him from my yoga class," said Pam, pausing to chew. "He was very flexible, considering his age."

"Men aren't usually flexible," said Lucy, picturing Bill's struggle to touch his toes.

"George had a lovely downward dog, and his cobra was amazing."

"How old was he?" Sue took a tiny bite of her sandwich.

"Not old enough to die. Fifties maybe?" said Rachel. "This bread is very good."

"That's about right." Pam nodded. "This whole sandwich is excellent."

Encouraged, Lucy took a bite and experienced a revelation. "It's real cheddar," she declared. "And the bread is so wholesome-tasting. It's really good, and I always heard English food is bad."

"So was he a full professor?" asked Sue. Her son-in-law Geoff had recently landed a position as an assistant professor at New York University.

"No. He was only an adjunct," said Pam. "Paid by the course, no benefits or anything."

"Really?"

"Yeah." Pam crumpled up the cellophane sandwich wrap. "You know how it is—a lot of liberal arts colleges are struggling financially these days. Winchester has a lot of adjuncts, but I did hear something about an opening in the English Department. Professor Crighton is due to retire, so maybe George would have gotten his job. He always scored really high on the student evaluations, and he was devoted to Winchester. He put in all sorts of extra time. He was even published." She stood up. "I don't know about you guys, but I don't want to spend all day sitting here. That stall with the scarves is calling my name."

Rachel turned her big brown eyes to Lucy. "How are you feeling?"

"Much better. Let's go shopping."

Pam was willing to pay the ten pounds the vendor was asking for three scarves, but Sue intervened and haggled until he agreed to accept eight pounds. Lucy ventured inside some of the antiques shops and found they extended far from the street front, winding through adjacent buildings in a higgledy-piggledy fashion, housing numerous dealers. She fell in love with a round breadboard that the seller assured her was a good value at thirty-five pounds. The woman had a number of them, ranging in price from ten to nearly one hundred pounds, so Lucy figured she could trust her expertise and paid the asking price.

Rachel had to be dragged away from the bread stall, where she insisted on buying four hot cross buns, and they all gathered in Tesco to buy the shampoo and body wash the hotel didn't supply. Sue lingered at the newsstand, stocking up on English magazines, while Lucy picked up a couple of tabloid newspapers. By then it was late afternoon and the market was winding down as stallholders began packing up their wares.

Sue glanced at her watch and yawned, setting off a little chain reaction among her friends. "I know. We should have afternoon tea and then head back to the hotel for an early night."

"I've always wanted to have high tea," enthused Pam.

"No, not high tea." Sue nodded wisely. "High tea is beans on toast, a working-class supper. What we want is afternoon tea with scones and cake and little sandwiches and a silver teapot."

Lucy was skeptical. "I don't think we'll find any establishments like that around here. These places all seem to use paper cups." She paused, remembering the many British mysteries she'd borrowed from the library, all aged and well thumbed by readers. "There's a chain called Lyons, or used to be."

Sue was thoughtful. "Maybe closer to the hotel," she said. But when they retraced their route back to the hotel and emerged, panting with exhaustion from the climb out of the Euston Square station, there seemed to be a surprising lack of tearooms. No restaurants at all, in fact, except for a dingy-looking Indian place. Coming to the end of their street, Sue admitted defeat. "How about some curry?" she asked.

Waking at two in the morning, Lucy tiptoed into the tiny bathroom and dug in her toiletries bag for the roll of antacid tablets she'd brought. She'd enjoyed the spicy Indian food, but now she had a terrible case of heartburn. She crunched a couple of the tablets while she peed, had a drink of water, and went back to bed, hoping she'd look better in the morning than she did now. Her reflection in the mirror over the sink wasn't encouraging; she had dark circles under her eyes, and she was certain she'd sprouted some new wrinkles.

Back in bed, she yawned and settled herself for sleep, but sleep didn't come. She was tired enough; there was no doubt about that. Her legs ached; her arms felt heavy. Every cell in her body seemed to be crying out for rest. All except her brain cells, which were annoyingly active and returned again and again to Temple's death, producing an image of his blanket-covered body whenever she closed her eyes.

Turning on her side, she stared at the windows, which were lighter patches of gray in the darkened room. She remembered how nervous she'd been going through security at Logan Airport, even though she'd checked the TSA website and packed according to the directions, filling a quart-sized ziplock bag with miniature versions of her favorite toiletries. She'd forgotten the water bottle she had tucked in her travel bag and had been forced to empty it, but the officer had been pleasant about it. George Temple hadn't been so lucky. The buzzer had sounded when he walked through the metal detector, and he'd actually been taken away by two officers, protesting loudly. "I never saw that before," he was saying as they hustled him along.

What on earth had they found? wondered Lucy, now staring at the white glass light fixture that hung from the ceiling, dimly glowing from the reflected light that came through the windows from the street. And what did they do to him? She'd been warned that TSA officers were empowered to conduct strip searches, and she'd made sure not to wear an underwire bra and had chosen elastic-waist pants without a zipper, just to be on the safe side.

No wonder Temple had seemed flustered when he returned and began rounding up the group and making sure everyone was there. Of course, Will Barfield was late and his mother's fretting had driven them all to distraction. "This isn't like him," she kept saying. "I hope he hasn't had some sort of accident."

By then Temple had begun coughing and sneezing and had used his inhaler at least once. Ann Smith had noticed and urged him to sit down and relax, taking deep regular breaths. He had complied and seemed to be recovering, until she tried to wrap him in her pashmina shawl so he'd be nice and warm. He'd protested and that had started a new fit of coughing.

Then the gate attendant had announced boarding and there was a great deal of movement, and Lucy lost track of Temple as she waited for her row number to be called. Dr. Cope had been right next to her at one point, she remembered, but if he noticed Temple's condition, he hadn't seemed concerned. Now that she thought about it, it seemed a bit odd. Temple's coughing had been very noticeable, and he'd attracted a lot of attention. At one point, a uniformed airline representative had even approached him, but Temple had produced his inhaler and apparently assured the official that he would be all right.

Of course, thought Lucy, embarrassment had no doubt played a part in Temple's refusal to accept assistance. She knew how silly she'd felt that afternoon, when she nearly fainted at the Portobello Market. The last thing she'd wanted was to make a scene.

Sighing, Lucy checked her watch. Three in the morning. Hours to go before it was time to get up. She should have accepted Sue's offer of a sleeping pill. Sue, who'd taken two, was sound asleep while Lucy was tossing and turning and burping up chicken korma. She rolled over, closed her eyes, and suddenly remembered Sue telling her the pills were on the sink in case she changed her mind. She had indeed changed her mind, she decided, throwing back the covers.

Chapter Four

When Lucy and Sue descended six flights of stairs to the little hotel's basement breakfast room on Sunday morning, they found that everyone from the group was already there, as were a smattering of other guests, sitting in twos and threes at little tables covered with red-and-white–checked cloths. They nodded and smiled as they wound their way through the dining room to the table for four where Pam and Rachel were waiting for them. As soon as they sat down, a young waitress arrived with pots of coffee and tea, and they both chose coffee, craving the caffeine. While they were drinking, Pam stood up and tapped her juice glass with a spoon.

"I have an announcement," she began in an official tone. "I received an e-mail from President Chapman this morning, and she sends her condolences to all of us. She was also able to find a substitute for George Temple—she is sending Professor Quentin Rea to take over the tour."

The name caught Lucy by surprise, and her empty cup rolled onto its side with a rattle as she set it on the saucer. She had taken a class in Victorian literature from Professor Rea some years ago and had found him terribly attractive. Of course, he was much younger then—they both were—but she'd always been a sucker for that preppy look of worn tweed jackets, frayed button-down shirts, and sun-streaked hair. She wondered if she'd still be attracted to him, not that she planned to do anything about it, she vowed, straightening the cup.

She hadn't done anything then, but she had been tempted, and she was sure that he had also found her attractive, and smiled at the memory.

"Lucy! Stop daydreaming!" It was Sue, hissing at her. "Our server wants to know if you want cereal."

Lucy blushed and turned to the girl who offered bran flakes, corn flakes, or Cheerios. Cheerios, here in England. Who knew? But Lucy chose bran flakes, taking the state of her digestion into account.

Pam was continuing her speech to the group. "Professor Rea won't arrive until tomorrow morning, so Dr. Chapman suggests we follow the itinerary George planned on our own. That means we go to the Tower of London this morning, break for lunch, and visit St. Paul's Cathedral in the afternoon. I suggest those who are interested gather in front of the hotel at nine-thirty and we'll go together on the Tube."

Pam was seating herself when the server arrived with Lucy's bowl of cereal. "This morning's breakfast is egg, bacon, and beans," said the girl.

"Okay," said Lucy, figuring that she might as well try the traditional English breakfast. Pam and Rachel declined the beans and Sue opted for nothing but toast.

The Smith family was seated at the table next to Pam, and Ann reached across and tapped her on the arm. "Since it's Sunday, I think we'll opt out of visiting the Tower," she said. She had dark circles under her eyes, and the gray sweater she was wearing only added to her careworn appearance. "We'll attend services at St. Martin in the Fields and then go on to the National Gallery." She paused. "Caroline loves art."

Lucy glanced at the red-haired girl, who seemed more interested in using a triangle of toast to mop up the egg and bean juice that remained on her plate than in discussing the day's program.

Her father, Tom, stabbed the map spread open before him on the table with a stubby finger. "We can take the Northern Line from Goodge Street. It's just a few stops. Ann doesn't feel up to much today, what with this jet lag and all."

Lucy thought he seemed a practical, take-charge sort of guy, rather like Bill, and she suddenly missed her husband.

"Fine with me," said Pam as their breakfasts arrived. She poked her fork at the generous slices of pink meat that were arranged alongside her fried egg. "This doesn't look like bacon."

"English bacon's different," said Sue, looking as if she wouldn't touch it with a ten-foot pole. As far as Lucy knew, Sue rarely ate solid food and seemed to exist on little more than black coffee and cocktails.

Rachel wasn't so fussy; she was digging right in. "It's very good."

Lucy tasted a forkful of beans and found them not so good. "Live and learn," she said with a grimace. In the future, she decided, she'd skip the beans.

"Don't like the beans?" It was Will Barfield, who was seated with his mother on the other side of their table, next to the wall. "I'll take them."

"Will!" protested Laura. She was dressed today in the same ladylike caramel-colored leather jacket she'd worn on the plane but had added a different scarf, green this time. "Don't be rude!"

"He's not rude," laughed Lucy, thinking of her son, Toby, and the huge amounts he ate as a teenager. "He's still growing." She spooned her beans onto her bread plate and passed it over. "It's a shame to waste them, and I'm certainly not going to eat them."

"Thanks," said Will, diving in. "You know, I'm not all that interested in this historical stuff," he said, raising a fork dripping with juicy beans and popping it into his mouth. "I heard the London Eye is really cool. I think I'd like to do that."

"Fine with me," said Pam.

"But, Will," protested his mother, slipping a pair of schoolmarmish wire-rimmed reading glasses on her nose and preparing to consult her guidebook. "You can't come to London and miss the Bloody Tower. I think you'd really like it—they say it has suits of armor worn by Henry the Eighth."

Will had plucked a tiny jar of marmalade from the little silver rack and was slathering it onto a triangle of toast. "Nah. I wanna do the Eye and then maybe hike over to the Tate Modern and that Millennium Bridge over the river. I saw it in a movie—it was neat."

Laura was studying the map in her guidebook. "Maybe you're right. The Millennium Bridge is next to the New Globe Theatre. I'd love to see that. It's a copy of Shakespeare's theater. Maybe we could even see a play there."

Will's face stiffened. "It's a pretty long walk, Mom." Lucy and her friends exchanged glances. It was clear to them that Will was trying to get away from his mother for the day. "Probably too much for you," he added.

"I walk all the time," she said, squashing his rebellion with a look as she removed her glasses and tucked them into a quilted case. "I walk miles every week with the dog."

"Okay," he said, accepting defeat with a sigh and pushing his chair back. "Let's go."

Laura popped happily to her feet. "Have a nice day," she said to the group in general before following her tall son out of the room.

Lucy watched them go, spreading a dab of butter on her toast and wondering how this little struggle would play out. It was only the second day of the trip and Will was already chafing at his mother's attempts to control him. He was obviously a kid who enjoyed his independence, and it seemed odd that he'd agreed to a trip with his mother. Most boys his age would choose to spend spring break in Mexico or Florida, or in a worst-case scenario, at home, where they had developed ways of deluding and eluding their parents and could hang out with their high school friends.

"He's a cute kid," said Rachel. "Reminds me of my Richie."

"Have you heard from Richie lately?" asked Lucy, who knew that Rachel's son was in Greece, working on an archaeological dig.

"Come to think of it, not since last month." She laughed. "He wanted income tax forms."

"That's something at least," complained Pam. "I haven't heard a word from Tim since Christmas." She paused. "Lucy's so lucky to have Toby living in town."

"It's true. I am lucky." Lucy put down her fork and dabbed at her mouth with her napkin. "But I have to remind myself not to hover. They may be nearby, but they need their own space." It was a lesson she thought Laura Barfield would have to learn, too, if she hoped to maintain a healthy relationship with her son.

Dr. Cope and Jennifer Fain were already waiting on the side-walk in front of the hotel when Lucy and her friends stepped outside at nine-thirty. The sky was overcast but the TV weatherman had promised later clearing, and the temperature was forecast to rise to twelve degrees Celsius—around fifty-four degrees Fahrenheit.

"Are we all here?" asked Pam, consulting her list.

"Autumn's still upstairs," said Jennifer.

"We'll wait for her, then," said Pam, unfolding her map of the Underground. "It looks like we can take the Northern Line from Euston Square."

"Lead on," said Lucy when the door of the hotel opened and Autumn clumped down the steps in her Dr. Martens. Today she was wearing black leggings that stopped at her ankles, a short black jersey dress, and a torn fishnet sweater.

"Do you think you'll be warm enough?" asked Pam, unable to stifle her motherly instincts.

Autumn's back stiffened and she glared at Pam as if she'd been accused of some dastardly crime. "I'll be fine."

"Okay," said Pam, backing off. "It looks like we're all here. The others have made separate plans."

"Well, this is nice," declared Dr. Cope. "I feel like Henry the Eighth, accompanied by six lovely ladies."

"Just as long as you treat us better than he treated his wives," said Rachel, falling into step beside him as they walked along Gower Street to the Tube station.

Crowds were already making their way to the Tower of London when they emerged from the Tower Hill Tube station into what had become a sunny day. As they joined the throng walking along the outer walls that ringed the spacious grassy moat, Lucy thought it must have been much the same throughout the centuries, especially when traitors and criminals were publicly executed on Tower Hill. Today's crowds weren't out for blood, however, but were drawn by the Tower's various attractions, including the crown jewels.

Despite the sunshine, it was chilly when they passed through the Middle Tower entrance into the castle complex. Lucy wasn't sure what she had expected but was somewhat surprised to find the Tower of London wasn't a single structure; rather, it was a number of buildings collected inside a double ring of walls that would frustrate an attacker. It was a true medieval fortress and reminded her of books about knights and castles she had read to Toby when he was small. Even today, she thought as they strolled along the shadowed path between the two walls, there was something grim about the place.

"The Traitor's Gate," said Dr. Cope, pausing in front of a semicircular opening in the outer wall, blocked with forbidding bars, that connected to the Thames beyond. It was here that prisoners had been delivered by boat.

"Imagine being brought through there, knowing you'd never get out," said Rachel.

"They used to put the heads of people they executed on top of the walls," continued Dr. Cope. "A grim reminder of the price of treason." He lifted his shoulders in a shrug. "And in those days, treason was whatever displeased the king."

"This is a terrible, evil place," said Jennifer, drawing the lapels of her pale blue jacket together with a delicate, ringed hand.

"Not really," said Rachel, who was studying her guidebook. "It says here it's like a little village. People actually live here. The Yeoman Warders—those are the guys in the funny red outfits—live here with their families."

"That's too cool," said Autumn, breaking her usual bored attitude to express a flicker of interest. "Look at that bird!" She was pointing to a super-sized crow, perched above the entry gate.

With its feathers fluffed out, it reminded Lucy of Autumn's spiky black hairdo and she smiled.

"That," said Rachel, "is a raven. The legend is that if the ravens ever leave the Tower, the kingdom will fall."

"I'd be worried if I were Prince Charles," said Sue.

Rachel smiled. "They're taking no chances—their wings are clipped."

"Seems like cheating to me," observed Lucy as they passed through yet another dank and chilly portal to emerge into a spacious green, grassy court. The gleaming White Tower, a large square fortress with a domed and turreted tower at each corner stood before them.

"It was built by William the Conqueror," said Rachel, amazed.

Lucy didn't know many dates but she did know this one. "In something like 1066?"

"Yeah. That's old," said Pam.

"The Hallett House, the oldest building in Tinker's Cove, was built in the eighteenth century," said Sue. "That White Tower is nearly a thousand years old."

"This is really something," said Rachel. "So where shall we start?"

Sue didn't hesitate. "The jewels, silly. Where else?"

A short line was already forming at the building housing the crown jewels, but the group happily joined it. Once inside, they discovered it was a bit like Disney World with a convoluted route that hid the length of the wait. The queue snaked past a flickering old black-and-white newsreel of Queen Elizabeth II's coronation, where she was decked out in a crown and ermine robe, as well as a number of other jewels, and carried an orb and scepter. Eventually they found themselves in a darkened room where a moving pathway carried viewers past the illuminated glass cases containing crowns and scepters glittering with thousands of diamonds, pearls, sapphires, emeralds, and rubies.

It all left Lucy rather cold, except for Queen Victoria's dainty little diamond topper, which looked like a miniature crown designed for a doll, but Sue was enthralled. When she came to the end of the people mover, she quickly ducked around and hopped on for another viewing.

"Pardon me," she said to the startled gentleman she stepped in front of.

"Not at all," he replied with famous British politeness.

But when she tried the same trick a second time, one of the Yeoman Warders stepped forward. "Madam, if you wish to see the jewels again, you will have to go to the end of the queue."

"Busted," announced Autumn, who was waiting with Lucy at the end.

"I don't care. It was worth it," insisted Sue. "If diamonds are a girl's best friend, the queen sure has a lot of friends."

Dr. Cope and Jennifer had drifted away from the others and were standing by a plaque embedded in the pavement, near a small stone church building, gazing at a withered bunch of roses that had been placed there. Lucy and the others went over to join them, and she realized the plaque marked the spot where the scaffold used for royal executions had once stood.

"Only very important prisoners were executed here," Dr. Cope was saying. "Or more controversial ones. It was more private since the public wasn't allowed in."

Lucy was reading the names embedded in a circle around the plaque: "Margaret Pole—Lady Salisbury; Catherine Howard; Anne Boleyn; Lady Jane Grey—"

"That poor girl was only seventeen . . . ," said Rachel, who devoured historical novels.

"Whatever did she do?" asked Jennifer.

"Nothing really," said Rachel. "She was the victim of an ambitious family. They managed to get her on the throne, but in the end they lost a battle and somebody else got the job—Mary Tudor, fondly known as Bloody Mary."

"They didn't have to kill her!" exclaimed Jennifer, looking pale.

Autumn had spotted one of the ravens, perched on a nearby fencepost, and waved her sweater at it, causing it to flap its wings and rise a few feet into the air, only to brush Jennifer's shoulder with its wing. Startled and frightened, Jennifer shrieked as the bird made a clumsy landing on the memorial plaque, where it stood like a grim reminder of the gruesome beheadings that had taken place there.

"Get it away!" she begged as tears rolled down her cheeks. "Make it go away."

"I don't think you're supposed to interfere with the ravens," said Lucy, reproving Autumn. "Let's check out the Medieval Palace and see what life was like back then."

"Yeah," said Autumn cynically. "If you managed to keep your head."

Chapter Five

"Now this is better," declared Sue as they wandered through the sparsely furnished but brightly decorated rooms of the Medieval Palace. A scratchy recording of lute music provided atmosphere.

Sue's interest was caught by a display case containing jewels and perfume bottles. "These things are pretty, but we can't really know what life was like back then, can we?"

"Not very pleasant, even at the best of times," speculated Rachel as they passed through the room where Sir Walter Raleigh wrote *History of the World* during his long imprisonment. "Imagine what this place was like in winter, with only a small fireplace to heat it."

Indeed, even though it was sunny and warm outside, it was chilly inside, where the stone walls held the cold and where sun couldn't penetrate the small windows. And these accommodations were deemed comfortable, a great improvement over those provided for less illustrious prisoners.

"I once read somewhere that life was so painful in the Middle Ages that tortures had to be really drastic to make an impression. Remember, this was before antibiotics and modern dentistry. There were no painkillers or anesthetics like we have now," said Dr. Cope. "Childbirth and infancy were perilous for women and children, and the men were fighting and riding horses and generally living dangerously. There was plague, I don't imagine the food was terribly wholesome, and the water wasn't fit to drink. People didn't bathe much. Their lives were short and painful. It's no wonder they put so much faith in religion and hoped for a better afterlife."

"It still seems terrible, the way those kings treated people. Poor Sir Walter was kept here for ten years." Jennifer had paused to read the explanatory placards.

"He committed treason," said Autumn. "It seems like everybody was committing treason."

Pam nodded. "They didn't have government like we do now, with an orderly transfer of power. Whoever was strongest and had the best army got to be king. There were plenty of people with a drop or two of royal blood, and they didn't have any trouble finding ambitious backers to support their claims."

"And if you backed the wrong guy, you lost your head," said Autumn as they paused inside a chilly tower with whitewashed walls whose signs pointed out inscriptions carved by prisoners.

They all fell silent as their eyes wandered over the carvings. It was too easy to imagine the prisoners' despair as they waited day after day to learn their fates, and their desire to leave some little scrawl proclaiming that they once lived and suffered for their beliefs.

It was a relief to emerge into the warm sunshine of the Wall Walk, which ran along the top section of the fortifications.

"Have we had enough of the Tower?" asked Rachel. "I believe there's a café down by the river."

Lucy was thoughtful as they made their way through the complex toward the river exit. Pam and Rachel were leading the way. Dr. Cope had fallen into step with Sue, and they were having a lively discussion. Autumn and Jennifer followed. Autumn was striding along in her thick-soled shoes, but Jennifer kept glancing at her companion anxiously, almost as if expecting a blow.

Maybe she was reading too much into Jennifer's body language, thought Lucy. Maybe she had bad posture from scoliosis or something, or maybe she was simply nervous and high-strung or had a blood-sugar problem. There could be lots of explanations for her extreme thinness, she told herself. Nevertheless, the way Autumn was dressed all in black with her spiky hair reminded Lucy of the Tower's nasty ravens, while Jennifer was like one of the little brown sparrows that flitted about nervously after crumbs, always keeping an eye out for the predatory ravens.

When Lucy joined her three friends at one of the riverside café's green-painted picnic tables, she realized she'd been on her feet for more than four hours. It felt good to sit with the sun warming her back and the River Thames sparkling in front of her. The view was splendid, featuring Tower Bridge with two tall stanchions that mimicked the nearby Tower of London. "It's hard to believe I'm really here," she said, feeling a sudden sense of dislocation. "I'm really in London."

"I know exactly what you mean," agreed Sue, taking a tiny bite of her panini. "I remember the first time I went to Paris. Sid and I were taking a taxi from the airport, and we drove right past the Eiffel Tower and the Louvre and Notre Dame, and I could hardly believe my eyes. I'd seen those things in books and movies, but it's quite different to see them in real life."

"I feel really lucky to be here," said Lucy, finding her thoughts turning to George Temple. "To be alive to see this, I mean."

"I wonder if George Temple had been to London before," said Rachel, echoing her thoughts.

"Oh, yes, I'm sure he had," said Pam. "He was quite a traveler. He led a trip like this every spring break, to different places, but quite often to London."

"That makes me feel a bit better, knowing he had a rich life," said Lucy.

Dr. Cope, who was seated at the next table, let out a harsh, barking laugh, and Lucy's eyes met Pam's. It seemed an odd reaction if he'd overheard them, but they had no reason to think he had. Maybe he was laughing at something his granddaughter said.

Lucy was so tired when they finally reached St. Paul's Cathedral that she headed straight for one of the chairs that filled the nave. Sue had assured them it wasn't worth taking the Tube, since St. Paul's was only one stop away from Tower Hill, but she had been deceived by the distortions of the Underground map. It was a different story aboveground, where they had to make their way through what seemed like miles of confusing streets, albeit with charming names like Fish Street Hill and Ironmonger Lane. This was the oldest part of London and still reflected the haphazard layout of the medieval town.

"We got quite a tour of the city," said Dr. Cope, lowering himself stiffly onto the seat next to her. He was breathing heavily as he cast his eyes around him, taking in the huge cathedral with its immense dome. His hands, holding the plan of the building, were resting on his thighs. "My goodness," he finally said.

"It's very grand," agreed Lucy, taking in the immense white and gold cathedral. "The dome is magnetic—you have to keep staring at it."

"I imagine that's the idea: to draw your eyes and your mind heavenward." He opened the brochure and began reading. "Well it's quite a climb to the top of the dome. I don't think I can do that."

"Me neither," said Lucy. "Not yet anyway. Shall we explore a bit around here?"

"Sure," said the doctor, rising with a grunt. "There are supposed to be carvings by Grinling Gibbons in the choir."

Looking around as they crossed the transept beneath the dome, Lucy saw the other members of the group dotted here and there in the cathedral. Autumn and Jennifer were also in the transept, staring up at the paintings in the dome. Rachel and Pam were admiring the elaborate carvings on the pulpit, and Sue was marching purposefully toward an aisle; Lucy suspected she was looking for a ladies' room.

Lucy found the choir a cozy contrast to the immense emptiness of the cathedral. Here in the enclosure behind the organ, there were wooden pews and carvings of fruit, flowers, and cherubs. Unlike the cathedral proper, which inspired awe, the choir encouraged reflection. Here your thoughts turned inward and you could assess the state of your soul.

"Are you a man of faith?" asked Lucy, turning to Dr. Cope.

"Not really. Medicine is a science, after all." He paused. "I guess I believe in the scientific method of hypothesis, tests, and conclusions based on evidence. I haven't seen any evidence of God. Quite the contrary, in fact."

Lucy was studying the adorable face of a Grinling Gibbons cherub puffing away on a trumpet. Though carved of wood, it seemed plump and soft enough to stroke. "Some scientists believe in God."

"Yes. They see the natural order of the universe as evidence of a master plan and conclude there must be a master inventor somewhere."

"Where is the question, I suppose," said Lucy with a smile.

"Exactly," agreed Dr. Cope. "It seems that you are also a doubter."

"I am. I don't believe in a higher power who judges what we do on earth. I think we must each make of our lives what we can. We must do the very best we can."

"In that case, we must each answer to our own personal conscience," said Dr. Cope. "That's quite radical, isn't it?"

"I guess it depends on each conscience," said Lucy. "Mine is actually rather conservative. I believe in the Golden Rule: Treat others as you wish to be treated."

"I used to think I had a clear understanding of right and wrong, but now I'm not so sure." Dr. Cope was staring at a faceted golden cross, whose trident-shaped rays caught the light and made it look like a radiant sun. His brow was furrowed and his expression troubled.

Lucy suspected he felt guilty about his failure to save George Temple. "You did everything you could to save him," she said.

He turned and looked at her, his blue eyes bright in his wrinkled, weathered face. "Did I? Do you really think so?"

"I do," said Lucy. "I blame myself. I should have realized he was in trouble much sooner and called for help."

The doctor raised his white, bushy eyebrows. "You do have a conservative conscience, but you shouldn't blame yourself. If I've learned anything at all in thirty-odd years of practice, it's that you can't save everybody. Death comes to us all, eventually. And you never know, perhaps his death was actually a blessing. Perhaps he would have developed Alzheimer's or cancer." They were walking back toward the transept and paused once again under the dome. "So now we have a choice: Shall we ascend to heaven or descend to the crypt?"

Across the way, Lucy saw a booth where tickets to the dome were sold. "I think I shall pay my money and attempt the ascension," she said.

"I, on the other hand, shall accept my fate as an unrepentant sinner and descend to the realm of the wicked and the doomed," said Dr. Cope.

According to the sign, there were 259 steps to the Whispering Gallery; 378 to the Stone Gallery on the outside of the dome; and 192 more steps to the Golden Gallery at the very top, which also offered 360-degree views of London.

"How high do you want to go?" asked Sue, joining her at the ticket window.

"In for a penny, in for a pound," declared Lucy, wondering how that particular phrase had popped into her head. "Might as well go all the way."

"Or die trying," said Sue, counting out the confusing coins that looked so much like American money but had entirely different values.

"People have been climbing these steps for hundreds of years," gasped Sue when they emerged at the Whispering Gallery. The stone steps were shallow, but they'd still had to pause several times on the way up to rest their legs and catch their breath. Even so, Lucy's thighs were burning and her left knee felt as if one of the Tower's torturers had inserted a red-hot skewer or two into it.

"This is it for me," declared Lucy, feeling a bit dizzy as she looked down at the cathedral's black-and-white checked floor so very far below.

"Well, I'm going on up," said Sue. "I want to get my money's worth."

"I'll wait for you here," said Lucy, eager to study the paintings and mosaics that decorated the dome. The paintings, on the upper portion of the dome, were sepia monochromes, rather like old photographs. She wasn't exactly sure who or what they portrayed: Moses? Isaiah? St. Paul? Whoever they were about, there was plenty of movement from flowing draperies and pennants, and there was a stirring scene of a shipwreck.

Also above her head, but below the paintings, were a number of white marble statues. From below they had seemed little more than chess pieces, but from up here they were huge. She dreaded to think what would happen if one of them toppled from its lofty perch to land on the cathedral floor below, and hoped they were fastened firmly in place.

From her vantage point in the gallery, she could look across to the opposite side and see the colorful mosaics tucked beneath the gallery. These were labeled, and she made out Ezekiel, apparently laying down the law on a stone tablet, and Jeremiah, consulting with an angel, as she proceeded around the gallery. She was just opposite St. Mark, seated on a lion and accompanied by two beautiful angels, when she heard a female voice, clear as a bell, from the other side of the dome. It was true, she realized—the Whispering Gallery was aptly named. You could hear people talking on the other side.

Curious about this phenomenon, she stood in place, listening intently.

"I saw what you did," said a voice that sounded a lot like Jennifer's. The wall blocked her view, so she couldn't quite make out the people on the other side, but she could see two little heads resembling Jennifer and Autumn.

The reply was hissed, little more than a whisper. "Like you're Little Miss Innocent! Give me a break!"

This time Lucy was sure the speaker was none other than Autumn, once again taunting Jennifer. The more she thought about it, the less she liked it and she wondered if she ought to have a word with Autumn. Not in a scolding way; maybe in a joking way. "Little birds in their nests agree," or something like that, a silly phrase that had suddenly popped into her head. From a movie perhaps, she wondered as she walked along the gallery. *Mary Poppins* maybe? But when she reached the other side, the girls were gone and Sue was waiting for her.

"You should have gone up, Lucy! The view was amazing and the guard said it's the clearest it's been in months."

"That's okay," said Lucy, whose knee was still bothering her. "Besides, this Whispering Gallery is pretty amazing. You really can hear people whispering on the other side."

Sue grinned wickedly. "What did you hear? Something naughty?"

"Maybe," said Lucy as they started down the stairs.

Lucy found herself seated next to Autumn and Jennifer as they took the Underground back to the hotel, but she hesitated to take a nannyish tone with them. Instead she made small talk, asking if they were roommates at college.

"No, we met at group," said Jennifer.

Lucy was puzzled. "What sort of group?"

Autumn leaned forward, speaking across Jennifer. "Not what you think. It's no big deal, just something they have for freshmen. We get together once a week and talk about how we're adjusting to school, time management, study skills, stuff like that."

"Sounds good," said Lucy, rising as the train pulled into Tottenham Court Road station, where they would change to the Northern Line. "I wish my daughter's school had something like that."

When they emerged at Goodge Street, Lucy noticed that Jennifer and Autumn were once again best of friends. They were walking with their heads together, and Autumn had her arm around Jennifer's waist.

"What's with those two?" asked Sue, falling into step beside Lucy. "One minute they're fighting and the next they're best friends."

"I noticed that, too," said Lucy, pausing to peek through a gate to admire the fenced gardens running behind the row houses. "Very weird."

"What's weird?" asked Rachel, joining them. "Hyacinths in March?"

"No, we were talking about the relationship between Jennifer and Autumn." The girls were well out of earshot, far ahead of them on the sidewalk and turning the corner onto Gower Street.

"It's almost a dominant-submissive sort of thing," said Sue.

"I don't think it's so odd," said Rachel, who was a psych major in college and never got over it. "College is a time for experimentation, discovering your real identity, and that includes your sexual identity."

"Do you think they're gay?" asked Pam, joining the group.

"Could be," said Rachel. "It wouldn't be the first time two women fell in love." She pointed to a hyacinth that had escaped the neat border and sprouted in the middle of a lawn. "Or maybe they're two outsiders who've found each other."

Chapter Six

There were no beans for breakfast on Monday; the menu was egg, bacon, and grilled tomato. Lucy discovered she loved grilled tomatoes, but Pam and Rachel were less enthusiastic. Sue stuck with black coffee and a triangle of toast.

After breakfast, the group lingered in the lounge, waiting for Quentin Rea, who was due to arrive at any moment. Lucy checked his flight on the computer the hotel provided for guests' use in the lounge and learned he had landed at Heathrow over two hours ago.

She also checked her e-mail, replying to Bill's update that all was well at home but everyone missed her with a chatty summary of her visit to the Tower and St. Paul's. When she sent it off, she noticed a new e-mail in her folder from Elizabeth.

News from Elizabeth was rarely good. Like most college students, she only bothered to contact her parents when she was in trouble or needed money. Lucy opened the message only to learn with dismay that the new dean at Chamberlain College was, in Elizabeth's words, "a stupid Fascist" who was threatening to remove Elizabeth from her post as a resident advisor. While Elizabeth was outraged at what she believed was the dean's unfairness, Lucy had a different reaction. She was concerned about her bank balance, because the position provided free room and board, which amounted to several thousand dollars. If Elizabeth lost her job, they would have to come up with the money. Just the thought of such a large, unexpected expense was enough to put a damper on her vacation.

Hearing voices in the hallway, Lucy wrote a quick reply asking for more information, then glanced up as Quentin Rea entered the lounge accompanied by a tall young woman. She had the sort of looks that turned heads, not so much because her features were outstanding—her nose was a bit too big, her lips thin—but because she knew how to present herself. Her black tailored pantsuit not only fit her slender figure to perfection but it also set off her buttery, shoulder-length blond hair. If she was wearing makeup, it was so expertly applied that you couldn't tell, apart from a dab of lip gloss and a swipe of mascara on her wide-set brown eyes. Remembering how tired she'd felt when she finally arrived at the hotel, Lucy wondered how this woman could look so remarkably fresh after spending the night on the red-eye from Boston.

Turning her attention to the professor, Lucy decided he hadn't aged well. He'd put on some weight in the years since she'd taken that course in Victorian literature, and his rumpled khaki pants and Harris Tweed jacket couldn't stretch to cover the round belly that stuck out like a baby bump. The longish, streaked hair that Lucy had found so attractive all those years ago had darkened into a slatey gray and had thinned as well, leaving a circular, pink bald patch at his crown. Of course, everybody got older, everyone aged, thought Lucy. The unfortunate thing in Quentin's case was that he hadn't accepted the fact and was still sporting the same look he'd adopted straight out of grad school as a young assistant professor. It had been devastatingly effective back then, but it didn't work now. He needed to buy pants with a larger waist; he needed a good haircut and a new pair of shoes. Long, bushy sideburns and loafers held together with duct tape looked ridiculous on a man approaching his fifties.

"There's nothing worse than preppy gone to seed," said Sue, leaning down to whisper in her ear.

Lucy laughed, closing out her e-mail account and pushing back her chair. Standing up, she caught Quentin's eye.

"Lucy Stone!"

Lucy was chagrined to feel her cheeks warming. All that had been long ago and had mostly been in her imagination. "Meet my friends," she said, quickly introducing Pam, Rachel, and Sue.

"Terrific, terrific," he murmured, glancing around the crowded lounge. "Is everyone here?"

Lucy did a quick head count. The Smith family were seated together on a big sofa; Caroline, ever the well-behaved daughter, was in the middle between her watchful parents. Dr. Cope and Laura Barfield were standing by the window, and Laura's son Will had taken Lucy's seat at the computer. Autumn and Jennifer had squeezed together into an armchair where they were giggling and looking through some of the tourist brochures provided by the hotel.

"We're all here," said Pam. "And we're very glad you could come and take over for George."

"Not at all," said Quentin. "I'm very happy to be here with you all, though of course I regret the circumstances that brought me here. This is Emma Temple," he said, indicating his companion. "She has come to make arrangements to return her father's body to the States."

If he'd announced he'd brought along an auditor from the Internal Revenue Service to inquire into their tax returns, he couldn't have gotten a more awkward reaction. The room fell silent and eyes were averted until Pam stepped forward and grabbed Emma's hand. "I think I speak for everyone when I say how very sorry we all are for your loss. If there's anything we can do to help, please don't hesitate to ask."

"You're very kind," said Emma, her glance passing to each of them, as a lawyer might assess a jury. "I don't anticipate any problems. I'm an attorney, so I'm familiar with situations like this. I expect to wrap things up fairly quickly."

"Dealing with the death of a parent is always difficult . . ." began Rachel.

Emma cleared her throat, eager to set the record straight. "My parents were divorced and I hadn't seen my father for many years. I can't pretend to be grief-stricken, but I do appreciate your concern." She turned to Quentin. "If you'll excuse me, I'd like to get settled in my room and leave you all to your tour. I have some phone calls to make."

As Emma left the room, there seemed to be a general relaxation of tension. People were uncomfortable with death, Lucy reasoned, and it was awkward to confront grieving family members. Even worse, perhaps, when the family member wasn't grieving.

"Well, then. Onward and upward as my dear mother likes to say." Quentin was ready to take charge. "I believe George made arrangements for an excursion to Hampton Court today. In fact, I noticed a minibus parked outside, and I spoke to the driver, who is waiting for us. So if you all want to get your things for the day, we can get this show on the road."

As always in London, the road was crowded and the minibus crawled through town. Lucy didn't mind the slow pace, because it gave her an opportunity to get the lay of the land. Passing through busy Leicester Square, she spotted the TKTS booth where theater tickets were sold for half price, and passing Green Park, she noticed a sign pointing the way to Buckingham Palace. This was all useful information that she filed away for future reference.

Sue was also taking notes. "That's the Wolseley," she said, pointing out a restaurant on Piccadilly. "Very fashionable."

"Looks expensive," said Lucy, noticing the Ritz Hotel on the next corner and the well-dressed men in bespoke suits with slim briefcases striding along purposefully on the sidewalk.

Sue had also noticed them. "Don't you wish people in America dressed better? All anybody seems to wear anymore is jeans."

"Jeans are just fine with me," said Lucy, looking down at her denim-clad legs, "and I've noticed plenty of people wearing them here in London, too."

"Only tourists," sniffed Sue.

Lucy laughed. "We're tourists. There's nothing wrong with that."

"Even Jane Austen was a tourist," said Quentin, joining the conversation. "It was quite the fashion in nineteenth-century England to tour the countryside and visit the stately houses. Elizabeth Bennett goes sightseeing in *Pride and Prejudice*. In fact, it's the sight of Mr. Darcy's impressive estate that prompts her to revise her previously unfavorable opinion of him and decide he's marriage material." He paused. "I think you will discover that Hampton Court is well worth a visit. It was built by Cardinal Wolsey and was the finest palace in England, a fact that didn't sit well with Henry the Eighth. He complained that the cardinal's home was far nicer than anything he had, compelling the cardinal to offer it to him. Henry didn't hesitate to seize it. He wanted something that would impress his new lover, Anne Boleyn." Quentin paused. "I guess we all know how that turned out."

"She was beheaded, wasn't she?" said Autumn. "We saw the monument at the Tower of London."

Quentin nodded. "Henry soured on the relationship when she failed to produce a male heir."

"Typical!" snorted Autumn. "Like that was her fault."

"Nowadays we know it's the father's sperm that determines the sex of the child," observed Dr. Cope. "They didn't know that in the sixteenth century."

"Was that why she died?" Jennifer's voice was low and her face pale. "Just because she didn't have any sons?"

"It was a bit more complicated than that. She was accused of treason and fornicating with her brother and just about anything her enemies could think of. But Henry had it done in true royal style." Quentin spoke with relish, enjoying showing off his knowledge. "Instead of letting the usual executioner go at her with an ax, which sometimes took more than a few whacks, he hired the famous swordsman of Calais to do the deed in the French manner. One quick swing of the sword and the problem was solved."

"I hated the Tower," whispered Jennifer. "It's a horrible place. You can almost hear those poor souls screaming."

"I imagine more than a few got exactly what they deserved," said Tom Smith.

"And others were sacrificed to royal whims," said Quentin. "At Hampton Court, they say, visitors sometimes encounter the ghost of Katherine Howard, still protesting her innocence."

"What happened to her?" asked Caroline, rousing from her usual lethargy and taking an interest.

"She was Henry the Eighth's fifth wife." Quentin ticked them off on his fingers. "Divorced, beheaded, died, divorced, *beheaded . . .*"

"Oh, no, not another," moaned Jennifer.

"Afraid so. She not only failed to produce an heir but she was also judged unfaithful to the king."

Sue raised a perfectly shaped eyebrow. "Seems a risky sort of thing to do with a husband like Henry."

"Who knows?" Quentin shrugged. "The court was full of rumors. It may not have been true. Unfortunately, Henry believed it, so it was 'Off with her head!' and this time there was no fancy French swordsman."

Jennifer was so pale Lucy was afraid she might pass out. "Tell us about the sixth wife," she suggested. "She outlived Henry, didn't she?"

Quentin smiled. "Catherine Parr. She did indeed. As the rhyme goes, she survived. She married again after Henry's death but unfortunately died of puerperal fever."

"A common occurrence in those days," said Dr. Cope.

"But don't think Hampton Court is anything like the Tower—it's a beautiful Tudor country estate that's been enlarged by subsequent kings and queens. It's situated on the Thames and has beautiful gardens, which I encourage you to explore. Because, it seems, we've arrived."

The driver swung the minibus into a drop-off area, and they disembarked, gathering in a small knot on the gravel pathway to wait while Quentin bought the tickets. Lucy found herself enjoying the fresh air and sunshine as she took in the splendid view. The gravel drive, which bisected a bright green lawn edged on one side by the meandering river, led to the quaintly towered and turreted structure of age-darkened red brick. It didn't seem very large or impressive from this angle, but rather like a castle you might see pictured in an illustrated book of fairy tales. Rapunzel would not have looked out of place letting her hair down from one of the twin towers that flanked the central gate.

When Quentin returned and distributed plans of the palace, she discovered it was a vast complex of buildings extending far beyond the Tudor façade and included a chapel, numerous enclosed courts, a Tudor kitchen, picture galleries, an orangery, halls for receiving state visitors, and once-private royal apartments.

"I'm afraid we got off to a rather late start this morning, so we don't have as much time as I'd like," said Quentin after checking his watch. "I suggest we stick together for a quick tour of the interior and then go our separate ways to the garden, lunch, the maze, whatever you like. We must all meet back here at exactly this spot at three o'clock. And I mean three o'clock and not a minute later because our driver has warned us that traffic will most likely be heavy and we must get back to London before our minibus turns into a pumpkin on the stroke of five."

This was met with nods and bemused smiles as they began making their way to the entrance with Quentin leading the way. Once inside, he led them upstairs and down through vast halls with elaborately plastered ceilings and along dark and chilly bricked corridors to the vast, smoky kitchens where two meals a day for hundreds of members of the royal household had been cooked every day on open fires. Lucy found it all fascinating and hung on to every word, but after they'd viewed the Chapel Royal and entered the Georgian area of the palace, she began to lose interest. All those Williams and Georges confused her, and she found herself longing to get outside to explore the garden and find the Great Vine. She'd recently read about it in a gardening magazine and was eager to see the famous old survivor for herself.

"These rooms were originally intended for Queen Mary the Second. She was coruler with her husband, William the Third, but they are better known to us as William and Mary, who the college is named after but were later used by Queen Caroline, George the Second's wife . . ." Quentin was rambling on, absorbed by a subject that he alone found fascinating. Without the titillation of sexual misalliances and royal beheadings, the group was becoming restless, and when Lucy saw Autumn and Jennifer slip away, she tapped Sue on the shoulder. "Let's go," she whispered. "I want to see the Great Vine."

When the group turned a corner into a little room with original linenfold paneling, Lucy and Sue headed in the opposite direction. By following a few signs, they soon found themselves outside, standing in front of a classically proportioned Georgian façade that bore no resemblance at all to the Tudor side of the building. This part of the redbrick palace had white trim and even rows of large windows that wouldn't have looked out of place on a New England college campus. It could even be a high school or a town hall.

"Whoa," said Sue, putting on her sunglasses, "talk about a time warp."

"Yeah," agreed Lucy, spotting a sign pointing to the Great Vine. "This way, come on. We can't miss this. It's hundreds of years old."

Sue was poring over the plan. "What exactly is it?"

"A grapevine. It was planted three hundred years ago."

Sue's eyebrows rose over her DKNY sunglasses. "So?"

"That's amazing. Just imagine. Three hundred years and it still produces grapes."

"Poor thing." Sue was marching along the walkway. "They ought to let it retire."

"Nope, it's like the queen. It has to carry on until it dies." Lucy waved her arm. "Just look at these gardens. They're beautiful."

As they walked along the side of the enormous palace, they could see various formal gardens laid out before them, many with lavishly planted beds packed with hyacinths and pansies, outlined by neatly clipped boxwood hedges.

"Their spring is way ahead of ours," said Lucy. "I haven't even seen a crocus at home."

"We don't really have spring in Maine," observed Sue. "We go straight from winter to mud and then it's summer and black flies."

Lucy had paused in front of an old-fashioned little greenhouse, surrounded by a patch of freshly turned earth. "This is it," she exclaimed, her voice full of awe. "The Great Vine."

"I only see dirt," said Sue.

"They don't plant anything here. The roots are beneath this soil, and they don't want anything to compete with the vine. Come on." She grabbed Sue's hand and pulled her toward the door.

Inside it was warm and humid, and the Great Vine was bare and leafless, its tendrils rising from a thick and knobby trunk and spreading beneath the greenhouse's glass roof.

Lucy exhaled slowly. "Isn't it magnificent?"

Sue was peering over her sunglasses, staring at the vine's rough brown bark. "I don't see it myself, but, then, I'm not much of a gardener. I suppose it's quite nice when it has leaves and grapes."

Lucy was crestfallen. "You don't like it?"

"I love it," said Sue, stifling a smile. "Now let's find this famous maze."

The walk to the maze took them past spacious lawns filled with thousands of naturalized daffodils, all in bloom. "Now this is more like it," said Sue. "I like a bit of color, and look at the way they all nod in the breeze. When I get home, I'm going to plant a whole lot of daffodils."

"You'll have to wait till fall," said Lucy.

Sue was doubtful. "Really?"

"Really. You plant them in the fall and they come up in the spring."

Sue chewed her lip. "I'll probably forget by then."

"I'll remind you." Lucy had stopped before a wall of living green. "This is it. The maze. The entrance must be around the side."

"It's bigger than I thought," said Sue. "What if we get lost and can't get out?"

"I have an excellent sense of direction," declared Lucy, stepping through the turnstile. "Follow me."

Once inside the maze, Lucy found she'd spoken too soon. The twists and turns of the paths soon confused her, and they came to several dead ends that required them to retrace their steps through the narrow alleys between the clipped hedge. The hedge was too tall to see over, but they could hear voices as other visitors laughed and called to each other. They recognized Autumn's voice, calling, "This way, come this way," and followed it to the center of the maze. But when they got there, they didn't find Autumn, only Jennifer, who was wiping tears from her eyes with her hands.

Lucy's motherly instincts were aroused and she produced a tissue from her bag. "What's the matter?"

"Nothing." The girl smiled wanly. "I had a little panic attack, but now that you're here, I'll be fine."

"Where's Autumn?" Sue gestured at the enclosed space, empty except for the three of them. "I heard her voice."

"She was here but she ran off." Jennifer's face was an angry red, in marked contrast to her usual pallor.

"Why did she do that?" asked Lucy, suspecting the girls had quarreled.

Jennifer licked her lips nervously and shrugged her bony shoulders. "You know how she is. She thought it would be fun to frighten me. She knew I was afraid I couldn't find my way out."

"That's rather mean," said Sue.

Jennifer was quick to defend Autumn. "Oh, she didn't mean anything by it." She tucked the used tissue into her pocket. "What does happen if you can't figure it out? Do they leave you here all night?"

"I don't think so." Sue was leading the way. "I imagine they keep count. That's probably what the turnstile is for."

"Oh." Jennifer giggled nervously. "Now I feel foolish. Why didn't I think of that?"

"They don't call it a maze for nothing," said Sue, pausing at a fork and trying to decide which way to go. "It's very disorienting."

"Go left," said Lucy. "When in doubt, go left."

Sue was doubtful. "Why?"

"Because it's natural to go right and the maze designer knows that."

"Okay," agreed Sue, turning the corner and discovering a sign pointing to the exit. "Look at that! Easy as pie."

"Pie!" exclaimed Lucy. "Do you realize we haven't had lunch yet? I'm starving."

"I could do with a bite myself," said Sue. "Let's head back to the entrance. I saw a sign for a café there."

Jennifer walked along with them. "Do you mind if I come, too?"

Lucy was impressed by her politeness and gave her a little hug. "Not at all."

It was quite some distance through the palace and back to the entrance gate, and then even farther to the Tiltyard Café, which was tucked behind a formal garden outside the palace. When Lucy saw the sign advertising Devonshire cream teas, she was encouraged.

"Look!" she exclaimed. "We can have afternoon tea."

The little café was packed. Every table inside and out was occupied by people of every size and description, speaking numerous languages, and all of whom seemed to be tucking into their afternoon snacks.

Jennifer's eyes were enormous as she watched the servers dipping out big scoops of Devonshire cream and strawberry jam that they arranged on plates alongside freshly baked scones. Even Sue was taking an interest. "When in England, do as the English," she said, joining the queue and taking a tray.

She'd no sooner picked it up than Quentin hailed them from the exit, where he was returning his empty dishes to the rack by the door. "Lucy!" he called. "It's three o'clock!"

Lucy's stomach growled in protest. "We'll get it to go," she promised.

"You don't have time! The bus is leaving!"

Jennifer was already hurrying across the café to Quentin, who was waiting for them by the door.

Sue replaced the tray with a thunk. "Just as well," she muttered. "Those things must be loaded with calories."

As they departed, Lucy's eye was caught by a pleasantly plump Indian woman in a sari who had bitten into a scone and was licking cream and jam off her lips, a blissful expression on her face. "We're zero for three," she reminded Sue as they followed Quentin and Jennifer down the gravel path toward the waiting minibus. "We couldn't find a tea shop on Saturday, we had a late lunch on Sunday, and today we didn't have time for tea. You wouldn't think it would be so hard, would you?"

"There, there." Sue was using her nanny voice. "This is England. I'm sure there will be lots more opportunities for afternoon tea."

"I sure hope so," grumbled Lucy, climbing aboard the minibus.

Chapter Seven

When Lucy took a seat on the minibus, she noticed Jennifer had spurned Autumn and was sitting with her grandfather. Autumn was sitting by herself, but when Quentin boarded, he took the seat next to her. Lucy was seated just behind him, which gave her a clear view of his pink and freckled bald spot.

Lucy knew that some women found baldness sexy—it was even fashionable for young men to shave their heads—but she wasn't a big fan of the look. She was glad that Bill still had a full head of hair and a thick beard, albeit dusted with gray. She thought of him fondly and wondered what he was doing at home and checked her watch. He was probably at work, she decided, and thinking about lunch. The thought made her feel a bit guilty since she wasn't home to pack that lunch for him. She wondered how he was managing with the girls, the dog, and the household chores, in addition to the remodeling job he'd taken on in one of the big shingle-style cottages on Shore Drive. The owners were very wealthy—and very demanding.

It was noisy in the minibus as the driver accelerated and turned into the road. The engine was loud and everybody was talking, comparing their experiences at Hampton Court. In the seat in front of her, Quentin was chatting with Autumn about Winchester College, and when there was a sudden drop in the general noise level, Lucy heard him offer to give her some career counseling. "It's not easy to decide what you want to be when you grow up," he was saying.

Ohmigosh, she thought, he's up to his old tricks. He'd used the same line with her, all those years ago, when she had taken that Victorian literature class. It all seemed foolish now, but she'd been a young mother then and had felt her sense of self slipping away as she struggled every day to meet her children's needs. When she'd decided to go back to school, it wasn't to satisfy her intellectual curiosity as much as to have something for herself. She'd enjoyed the course, had even liked writing papers, but what had kept her coming back week after week was the opportunity to see the handsome young professor.

It was nothing more than a crush, but he noticed her interest and invited her to lunch at the town's poshest restaurant, the Queen Victoria Inn. Another thought popped into her head—the image of the woman in the café licking cream off her lip. Quentin had done the same thing then, and she'd found it exciting. Much to her shame, she remembered, she accepted his invitation to go to his apartment. He said he wanted to show her some photos he'd taken of Elizabeth Barrett Browning's flat in Florence. She never got a glimpse of the photos, but he had kissed her, more than once.

The memory made her squirm in her seat, earning her a curious look from Sue. "Ants in your pants?" she asked.

"I've got a backache." It was true, she realized. Being a tourist was hard work, and all that walking and standing was taking a toll.

"Me too." Sue raised her arms above her head and stretched, arching her back. "And I'm really hungry."

Quentin overheard her and made an announcement. "I've made reservations for dinner tonight for all of us at Ye Olde English Roast Beef," he told the group. "I've invited Emma Temple, too. I thought eating dinner together would give us all an opportunity for closure. We can share our thoughts and feelings about George's unexpected and tragic death and, hopefully, move on."

"I don't know," objected Ann Smith in a quavery voice. "There was that, well, I don't quite remember what it was about, but there was something about English beef not being safe to eat."

Rachel remembered. "Mad cow disease."

"That's right!" Autumn was eager to share the gruesome details. "You eat the meat and forty years later your brain turns to mush and you become a drooling idiot. We can't eat there."

"We certainly can," said Dr. Cope. "The British government dealt very effectively with that outbreak, and British beef is now one hundred percent safe to eat."

Laura Barfield was retying the blue scarf she had tucked into her jacket. "I know somebody who can't give blood because he was in England during that outbreak."

"A wise precaution, I'm sure," admitted Dr. Cope. "But the actual chance of infection was very low, even during the height of the outbreak. You have more to fear from the flu that arrives every winter."

"Well, then, we'll go ahead to the steak house." Quentin paused and, hearing a murmur of dissent, continued. "I'm sure they serve fish and chicken as well as beef."

Tom Smith raised a hand, as if in school. "Is the dinner included in the tour or will we have to split the check?"

"Good point. We'll split the check." Quentin was already turning his attention back to Autumn, who was bent over her iPhone. "Those are fantastic, aren't they? Super for e-mail."

Autumn was focused on the screen. "I'm not e-mailing. I'm tweeting."

"Tweeting? What's that?"

She turned and looked at him, her expression a mixture of shock and dismay. "Don't you know about Twitter?"

Oh, dear, thought Lucy. *Poor Quentin. His age is showing.*

When they all gathered at the long table that had been reserved for them at Ye Olde English Roast Beef, Lucy discovered Quentin was an equal-opportunity flirt. As soon as he spotted her coming through the door with her friends, he invited her to sit beside him. There was room for all four of them, so she could hardly refuse. Pulling out the chair, she noticed a couple of aged French fries curled up on the leatherette seat and brushed them off with her napkin.

Once seated, she took a look around and discovered the place had seen better days. Dated Tiffany lamps hung over the scuffed tables, the mirrors that lined the walls were streaked and dirty, and the stuffed head of an Aberdeen bull that hung over the bar seemed to have a bad case of mange, which was giving him a rather wild-eyed expression.

"The mad cow himself," said Sue.

"I need new silverware," said Rachel, holding up a fork for examination. If it had gone through the dishwasher, the dishwasher was in need of repair.

Lucy was checking her own place setting when Emma Temple arrived, seating herself in the last vacant seat, directly opposite Quentin. The rest of the group was arranged on Quentin's other side: Autumn was next to him, separated from Jennifer by Laura and Dr. Cope. Will was at the end of the table and the Smiths were seated between Will and Emma. As always, Caroline was positioned protectively between her parents, which struck Lucy as slightly ridiculous. The girl was every bit as big as her father and seemed quite capable of taking care of herself.

After a few pleasantries and greetings, everyone got busy studying their menus. There was no rush. Lucy had practically learned it by heart before the waiter appeared. He didn't seem old enough to be working—his face was spotty with pimples—but he quickly took charge.

"I'll replace that fork for you, madam," he said smoothly when Rachel displayed the offending piece of cutlery, and quickly moved on to the important business at hand. "Would you like to start with something from the bar?"

Once they'd all placed their orders, Quentin leaned toward Lucy in a rather intimate manner. "If I remember correctly, you're something of an investigative reporter."

Hearing this, Laura Barfield's head snapped around and she stared at Lucy. Conversation had stopped and Lucy found everyone waiting for her reply. "Not really, although I do write a little bit for the Tinker's Cove weekly newspaper, the *Pennysaver.* Pam here is married to the owner."

"Don't be so modest." Quentin turned to the table at large. "Lucy cracked a case that had the police completely baffled. A murder."

Lucy could have killed him. The last thing she wanted was to be the center of attention. "It was a sad, tragic incident," she said, "and not really suitable for dinner table conversation."

"I quite agree," said Laura primly. "I was brought up to avoid controversy at dinner. Religion, politics, and money were all strictly banned at my mother's table." She paused, turning to Emma. "How was your day?"

Emma leaned to the side, making room for the waiter to put down her glass of white wine. "Thank you for asking. I'm afraid I encountered a bit more red tape than I expected."

"That is too bad." Laura seemed determined to keep the polite chatter going. "It's really the curse of the modern world, don't you think? Life has gotten so complicated. I recently changed my Internet service, and I can't tell you how confusing it was."

"Too many choices—that's the problem." Dr. Cope was twirling his old-fashioned, waiting for everyone to be served.

"You're exactly right," agreed Tom Smith. "First thing I have to do when I get home is my income tax. I'm not looking forward to that!"

The waiter had set down the last glass and Quentin was on his feet. "I'd like to propose a toast to our dear friend and colleague George Temple."

A few glances were exchanged but everyone raised their glass.

"*Requiescat in pace.*" Quentin took a big gulp of his red wine.

"Amen," said Rachel, prompting a responsive murmur and a few nods as everyone took a swallow.

Lucy felt badly for Emma, who she suspected might rather not be reminded of her father's death, but the young woman didn't seem upset. She joined the others in raising her glass and downed a hearty swallow before turning to Ann Smith, who was seated beside her, and referring to the menu. "What looks good?"

The next few minutes were spent placing their orders, but when the waiter ambled off to the kitchen, Lucy seized the opportunity to ask Quentin about George Temple. "Did you know George well?"

"Not well, no," he said, speaking slowly and making plenty of eye contact. "Although he had been at the college for some time. He arrived shortly after I started there, perhaps in the early nineties. He was middle-aged then. I think he had changed careers in midlife. He was popular with the students, and he led one of these trips every year, but he wasn't a true academic. His knowledge was wide but not deep, if you know what I mean." He smiled at Emma. "But that's not to say he wasn't a committed, caring teacher, quite competent to teach introductory-level courses. He was an adjunct, you know, not on the tenure track."

"That's not what I heard," said Lucy, remembering her conversation with Pam. "I heard he was being considered for some professor's job."

Quentin chuckled and promptly changed the subject. "What do you think of the English newspapers?"

"Pretty racy if you ask me," said Tom Smith with a leer. "Topless girls, right on page three."

Ann didn't approve. "Oh, Tom," she said. "Not in front of—"

"The kids?" Tom finished the sentence for her. "I imagine they could teach us a few things."

The food took a while to come, giving them all time to order a second round of drinks, which Lucy suspected might be intentional on the part of the restaurant. Quentin remained focused on Lucy, saying he'd followed her career in the *Pennysaver.*

"Not much of a career, really. I don't get to write as much as I'd like. I mostly edit the events listings." Lucy giggled; she was tired and that second glass of wine was going straight to her head.

"And what about your family?" Quentin was doing that thing again, running his tongue over his upper lip.

"The kids are growing up. Toby is married and has a baby boy."

Quentin's eyebrows lifted. "Don't tell me you're a grandmother?"

Lucy laughed. She had to admit it was nice to have someone paying attention to her. She loved Bill, but he did tend to take her for granted.

"And your husband?"

Lucy felt that Quentin was testing the waters, and it was time to let him know these seas were definitely chilly. "Bill is keeping the home fires burning, keeping an eye on our youngest girls."

Quentin gave her that half smile of his. "Sounds like you have the perfect family."

Lucy thought of Elizabeth's e-mail. "Not perfect." Quentin leaned a bit closer, apparently taking this as a sign of encouragement. "But okay," she added, pulling away from him.

She was relieved when he turned to his other side and began talking to Autumn. Conversation was lagging, despite Laura's gallant efforts at polite small talk, and more than one member of the tour was yawning when the waiter finally began delivering their dinners. Dr. Cope and Quentin had stuck to their guns and ordered steaks, which looked to be a mistake since the meat was overcooked. Ann Smith's broiled Dover sole, on the other hand, didn't seem to have more than a passing acquaintance with the flame and was still pink and glistening. When she asked the waiter to take it back for another pass under the broiler, he warned her that the chef would be insulted.

Ann wasn't about to insist. "Oh, dear, I guess it's all right." She was picking up her fork when her husband snatched the plate away.

"Don't be ridiculous," he told the waiter. "This hasn't been properly cooked."

The kid took the plate, perching it dangerously close to the edge of the tray, while continuing to distribute the other dishes. He finished passing out the chicken and pasta dishes the others had ordered before taking the fish back to the kitchen.

The younger members of the party immediately began eating, but the others sat waiting for the waiter to bring Ann's plate back.

"Please don't wait for me," she urged. "Your food will get cold."

"Have some of my pasta," offered Rachel, picking up her bread and butter plate and spooning some pasta primavera onto it.

"We didn't get any rolls," observed Lucy.

Sue had taken a bite of chicken, then put down her fork. "This chicken is weird. It's some sort of processed meat."

"Well, the steak is delicious," insisted Quentin, chewing energetically.

"I wouldn't go quite that far," said Dr. Cope.

"English food isn't supposed to be very good," said Emma, carefully cutting away the brown edges of a piece of broccoli.

The waiter returned with Ann's sole, which was now as brown

and tough as a cedar shingle. "Can you get us some bread or rolls?" asked Lucy.

The waiter squinted. "Costs extra, you know."

"We'll pay," said Pam in a no-nonsense tone. "And don't forget the butter."

They had just about finished eating as much of the awful food as they could manage when the waiter returned with a basket of sliced soft white sandwich bread. It was passed along quickly as everyone took a slice, hoping to gain enough sustenance to survive until breakfast.

"Can I interest you in dessert or coffee?" inquired the waiter, pencil poised to take their orders.

"None for me," said Lucy, rising to go to the restroom. If the dinner was anything to go by, the coffee was sure to be thin and lukewarm, she thought as she groped her way down the poorly lit stairway. The door to the ladies' room was missing the letter *L* but when she entered, it was brightly lit, which was unfortunate considering the state of the facilities. She wrinkled her nose at the unpleasant smell and cautiously pushed open the stall door, expecting to find a filthy situation. The toilet was passably clean, however, and she was sitting on it when she heard the outer door open and recognized Jennifer's and Caroline's voices.

She leaned forward, straining to hear what they were saying, but only caught a few words: "Autumn . . . who does she . . . like it was her idea . . ."

Lucy zipped up her jeans, flushed the toilet, and pushed open the door, catching a glimpse of the two girls with their heads together. Realizing they weren't alone, they suddenly stopped talking and Caroline rushed past her into the single stall.

"I didn't mean to startle you," said Lucy, leaning over the grubby sink and turning on the rusty faucet to wash her hands.

Jennifer was brushing her long blond hair, absorbed by her own reflection in the cracked mirror. "No problem," she said. Her voice was cool and assured, and it struck Lucy that she hadn't heard her use that tone before now, and certainly not when she was talking to Autumn.

Lucy found a clean spot on the roller towel—a relic of the past that she hadn't seen in years—and dried her hands. "See you later," she said, leaving the room. As she made her way up the dusty stairs with the broken rubber treads, she had the uncomfortable feeling that something wasn't quite right but attributed it to her digestion.

"We'll be lucky if we don't come down with food poisoning," she told Sue as she added her twenty-pound note to the pile in the center of the table.

Sue shoved her mostly untouched plate away and glanced at the stuffed bull's head. "We should have risked mad cow disease."

Chapter Eight

When the morning sun brightened the gap in the flowered curtains the next morning, Lucy was surprised to find she had slept through the night and felt fine. Jet lag was apparently a thing of the past. It was only six, though, and Sue was still asleep, so Lucy pulled a sweater over her pajamas and tiptoed out of the room, intending to get a cup of coffee from the machine in the lounge. Some of the rooms didn't have bathrooms, and there were shared facilities off the stair landing. She paused in one on the way downstairs, pleased that she didn't have to disturb Sue by using the loo in their room.

The lounge was deserted at this early hour. The couches and easy chairs, upholstered in varying shades of red, were somewhat rumpled and still bearing the imprints of last night's occupants. Lucy prepared her coffee and took it over to the computer, enjoying a few sips while she waited for the PC to warm up and let her log on. In a few minutes, she'd finished her coffee and was scrolling through her e-mail, deleting all the junk mail. She wrote a funny account of the horrible Ye Olde English Roast Beef restaurant to Bill and sent it and was about to log off when a message from Elizabeth popped up.

What on earth was the girl doing, writing e-mails at two in the morning? Lucy shook her head in dismay as she opened the message, which was written entirely in capital letters. Elizabeth was clearly upset.

MOM I HAD THAT MEETING WITH THE DEAN AND SHE'S REALLY A STUPID WOMAN WHO DOESN'T KNOW ANYTHING ABOUT OUR SCHOOL TRADITIONS. THE ENTIRE SENIOR CLASS ALWAYS HAS A CANDLELIGHT PROCESSION DOWN NEWBURY STREET TO THE PUBLIC GARDEN THE NIGHT BEFORE GRADUATION. THEN WE ALL STAND AROUND THE LAKE THERE WITH CANDLES AND SING THE ALMA MATER. WE'VE BEEN DOING IT FOR OVER A HUNDRED YEARS AND NOW THIS AWFUL WOMAN SAYS WE CAN'T DO IT. HONESTLY I'D LIKE TO KILL HER!!!

Lucy got up and fixed herself another cup of coffee while trying to think how to reply. Sipping thoughtfully, she stood for a minute in front of the windows, looking out at the empty street and the neat row houses on the opposite side. She had such high hopes for Elizabeth. She hoped the girl wasn't going to sabotage herself before she got started in life.

Dear Elizabeth,

I understand that you're upset about the changes the dean has proposed, but you need to remember that the world has changed quite a lot in the past hundred years. I'm sure the dean is concerned about the students' safety as well as liability issues. The school would be responsible if there was an accident and somebody got burned.

I hope you were polite during your meeting. Perhaps you should consider apologizing and trying to work out a compromise of some sort.

You need to keep your RA job—we can't afford the additional expense if you lose it.
Stay in touch.
Love,
Mom

Lucy reread the message a few times, then clicked SEND, at the same time sending up a little wish that it would all work out. She picked up her half-full cup of coffee and made a fresh one for Sue, then started up the stairs to their room.

Sue was just waking up when Lucy opened the door. "You're an angel," she said when Lucy set the coffee on her nightstand. After she'd had a few swallows, she stretched her arms over her head. "So what are we doing today?"

"The Victoria and Albert Museum," said Lucy, grabbing her towel and heading for the shower.

"The Victoria and Albert Museum is the world's largest with over seven miles of galleries," said Quentin. The group was seated together in one end of a carriage on the Piccadilly Line, and he was standing above them, hanging on to a pole as he delivered a brief introductory lecture. "It was the vision of Prince Albert to create a collection that would be available to all people to inspire and inform them. Some of the highlights include the Raphael Room, the British Galleries, and the Islamic and Indian Galleries."

Sue was studying her guidebook. "It's also quite near Harrods."

Quentin sighed. "Yes, it is."

"We'll give it a quick look," said Sue, speaking to her friends and keeping her voice low, as if plotting a conspiracy. "Then we'll go shopping. Harrods is the world's most famous, most fabulous department store."

Her fellow conspirators weren't convinced. "I want to see the Great Bed of Ware," protested Pam.

"I want to see it all," said Rachel.

Lucy noticed Sue's expression darkening—she liked to get her way. "There's that exhibit of hats you were talking about," she reminded her friend.

"Okay." Sue was amenable. "I'll look at the hats while you all do the boring stuff."

Lucy felt rather overwhelmed when they arrived at the museum and paused under the enormous Dale Chihuly glass sculpture that looked like a nest of snakes. She unfolded a floor plan and studied it, trying to decide where to begin.

"I think we should start with the British Galleries," suggested Pam, looking over her shoulder.

"I imagine that's where they keep the Great Bed of Ware," said Rachel, amused.

"And Grinling Gibbons's cravat—it's a necktie entirely carved of wood. I saw it in a magazine." Pam was bouncing on her toes, as excited as a kid at an amusement park.

"Doesn't sound very comfortable to me," observed Sue. "I'll stick to hats."

"I always get lost in museums," confessed Lucy. "We better have a meeting place, just in case. Let's meet in the café at one."

Sue liked that idea. "Then we can decide if you want to continue here at the museum or go on to Harrods where they have the really good stuff—and you can buy it."

"Don't hesitate to let us know what you'd like to do," cracked Rachel. "Just speak up."

"You'll see. I'm right," predicted Sue, marching off to buy a ticket for the special exhibition.

Lucy and the others headed for the British Galleries, but when Lucy paused to study a display of Victorian tableware, she lost track of Pam and Rachel. A few twists and turns took her to a roomful of antique medical instruments, and she soon found herself both fascinated and appalled by treatments once considered effective, such as purging and bloodletting. Shockingly, some of the crudest apparatuses, like surgical saws and obstetrical forceps, were still in use today.

Lucy was staring at a jar of leeches preserved in formaldehyde when Ann Smith joined her. "Disgusting, aren't they?" observed Ann.

"They sure are," agreed Lucy, wondering that Ann had managed to separate herself from her husband and daughter.

The mystery was soon solved. "Have you seen Tom and Caroline? I seem to have lost them."

"It's easy to do here," said Lucy. "I lost my friends, too. Shall we stick together?"

Ann was eager to accept her offer. "I'd appreciate it. I get a little panicky when I'm alone."

"I guess we all do," said Lucy, who didn't really think that at all. It seemed to her that she rarely had a moment to herself, and she liked being alone now and then.

Ann's gaze had fallen on a glass case containing a glittering display of saws and scalpels, and she seemed to physically shrink. "Actually, I think I've seen enough here."

Lucy was agreeable. "Me too. This exhibit is enough to make you appreciate modern medicine."

"I suppose." Ann wasn't looking at either side as they passed through the gallery but kept her eyes lowered, studying the floor tiles.

"They say George Washington's doctors actually killed him by bleeding him too much." Lucy was just making conversation and didn't expect the reaction she got.

Ann whirled around. Her thin body was quivering beneath the worn beige sweater and shapeless brown pants that were too big for her, and red circles had appeared on her cheeks. "Everybody talks about the miracles of modern medicine and says how Americans have the best medical system in the world, but it's not true," she declared, sounding like she'd just bitten into a very sour lemon. "Believe me, they can't save everyone, and they don't even try if you don't have the money to pay. And medical insurance—that's a joke! They take your money, all right, but when you try to file a claim, they find ways to disqualify you."

"It's terrible, I know," said Lucy, who knew all about the problems with medical insurance. Bill was self-employed, and their premium had recently passed their mortgage to become their largest monthly expense. She grudgingly wrote the check every month, but she had no illusions that even the best health insurance policy could guarantee to cure everyone. "Dr. Cope did his best but he couldn't save George Temple."

"Temple! Is that who you think I'm talking about?"

Ann was agitated, quivering with emotion, but exactly what emotion? Lucy wasn't sure what was upsetting her. She kept her voice calm, fearful of agitating her further. "What's the trouble?" she asked. "Can I help?"

Ann laughed, a sudden, harsh explosion of sound. "Help! If only." A sob escaped from between her lips and she pressed them together. "Nobody could help my baby. My baby boy."

"I'm so sorry." Lucy suddenly understood. The Smiths had lost a child. No wonder they clung so tightly to Caroline. She felt a huge surge of sympathy for Ann, knowing that her greatest fear was losing one of her children.

"He died when he was one."

Lucy thought of her grandson Patrick, who would soon have his first birthday. She thought of his soft, fair hair and his chubby wrists and dimpled cheeks, and she knew she couldn't bear to lose him. "That's terrible," she said.

Ann had grabbed Lucy's arm, and her grip tightened. "It was my fault."

"These things happen." Lucy was beginning to worry that Ann might go completely to pieces and looked around the empty gallery, hoping to see Tom and Caroline coming in search of her. Where were they? Where was everybody? Thousands of people come to the V&A every day. How come none of them were coming to this exhibit? Ann needed help—that much was obvious—and Lucy didn't know what to do.

"It didn't have to happen." Ann's eyes were open but she wasn't seeing Lucy. She was in a trance. The words kept coming, as if once started on this story she couldn't stop. "It was the brakes. We knew they were going, but money, there was never enough money back then, so we kept putting it off. It was always next week—we'd get it done next week. And then it was too late. Caroline was in the hospital for a month. I was there even longer, until the insurance money ran out and they sent me home. That was when they told me that little Bobby was gone. They'd been afraid to tell me before."

Ann was now leaning on Lucy for support, and Lucy felt as if Ann might collapse at any moment, taking them both down.

"When I got home, there was nothing left of Bobby except a little stone in the cemetery. Tom had even cleaned out his room. He said he thought it would be easier for me."

Lucy felt as if her heart were being ripped from her chest as she led Ann to a bench in the stairwell. "Why don't you sit for a minute?" she suggested, lowering the woman onto the seat as if she were a fragile old lady. Then she seated herself beside Ann and took her hand, patting it. That's how they were when Tom and Caroline came up the steps, reminding Lucy of the cavalry in an old Western movie. Like the folks inside the circle of wagons, she felt a huge sense of relief.

"What's happened?" asked Tom, rushing to his wife's side. Behind him, Caroline was breathing heavily from the exertion of getting her extra weight up the stairs.

"Ann was upset by this medical exhibit," said Lucy, standing up. She couldn't wait to get away. "I have to meet my friends in the café," she said, apologizing for her abrupt departure.

Lucy found her friends seated at a table in a part of the café that was decorated in what she now knew, thanks to her brief foray into the British Galleries, as the Arts and Crafts style. Stained glass, colorful tiles, and heavy wood paneling created a cozy nook in the huge, bustling café, where you fetched your food from various serving stations. The girls had already bought cups of tea and were waiting for her before getting their food. Sue wanted only a small salad, so she stayed at the table to save their seats while they got in line at one of the busy cafeteria counters.

"What happened to you?" asked Rachel as they waited to place their orders.

"I don't know. I was looking at some silver and then I couldn't find you, and then I got sidetracked by Ann Smith." Lucy didn't want to say more until she'd sorted out her own emotions, which were still in turmoil. She felt badly for Ann, of course, but she also resented the way Ann had burdened her with such an unhappy story.

"I hope you didn't miss the Great Bed of Ware." Pam was studying the list of menu choices above the counter.

"I think I did. How great was it?"

Pam smiled. "Pretty great. You could fit the whole family in that bed."

"Including grandma, the dog, and a chicken or twelve," added Rachel.

"Which they probably did," said Lucy, appreciating her friends' humor.

"What can I get you?" asked the server, a chubby-cheeked woman.

"Cottage pie." After the unfortunate dinner at Ye Olde English Roast Beef, Lucy had decided the best strategy was to eat heartily when food was available and affordable, and looked good.

Pam and Rachel agreed. "Make that three," said Pam. "And a small salad."

"What exactly keeps Sue going?" asked Pam as they carried their heavily loaded trays back to their table. "What does she run on?"

Lucy shrugged. "Don't ask me. It's nothing but black coffee, salad, and wine, but she has plenty of energy. I can't keep up with her."

"I worry about her." Rachel shook her head. "It's not healthy."

"She's never sick," observed Pam.

"She looks great." The three stopped, simultaneously dropping their jaws, spotting Sue in conversation with a handsome man dressed in a beautifully tailored suit. He had one hand on the back of a chair and was leaning forward, practically dripping charm all over the table.

The three exchanged glances and marched forward in unison. "Here's your salad," said Lucy, placing it in front of Sue.

"These are my friends," said Sue with a graceful wave of her well-tended hand. "Pam, Rachel, and Lucy, this is Perry." She paused, savoring the moment. "He's an earl."

"Nice to meet you." Lucy felt a bit like the upstairs maid, standing there holding her tray. "Are we supposed to curtsy or something?"

"Not a bit. All that's rather gone out of style these days." There was a touch of gray at his temples, his eyes were blue, and his smile revealed a mess of crooked teeth. His gaze returned to Sue. "If you're interested in my collection, just ring me."

Then he was gone and the girls were plunking themselves down at the table, giggling like middle schoolers. "And what exactly does the earl collect?" inquired Pam. "Etchings?"

Sue was shaking her head. "I married too young. If I'd only known this day would come, I would have saved myself." She speared a piece of lettuce with her fork. "And we have so much in common. I like castles and he has a castle. I like hats and he collects hats, with an emphasis on hats with feathers," she said, provoking gales of laughter.

"I guess he's safe enough, then," observed Rachel drily.

"It's good to know we don't need to worry about protecting your virtue," added Pam.

"I wouldn't be so sure," said Lucy. "He seemed awfully interested."

"No," sighed Sue. "He's after my feather fascinator." Seeing their blank looks, Sue continued. "You know, the little hat I wore at Lizzy Muse's wedding. There was one quite like it in the show, and apparently Camilla wore one at her wedding to Prince Charles. Perry says it was divine, and he tried to buy it but Camilla won't sell. Sentimental reasons, he says." She chewed slowly. "I might sell him mine."

Pam was buttering a roll. "She's obviously lost her mind."

Lucy nodded. "There's only one thing that will bring her back."

"Retail therapy," suggested Rachel.

Sue gave a shaky little sigh. "I do think it's my only hope."

When they joined the stream of people pushing into Harrods—Lucy was quickly learning that people from many other countries do not necessarily have the same sense of personal space that Americans do—they passed glass cases displaying all sorts of luxury items: sunglasses costing hundreds of pounds, handbags costing thousands, watches costing tens of thousands. It was a bit overwhelming until you realized that nobody was buying. This was a temple to consumerism, and the high-priced goods were designed to awe the tourists who streamed past, nudging each other and whispering the astronomical prices.

You would have thought they were in church, thought Lucy with disapproval. "Let's start with the famous food hall."

"I've heard it's amazing," agreed Rachel.

"I did not come to Harrods to go to the supermarket," protested Sue. "I want to see the designer clothes."

"And I want to use the luxury loo," said Pam. "We need a plan."

"I have one," said Sue, consulting her guidebook. "They have a tearoom. Let's meet there at four-thirty."

The four then split up, Pam and Sue taking an elevator up and Lucy and Rachel taking one down to the cavernous food hall.

Seeing the white tile walls with their mosaics picturing foodstuffs and the refrigerated cases containing every sort of meat, Lucy felt she was in familiar surroundings. She shopped for groceries every week, and Harrods food hall wasn't that much different from the IGA in Tinker's Cove. Except, of course, that it was bigger and had a greater variety of products, and the prices were much higher.

"Imagine," said Rachel. "Thirty-two pounds for a hunk of meat."

Lucy was not about to be discouraged. She oohed in delight when she found quail eggs for sale, she admired the glistening fresh fish, and she exclaimed over the fresh-baked bread and rolls. Unable to resist the temptation to buy, she purchased four apples and four oranges in the produce section and was delighted when the clerk wrapped them in one of the highly desirable green plastic carry bags with the Harrods name in gold.

Rachel wanted to get some books for Miss Tilley, so they found an escalator and ascended, rising past a statue of a young man and woman with their arms stretched toward a soaring seagull. Lucy studied it, realizing with shock that the figures were representations of Princess Diana and her boyfriend, Dodi Fayed. Reaching the landing, she saw there was a book in which visitors could inscribe their names, just like the guestbooks provided at the funeral home back in Tinker's Cove. But this wasn't a funeral home;

it was a department store and hardly seemed a suitable place for a memorial.

Stunned, she turned to Rachel. “Isn’t this the tackiest thing you’ve ever seen?”

Rachel gave a little half smile. “The man who owns Harrods is Dodi’s father. It’s his way of making sure his son isn’t forgotten.”

Lucy stepped off the escalator and through the archway leading to the book department, among others. “It seems an odd way to do it.”

“People grieve differently, but I don’t think anybody ever gets over the loss of a child, even if that child is grown.”

Lucy reached for the spot on her arm where Ann Smith had gripped it, noticing it was a little tender. She thought of her four children and of Toby’s wife, Molly, and their son Patrick, hoping they were all healthy and happy, and she knew that if she were to lose one of them, she would grieve until the day she died.

Chapter Nine

While Rachel was looking for English mysteries to bring back to Miss Tilley, Lucy wandered into the toy department where she looked for a birthday present for Patrick. When she found a little stuffed Paddington Bear to go along with the first book in the series, she bought it, getting another Harrods bag in the bargain. Then they wandered through the housewares, deploring the fact that crockery, no matter how adorable, was an impractical souvenir, being both heavy and liable to break. At four-thirty, they went to the tearoom as planned, only to discover Sue and Pam standing in front of a door with a closed sign.

"It's undergoing renovations," said Sue. "This store has more than thirty restaurants and they have to close the tearoom."

Pam was indignant. "How many days have we been here? Three? Four? And we haven't had afternoon tea yet. What's happened to England?"

"We can go to the pub or the Asian grill or the pizza palace," suggested Rachel. "What about the coffee bar?"

Sue was pouting. "I want tea. I'm in England and I want tea."

"I have an idea," said Lucy. "Meet me at the Tube station in half an hour."

"Let's meet at six," said Sue, who had found some interesting information in her guidebook. "There are lots more stores around here. Harvey Nichols. Habitat. Burberry. If we can't have tea, we might as well shop."

"We can't afford those places," protested Pam.

"But you can always dream," said Sue, marching off with Pam and Rachel following in her wake.

Lucy found a very tired trio drooping on a bench when she arrived at the Tube station a few minutes after six, laden with more Harrods bags.

Sue looked at the bulging green bags suspiciously. "This isn't like you, Lucy. What have you been buying?"

"Food," said Lucy. "Good, wholesome food. Cheese and fruit and salads and bread and even some nice tea—I figured we could get hot water from that weird machine in the lounge. Oh, and I got a couple bottles of wine, too. We'll eat in tonight."

"Good idea." Pam was rising to her feet as the train slid into the station. "I'm too tired to go out."

Rachel secured her purse under her arm as she boarded the train. "And I'm sick of paying too much money for really bad food."

"Did you say tea?" asked Sue, perking up.

"Yes, dear. I found your favorite Lapsang Souchong."

"You really are a pal," observed Sue, sinking into the seat a handsome man in a tan trench coat promptly vacated for her.

Back at the hotel, they all crowded into Lucy and Sue's room where Lucy spread out the food on her bed, picnic style. Sue poured the wine into bathroom tumblers. Lucy tugged her swollen feet out of her shoes and tucked a pillow behind her aching back, reclining against the headboard.

Rachel and Pam brought in pillows and a chair from their room, and soon they were all comfortably settled.

"So what did you think of Harrods?" Lucy asked Sue. "Was it everything you dreamed of?"

Sue was spreading some pâté on a bit of bread. "And more. Especially when it came to prices. I didn't buy anything. I just couldn't do it."

"Even I broke down and bought this," declared Pam, holding up a gaudy flower-printed tote bag with the Harrods logo prominently embroidered beneath the handles in gold thread.

Lucy gulped. "For you?"

"That's not your style at all," observed Sue.

"No. Not for me. It's a gift for Phyllis."

Phyllis, the receptionist at the *Pennysaver,* was known for her flamboyant taste. "She'll love it," said Lucy.

"I got a good deal on books," said Rachel, digging into a container of bean salad with a plastic fork. "If you bought two, you got a third free—and I know Miss T hasn't read them."

Lucy's keen detective mind recalled seeing Sue with a small bag. "You did buy something, though," she said, looking at her friend accusingly. "What is it?"

"I'm guilty as charged," admitted Sue. "I found a lovely camisole in Harvey Nichols." She held up the wisp of lace for the girls to admire. "It was expensive but I think it was a good value."

The other three exchanged doubtful glances. High fashion in Tinker's Cove usually meant something warm and woolly.

"Really! It was less expensive than it might have been, because I found it in the lingerie department. And I can wear it lots of ways: underwear, nightwear, even under a suit to dress it up for evening."

Lucy was dipping into the salad, trying to imagine a situation in which she might wear something like the camisole and failing. "I bought a Paddington Bear for Patrick," she said. Thinking of her chubby little grandson reminded her of Ann Smith's terrible loss, and she felt a bit guilty for the way she had fled from the distraught woman.

"What do you think of the tour so far?" asked Pam, holding out her glass for a refill. "The people, I mean."

Sue was pouring the wine. "Quentin's got a thing for Lucy, that's for sure."

Lucy held out her glass, too. "He's got a thing for anything female. Didn't you notice him flirting with Autumn?"

"That girl is trouble," said Pam.

"She definitely has some serious issues," observed Rachel. "And so does Jennifer. I think she's anorexic."

"Her grandfather keeps a close eye on her," said Lucy.

"And Laura Barfield sure keeps tabs on her son," said Pam. "Poor Will—he's desperate to escape."

"I wonder what happened to his father," mused Lucy. "I wouldn't want to raise a son without a husband."

"Maybe he just didn't come on the trip," speculated Sue. "The Smiths are certainly a tight little family unit. I can't imagine Sidra ever clinging to Sid and me the way Caroline sticks to her parents."

Lucy put down her glass. "I ran into Ann in this gruesome exhibit of surgical tools. She'd gotten separated from Tom and Caroline and was frantic over it. She told me she had a little boy who died in an auto accident when he was a baby. She was pretty upset."

"Why was she telling you that?" asked Sue.

"I don't know, really. My sympathetic face?" Lucy tried to make light of it but couldn't quite carry it off. "It was pretty strange. I mean, it must have happened at least eighteen years ago. She said Caroline was a baby when it happened."

"You'd think she'd be over it by now," said Sue.

Rachel ran her finger around the rim of her glass. "The loss of a child stays with you forever. It changes your personality, your outlook on life, your relationships. It's like an emotional earthquake. Nothing is the same afterward."

Lucy thought of the statue of Diana and Dodi, soaring heavenward along with a seagull and decided it was an attempt, perhaps a futile attempt, to recast their terrible fate into something more acceptable. She supposed a lot of people would rather think of them as happy spirits than recall the sordid details of that crash in a filthy Paris tunnel.

Falling silent, they heard a soft knock on the door. When Sue opened it, she found Emma Temple standing there, holding a white blouse.

"Oh, I'm sorry to barge in like this," she said, retreating.

"No, no. Come in," invited Lucy. "What can we do for you?"

"I'm looking for a needle and thread. A button is coming loose on this blouse and I want to wear it tomorrow."

Pam, always as prepared as a good scout, popped up. "I've got a sewing kit in my room. I'll be right back."

"Oh, don't go to any trouble . . ."

"It's no trouble—it's right next door. Have some wine while I get it."

"Yes, do," said Lucy, noticing that Emma's eyes were lingering over the picnic spread out on the bed. "And some food. We've got plenty."

Emma swallowed. "Are you sure?"

"Absolutely," said Rachel. "We can't eat it all, and we have no way of keeping it."

"I'm starving," admitted Emma. "I simply couldn't face Ye Olde English Roast Beef again."

"Dive in—I hope you don't mind fingers. We're a bit short on cutlery." Lucy eased herself off the bed carefully so as not to spill anything and went into the bathroom for another glass. Emerging, she held it aloft. "Some chardonnay?"

"Actually, I'd prefer water." Emma was spreading some pâté on a hunk of baguette.

Sue was on her feet, too. "I was just going downstairs to get some hot water for tea. Would you like some?"

"Tea would be heaven," Emma said. "I've had a really tiring day."

She did look exhausted, thought Lucy. Emma had pulled her hair back into a sloppy ponytail, and her makeup had worn off to reveal pale, colorless lips and dark circles under her eyes. Beneath that glossy professional surface, she was really only a very young, vulnerable girl. "Were you able to make all the, um, arrangements?" she asked.

"Yes." Emma flashed a quick smile of thanks to Pam when she returned with a little plastic case containing threaded needles. "These are great. I don't know if I could see to thread a needle, my eyes are that tired," she said, choosing the white one. "I can't wait to take out my contacts."

"Let me do that," said Lucy, taking the blouse. "I'll sew while you eat."

In a matter of minutes, she had stitched the loose button back in place and bitten off the thread.

"That was fast," said Emma as Sue returned with five paper

cups of tea precariously balanced on a guidebook she was using as a makeshift tray.

"I made some for everybody, to save another trip downstairs," she explained between gasps for breath. "Or another climb upstairs."

"Do we have dessert?" asked Rachel, glancing at a small white box tied with string.

"Cookies!" exclaimed Lucy, lifting the lid. "Scottish shortbread."

"Perfect!" declared Rachel, choosing a petticoat tail and taking a bite. "I can't believe Ye Olde English Roast Beef is the only restaurant in London. There must be better places."

"This is my first trip to London," said Emma, sipping her tea. "I have to say it's been a bit of a disappointment. I'm glad I'm going home tomorrow."

"London's great," declared Sue. "I think your perception may be colored by your sad mission. You haven't had time to shop or see the sights or go to the theater."

Rachel nodded in agreement. "It's always hard to lose a parent."

Emma shook her head. "Honestly, he was like a stranger to me."

Rachel was having none of that; she knew all about the tricks the mind could play. "Sometimes being estranged makes it even harder."

Emma sniffed. "Unresolved issues?"

"Exactly." Rachel was reaching for another cookie.

"Frankly, I think I'm suffering more from jet lag than grief." She sighed. "Plus the frustration of dealing with very polite but very obstinate bureaucrats."

They all laughed and Lucy took advantage of the moment to pose a question that had been bothering her. "Is the coroner still satisfied that anaphylactic shock was the cause of death?"

Emma's big blue eyes widened in surprise. "Why, yes. Isn't that what happened? Some of you were right there, weren't you?"

"Right there," said Sue. "Just across the aisle."

Emma's face softened. "That must have been terrible for you."

Sue was philosophical. "They gave us free drinks."

Lucy was shocked at Sue's rudeness, fearing Emma would be insulted. But instead, she tilted her head back and laughed. "That's exactly what my mother said when she heard. She said that if the airline gave everyone free drinks because he died, it would be the nicest thing he ever did."

No one quite knew how to react—except Sue. "That must have been one really nasty divorce."

Emma nodded. "I think so. It all happened when I was quite small. I don't remember anything about it. It's always been just Mom and me, but that's the way it was for a lot of kids in my school. Some had stepparents they hated, so I figured I was pretty lucky to have Mom all to myself. We always got along fine; we're a lot alike. And Mom made a good living as a court reporter. That's how I got interested in the law—sometimes she'd bring me along if it was an interesting case."

Sue drained her teacup. "So there was no picture of Dad on the mantel?"

"No Dad at all." Emma grinned. "Really, I could have been the product of an immaculate conception. No Dad, no men. Mom wasn't interested in dating. One time I asked her about it, and she said once was enough and that was all I could get out of her."

Rachel tapped her lip with a finger. "Did she discourage you from dating?"

"Not in so many words, but she did keep me pretty busy. School was a top priority, and there were lots of dance and music lessons, soccer, Girl Scouts. She always said it was important for me to be able to support myself and not to expect some Prince Charming to rescue me."

Lucy approved. "That's good advice. That's what I tell my girls."

Rachel was thoughtful. "But weren't you curious about your father?"

"Yeah," agreed Pam. "Didn't you want to know if heart disease or cancer or hemophilia ran in his family?"

Emma laughed. "I think I'm a little too young to worry about that stuff, but it's a good point. I know he had allergies, that's for sure, but I don't seem to have any." She paused. "Maybe now that he's gone, Mom will be more willing to talk about him. I definitely would like to know more about him."

Pam was fingering the sewing case. "For what it's worth, I can tell you he was well liked at Winchester College. I never heard anyone say a bad word about him. He always got high marks on the student evaluations every year, even the underground one the students do. They said his classes were interesting, and he took an interest in the students. And he was popular with the faculty, too. I teach a yoga class, evening school, you know, and he was a regular. He was very good, very flexible." Pam's expression was thoughtful as she trolled for memories. "He had a nice attitude, serious but not too serious. I'll miss him."

Emma impulsively wrapped an arm around Pam's shoulder and hugged her. "Thank you. That means a lot to me." She got to her feet. "I really need to turn in. I've got to be at Heathrow at five tomorrow morning. Thanks for everything."

"You're welcome," said Pam. "Have a safe trip."

"Safe home," said Lucy, beginning to clear away the food wrappers in hopes that the others would take the hint. She was tired and talked out; she wanted to sleep. But when she'd brushed her teeth and slid between the sheets, she found her mind was a whirl of conflicting images. George Temple had seemed like a nice enough person; that's certainly how Pam had seen him, but not his wife. Why had she cut him out of her life so completely? What had he done?

Chapter Ten

There was definitely a different atmosphere in the breakfast room Wednesday morning. Lucy noticed it as soon as she and Sue entered. Instead of the usual hushed silence, there was a lively buzz of conversation. When she seated herself and glanced about, she noticed that everyone from the tour was there, except Quentin and, of course, Emma, who had had to catch an early flight back to the United States. This was a definite departure from the usual order of things—Autumn, Will, and Jennifer had taken to skipping breakfast the last couple of mornings, presumably so they could sleep in as long as possible. But today all three were gathered at a table, chirping away as bright as birds.

"Am I hallucinating or is something different?" asked Lucy as the waitress brought their pot of coffee and filled their cups.

Sue was lifting her cup. "I guess they're excited about going to Brighton."

Lucy took a sip of coffee and considered. The itinerary for the day was a bus trip to the famous seaside town, where they would tour the Royal Pavilion. Lucy knew a bit about the town from reading English mysteries: It featured a honky-tonk pier as well as the Pavilion, which was an architectural marvel built as a private pleasure palace by some prince. "I don't think that's it," she said.

"It's like some big cloud has lifted." She lowered her voice. "Do you think it's because Emma's gone?"

"Could be, but I think it's more likely they're excited about the roller coaster." Sue was refilling her cup. "I can't say I share their enthusiasm. It sounds hideous: a fusty old historical building and an amusement park. It's not really my sort of thing."

"There's shopping, too." Lucy had checked her guidebook. "Adorable boutiques in an area known as the Lanes."

Sue perked up, causing Lucy to wonder if it was the caffeine or the possibility of more shopping. Pam and Lucy joined them, and the waitress announced today's breakfast was egg, bacon, and sausage.

"Oh, my, that's a lot of protein," said Pam.

"Fat, you mean," said Sue. "Just toast for me."

Lucy was ready for a change. "I'll have the egg and sausage, but no bacon."

"Bran cereal for me," said Rachel.

"I'm going for the whole kit and caboodle," declared Pam. "It looks like we have a busy day ahead of us." She drank some coffee. "They say Brighton is known for its fish-and-chips shops."

"And the candy—Brighton rock." Lucy was watching as Quentin made his entrance, pausing in the doorway before joining the three students at their table. Will and Jennifer reacted as Lucy expected, straightening up and giving him polite smiles. He was a professor after all, and they were hoping to earn a couple of credits on this trip. Autumn, however, kept her elbows on the table and gave him a slow smile, as if they shared a secret.

Quentin didn't sit down, however, but picked up a spoon and tapped his glass, causing conversation to cease.

"Just a quick announcement. We will depart by minibus, or minicoach as they call it here, at precisely nine o'clock, so don't be late." He waved a warning finger, which Autumn seemed to find hilarious. He raised an eyebrow in her direction and continued. "Also, on a more serious note, I'm sure you know that Emma Temple has left our little group and is now returning to the States. As far as I know, the family is not planning a funeral service, but President Chapman has asked me to inform you that the college will be holding a memorial service on April third, the Friday after we return. She—and I join her in this—hope you will all be able to attend."

The silence that followed this somber announcement was broken by a loud guffaw, and everyone turned to see Tom Smith clapping a hand over his mouth. His wife, Ann, was glaring at him and he quickly apologized. "Sorry. I know that was terribly inappropriate. I was thinking of something amusing that happened yesterday."

Ann did her best to smile, as if she was also recalling the incident. "Yes, we saw the most proper British gentleman on the Tube yesterday, you know the type, in a suit and tie and even an umbrella and a bowler hat, and he had a big piece of newspaper stuck to his shoe!"

She and Tom shared a rather forced laugh, but all they got from the others was a scattering of fleeting smiles. Their story struck Lucy as false; when she left the family at the museum, they hardly seemed to be in a mood to notice such a sight, much less find the least bit of humor in it. But maybe she was wrong, she admitted to herself as the waitress set down a plate loaded with the usual egg and two plump sausages. If she'd learned anything in this life, it was that people often behaved strangely and in ways you didn't expect.

"How's the sausage?" asked Rachel, digging into her bran flakes. "It doesn't look like our sausage."

Indeed it didn't. It was a richer brown color and plumper. Lucy cut a piece, finding it firmer than she expected, and popped it into her mouth. "Not as fatty- tasting and with a hint of spice, nutmeg maybe." She chewed. "It's good. Different, but good."

Sue was pushing her chair away from the table and rising. "I don't know about you guys, but I need to get myself organized for the day," she said, glancing at the sunlight streaming through the window set high in the basement wall. "Don't forget your sunblock!"

"Sunblock?" mused Pam when she'd gone. "Who brings sunblock to England?"

"Sue." Lucy was polishing off her second sausage. "Only Sue."

* * *

As always, traffic was heavy and the minicoach progressed with stops and starts through London. The sun made it stuffy in the bus, and Lucy nodded off, waking to find they had reached open countryside and were passing rolling fields divided by hedgerows. This was the England she'd seen so often in movies, generally with a red-coated party of hunters on horseback racing after a pack of baying hounds. Foxhunting had been outlawed, however, so today the hunters were only in her imagination and the horses were grazing peacefully in lush green fields.

She watched the passing scene, noticing how the sky became brighter and the landscape seemed to open up, somehow seeming airier, as they passed a road sign indicating the turn to Brighton. Soon they were winding their way through narrow streets, past shops and houses, until they arrived at the bus drop-off by the Brighton Pier. There they disembarked and gathered on the sidewalk as Quentin fussed about, keeping his troops in order.

"It's a short walk to the Pavilion, which we will tour as a group, and then I will dismiss you to spend the rest of the day as you wish. The bus will pick us up here at this spot at five-thirty." He raised his finger in a gesture that was becoming familiar. "I suggest you look around and familiarize yourself with the area so there will be no confusion when it's time to leave." He waited a moment as they all gazed around, then led them on to the Royal Pavilion.

"We're not in Tinker's Cove anymore," observed Sue as they followed along with the rest of the group, and Lucy knew exactly what she meant. Brighton and Tinker's Cove were both resort towns, perched on the shore, but they had little in common. Tinker's Cove was at heart a country town, with one traffic light. Only a few streets even had sidewalks, which tended to be winding, ramshackle affairs made of various materials—asphalt here, concrete there, and, now and then, a slab of granite. The shops and houses were built of wood with clapboard or cedar shingles for siding. They tended to be one or two stories tall, with peaked roofs. Some dated from the eighteenth and nineteenth centuries, while others were more recent, generally ranches and a few McMansions.

Brighton, on the other hand, was a busy city, and they were walking on a smooth concrete sidewalk past bus stops and traffic lights. There was a constant hum of traffic rounding the rotary in front of the pier and lots of motorcycles. The buildings, uniformly tall and square, were made of white stone. If it weren't for the brightness and the tangy seaside air, Lucy would have thought she was back in London.

Rounding a corner, they got their first view of the Royal Pavilion, also built of white stone but certainly not foursquare like the others: This fantasy had sprung tall turrets and bulging domes that gave it a fairy-tale atmosphere. Unlike the Tower, there were no walls enclosing this royal domicile, only an iron fence that gave passersby a clear view of the garden. It was sizable, but not enormous, and neither was the Royal Pavilion itself. Lucy thought it had a suburban air to it, as opposed to the heavily fortified Tower of London and the expansive complex at Hampton Court.

Quentin was eager to explain the building's significance, gathering them all in the front entrance. "This was a party house built by the prince regent, a place where he could gather with his friends without the formality of the royal court. He considered himself a bit of a connoisseur of the arts and chose the very new and exciting style that was taking nineteenth-century England by storm: Orientalism. But remember, this is an English adaptation of Oriental style, taken from drawings and written descriptions since few architects and artists had actually been to China or Japan."

Once inside, they were given audioguides that led them along a prescribed circuit. In the enormous dining room, they all stared in awe at the massive table, set for thirty people, and the amazing chandelier. "I really must remodel," quipped Sue, gazing at the glittering fantasia that combined English crystal with Asian dragons.

The group drifted apart as members followed the audioguides at their own pace, stopping to linger as various items caught their interest. Lucy noticed that Autumn's major interest seemed to be sticking as close as possible to Will and wondered if she were making a play for him or perhaps trying to make Quentin jealous. Jennifer tagged along with them but was obviously the odd one out.

"It was okay," said Pam when they emerged into the gift shop, "but it seems like it would take a lot of dusting."

"Like you dust!" scoffed Sue.

Rachel jumped to her defense. "I've seen Pam dust. Once when I stopped by at her house, she answered the door holding a feather duster."

"Ah." Lucy knew that appearances could be deceiving. "You saw her with a duster, but did you actually see her use it?"

Pam quickly changed the subject. "I don't know about you guys, but I'm ready for some fish and chips. When we got off the bus, I saw a place advertising 'world famous fish and chips.' "

Harry Ramsden's was located on a corner opposite the Brighton Pier and was clean and spacious inside. Lucy was a bit disappointed when she was presented with a laminated menu instead of a chalkboard, and the fish and chips were served on a plate instead of wrapped in a sheet of newspaper, but there were consolations.

"They serve wine!" exclaimed Sue, ordering a dry white.

Pam was excited about something else. "And the fish comes with mushy peas! I've always wanted to try them."

When their meals were served, they discovered that she was right. Each portion of battered fried fish and French fries was accompanied by a little round bowl full of astonishingly bright green mush.

Lucy poked her peas suspiciously with her fork. "I never saw peas this color. They look radioactive."

"They're almost glowing," agreed Rachel.

Pam was not to be deterred. She dug in eagerly and lifted a big forkful to her mouth, but her expression of delighted anticipation soon turned to disappointment. "They taste like baby food."

Lucy wasn't tempted by the peas but found the fish delicious.

Sue sprinkled her fries liberally with malt vinegar and nibbled on one, sipping her wine. "So much better than fries with ketchup—and fewer calories."

"Chips," corrected Lucy, remembering those mysteries she loved so much. "They call them chips here. And potato chips are crisps."

"Whatever." Sue waved a graceful hand and ordered another glass of wine.

When they left the restaurant, they discovered the sun had gone and clouds had moved in. The air was cold and heavy with moisture that clung to their faces, chilling them.

"Just like home," said Lucy, shrugging into her jacket.

"It's good for the complexion." Sue studied her map, then pointed a finger. "The Lanes are thataway."

Retracing their steps toward the Royal Pavilion, they entered a narrow alley between two substantial white stone buildings and found themselves in a maze of tiny streets that twisted this way and that. It was like stumbling into a medieval village; the narrow streets were filled with groups of chattering shoppers wandering from store to store.

"What if there was a fire!" Rachel seemed to be sniffing for smoke. "A fire truck could never get in here!"

"They must have special apparatuses," declared Sue. "Look! Cath Kidston!"

"What is Cath Kidston?" asked Pam.

"You will love it." Sue grabbed Pam's hand and pulled her toward the store.

They all loved Cath Kidston, which offered household linens printed with colorful vintage designs. There were items for children—bibs and bedding and clothing, covered with bunnies and kittens for girls and fifties-style cowboys for boys. Kitchenware was abloom with flowers of all sorts, but most especially roses, in gorgeous pastel colors.

Lucy could have bought out the shop but contented herself with a cowboy bib for Patrick, and Rachel limited herself to a packet of printed tissues. Pam, on the other hand, emerged with an enormous shopping bag bulging with tablecloths and napkins and dish towels and a seriously depleted wallet.

Only Sue had resisted. "Not my style. Too flowery." Noticing Pam's disappointment, she quickly added, "But I understand the appeal. Very cute."

Continuing on, they found a jewelry store that was having a closeout sale, offering everything at 90 percent off. They quickly joined the eager throng pawing through the bins and boxes. After a few minutes, Lucy concluded the stuff wasn't to her liking, and she was uncomfortable in such tight quarters. She went back outside to get a bit of air and noticed an antiques shop across the way.

Unable to resist, she opened the door, setting a little bell to jangling. It reminded her of a similar bell on the door at the *Pennysaver* office, and she felt immediately at home. The storekeeper was sitting at a desk off to one side and looked up from the newspaper she was reading, giving her a welcoming nod. "Looking for anything in particular?"

Lucy shook her head. "Just browsing."

Much to her surprise, the little shop seemed to go on and on. She wandered through room after room, past shelves of china and old toys, tarnished silver tea sets, battered and rusty tins that once contained Lyle's Golden Syrup and Horlicks powder. She paused to flip through a box of old prints and gazed longingly at an antique "Souvenir of Brighton" plate priced at thirty-five pounds. That was something like fifty dollars. Could she bargain for a better price? She was just reaching for the plate to examine it more closely when she heard a familiar voice.

"Lucy!"

She turned her head and saw Quentin, a book open in his hand, standing in front of a shelf packed with more old books in faded covers.

"Anything interesting?" she asked.

"Nothing as interesting as you," he said, making eye contact. "How did you manage to get away from the Three Musketeers?"

She laughed. "They're looking at jewelry. There's a big sale across the way."

He replaced the book. "And you don't like jewelry?"

"I like antiques more." Lucy picked up the plate. "And it was awfully crowded in there."

He lifted his head in surprise. "You suffer from claustrophobia?"

Lucy studied the plate. Search as she might, she couldn't find any cracks. "A little bit."

"Why don't we head for the Pier, then, and get some fresh air?"

Lucy was wondering if the plate was perhaps a bit too perfect. Could it be a fake? "Sounds good," she said, replacing the plate.

Quentin took her elbow. "Do you need to check with your friends?"

Lucy shook her head. "They know I can take care of myself."

The clouds thinned when they left the store and began weaving their way through the crowded lanes, and for a moment or two there was enough sunshine to create shadows. Lucy could see her silhouette and Quentin's, stretching before them on the wide sidewalk as they walked along the busy main road to the pier. From this angle, it seemed a flimsy structure, perched on stilts and extending some distance into the blue-gray water.

"It doesn't look very safe." Looking along the shore, Lucy could see the remains of an earlier pier that had collapsed, leaving ragged and dangerous-looking beams poking out of the gray waves.

Quentin slipped his arm around Lucy's waist. "The British are very safety conscious. Mind the gap and all that. I'm sure it's inspected regularly."

They passed under the metal archway welcoming them to the pier and walked along the boardwalk, passing shacks that sold food and candy. Lucy wasn't interested in them; she wanted to walk along the white-painted railing and take in the view. They paused for a moment, a chilly breeze ruffling their hair, looking along the beach where families were gathered in little clusters along the water. A busy road ran behind the beach, lined with substantial white hotels.

"It's a whole different attitude," said Lucy, thinking of the shingle-style Queen Victoria Inn in Tinker's Cove where guests lingered in rocking chairs to enjoy the view. "They don't have porches."

"No wonder," said Quentin, drawing her closer as the sun again disappeared and a light drizzle began to fall. "It's freezing here."

Lucy pulled away, wrapping her arms around herself. Her interest was caught by a pair of elderly women, dressed as if for church in suits and heels, walking arm in arm along the pier. "Look at them, they're wearing their best bib and tucker."

Quentin touched her chin. "That's what I love about you, Lucy. *Bib and tucker.* You really have a way with words."

Lucy took a step backward, uncomfortable with the direction this was going and resumed walking. "People here do seem to dress more formally than we do in America. I haven't seen anybody in a tracksuit."

Quentin fell into step beside her. "I got into a conversation with a woman at Hampton Court. We were sitting on the same bench, in the garden. She was asking about our itinerary, and when I told her we were going to Brighton, she began to reminisce about childhood family excursions. She said everyone dressed up to go to the seaside; they wore their best clothes—the men even wore suits. They'd sit there on the shingle—that's what they call the beach—and spread out a picnic. If it was hot, the men would take off their shoes and socks and roll up their trousers to wade in the water. If it was sunny, they'd knot their handkerchiefs to make little hats to protect their heads." He paused, holding the door for her as they entered an enormous enclosed arcade filled with ringing and buzzing games. "It was a different world."

The arcade was crowded with people who had been driven inside by the weather, and Lucy was jostled by a group of laughing teens. "It's a bit—"

"I know." Quentin took her elbow. "Claustrophobic. But I see light ahead."

They made their way past the pinball machines and barkers and emerged onto the far end of the pier near the merry-go-round. Even in this weather they could hear screams from thrill seekers on the roller coaster. A refreshment area offered shelter from the weather behind a wall of glass, and that's where Lucy spotted her two ladies, each enjoying a glass of beer.

"That place seems respectable enough." Quentin's smile was teasing.

"I am a married lady and a mother of four," Lucy reminded him. "I have my reputation to consider."

Quentin opened the door for her. "And how is the family?"

Lucy's thoughts immediately turned to Elizabeth. "My oldest daughter—she's an RA at Chamberlain College—is in trouble with the new dean."

Quentin was holding a chair for her. "I know from experience that deans, especially new ones, can be very annoying."

Lucy laughed and sat down. Quentin took the opposite chair, and she studied his face. It was a nice face, she decided, and you couldn't see the bald spot from this angle. He had laugh lines spreading from his eyes, his smile was easy, and he had a good sense of humor. Lucy had to admit she was finding it hard to resist him.

Chapter Eleven

"Winchester seems to take better care of its students than Chamberlain," she said, smiling.

He furrowed his brow. "Why do you think that?"

"Well, Autumn and Jennifer told me they're in a support group to help freshmen adjust to college life."

Quentin laughed. "Is that what they call it?"

Lucy gave him a sideways look. "Isn't that what it is?"

"Not quite." Quentin raised a hand, signaling the waiter. "It's more of a last-ditch effort by the college to avoid expelling them."

Lucy thought this over as the waiter approached to take their order.

"A pint of bitter for me," said Quentin.

Lucy had spotted an advertising poster that caught her interest. "What's shandy?"

"It's a mix of lemonade and beer." Seeing her doubtful expression, he continued. "It's quite good. Ladies enjoy it."

"In for a penny, in for a pound—I'll try it," said Lucy, causing Quentin to grin. "I've got a million of them." She paused, gazing out at the flat gray expanse of water. "So what exactly is this program?"

"It's an intensive group therapy session for students who are considered high risk. I don't know the exact circumstances that led to their enrollment in the program, but"—he leaned across the table—"I have heard the campus scuttlebutt."

"Ah!" Lucy jabbed a finger in the air. "That's one for you: scuttlebutt."

Quentin waited a moment for the waiter to place their drinks on the table, then raised his thumbprint mug in a toast. Lucy raised her glass, too, and tapped his. "Here's to kindred spirits," he said.

That seemed harmless enough, thought Lucy. "Kindred spirits." She took a cautious sip of her drink and found it exactly as described, fizzy and lemony, with a beerish tang. It was good. "So what's the scuttlebutt on these kids?"

"I don't know if there's any truth to these stories or not—you know what a college campus is like. It's a small, enclosed community and people talk about each other."

"Just like Tinker's Cove," said Lucy.

"Exactly. Sometimes these rumors are true and sometimes they're not. You have to take them with a grain of salt. But I do happen to know for a fact that Autumn did assault her roommate, because the girl came to me to complain covered with scratches and a black eye."

"Oh my," said Lucy, reaching for her glass.

"Yeah." Quentin nodded. "The upshot of that was they both got single rooms and Autumn got sent to the group."

"What about Jennifer?"

"I don't actually know but I'm guessing anorexia and anxiety. I think she has real mental health issues."

"It's too bad. She's such a pretty little thing. She ought to be enjoying her youth."

Quentin was thoughtful. "The longer I've been teaching, the more I've come to understand that very few kids do enjoy their youth. It's something we look back on with nostalgia, thinking only that we had a full head of hair or a flat stomach and forgetting how miserable we really were."

"You have a point. But what about Will? He's a handsome kid and seems to be having a pretty good time."

"Too good." Quentin had drained his pint and was signaling for another. "He's a real party boy. He not only got himself put on academic probation because of his grades but he also got arrested for drunk driving. And there's a nasty rumor about a monkey—I don't know the details. He's this close"—Quentin almost pressed his thumb and forefinger together—"to getting kicked out."

"No wonder his mother doesn't want to let him out of her sight," said Lucy.

"He's been doing better." Quentin paused as the waiter delivered the fresh pint and took away the empty one. "And then there's Caroline. Kids on campus call her the Tuber."

"That's cruel." Lucy suspected that one of the attractions of teaching was that it allowed Quentin to indulge an unpleasant streak of immaturity.

"You're right. We don't really know what she's like. The poor girl is obviously taking some powerful psychotropic drugs. She may look like a zombie, but they seem to be getting her through the days."

Quentin's explanation made a lot of sense to Lucy. No wonder Caroline seemed so subdued, and her parents' clinging concern suddenly made sense.

"It's a shame that all four signed up for this trip," continued Quentin, shifting his gaze away from her and studying the coaster under his beer.

"How so?"

He raised his eyes to meet hers. "Once the word got out that they were coming, nobody else wanted to sign up. George almost had to cancel the whole thing. Then Pam got you guys to come and that gave him a dozen—just enough people to make it worthwhile." He nodded. "These trips usually attract about thirty or forty people."

Lucy was stunned. "You mean we're responsible? That poor George would have been home in Tinker's Cove and most probably wouldn't have had an allergy attack or if he did would have gotten treatment in time?"

Quentin's warm hand covered hers. "Don't be silly. When your time's up, it's up."

Lucy snatched her hand away. "Not at all. The rescue squad is terrific. We get grateful letters all the time at the *Pennysaver.* They could have saved him."

"If they'd been called in time, but George was stubborn. He wouldn't have allowed it. And believe me, he died doing what he loved. If he'd had his choice, I'm sure he would rather have died exactly the way he did, en route to his beloved England."

Lucy didn't agree. She remembered the terrified, frantic expression on George's face when he reached out to her for help on the plane. He was fighting for every breath; he was fighting for his life. Lucy also had had another thought, one that had troubled her for some time. She thought of the awkward silences whenever his name was mentioned, the inappropriate bursts of laughter, and the palpable sense of relief she'd noticed in the breakfast room after Emma's departure.

"You know, for somebody who went to so much trouble for others, George doesn't seem to have been very popular with the folks on this tour. There seems a real absence of, well, I don't know, compassion, for lack of a better word. Have you noticed?"

"Can't say I have," he said, draining his mug and pushing his chair back. "Let's see what's at the end of the pier."

Lucy was agreeable. The pub was musty from its humid location on the pier, and she was ready for some fresh air. "Good idea."

She was thoughtful as they went outside and wandered past the merry-go-round and other attractions. The rattling roller coaster took up the entire end of the pier, so there was no view of the sea, but there was plenty of activity to interest a people-watcher like Lucy: moms comforting cranky babies, boyfriends teasing girlfriends and attempting to lure them onto the thrill rides, dads with toddlers perched on their shoulders, a couple of old duffers contentedly puffing away on stinky cigars that were probably forbidden at home.

Watching all these people enjoying themselves, Lucy pondered Quentin's assertion that George had died the way "he would have wanted." She'd often heard similar phrases in the course of her work as a reporter interviewing family members for obituaries. "Well, Mom is probably happier now she's with Dad," a daughter would say, and Lucy would remember a merry widow who enjoyed her volunteer job at the historical society and her weekly bridge game. Or "His suffering is over—he never did get used to that titanium hip," and Lucy would remember the enthusiastic bowler she'd interviewed for a story on the senior bowling league.

It was natural enough, she supposed. People looked for comfort when confronted with the inevitability of death; they were looking for a bright side. Some people even believed in heaven and an afterlife of perfect happiness, whatever that was. Personally, Lucy found the promises of heavenly reunions somewhat unnerving—would she encounter her mother before or after the Alzheimer's took over? If before, she would have to endure an eternity of carping criticism; if after, a sweeter, confused stranger.

"You're miles away," said Quentin as they propped their arms on the railing and gazed at the choppy gray water. The wind had picked up and had blown a lock of hair across her face. He gently smoothed it away and leaned toward her, and she suddenly realized he was going to kiss her.

"I guess we should head back," she said, pulling away and turning to go, but the way past the merry-go-round was suddenly blocked by a crew of EMTs rushing toward the roller coaster. Behind them the crowd surged forward, eager to see what all the fuss was about. As the crowd pressed around her, Lucy was jostled and Quentin positioned himself protectively, wrapping an arm around her shoulder. For once Lucy didn't resist, but strained onto her tiptoes, trying to see what was happening.

The rescue crew, carrying cases of equipment and pushing a wheeled stretcher, had disappeared into an area beneath the roller coaster that was blocked from public access.

"Bet it's a jumper," said a woman with frizzy bleached blond hair.

"A jumper?" Lucy leaned over the railing and spotted one of the rescuers descending a ladder fixed to one of the supporting pilings beneath the pier. Leaning a bit farther, she saw, or thought she saw, a face beneath the surface of the water and perhaps a glimpse of a shoulder.

Then, as she watched, a rescue swimmer in a wet suit lowered himself from a ladder into the water and began swimming toward the spot where she'd seen the face, and another rescuer quickly followed. When he was in the water, others on the pier began lowering a metal basket equipped with floats on either side. Lucy could only imagine how cold the water must be, even with the wet suits, and was struck by the rescuers' selfless efforts to save the jumper.

It was hushed on the pier as the people along the railing strained to watch and pass along the rescuers' progress to the others. " 'E's got 'er now!" declared someone with a Cockney accent, and Lucy saw the swimmer had seized the jumper in the familiar cross-chest hold she'd learned herself in a Red Cross lifesaving class when she was a teen. "They're puttin' 'er in the basket," announced the Cockney. "Oops, bit of a slip there."

The crowd gasped as the limp, plump body rolled out of the basket, only to be seized once again by the rescuers. This time they were successful, and the crew atop the pier began raising the basket, straining against its weight. As soon as the victim was hoisted onto the pier, one of the EMTs immediately began CPR. The two rescuers who'd gone into the water were wrapped in blankets and given hot drinks; they joined the crowd watching the EMTs attempt to revive the girl. Lucy stared at a pair of plump, hairless white legs. One chubby foot was bare, the other covered with an ugly white running shoe. A chunky, clumsy shoe that somehow seemed familiar.

She reached for Quentin's sleeve. "Could that be Caroline?"

His cheeks, rosy from the alcohol, suddenly drained of color. "Ohmigod."

"She's comin' 'round." The word spread through the crowd as Quentin began pushing his way forward.

"Hey, there!" protested one woman. "We were here first!"

For a moment Lucy thought of the crowds that had once flocked to Tower Hill to witness the gruesome public executions that took place there, and she stepped back against the railing. What was she doing here? Why had she joined this group of ghouls?

"I think I may know the victim," said Quentin. "Please let me through."

The ghouls were suddenly transformed into caring, concerned citizens. "Let 'im through," they were saying, stepping aside. "'E says 'e knows 'er."

Stepping forward, Lucy grabbed the back of Quentin's jacket and followed him through the crowd until they were directly behind the EMTs gathered around the victim. Quentin tapped one on the shoulder, and when he turned around, Lucy got a good look at the girl's face. It was round and somewhat bloated with strands of wet brownish red hair clinging to her forehead, but it was unmistakably Caroline Smith.

"I have information about the victim," said Quentin.

"Come with me," said a policeman, pulling out a notebook. While Quentin supplied Caroline's particulars, Lucy watched as an oxygen mask was slipped over her face and the crew of rescuers lifted the wire basket onto a gurney and began wheeling it through the crowd. Quentin followed, answering the officer's questions as he went, and Lucy tagged along, occasionally supplying a bit of information.

An ambulance was waiting when they emerged from the enclosed arcade, and Caroline was quickly bundled inside.

"I'll have to go with her." Quentin didn't look happy about it. "You must find her parents and tell them what happened."

"Where are you taking her? They'll want to go to the hospital."

"Brighton General, ma'am." The EMT closed one of the rear doors.

"But how will you get back to London?"

"I don't know. The train . . ." Quentin paused, realizing the

EMT was waiting impatiently for him to get into the ambulance. "I've gotta go. You can tell the others what's happened, get them back to the hotel."

Then he was inside and the second door slammed shut. The ambulance took off, siren wailing and lights flashing. Lucy stood watching it leave and wondering how she was ever going to find Tom and Ann in this crowded holiday town. Where would they be? Were they frantically looking for Caroline? Or had they agreed to go their separate ways, planning to meet later? She had no idea.

Lucy retraced her steps along the pier, realizing it gave her a good vantage point from which to search the beach. She went from one side to the other, standing at the railing and looking down at the handful of people scattered on the pebbly beach. They were mostly walkers, hardy types, striding along the water's edge to take the air, but some were huddled in little groups with blankets held over their heads to ward off the drizzle. She tried to remember what the Smiths were wearing and failed completely. No, she reminded herself, they were traveling and were probably wearing the same jackets they'd worn to the museum. She concentrated hard, trying to remember how they'd looked in the stairwell at the V&A.

Ann had been in brown, she remembered. Brown pants and a beige sweater. No good, she must have worn a jacket of some sort today. But what about Tom? Leather? A black leather jacket? Yes. So she should keep her eyes peeled for a stocky man in a black leather jacket and a beigy brownish woman.

Lucy turned around and scanned the passing crowd. Lots of leather jackets, lots of beigy women. This was not working, she decided. There was nothing to do except to keep walking and hope she spotted them, or perhaps someone else from the tour who might have seen them. She decided to take a systematic approach and began by hiking along the wide sidewalk that bordered the beach, first heading to the left and then coming back to cover the area on the other side of the pier.

The crowd was thick, especially where portions of the sidewalk were allotted to motorcycle parking. It was a little clearer on the bike path, but there she ran the danger of being run over by a biker. She hiked on, uphill, until she reached a little covered pavilion with a couple of benches, where she sat to catch her breath and watch the passing crowd. After a few minutes, she began to feel guilty about sitting there while the Smiths were unaware of their daughter's plight, and she got up and began walking back toward the pier. She scanned each face but didn't recognize Tom and Ann.

At least she was going downhill, and the crowd on the other side of the pier, past the aquarium, was thinner. The aquarium, she realized, might have caught the Smiths' interest, so she lingered for a while by the entrance, watching the people who came and went. When she noticed a woman paying for her admission with a charge card, she had a sudden brainstorm. When they'd finished their transaction, she went up to the ticket window.

"This is a bit unusual," she began, speaking to a middle-aged woman with a pixie haircut. "But I'm here with a tour group from America, and one of our members just went off the pier."

The woman nodded, her expresson sympathetic. "They do it all the time. It's the number-one location for suicides in the UK."

"Really?" Lucy was shocked. "Are they often successful?"

"They can usually save the daytime ones, but the nighttime . . ." She shook her head. "The currents are something terrible here." She leaned forward. "Did they save your friend?"

"Yes. I think so." Lucy realized she'd digressed. "But I'm trying to find her family, her parents. They're on the tour, too."

"And you wondered if they'd come in here?" The woman shook her head. "I don't know that I'd remember them, even if I knew what they looked like. A lot of people come here. Beats me. It's just a bunch o' fish."

"I was thinking they might've charged their tickets," said Lucy.

"Good idea!" The woman produced a thick packet of charge slips. "What's their name?"

"Smith," said Lucy. "Ann and Tom Smith."

"Couldn't be more common if they'd made it up, could it?" The woman was flipping through the slips. "Smith, Gerald, no; Smith,

Patricia, no; Smithson, William, no." Suddenly she stopped. "Here you go, luv. Thomas Smith. Two adults."

"Are they still inside? Can you tell?"

"Maybe. They went in about an hour ago."

That seemed about right, Lucy realized. They'd probably split up, Mom and Dad going to the aquarium and Caroline, seizing the moment, for whatever reason, to end her life. Lucy reached for her wallet, but the woman waved her hand. "Go on in that door, the one marked 'exit.' Work your way through backward—and good luck, dearie."

Lucy smiled her thanks and went to wait by the exit for somebody to come out so she could grab the door and dart inside, which she was shortly able to do. Once inside, it was dark and dank and a bit smelly. Tanks of blue and green water containing various forms of sea life glowed in the walls. Lucy waited a few minutes for her eyes to adjust to the darkness, then began searching for Tom and Ann. She found them in front of a tank containing an octopus.

"Hi!" she said, approaching them and wondering how to begin. Probably the most direct way would be best, she decided. "I've got some bad news for you."

Ann seemed to sway on her feet, and Tom grabbed her elbow to steady her. Behind them the startled octopus scooted into its rocky shelter. "Is it Caroline?" he asked.

"I'm afraid so. They just pulled her out of the water."

Ann slumped against her husband, her eyes closed. "Is she . . . ?"

"She's alive," said Lucy. "They took her to the hospital. Quentin went in the ambulance with her."

Tom's face hardened. "What was he—?"

Lucy quickly defended him. "He was with me—we just happened to be there. It was very fortunate."

Ann was clinging to her husband's arm. "We have to go to her."

"Yes, I think your best bet is a taxi." Lucy was escorting them to the exit. "She's at Brighton General."

"Thank you, thank you for finding us," said Ann as they made their way through the swinging doors and out into the darkening afternoon. Lucy gave the woman in the ticket booth a wave as they crossed the crowded sidewalk to the curb where a couple of taxis were waiting. She opened the door and held it for them, waiting until they were settled and then telling the driver to take them to the hospital.

Then she raised her arm in a parting wave and watched the taxi pull out into traffic, taking them to an uncertain future.

Completely drained, she sighed, then spotted Harry Ramsden's across the way. Maybe they'd give her a cup of tea.

Chapter Twelve

The lunchtime crowd had long since dispersed, and only a handful of people were seated at tables inside the fish and chips restaurant, most of them with pots of tea. When a server told her she could sit where she pleased, Lucy chose a table for two near the window, where she could keep an eye out for her friends. As soon as she sat down, she felt enormously tired, as if she'd run a marathon, and her hands began to shake.

"What can I get you, luv?" The server was a spry fellow in his sixties with a military haircut.

"Just tea, please."

"Filthy weather out there, ain't it? Sure you wouldn't like a bit of sweet? We've got sticky toffee pudding and spotted dick—fruit crumble, too."

Lucy hadn't the faintest idea what he was talking about.

"They come with your choice of custard cream or vanilla ice cream."

The very thought of anything with custard made her feel queasy. "I'll stick to tea," she said.

"Very well."

He left and she stared out the window, watching the people hurrying by, heads lowered against the drizzle and clutching the collars of their lightweight spring jackets. They'd been tricked by the sunny morning weather, which hadn't lived up to its promise. Now the day had turned gray and cold, with drizzle and showers, just the way it often did in Maine.

"It's too bad, really. All them folks hoping for a nice holiday by the seaside." The server put a pot of tea and a cup and saucer in front of her, along with a pitcher of milk and a china box containing packets of sugar and sweetener. "I heard there was a bit of a fuss on the pier."

"There was. They had to pull a young woman out of the water."

"A jumper?"

Lucy considered. "That's a good question." She remembered teasing Pam, or maybe it was Sue, that just because she was holding a duster didn't mean she actually used it. Everybody seemed to assume that since Caroline was fished out of the ocean that she must have jumped voluntarily, but that wasn't necessarily the case. Maybe she hadn't jumped; maybe she'd been pushed, although it did seem unlikely due to the sturdy, chest-high railing.

"I saw the ambulance. They took right off, so she must've been breathing." He lifted the pot and filled Lucy's cup. "They don't rush with the goners."

"I hope she'll be all right," said Lucy, wrapping her hands around the warm cup. "I heard this happens quite a bit."

The server's tanned, wrinkled face was solemn. "Too often, if you ask me. England's changed, you know. Used to be everybody kept a stiff upper lip, keep calm and carry on, that sort of thing. When Princess Diana died, that all changed." He put the pot down. "I liked the old way better."

Using both hands, Lucy lifted the cup to her lips and took a sip. Despite her efforts to control the trembling, the sharp-eyed waiter noticed. "Don't tell me you know the jumper?"

The cup clattered in the saucer as Lucy set it down. "I do."

"Dear me. That's dreadful." He glanced out the window. "A friend of yours?"

"Not exactly. I'm here with a group from an American college. She's a student there."

"A young person." He clucked his tongue. "That's a shame."

Lucy nodded. What sort of mind-set prompted a healthy young person to jump off a pier that was thirty or forty feet above the water? Why had her future seemed so bleak?

The waiter tapped his tray. "Tea's on the house," he said before turning to greet a new customer.

Lucy stirred some sugar into her cup and drained it, then refilled it from the pot. She was feeling better; the trembling had stopped and she was even wondering what spotted dick could possibly be when she saw a familiar face on the opposite side of the street, waiting at the crosswalk for the light to change. It was Autumn and she wasn't alone. Will was standing beside her. They didn't seem like a couple, however. Autumn was scowling, shaking her head, and Will was bent over her, talking to her, trying to convince her of something. At least that's what it looked like. And they seemed to be coming from the pier—where else could they have been in this foul weather? Unless they'd been in the aquarium, which Lucy didn't think was likely. The arcade seemed more their style. Lucy wondered how long they'd been there. Had they been on the pier when Caroline jumped?

The sky was darkening and Lucy checked her watch, realizing with a start that it was almost five and she needed to get over to the bus drop-off to meet the minivan. She hurried out of the restaurant and dashed across the street, but when she rounded the corner, she was surprised to discover the group had already gathered, waiting. It was a much smaller group, of course, without Quentin and the Smiths—only Lucy's three friends, Dr. Cope and Jennifer, Laura Barfield, Will, and Autumn.

"Where were you?" demanded Sue when Lucy was within shouting distance. Her tone was accusatory, and Lucy felt guilty, realizing she shouldn't have spent so much time with Quentin. She'd enjoyed herself but perhaps she'd led him on without meaning to.

She was saved from answering when the minivan pulled up and they all hurried to get on board, complaining about the way the weather had turned so cold. When everyone was seated, Lucy delivered her little speech.

"I'm sorry to tell you there's been an accident—Caroline Smith was taken to the hospital by ambulance. Her parents are with her and so is Professor Rea. He asked me to see that we all get back to the hotel tonight." Lucy took a head count but wasn't at all sure she'd got it right. "I think we're all here. Is anybody missing except for the Smiths and Professor Rea?"

Nobody was paying attention; they were all buzzing about the accident.

Rachel came to her rescue. "Speak now or forever hold your peace," she said, pronouncing their names and counting them up on her fingers. "I make nine. With the missing four, that's thirteen. We're all here," she told the driver, who began pulling out into traffic.

"Thirteen!" Lucy slid into her seat next to Sue. "I hadn't realized."

"It's unlucky." Pam nodded seriously. "No wonder we've had so much trouble. First poor Professor Temple and now Caroline. What happened? Was it an accident? The traffic here is terrible."

The group was silent—everyone was listening—but Lucy wasn't sure how much to tell. Then again, she decided, it was a public event. It had all taken place in the clear light of day. There was no question of confidentiality here, no request to keep the incident off the record. On the other hand, she could only tell what she knew for sure. "Rescuers pulled Caroline out of the water beneath the pier and rushed her to the hospital. That's all I know."

Jennifer's face was paler than usual. "Did she jump?"

"I really don't know how she got into the water. I didn't see that part."

Laura leaned forward, her expression anxious. "Will she be all right?"

"I don't know that either. They were giving her oxygen when they put her in the ambulance."

"There may well be considerable trauma, internal injuries, broken bones," advised Dr. Cope. "It depends on how she hit the water. From a certain height, the impact can be the same as hitting concrete."

They were all silent. Lucy glanced over her shoulder, looking for Will and Autumn. They were seated together in the very back. Autumn was bobbing slightly, listening to her iPod, and Will was staring out the window, scratching at his chin.

"Look, even here," said Sue, pointing out the window as they passed the Gap and McDonald's.

A little bit of home, thought Lucy. She should have been pleased, reassured, even, but she only felt depressed.

"Caroline didn't seem like a very happy girl." Laura Barfield's tone was thoughtful. "But I'm sure she didn't mean to kill herself. This was probably one of those cries for help."

Across the aisle, Rachel caught Lucy's eye. "I think so, too," she said. "This may be a turning point for her. She may get the care she needs."

"She was lucky." Dr. Cope put his arm around Jennifer's shoulder and pulled her close to him. "I've seen a number of suicides in my time, and the ones who survive always say the same thing—that as soon as they jumped or pulled the trigger or shoved the chair out from under their feet, they realized they'd made a terrible mistake. They wanted to live after all."

They were in the countryside again, and the clouds had parted to let the last rays of sunshine bathe the green fields in golden light. Here and there, flocks of sheep were scattered like cotton balls spilled on a green carpet; many of the ewes had little lambs resting beside them. It was like something out of a Cath Kidston print or a Kate Greenaway illustration, and Lucy hoped the little lambs were being raised for wool and not the dinner table.

As if reading her thoughts, Sue covered her hand with her own. "Wool, sweetheart, they're going to give bags and bags for the master and the maid. . . ."

Lucy managed a little smile, spotting a kid with a backpack wheeling his bike up a steep drive toward a thatched cottage, the windows blazing red from the setting sun. "And one for the little boy who lives *up* the lane."

Dinner that night was better. Rachel had spoken with the chambermaid and learned there were a number of restaurants on nearby

Charlotte Street, and since they'd had a hearty fish and chips lunch, they opted for pizza and salads at Pizza Express, along with big glasses of red wine. Back at the hotel, Lucy went straight to the lounge to check her e-mail, but there was no word from Elizabeth. Bill, however, had calculated the amount they would owe if she lost her resident advisor position: It was nearly five thousand dollars.

"Better watch your spending!" he advised, and Lucy wasn't sure if he was joking or not. She was signing off, a lengthy process on this cranky old computer, when Autumn came in and switched on the TV. Lucy's interest was caught by an outrageous performer with peroxide hair in a shiny violet suit, and she watched, amazed, as he welcomed an American country music star to the show. Fascinated, she joined Autumn on one of the battered red sofas.

"Isn't that Dewey Pike?" she asked. The singer, who was wearing a red, white, and blue shirt; cowboy boots; and a ten-gallon hat, clearly hadn't known what he was in for when he agreed to do the show. The host, Graham Norton, got right down to business, asking Dewey if he was gay or straight.

Autumn was in stitches. "This guy's all about guns and pickup trucks and the flag—look what he's wearing—and Graham Norton wants to eat him up!"

Dewey, however, was more sophisticated than he looked. He winked at Norton, said he was open to new experiences, and offered to sing a song. Norton was happy to oblige, setting the singer in front of a shimmering curtain for his performance. Dewey was well into his hit song about a woman who done him wrong when the glittery silver curtain opened to reveal Norton, dressed in drag, swooning and shimmying behind him. The live studio audience went wild. Dewey caught on and began singing to Norton, ending by wrapping him in his arms and planting a big kiss as they went to commercial.

"That guy was way cooler than I expected," said Autumn.

"He's in show biz." Lucy shrugged. "That super-patriot persona is probably just an act. For all we know, he's a registered Democrat."

"No. He campaigned for McCain."

Lucy hadn't expected Autumn to be so well informed, but she wasn't about to talk politics. The subject had become so divisive lately. Instead she changed the subject. "Are you enjoying the tour?" she asked.

"Yeah. England's a lot more modern than I expected."

Lucy wondered if Autumn had expected the England of costume dramas, then revised her thinking. By old-fashioned, Autumn probably meant Guy Ritchie films.

"Is this your first trip out of the U.S.?"

"Yeah." Autumn snorted. "The people I was living with, my foster parents, they were mostly interested in getting that check from the state every month. They weren't exactly into education and enrichment. It was more about keeping gas in the car and Kraft mac 'n' cheese on the table."

"But you got into college, right?"

"No thanks to them. The guidance counselor helped me out, made me apply and told me about scholarships and loans." Seeing that the show was over and the news was next, Autumn clicked the remote and turned off the TV. "The Rotary Club gave me money for this trip, in case you were wondering. Professor Rea wrote them a letter."

Lucy wasn't surprised by her defensive attitude; it was understandable for a kid who'd been through the foster care system and had to fight for everything. "I have a daughter in college, so I know how expensive it is." She scowled. "She's fighting with the dean and may lose her RA job and the free room and board."

"That job sucks. I hate my RA. She's always snooping around, looking for drugs and stuff."

Lucy had a sudden insight. "That may be the problem. I can't imagine Elizabeth doing that. She couldn't care less."

"Where does she go to school?"

"Chamberlain College in Boston."

"I'd like to go somewhere like that. I might transfer. Tinker's Cove is dead."

Lucy nodded in agreement. The little town was quiet, especially in winter. "I guess it's pretty claustrophobic. Everybody knows everybody at a small school like Winchester." She paused. "Did you have any classes with Caroline?"

"No." Autumn clicked the TV back on and began watching a margarine commercial with great interest.

"I heard she wasn't very popular."

Autumn ignored her, flipping to another channel and a dog food commercial.

"I'm just wondering because of what happened today. Do you think she was suicidal? I'm just asking because you were both in that support group. Did she ever say anything about life not being worth it, anything like that?"

Autumn was watching a news segment about a sewage treatment plant in Manchester with great apparent interest. "She was, you know, weird."

"What do you mean?"

"Uh, look, I don't want to talk about it."

Lucy wondered if Autumn had encountered Caroline on the pier, and if something had happened that might have caused Caroline to take the desperate measure of jumping. Considering the way Autumn had tormented Jennifer at the Tower of London, it seemed at least a remote possibility. "If you know anything about what happened to Caroline, you need to speak up," said Lucy. "She could have died. She might still."

"Look, that's got nothing to do with me!" The rings and studs that dotted Autumn's face seemed to be bristling. "And just for the record, I had nothing to do with that creepy old professor's death either. It was an accident. I didn't mean to knock the medicine thing out of his hand, but it probably wouldn't have made any difference anyway. He was really old."

"Accidents happen," said Lucy, hoping to calm Autumn's temper. She actually thought Autumn and Jennifer had behaved badly on the plane. Their reckless behavior had certainly contributed to Temple's death, even if it hadn't caused it.

"Jennifer had the peanuts, you know." Autumn's tone was self-righteous. "How was she supposed to know he had a peanut allergy?"

Lucy's jaw dropped. Why hadn't she thought of that? Not only had they been dancing around in their seats, but they'd been shaking that bag of trail mix, spreading peanut dust in the air. "You should have known better."

"Well, I know now." Autumn practically spat out the words. "But I didn't know then. We were just excited about the trip and having a good time."

Lucy thought things were getting a little intense. It was time to change the subject. "Did you enjoy Brighton? I saw you and Will leaving the pier. . . ."

"So what?"

Lucy had intended to say what a nice couple they made, but her maneuver backfired.

Autumn turned on her with the ferocity of a feral cat. "I suppose you think we pushed Caroline into the water, too."

Lucy drew back into herself. "Not at all. I didn't think that. I was just making conversation. Everybody seemed to be having a lot of fun on the rides and all."

"I wouldn't call it fun. Roller coasters make me puke. And I couldn't get rid of Will. He was stinking drunk, you know. He was all over me, pawing me. I hate when guys do that. He's so immature."

Lucy was shocked and fascinated by Autumn's sudden change. At first she could hardly get a word out of her, but now the girl was on a roll. It was all pouring out, and Lucy wondered if she was the first person who'd ever listened to her.

"Guys are such creeps. It's like they just assume if you don't wear little pink blouses and pearl earrings that you're some sort of slut, that you'll do anything they want. And they always want it—anywhere, anytime. In the backseat, up against a wall, on a stinky old frat house couch." She paused, considering a new possibility. "I bet that's it, you know. I wouldn't be surprised at all. It's obvious." The stream of words stopped abruptly and she sat primly, lips pressed together.

"What's obvious?"

"Will and Caroline, that's what. He must've lured her to one of those secluded spots there underneath the roller coaster. A guy like Will would think he was doing her a favor, giving a fat girl a big opportunity. And when it turned out she didn't appreciate the wonderful chance to, you know, do whatever with him, he probably got mad, and maybe she tried to fight him off or something and he ended up pushing her into the water." She looked at Lucy. "I can just see it, can't you?"

Unfortunately, Lucy could.

Chapter Thirteen

The breakfast room was once again terribly quiet when Lucy and Sue went down on Thursday morning. They soon discovered the reason: Tom Smith was standing by the kitchen door, requesting trays to take up to his wife and daughter.

Lucy went right up to him. "How is Caroline?"

"She's doing pretty well," he said. There were dark circles under his eyes, and he seemed to have lost about twenty pounds in one night. "She broke her arm and is covered with bruises. She's in a lot of pain, but at the hospital they all said how lucky she was."

"And when did you get back?"

"Around midnight. We hired a town car. It was expensive, but Caroline was in no shape to take the train, and Professor Rea offered to split the cost."

One question was on everyone's mind, but Lucy didn't mention it. She just couldn't bring herself to ask how Caroline managed to end up in the water. Instead she said, "That's good news. We were all worried about her. I hope she makes a speedy recovery."

When she joined Sue at the table, she was met with an accusation. "You waffled."

Lucy nodded. "I know. But how could I? The poor man is obviously shattered."

"And you call yourself a reporter!"

Lucy picked up the coffeepot and filled her cup. "I'm on vacation. If you want to know so badly, you ask him."

Sue shook her head. "No, I was brought up to never ask personal questions."

Hearing that, Lucy was chuckling when Quentin Rea arrived, practically bumping into Tom in the doorway. Tom was carrying the heavy breakfast tray the kitchen had prepared for him.

"Glad you're up and about," said Quentin. "I was wondering if you'll be coming along to Westminster Abbey and the War Rooms?"

Tom didn't answer. He was looking over Quentin's shoulder, into the hallway, at Autumn. The girl no sooner spotted Tom than she whirled around and darted back upstairs.

"I'm coming," said Tom. "Ann insisted. She knows how much I was looking forward to seeing Churchill's command center. She's going to stay here with Caroline."

"I'll see if the hotel can provide them with some lunch," said Quentin.

"That would be great," said Tom, heading down the hall.

Lucy turned her attention to the waitress, who had arrived to take their order. "This morning it's eggs, bacon, and beans," she said.

"No beans for me," said Lucy. She couldn't help wondering if Caroline was tucking into the complete breakfast or if in her fragile emotional state she was daintily nibbling a bit of toast. If her past behavior was anything to go by, she was going for the beans.

"I don't buy it," she said to Sue as Pam and Rachel joined them. "I just don't see Caroline as the suicidal type."

Westminster Abbey was a gorgeous remnant from the Middle Ages, surrounded by soulless modern buildings made of glass and steel. There was no expansive lawn here, no encircling wall. Only a small patch of grass and some sidewalk protected the Abbey from the noisy traffic on Victoria Street, where buses and taxis streamed past Big Ben on their way to Westminster Bridge and busy Waterloo station on the other side of the Thames. Across the street, plastic orange barricades and a large police presence awaited the protesters who regularly filled Parliament Square.

It was all hustle and bustle and honking horns and diesel engines outside, but inside the Abbey it was quiet as death. Tourists spoke in hushed voices as they wandered among the tombs of the royal and great, closely observed by robed clergy and volunteers sporting official badges on their dark clothing. A priest climbed the pulpit every now and then to remind all those present that this was a house of worship and to invite them to participate in a moment of silence and prayer.

Lucy and the girls were gathered together at the front of the nave near the Tomb of the Unknown Soldier, heads bowed along with everyone else, when they heard Will's voice ring out, echoing in the huge vaulted space. "Dr. Livingstone, I presume?" he cracked, then laughed. Nearby, one of the volunteers rolled her eyes. Lucy wondered how many times a day she heard the same bad joke.

Nevertheless, when the moment of silence ended, Lucy headed straight for the plaque marking Livingstone's resting place. BROUGHT BY FAITHFUL HANDS OVER LAND AND SEA HERE RESTS DAVID LIVINGSTONE, MISSIONARY, TRAVELER, PHILANTHROPIST. FOR 30 YEARS HIS LIFE WAS SPENT IN AN UNWEARIED EFFORT TO EVANGELIZE THE NATIVE RACES, TO EXPLORE THE UNDISCOVERED SECRETS, TO ABOLISH THE DESOLATING SLAVE TRADE OF CENTRAL AFRICA.

"I didn't know that," said Rachel. "I thought he was just an explorer."

"Me either." Lucy raised her eyes to look at the massive stone walls of the nave, rising high above her and blocking out the sun. "Poor man, if he'd had his druthers, I bet he would have preferred to be buried in Africa."

"He was a national hero," said Quentin, joining them. "It's a great honor to be buried here. They wouldn't let Byron in, you know. He was considered immoral—he set a bad example by falling in love with his half sister Augusta."

"Unlike the Unknown Soldier, who went off to fight for God and country." Pam paused, fingering the peace symbol charm she'd clipped to her handbag. "I guess the Germans worship a different God from the English."

"If we've learned anything on this trip, it's that God is an Englishman." Quentin caught Lucy's eye and smiled at her. "There's lots more to see. Follow me." Falling into step behind him, they crossed the nave to the south transept, stopping in front of a number of plaques bearing writers' names. "This is the Poets' Corner."

Standing together in a little group, their eyes wandered from one carved name to another: Dickens, Tennyson, Auden, Browning.

"Where's Elizabeth Barrett?" asked Sue.

Quentin had the answer. "In Florence."

"That's so sad," said Lucy. "They ought to be together."

"There are some odd pairings," said Quentin. "Elizabeth I and Mary are next to each other. It's true they were half sisters, but they didn't get along."

"That's odd," said Laura, joining them. "Elizabeth had Mary's head cut off, didn't she?" Will was tagging along with his mother but didn't seem to like it much. He was fidgeting, bouncing on the balls of his feet, and she gave him a warning look. "Listen to the professor and you might learn something."

"That's a common misconception," said Quentin. "Mary died a natural death from illness. Elizabeth executed Mary, Queen of Scots. Her son brought her body here when he became king. It was kind of a slap in the face to Elizabeth. He even made sure his mother's tomb was much prettier and more fashionable than Elizabeth's."

"Who was Bloody Mary?" Laura was keeping an eye on Will, who had begun to drift away toward a door leading to the cloister.

"Mary Tudor, Elizabeth's half sister." Quentin grimaced. "It was a well-deserved nickname. She executed more than three hundred Protestants, mostly by burning them alive."

"I don't like it here," said Lucy, shuddering. "It's a big old mausoleum." She unfolded the brochure she'd been given with her admission button and noticed a green patch, the College Garden. "I think I'll check out the garden."

"Don't you want to see Elizabeth's tomb?" Quentin seemed disappointed.

"Not really." She left the others, who were following Quentin to the Lady Chapel, and stepped through the same door Will had taken. She found herself in a chilly corridor, open on one side to the cloister. A sign pointed the way to the Chapter House and she followed it, finding herself in a simpler and more serene part of the Abbey. It was an octagon-shaped room, the walls filled with stained-glass windows. There was nothing inside except a few explanatory signs pointing visitors to the faded decorative paintings on the rough stone walls.

Unlike the rest of the Abbey, this room was full of light, and she lingered, studying the windows that had been damaged by German bombers during World War II. Standing there, she was struck by the incongruity of this building supposedly devoted to faith and prayer that was so full of reminders of war and death. She was thinking of soldiers who fought for God and country, kings and queens who executed their rivals, and planes that rained nighttime terror down on innocent people. It was too depressing. She had to find that garden.

But when she finally discovered it, she found a notice on the door advising it was closed for the day. Retracing her steps, she encountered Will and his mother in the cloister. Laura was holding Will's sleeve and speaking earnestly to him, but she stopped abruptly when she spotted Lucy.

"You should have stayed with us," she said. "That's what I was just telling Will. Professor Rea makes it all so interesting. He said Mary and Elizabeth really hated each other but they're buried together, side by side."

"Talk about rolling in your grave—they're probably tearing each others' hair out," said Lucy.

Laura gave a funny little chuckle and slipped her arm firmly through her son's. "Family members should care for each other. Don't you agree?"

Will was looking across the cloister to the other side, where Autumn was leaning against a stone pillar. Dressed in her habitual black, she looked a bit like a witch and every bit as out of place as a genuine witch would be in this Christian shrine.

Lucy turned to Laura, noting her anxious expression. "I think we should all care for one another. We're all on this little overheated planet together, after all. We all have the same needs and hopes. It's time we put our differences aside and work together to make life better for everyone."

"Like Livingstone," said Will, detaching himself from his mother and heading toward Autumn.

Laura watched him go. "I worry about that boy," she said.

Lucy thought she was right to worry but didn't say so. "Come on, let's find the others," she said.

Lucy wasn't in the mood to see the Cabinet War Rooms but went along with the group since the admission fee was included in the tour. She didn't want to dwell on the terrible loss of life caused by World War II but focused instead on the homely details of Churchill's simple living quarters: the kettle on the old-fashioned stove, the dining table and chairs that were just like those she remembered seeing as a child in her great-aunt Mary's house in Ludlow, Massachusetts.

As they trooped through the underground rooms, Lucy noticed that Autumn and Will kept their distance from Tom Smith, who pointedly ignored them. He was a big Churchill fan and expressed his enthusiasm in the museum devoted to his life. "He fought in the Boer War, you know," declared Tom. "He wasn't just a politician; he was a real soldier. He'd seen combat himself—he knew what it was all about."

"He was an artist, too," said Rachel, pausing before a landscape painting of green fields.

"And they say he was a real family man," added Laura with a glance at Will.

He and Autumn were whispering together in a corner.

"He adored his wife, Clementine." Sue was staring critically at a photo of a rather plump, middle-aged woman. "You'd think she would have done more with herself."

"He loved her the way she was. They were married for more than fifty years," observed Pam.

"If it wasn't for the old bulldog, Hitler might've won the war," said Tom. "The Blitz took a terrible toll on London."

"And the Allies did even worse to Dresden and Berlin, but you don't hear about that," said Pam, who was a staunch member of the Mothers March for Peace. "And we're the ones who dropped the atom bomb on Japan."

"It had to be done," said Dr. Cope. "The war would have dragged on much longer and many more lives would have been lost."

"Churchill was right about Hitler," said Tom. "He knew from the beginning that appeasement wouldn't work."

Lucy was growing impatient with all this talk. "Hitler got his in the end," she said. "I'm ready for lunch."

"Hitler committed suicide—he took his own life," said Dr. Cope. "He never faced a war crimes tribunal. He was never punished for the terrible things he did. By committing suicide, he denied the survivors even the small satisfaction of seeing him disgraced and punished."

Tom Smith agreed. "The Italians strung up Mussolini. They tore him apart. Literally. They realized he'd led them astray and they took it out on Il Duce. The Germans never did. They collaborated; they followed orders. They're just as guilty as Hitler because they didn't stop him."

"Tom Cruise tried," said Sue, and everyone turned to look at her. "In that movie, I mean. German officers plotted to kill Hitler but the bomb misfired and they were all rounded up and killed."

"They were betrayed," said Dr. Cope, addressing the group in a serious tone that struck Lucy as sounding more like a warning than a casual observation.

"Something's going on," she said, unwrapping the sandwich she'd bought in a Pret A Manger shop. She was sitting on a bench along with her three friends in St. James's Park, watching the ducks and pelicans gathered at the edge of the lake, looking for handouts. It was a sunny afternoon and the friends had decided it was much too nice a day to spend in the Tate Britain museum, which was where the rest of the group had gone.

"What do you mean?" asked Sue, who was sipping a bottle of iced tea.

"There's some kind of tension. Don't you feel it?"

"Not really," said Pam, ripping open a bag of salt-and-vinegar crisps. "It's a tour. There's bound to be personality clashes."

"Pam's right," said Rachel, biting into her egg and cress sandwich. "Whenever you put a random group of people together, there's bound to be conflict. Dr. Cope is serious and intellectual; he has a scientific bent. Tom Smith is more of a man's man. I bet he's a big sports fan, too. Poor Laura is trying to keep tabs on Will. . . ."

"Autumn says he's got a drinking problem," said Lucy, wondering if that was why Laura was so worried about her son.

"Or maybe just an immaturity problem," said Pam.

"Poor Quentin's really got his hands full," said Rachel.

Sue grinned wickedly, glancing at Lucy. "He'd like to get his hands on you, that's for sure. You should have seen the way he watched you when you left us in the Abbey."

"Yeah, Lucy, what were you two doing in Brighton?" asked Pam.

They were all looking at her, and Lucy felt she had to defend herself. "Nothing. We didn't do anything. We had a drink, that was all." She smoothed her paper napkin. "He's barking up the wrong tree if he's after me. I'm another Clementine Churchill, loyal to a fault."

"Just as long as you don't start looking like her," muttered Sue, sending them all into gales of laughter.

Chapter Fourteen

The group was scheduled to see *The Mousetrap* on Thursday night, but the choice didn't sit well with Rachel.

"Why do we have to see an old chestnut like that?" she asked as the four friends waited in the lounge for the rest of the group. "London's known for wonderful, cutting-edge theater and we're stuck with this old thing."

"I agree," said Quentin, rising from his seat at the computer and joining them. "But George apparently felt that no trip to London was complete without seeing it. And it's certainly a safe choice with nothing to offend anyone."

He gave a slight tilt of his head to the doorway, where the Smith family had just appeared. Tom and Ann were on either side of Caroline, whose arm was in a blue sling. She seemed more stolid and robotic than ever. Lucy figured her glassy eyes and listlessness were due to medication, but apart from that and the broken arm, she seemed none the worse for her dunking.

There were plenty of free seats in the lounge, but only the saggy old couch provided seating for three. Lucy was wondering why Tom Smith was staring at her in that pointed manner and, receiving a sharp jab in the ribs from Rachel, realized he wanted them to give up their seats.

Lucy thought it was ridiculous, but she got up and moved to an equally saggy armchair on the opposite side of the room. Sue, she saw, was rolling her eyes at the maneuver.

Rachel, true to her nature, was full of sympathy. "It's great to have you back with the group," she told Caroline. "How are you feeling?"

Caroline was slow to answer. "Okay, I guess."

Rachel received this news with a delighted smile. "That's wonderful. I'm sure you'll enjoy the show."

Her efforts to engage Caroline in conversation were not received well by her parents, however. Tom was glaring at her beneath bristly eyebrows, and Ann was nervously stroking Caroline's hand, as if this harmless bit of small talk might trigger an emotional breakdown.

Ann's anxiety increased when Will and his mother arrived; she practically leaped out of her seat when Will demanded to know if they'd have to stand for "God Save the Queen."

"I think that stopped when World War II ended," said Quentin. "But the theaters do have bars. That hasn't changed."

"Really," sighed Laura. "Must they have alcohol available at every event?"

"I thought England would be stuffy," said Autumn, "but it's great. They drink, they smoke, and they swear."

Quentin's face lit up. "So the UK's okay with you?"

"It's bloody marvelous," declared Autumn, practically sending the Smiths into paroxysms of propriety. Tom humphed and Ann straightened her back and pursed her lips in disapproval.

Dr. Cope, however, chuckled as he settled himself in the last available chair. "I was here in the sixties," he said as Jennifer perched on the arm of his chair. "Studying, you know. I tell you, it was difficult to keep my mind on the intricacies of the endocrine system with all those birds popping about in miniskirts. It was a great time to be in London."

"Were you a mod or a rocker?" asked Sue with a naughty grin.

Dr. Cope sighed. "Neither, I'm afraid. I was a grind."

"You made the right choice," said Quentin, assuming a professorial air. "The mods and rockers are gone but the endocrine system is eternal." He stood up. "I think we're all here, so we can get this show on the road—pun intended! We can walk together over to the Goodge Street station. It's just two stops to Leicester Square."

"I've arranged for a taxi," said Tom with a nod to his daughter.

Ann was quick to defend her daughter. "It's not anything to do with Caroline," she declared. "I don't like the noise and the smell of the Underground."

"Of course," said Quentin diplomatically. "We'll see you at the theater, then."

When they emerged from the theater into the narrow neon-lit street, which was slick from an evening shower, Sue insisted they stop at a nearby pub for a drink. "Otherwise, I'm sure I couldn't be trusted not to reveal the surprise ending of the play."

She was referring to the fact that everyone in the audience had been asked not to reveal the killer's identity, thereby spoiling the surprise for future audiences.

"After twenty-three thousand performances, I suspect the secret is out," said Rachel.

"Were you surprised, Lucy?" asked Pam. "You're the reporter, after all. Did you suspect the, well"—she dropped her voice to a whisper—"the *you-know-who* wasn't what he seemed to be?"

The three turned to look at her and Lucy blushed. "That play was written by a master—there were a lot of red herrings."

"She didn't guess!" crowed Sue.

Lucy turned the tables on her friend. "Did you?"

Sue didn't answer; she was busy pushing her way into the crowded pub.

The crowd was mostly in the front, near the bar; they discovered plenty of free tables in the rear. They were gathered around one, sipping white wine and nibbling assorted flavors of crisps, when they spotted Dr. Cope standing awkwardly with a pint of beer in his hand. Pam waved him over and he joined them, followed by his granddaughter Jennifer and Will Barfield.

"Where's your mother?" Lucy blurted it out without thinking.

"Laura was tired and went back to the hotel with the Smiths," said Dr. Cope.

Will didn't seem to be missing his mother at all. He was busy whispering in Jennifer's ear and had draped his arm along the top of the banquette where it rested behind her. Dr. Cope noticed, his face hardening in displeasure, but he didn't say anything. Instead, he turned to Rachel. "Did you enjoy the play?"

"I didn't expect to, but I did," she said. "I guess there's a reason why it's lasted all these years."

"You can't argue with success," declared Quentin, arriving with Autumn and pulling up chairs for both of them. "Do you know why it's called *The Mousetrap*?"

Nobody did.

Quentin wasn't shy about telling them. "It's based on a short story called 'Three Blind Mice,' which doesn't quite have the snap of *The Mousetrap.* Pun intended!"

At this, Autumn groaned, but Quentin continued. "*The Mousetrap* is the name of the play in *Hamlet,* which is designed 'to catch the conscience of the king.' "

"From what I've seen, none of these kings, or the queens either, had much in the way of consciences," said Lucy, draining her glass.

"It's a funny thing about consciences," said Dr. Cope. "Some people have them and some seem not to have them at all. They just carry on without a care, conveniently ignoring the damage they've done."

Lucy suspected he was directing this to Will, issuing a warning to be careful of Jennifer's emotions. If so, he had missed his target—Will's arm was now draped across the girl's shoulders.

Pam was trying a prawn-flavored crisp. "But Maureen Lynn—the abuser in the play—she went to prison. She paid for her crime. I don't see why you-know-who had to kill her."

"Some crimes can't be forgiven," said Dr. Cope.

"Two wrongs don't make a right," insisted Pam. "And you-know-who wrecked his own life—now he'll get sent to jail."

"Or even hanged," said Quentin. "The death penalty was in force when the play was written."

"I expect he felt so strongly about taking his revenge that he was willing to face the consequences," said Dr. Cope, placidly twirling his empty glass.

"My husband, Bob, he's a lawyer," said Rachel. "Bob says the law really has nothing to do with moral truth. It's a system. It's better than nothing, but it doesn't allow for every situation. Sometimes there are mitigating circumstances, like abused women who kill their abusers, situations like that."

"That's exactly the point Agatha Christie makes in *Murder on the Orient Express,*" said Pam. "I love that book, because justice—real justice—triumphs in the end. Poirot solves the case but decides the twelve have acted as a jury. The dead man deserved what he got, and Poirot decides they shouldn't be punished."

Dr. Cope had turned rather pale, and Lucy turned to see Will was nuzzling Jennifer's neck.

But it was Autumn who spoke up, her voice charged with emotion. "Anything can happen in books—authors make things end the way they want." Her voice dropped. "Something like that could never happen in real life."

"Point taken," said Quentin, popping up. "I need to get drinks for myself and Autumn. Can I get you all another round?"

No one had any objection and he soon returned carrying a tray loaded with drinks. Conversation flowed as everyone had a good time, freed from Laura's sense of propriety and the Smiths' dampening influence. Lucy found her thoughts wandering, recalling Christie's intricate plot in which twelve seemingly unrelated travelers come together on the Orient Express to execute a kidnapper.

Her mind was awhirl as she stared into her glass, watching how the surface of the wine reflected the light from the wall sconce behind her, refracting differently as she moved the goblet. Was it the same with this tour? Had this odd group of travelers come together to exact revenge by killing George Temple?

It was possible, she realized, if they'd known about his allergies. Thinking back to the events at the airport, she could see a clever set of circumstances that could have been designed to trigger and exacerbate an attack. First there was the trouble at security, when officers found something in Temple's pocket that required them to question him, perhaps even search him. Something that he claimed he hadn't known about. What was it?

When he returned to the group at the gate, he was already exhibiting symptoms. Ann Smith had rushed to his aid as he sat, struggling to catch his breath, by wrapping her pashmina around him. But this effort to soothe and relax Temple had backfired; his breathing only got worse.

That situation had accelerated when Laura Barfield frantically announced her son Will was missing, just as the boarding process began. She was practically hysterical, pleading with Temple to make the airline delay the flight, something that he had no power to do. Her panic was contagious; everyone in the group was upset by the time Will arrived, nonchalantly explaining he'd been in the bookshop and had lost track of the time.

And then, of course, there was the business with Jennifer and Autumn that Lucy had witnessed. It could have been a series of accidents—that's what it had seemed like at the time—but what if the girls had behaved deliberately? What if they'd known about Temple's peanut allergy and made sure to shake the trail mix, releasing the peanut dust into the air? And what if Autumn had purposely knocked the inhaler out of his hand?

But there Lucy felt she'd gone too far. These two young girls had their own problems; it hardly seemed likely they would plot to kill a respected teacher. Why would they do such a thing? And if this was indeed some sort of macabre plot, Dr. Cope would have had to be involved, and Lucy had seen him use the EpiPen with her own eyes. And furthermore, she'd seen his serious expression when he announced that Temple was dead. She was convinced the doctor was not one who took death lightly.

She looked across the table at Dr. Cope, noticing his usually severe expression had brightened with the appearance of two red patches on his cheeks. He was clearly enjoying himself—and the pub's best bitter. He'd even forgotten to keep an eye on Jennifer, who was kissing Will.

Back at the hotel, Sue was brushing her teeth and Lucy was turning down her bed when Pam knocked gently on their door. "Can I come in? I need a Band-Aid." She held up her finger, which was wrapped in a wad of toilet paper.

"How did that happen?" Lucy was examining the cut.

"I dropped a bathroom glass and cut myself when I was picking up the pieces." She shook her head. "I can't believe I didn't bring any—I always have a couple in my purse."

"No problem, I've got some." Lucy pulled a ziplock bag out of her handbag and produced a little plastic first-aid kit. "I've even got antibiotic cream."

Pam was dabbing at her finger with the toilet paper. The bleeding had slowed, and after a few dabs, Lucy was able to apply the ointment and stick on a Band-Aid.

"She's a real Nurse Nancy." Sue had popped out of the bathroom and was watching the operation with interest.

"More like Nancy Drew." Pam was tossing the bloody bit of paper into the wastebasket. "Did you see her at the pub? That suspicious mind of hers was in overdrive."

"We should never have allowed her to see a mystery. She really can't handle them." Sue sat on her bed. "Well, are you going to tell us or not?"

"It wasn't *The Mousetrap,*" said Lucy. "I'm thinking more of *Murder on the Orient Express.*"

Pam and Sue exchanged glances. "You think they—meaning everybody on the tour except us four—plotted together to kill George Temple?" demanded Sue.

"That's the craziest thing I ever heard." Pam was studying her finger. "Everybody at Winchester loved him."

"I agree with Herr Doktor Professor Shtillings." Sue had adopted a phony German accent. "It is crazy. She has these recurring episodes in which she sees murderers everywhere. It's a form of paranoia."

"Or maybe schizophrenia," added Pam with a sharp nod.

"There is only one cure that I know of," continued Sue.

"Und vat is dat?" Pam was enjoying herself.

"Shopping! She must go to Topshop, and the sooner the better."

"I agree, Herr Doctor." Pam was yawning, heading for the door. "Until tomorrow, then."

"Wait a minute." Lucy was tapping her chin. "In *Murder on the Orient Express,* and *The Mousetrap*, too, the murder, the act of retribution, takes place long after the original crime, right?"

"Oh, Doktor, it is vurse, far vurse, than I thought." Pam was shaking her head.

"It's the vurst!" exclaimed Sue, laughing hysterically. "It's the bratvurst!"

Lucy was laughing, too. "Cut it out. I'm serious. The George Temple you knew at Winchester was a nice guy, but maybe he wasn't always a nice guy. Maybe he has a past. Maybe he did something unforgivable. Dr. Cope was sort of talking like that, wasn't he? About people not having consciences, not caring that they'd wrecked other people's lives?"

"He was just speaking generally," protested Sue. "Making small talk. We'd just seen a murder mystery."

"I know," admitted Lucy. "But I've got this feeling. I just can't shake it."

Pam held up a finger. "Dis is progress, Doktor. She admits she may be delusional."

"It's a first step," agreed Sue.

"Okay, if I'm delusional, prove it," challenged Lucy.

Pam sighed. "And how am I supposed to do that?"

"Ask Ted to do a bit of research. He's the chief reporter at the *Pennysaver. . . .*"

"Editor and publisher to you," said Pam.

"He loves reporting most of all," said Lucy. "He'll enjoy doing a little digging. It will keep him out of trouble until you get home."

"Okay," said Pam, "but in the meantime, you must agree to treatment."

"If you insist," agreed Lucy. "But I'm afraid I may have maxed out my credit cards."

Chapter Fifteen

When Lucy awoke on Friday morning, she found Sue's bed was empty. Reaching for her watch, she realized with a shock that it was close to nine o'clock. How had this happened? She never slept this late. Folding back the covers and swinging her legs out of bed, she yawned and scratched her head, trying to remember the day's itinerary. It came to her as she stood in the bathroom, studying her puffy face in the mirror over the sink: Windsor Castle. They were supposed to go to Windsor, and the bus was leaving at nine o'clock. Hurrying over to the window, she was just in time to see it pulling away from the curb and driving down the street.

She was throwing some clothes on, intending to find out what was going on, when Sue arrived with a cup of coffee for her. "I hope you don't mind. I made an executive decision."

Lucy took the cup. "What about Windsor?"

"It's just another musty old castle," said Sue with a shrug. "And you were sleeping so soundly, snoring away. . . ."

"I don't snore."

Sue cocked an eyebrow. "Sweetie, I hate to break it to you, but you do. Just a little bit, now and then. It's actually more of a ladylike little snuffle. Positively mouselike."

Lucy took a swallow of coffee. "This mouse wanted to see Windsor Castle."

"Mother knows best, dear. Trust me on this. Time is running out and we haven't had time for any serious shopping."

"What do you call Harrods? That was pretty serious shopping."

Sue shook her head. "I happen to know that all you've bought are those sad little odds and ends from Portobello and a toy bear. What about the girls? Aren't you going to get anything for them? And Bill? What about him? He deserves something for keeping the home fires burning and all that."

"There are shops in Windsor," protested Lucy.

"No, dear. We all talked it over and decided you definitely need a break from the group and your wicked suspicions. And some of us want a decent breakfast."

That was the last straw. Lucy realized she'd missed breakfast. "No eggs and bacon?"

Sue patted her on the shoulder. "We're going to go out and get some nice fruit and yogurt and get you back on the right track." She spoke in a soothing voice, as one might to a fretful invalid. "And if you're good, maybe a bit of wholemeal toast with jam."

Lucy knew when she was beat. "All right, Mother."

"Now finish your coffee and get dressed like a good girl. We're meeting downstairs in fifteen minutes."

Pam was sitting at the computer terminal in the corner when Lucy arrived in the lounge a half hour later.

"It's about time you got here," said Sue, who was flipping through a magazine.

"What is the matter with this thing?" muttered Pam.

Rachel put down the guidebook she was reading and went over to her. "What's the problem?"

"I've got this attachment, and I want to print it, but it won't cooperate."

"Let me try," suggested Rachel, reaching for the mouse. She clicked a few times, then shook her head. "It's got a virus scan going or something. It's too busy to bother with your attachment."

"How long will it take?" asked Sue.

"I don't know. It says it will complete waiting tasks when the scan is complete. We might as well go. Your attachment will be here when we get back."

Pam considered. "I don't want people reading my e-mail."

"Don't be silly," said Sue, impatient to get going. "Who's going to be interested in your boring e-mail?"

"Just close it out and do it later," said Lucy. "I'm starving."

"Good idea, Lucy." Pam clicked the little X in the corner of the screen and hopped up. "There's a Starbucks in that bookshop across the way—let's go there and get some decent coffee."

Lucy felt a lot better after she'd eaten, and she had to admit her friends were right about Starbucks, which was a big improvement over the watery orange juice, weak coffee, and greasy eggs the hotel provided.

"I kinda missed the bacon," she teased as they emerged from the Underground at Oxford Circus.

Sue ignored her, as her gaze was focused on the Topshop sign as if she'd finally found the Holy Grail. "There it is." She sighed in rapture before leading the charge across busy Oxford Street.

Once inside, Lucy found the loud rock music and jumbled displays disorienting.

"This is the perfect place to find something for Sara and Zoe," said Pam, joining Sue in energetically flipping through racks of colorful shirts.

Lucy moved a few hangers in a halfhearted way, then turned to Rachel, who looked uncomfortable. "Let's find the ladies' loo," she suggested, and Rachel agreed.

"Too much coffee this morning," she said as they stepped onto the escalator for the descent to the lower level.

"Too much music," said Lucy.

Much to their surprise, when they emerged from the ladies' room, they found a café where they could sit in comfort and gather their thoughts.

"There are a lot of other shops around here," said Rachel. "Maybe we could meet them later."

"I saw Marks and Spencer," said Lucy. "Bill needs some underwear."

"My guidebook says Marks and Sparks, that's its nickname, is the place for underwear."

"We better go find them and figure out where to meet."

The store had become crowded, filled with chattering girls darting from one rack to another, like distracted honeybees in a flower garden. There was no sign of Sue, but they did find Pam pawing through a bin of colorful scarves.

"Can you believe it? Twenty pounds for this!" She held up a garish black and yellow striped number. "Sue said this place had great bargains but I haven't found any."

"We're going on to Marks and Spencer," said Rachel. "Want to come?"

"No, I want to find Liberty. It's around here somewhere."

"Okay, let's say we all meet back here, out front, in an hour. Okay?"

"Sounds good to me," said Pam, digging down and pulling up a polka-dot scarf, which she held up. "What do you think?"

Lucy and Rachel both shook their heads no.

When the four friends met at the appointed place, only a quarter of an hour late, they all had something to show for their time. Rachel had found some colorful glass and brass knobs on sale at Liberty, and Pam had discovered a shop selling natural cosmetics where she splurged on skin lotion and bath bombs. Lucy had found briefs at Marks and Spencer for Bill, and faux Burberry scarves that she bought from a street vendor who was selling them for about five dollars each. Back in Tinker's Cove, nobody would know the difference.

Sue wasn't impressed. "Oh, Lucy, anyone can see that's not really a Burberry scarf."

Lucy studied the pink plaid strip of acrylic fabric. "I don't care. I think they're pretty and I got one in every color." She pulled out a gray and black one. "This one's for Toby."

Sue examined it. "You know, that's not bad. It's this season's color." She came to a quick decision. "Where'd you get it?"

"Over there." Lucy pointed across the street, where the vendor had set up a portable table displaying his wares.

"Let's go." Sue was leading the way with the others following in her wake. Lucy and Rachel were just behind her, crossing the street as the light began to blink. Pam, who'd dropped her bag and stopped to scoop it up, was running after them and just made it to the crowded pedestrian island in the middle of the street before buses and taxis began surging past. She was perched at the very edge of the island, barely on it. One moment she was there and the next she'd fallen backward, into the path of a cab that was speeding to catch the green light. The driver swerved and avoided her, passing with a blare of the horn.

"Oh my goodness," said a gentleman, stooping to help Pam get on her feet and back onto the curbed island. "You must be American—Americans always forget to look right."

"No, no," insisted Pam, shaking her head as her friends gathered around her. "I wasn't crossing. I was on the island. I was pushed off."

"Did you see who did it?" asked Lucy.

"I didn't. I was looking at the light, waiting for it to turn and keeping an eye on you guys so I wouldn't get separated from you. Then, all of a sudden, I felt a jab from my left side and over I went."

"She's right—I saw him," said a tiny Indian woman dressed in a red sari topped with a Western-style jacket.

"What did he look like?" asked Lucy

"Young and tall." She considered a moment. "I don't think he did it on purpose. These islands get so crowded. I think it was an accident."

"Yes, I'm sure that's what it was," said Pam. "It was an accident."

But as they crossed the other half of the road, Lucy wondered. The woman's description of a tall young man could fit Will. Of course, it could also fit a lot of people, but Autumn had speculated that Will had pushed Caroline off the pier. Trailing along behind the others, Lucy thought it was one heck of a coincidence. Or was it? It would be easy to find out if Will went along with the group to Windsor or if he'd taken off on his own. She was thinking about that when she caught up with the others, who were waiting outside a pub.

"Pam's twisted her ankle," said Sue, "so we thought we'd grab some lunch in here and see if she recovers."

"Fine with me," said Lucy as they filed into the mahogany and red plush interior. She perched on a banquette with Pam while Sue and Rachel went to the bar to get drinks and order their food.

"Salads all round," announced Sue, returning with a glass of white wine in each hand.

"The menu's pretty limited," added Rachel, who also had a wineglass in each hand."

"It's just nice to sit," said Lucy. "How's the ankle?"

"Fine, as long as I don't put any weight on it." Pam sighed. "I hate to spoil your day."

Lucy was pawing through her bag looking for the little tin of painkillers she always carried. She finally produced it after a prolonged search, finding it lurking beneath a business card.

"Take two," she told Pam, passing over the tin and giving the card a quick glance. It was a bit crumpled but still quite legible; it was the card the Scotland Yard detective had given her after interviewing her on the plane.

She debated whether to discuss her discovery with the girls for a moment, then decided not. There'd been too much discussion; it was time to put her suspicions to the test. If he thought she was on to something, he'd talk to her. If not, she'd forget the whole thing. Anyway, the chance that he would actually be at his desk and answer his phone was exceedingly slim. She could live with that, but she had to try. Without a word to the others, she got up and went over to the pay phone that hung on the wall, dropped in some coins, and dialed.

"Neal here." The voice was firm and brusque, businesslike, to the point.

"I'm Lucy Stone. You questioned me about George Temple, the man who died on the plane from America. . . . You gave me your card, in case I thought of anything more."

"Umm, right." Neal didn't sound very interested. "This was . . . when?"

"Just about a week ago," said Lucy, a bit annoyed. How many people died on flights en route to the UK? You'd think he would remember.

"Uh, sorry. I was multitasking. Now what's this about?"

"George Temple. The man who died on the airplane. I may have some new information."

"Go on."

"I think he was murdered."

"Well, I guess you better come round, then, and tell me about it. I'm here until six o'clock."

Lucy didn't need any encouragement. "I'll be there in about an hour," she said.

"What was that all about?" inquired Sue, putting down her fork. She'd been poking halfheartedly at a blob of tuna salad that was nestled in a bed of iceberg lettuce along with some pineapple chunks and a scoop of mayonnaise.

"What's this?" The same dish was waiting for Lucy.

"It's the pub version of a salad," said Pam, who was cutting up her lettuce chunks with a knife and fork. "It's not bad."

"It's full of calories," said Sue. "The tuna is loaded with mayo."

"And they give you extra, in case you need a bit more to clog up your arteries for good," said Rachel.

"Between those greasy breakfasts and lunches like this, it's a miracle they don't all drop dead in the streets," said Lucy, spearing a pineapple chunk.

"You haven't told us who you were calling," reminded Sue.

"Don't laugh," warned Lucy. "I called that Scotland Yard detective. I found his card in my purse."

Sue gave her a look. "Just to chat?"

"Oh, come on." Lucy felt defensive. "You've got to admit there've been an awful lot of so-called accidents on this trip. I don't think the average tour to London includes a sudden death in the air, a leap off the Brighton pier, and a near-miss auto accident."

Pam nodded. "And there's the atmosphere—like everybody's hiding something."

Lucy leaned forward. "You've felt it, too?"

"Not really," admitted Pam, "but you keep talking about it and I'm beginning to think you're right." She gave a sharp nod. "I was definitely pushed into traffic. I'm absolutely certain about that."

"Want to come to Scotland Yard with me?"

"If we take a taxi—I don't think I can manage the Tube with my ankle."

"While you do that, Sue and I can go to the Natural History Museum," suggested Rachel. "I've been wanting to go."

Sue looked at her as if she were crazy. "Don't be silly, darling. There's a marvelous gallery around here, just a street or two over, that's an absolute can't-miss. It's got fashion—"

Rachel's good nature was being stretched. "Fashion isn't really my thing. . . ."

"You can say that again." Sue was looking at her empty glass, considering whether to have another. "Just joking, sweetie. No, the reason this gallery is so special is that it has nature stuff, too. Skulls and twigs and things."

Rachel knew when she was beat. "If you say so."

Lucy couldn't help it—she was excited when the taxi pulled up in front of the revolving New Scotland Yard sign she'd seen in so many British crime dramas on TV. And here she was, actually at Scotland Yard, to assist on a case. But first, she had to help Pam out of the cab and pay the fare. After that, there was quite a bit of security to negotiate and miles of corridors, which Pam insisted were fine but which Lucy knew must be terribly painful for her. It was a great relief when they finally reached Inspector John Neal's office.

The office was very small, painted green, but very neat, and it had a wonderful view of the Thames. Neal, who had hung his suit jacket on a coat tree and had rolled up his shirtsleeves and loosened his necktie, immediately noticed Pam's swollen ankle and leaped from behind his desk to hold a chair for her. She expelled a huge sigh as she settled herself. Lucy, sitting beside her, noticed and felt guilty for dragging her along on what was probably a wild-goose chase.

"Soo, Mrs. Stone, you say you have new information about

George Temple's death, which the medical examiner and the coroner have determined to be the result of an asthma attack."

Lucy spoke slowly and carefully. "I think the attack was caused by the tour members. I think they did things on purpose that would cause him to have a reaction."

Neal didn't seem convinced. "Really? How so?"

Lucy ticked off the events at the airport, the peanut granola, and the incident with his inhaler. Seeing that she wasn't making much of an impression, she made a reckless accusation. "Even the EpiPen could have been faked," she added.

Pam was shaking her head. "I don't think Dr. Cope is involved, but I do think something weird is going on. Caroline Smith was pushed off the pier, and I was knocked into traffic today, twisting my ankle."

"Foreigners always forget to look right," said Neal, leaning back in his chair. He'd formed a little tent with his fingers and seemed to be enjoying himself.

"I was pushed," insisted Pam. "It was not a matter of not looking in the right direction."

Neal smiled. "And have you been having a nice time in London? Seeing the sights?"

Lucy didn't like the direction this was taking. "London's fine; it's the group that's worrisome," she said.

"I fear that is often the case when an oddly assorted group of people travel together. Tensions often arise." He paused. "I wonder, have you been to the theater?"

Pam and Lucy nodded.

"I mention it, because the incidents you've described to me almost seem like the plot of a play. You didn't perhaps see a thriller?"

"We saw *The Mousetrap.*" Lucy felt as if she were signing a confession.

"Aha." Neal nodded. "Case solved. I think we can put your suspicions down to less than congenial company and overwrought imaginations." He stood. "I'll be happy to call a cab for you, and I think we can rustle up a wheelchair to get you back downstairs."

Pam was touched by his consideration. "Thank you so much."

Lucy less so. "Thanks for your time," she grumbled.

* * *

Back at the hotel, Lucy and Pam stopped in the lounge and had a cup of tea to fortify themselves for the climb upstairs. Pam insisted she could manage by taking each stair with her good leg and hanging on to the railing for support. Lucy was doubtful.

"Maybe we can get you a room on a lower floor," she suggested, heading over to the computer where she planned to check her e-mail. A stack of papers on the printer caught her eye, and she glanced at them, finding they were from Ted.

"Here's your e-mail," she said, taking the pages over to Pam.

"Oh, good, this is that story about Tim's project in New Orleans," she said, flipping through the papers. "Oh, and Ted says he'll get on that George Temple research for you when he has a minute."

"Tell him thanks for me," said Lucy, closing out her e-mail account. No word from Elizabeth. Oh, well, she decided. No news was good news. At least she hoped it was.

Chapter Sixteen

"Don't you think there was something positively sinister about that place?" asked Sue, holding the hotel door for her friends who were returning from dinner at a highly recommended French restaurant.

"The food was awfully good," said Rachel.

"And it was the closest one—I was glad not to have to walk very far," said Pam.

"But those waiters . . ." Lucy shuddered. "I didn't like the way they stood around, watching. It was weird."

"Like in a movie, when they're focusing on supposedly everyday activities to build the tension." Sue gave a knowing nod.

"Maybe it was just everyday stuff," said Pam. "I think you're overreacting. It's just that we were early and they didn't have much to do. The place was just starting to hop when we were ready to leave."

Sue yawned. "I don't know about you guys, but I'm beat. I think I'll go on up to bed."

"Me too," said Rachel, starting up the stairs and leaving Lucy and Pam in the foyer.

"I'm not tired yet. I slept in this morning," said Lucy. "Besides, I'd like to check my e-mail again."

"I'm not ready to face the climb," said Pam. "Let's see what's doing in the lounge."

When they entered, they found a card table had been set up and Laura Barfield, Ann Smith, and Dr. Cope were all playing Scrabble. Pam immediately hobbled over.

"Do you mind if I join? I love Scrabble," she said.

"I don't mind at all. You're quite welcome," said Ann.

"But you'll be at a disadvantage," warned Dr. Cope, studying his tiles. "We've already racked up quite a few points."

"Not a problem." Pam was lowering herself into the fourth chair. "I don't care about winning—I just like to play."

Not a problem at all, thought Lucy, seating herself at the computer. If she were a betting person, she'd put her money on Pam, even with a late start. She was an absolute fiend at Scrabble, never missing an opportunity for a triple-word score, preferably one with an *X*.

"Did you all enjoy Windsor?" Pam was busy arranging her tiles on the little wooden rack.

"It's a bit of a factory—they move you right along," said Ann, putting down some tiles. "There. *Ambiguity.* And a double-word score."

"Very nice," said Dr. Cope. "Afraid all I can come up with is *yak*."

"Did you get a look at Eton?" inquired Lucy, waiting for the computer to connect and authorize.

"*Student,*" crowed Laura, laying down the letters. "Thanks, Lucy."

"No, the weather was foul and the hike up the hill to the castle entrance was rather strenuous, so we ended up having a long lunch at a nearby pub." Dr. Cope looked at Pam. "It doesn't seem to me we've left you much room to maneuver."

Lucy had opened her account but once again found no message from Elizabeth. Bill, however, had sent a long, rambling note about Zoe's big track meet against the rival Gilead Giants and Sara's problems with her history term paper. She was busy writing back with congratulations for Zoe and helpful hints for Sara when there was a sudden upset at the Scrabble table and the board went flying, scattering wooden tiles every which way.

"Oh my goodness! I didn't mean to do that!" Laura was on her knees, gathering up the little wooden squares.

"Let me help." Dr. Cope dropped to the floor to help. "We better find them all."

Ann was also stooping and picking up the game pieces. "We don't want to spoil the game."

"I wish I could help," said Pam. "But I'm on the disabled list."

Dr. Cope looked up at her. "What's the problem?"

"I twisted my ankle. I expect it will be better tomorrow."

"Better let me take a look at it."

Pam smiled as he hobbled across the floor on his knees. "Sorry—I'm already married."

"If you would just lift your pants leg," he said, smiling at her joke as he took her ankle in his hand. "It's definitely swollen. Does this hurt?"

"Aah," protested Pam.

"Doesn't seem too serious to me. Try to stay off it as much as you can. Ibuprofen will help with the pain and reduce inflammation."

"Thank you, Doctor," said Pam. "Shall we try another game?"

Ann was already back at the table, flipping the tiles so the letters faced down.

"I think I'm done for the night," said Laura, dropping a handful of tiles on the table and dashing for the arched doorway.

Lucy, who was rising from her seat at the computer and relocating to the sofa, watched her sudden departure and caught a glimpse of Will taking the stairs two at a time, with his mother hurrying after him. A moment later, Jennifer wandered into the lounge with her usual uncertain attitude and seated herself on the sofa.

"Do you mind if I sit here?" she asked, tugging at a lock of hair.

"Not at all," said Lucy. "There's room for two." She paused, reaching for a magazine. She opened it and began turning the pages. "Did you enjoy Windsor?"

"The castle is like a fairy tale," said Jennifer. "I'd like to live there." She blushed. "I guess every girl wants to be a princess."

At the card table, Ann Smith, Pam, and Dr. Cope were choosing their letters and arranging them on their racks for a fresh game.

"A princess in a castle needs a gallant champion," said Pam. "Any prospects?"

Jennifer laughed. "Not a one."

"Not even Will?" asked Lucy, keeping her eyes on the magazine.

"He didn't come. He wanted to see some dungeon thing here in London."

Lucy's and Pam's eyes met as Dr. Cope slapped down all of his tiles on the board.

"Look at that: *dragons.*" He chuckled as he filled his rack again. "Will the Dragon Slayer."

Jennifer was looking uncomfortable, so Lucy decided to change the subject. "Are you looking forward to getting back to school?" she asked.

"I've really been enjoying the trip, but now that we're nearing the end, I have to admit I've been thinking about all the work that's waiting for me back at school. Finals are coming up soon."

"My daughter's going to graduate in a few weeks," said Lucy, "if she manages to stay out of trouble."

"Where does she go?"

"Chamberlain, in Boston. She's an RA. At least she was. She hasn't been getting along with the new dean, and I wouldn't be surprised if she lost her position."

Jennifer turned to her. "Are you angry with her?"

Lucy considered the question as tiles clicked in the background. "A little bit, I guess, but this sort of thing is nothing new. Elizabeth's always been a challenging kid."

"She's lucky to have such understanding parents. At school it seems kids are always at odds and fighting with their parents. Nobody at school ever says anything nice about their parents. They resent them."

Lucy didn't have any trouble imagining this. "What about you? Do you say bad things about your family?"

Jennifer shook her head. "No. Gramps and I are real close." She turned her head and winked at him, and he winked back. "My father died when I was a baby, and Mom and I moved in with Gramps. He's been super."

"It's been a pleasure, my dear." He was watching Pam put down her tiles and groaned. "You are a devil," he said, toting up her score. "Eighty-seven. How do you do it?"

"Practice. I play a lot with my husband. He's a newspaper editor."

"Humph." Dr. Cope was studying the letters on his rack. "I call that an unfair advantage."

Ann's usually worried expression seemed to deepen. "What newspaper?"

"Tinker's Cove," said Pam automatically, replacing the tiles she'd used.

Lucy yawned and stood up, deciding to give her e-mail one more try before heading up to bed. "Cross your fingers for me—I'm giving Elizabeth one more chance before I turn in for the night."

"Consider them crossed," said Pam, busy rearranging the letters on her rack.

The computer was much faster this time, and Lucy got right into her e-mail account. There was no news from Elizabeth, but there was one from Ted. Opening it, she found he'd done the research about George Temple that Pam had requested.

> I had to go back quite a few years, all the way back to the savings and loan crisis in the nineties. He lost his job as a bank president. He was basically fired by the board of directors and went into business for himself as an investment advisor. The fact that he'd been fired was kept secret, and quite a lot of bank customers signed on with him, but he wasn't any better with investments than he was with banking. When the investments he recommended started losing value, he began falsifying the statements and inevitably began using good money to cover bad. The business turned into a Ponzi scheme. It

all came apart in 1991 when a client began to suspect something was fishy and complained to the state. An investigation followed, and a lot of people who thought they were prudent investors learned they were broke, and Temple was convicted of fraud. He had a sympathetic judge—a lot of eminent types testified on his behalf, saying he never meant to hurt anyone, that he was just trying to keep things afloat until the market recovered—and he went to jail for a couple of years.

When he got out, he went back to school and got a master's degree in history, cum laude, no less. Those same friends who testified on his behalf helped again and found him the job at Winchester College, where he seems to have been a great success. I called the college president, who says his death is a great loss to the school; Temple was even being considered for a professorship, something she said was long overdue. She also said a memorial service is planned for next week. If I learn anything more, I'll pass it along.

Meanwhile, Lucy, the work is piling up on your desk!

Lucy grimaced, picturing the stack of papers that she would face when she returned, and hit the PRINT button. Instead of obediently printing the page for her, the printer began beeping, alerting her to a paper jam. When she cleared it and tossed the offending paper into the nearby wastebasket she noticed a couple of sheets that looked familiar. Bending down to retrieve them she realized they were copies of the same attachment from Ted that she was printing. Ted must have sent the information to Pam as well, and Pam's copy had printed earlier that day when the virus scan was complete. Which meant, thought Lucy, that somebody else had found it.

"I guess I'll say good night," she said to the room in general as she bundled the papers together.

Pam gave an ostentatious yawn. "You know, I think I'll head upstairs, too. All this thinking has plum worn me out." She added her tiles to the others spread out on the table. "It was fun. I hope we can do it again."

"Absolutely," said Dr. Cope. "You've certainly raised the level of the game."

"Sleep well," said Ann.

Lucy and Pam climbed the stairs in silence, except for the occasional groan from Pam, until they reached the top floor. There, she caught Lucy's arm. "A funny thing happened during the game."

Lucy was interested. "Really?"

Pam gave her a knowing look. "Remember when the board spilled?"

"Yeah."

"Laura knocked it on purpose."

"Why? Is she a sore loser?"

"I think it was the word I put down. The minute she saw it, she went all white."

"Interesting. What was the word?"

Pam paused for emphasis. *"Murder."*

"That is very interesting," said Lucy. "And there was another interesting thing. Did you notice? Will didn't go to Windsor. He stayed in London today."

"I noticed that, too." Pam shrugged. "But why would he want to knock me into the street?"

"Remember your attachment from Ted, the one you couldn't get? Well here it is," said Lucy, handing the papers to Pam. "It came through on the printer. I found it in the trash—somebody didn't want you to see it."

"You really think there was some sort of conspiracy to kill George?"

"Tell me what you think after you read it. It's pretty interesting stuff."

"See you in the morning." Pam was already reading as she limped across the hall to her room.

Opening the door to the room she shared with Sue, Lucy found the lights were on but Sue had fallen asleep with an open magazine spread out on her chest. Her mouth was open, and in the harsh light of the bedside lamp, she looked much older than she did in daytime, when her face was carefully made up. Even Sue, thought Lucy as she carefully lifted the magazine off her chest and turned off the light, was beginning to show her age.

They all were, she mused as she brushed her teeth and washed her face and carefully applied her drugstore night cream. Then, tucking herself into bed, she reached for the mystery she was reading. She found it difficult to concentrate on the story, however, as her thoughts returned over and over to George Temple's death.

Perhaps Inspector Neal was right and she did have an overactive imagination, but she had learned to trust her instincts, and they were telling her that something was odd about this tour. People were jumpy; their reactions didn't seem quite normal. There was Tom Smith's inappropriate guffaw when Quentin announced the memorial service for Temple, and there was Laura Barfield's startled reaction when Pam used the word *murder* in the Scrabble game. And these were just small incidents. Lucy's mind began to whirl, remembering Autumn's warning to Jennifer in the Whispering Gallery at St. Paul's and the way she'd teased her with the ravens at the Tower of London. And, of course, there was Caroline's tumble off the Brighton Pier. Autumn had been quick to suggest Will had something to do with it, but did he? And had he spent the day playing some fantasy game, or had he read the e-mail and decided to follow Pam instead? And if he did indeed push Pam into traffic, was he issuing a warning or intending to kill her?

Lucy didn't know the answers to any of these questions. She closed her book, turned off the light, and rolled over, intending to go to sleep. She closed her eyes but couldn't stop the film that was running in her mind. It was the faces of the tour members, one after another, all expressing sorrow, anger, anxiety. If someone had asked her to sum up the group in a word, it would be *tense.* They were all nervous and jumpy; it was in the air and it was contagious. It kept you awake at night, she decided, flopping on her back and opening her eyes to stare at the ceiling.

She had learned one thing, though, that might explain everything. George Temple had a history. Before he was the esteemed instructor at Winchester College, he'd been involved in financial misconduct. He'd even gone to jail. He'd been punished. Lucy yawned. And it had all taken place a long time ago. It was history, a footnote in the cycle of booms, bubbles, and recessions. That's what Lucy was thinking of, bubbles and dollar signs, when she finally drifted off to sleep.

Chapter Seventeen

Friday morning, the group departed on the minibus for Bath, which Quentin made a point of announcing was properly pronounced *Baaath.*

"Bath is rich in historic and literary associations," he began from his perch in the front of the minibus. "The original Roman baths for which the city is named are well preserved and offer a fascinating glimpse into ancient times. But for many of us, including myself, it is the city's association with Jane Austen that most fascinates. Those of you who have read *Persuasion* and *Northanger Abbey* know that she used the city as a setting for part of the action. The famous Pump Room is still in business serving tea."

"Tea!" Sue gave Lucy and Pam a little nod. "We'll finally get our afternoon tea."

"And on the way we'll stop at Salisbury Cathedral. It has the tallest spire in England," he said, pausing when Autumn and Will groaned in protest.

"I know, we have seen a lot of churches, but this one has quite a nice lunchroom where we can get something to eat, and it has one of the four existing copies of the Magna Carta. And on the way home, we're going to pause at Stonehenge. I'm hoping to time it so we can see the sunset there."

For once Will seemed interested in the itinerary. "They did human sacrifices there, right?"

"Perhaps," admitted Quentin. "No one knows for sure what the circle was used for." His eyebrows rose. "That's what makes it so fascinating, for me at least: the mystery."

"I believe it has something to do with the solstice—a calendar of sorts," suggested Dr. Cope.

Lucy was listening, watching the street scene as the minibus wove its way through the city. People were walking along purposefully, probably on their way to work. She had enjoyed the trip—she loved being in a different country—but she was eager to get home. She missed Bill and the kids, she was worried about Elizabeth, and she missed her job. Back in Tinker's Cove, she was sure of herself. She knew her roles as wife and mother and reporter. Here, it was different. She couldn't escape the feeling that something was very odd about this group of tourists, but she wasn't comfortable crossing the line and investigating them. It wasn't her business to pry into their lives—or was it? If there had been a conspiracy to murder Temple, wasn't it her duty to expose it? After all, murder wasn't only a crime against the victim; it was a crime against society as a whole.

"I read the attachment." Pam had cupped her hand around Lucy's ear and was whispering.

"What do you think about it?"

"Well, it was a long time ago." Pam's voice was low. "People change. He was tried and punished. As far as I'm concerned, he paid his debt to society."

Lucy nodded. "We've all done bad things."

"And it's not like he killed somebody or anything," continued Pam. "It was only money. White-collar crime."

From the window, she saw a couple of men walking along on the sidewalk, togged out in dark suits and carrying briefcases and umbrellas. They looked terribly respectable, irreproachable even, headed no doubt for jobs in the City, as London's financial district was known. "Not exactly a home invasion," said Lucy, thinking of a violent episode that had recently taken place in a neighboring town.

"Or a serial killer." Pam shifted in her seat and flexed her ankle. "My ankle is much better today," she added. "But I am glad for the minibus. And it's nice to get out of the city and see some more of the countryside."

Lucy agreed. One of the things that had surprised her most about England was the large amount of unspoiled countryside. She loved seeing the rolling green fields dotted with sheep or cows and sometimes horses. There was much more than in Maine, where family farms were going the way of the dodo, replaced either by strip malls or gradually overtaken by trees and reverting to forest.

Of course, in England they still had open markets where small farmers could sell their produce. In Maine, farmer's markets were just beginning to sprout, and there was nothing like Portobello, where the stalls with meat and eggs and vegetables were mixed right in with the used clothing and antiques. She settled back in her seat, intending to enjoy the ride, but her thoughts kept straying from the pastoral scenes outside to the group inside the minibus.

Only money. That's what Pam had said, but that was an oversimplification. It was never "only money" or "only my house—thank heaven we're all still alive." After the shock of the hurricane or tornado or fire wore off, there you were with nothing but the clothes on your back. She and Bill had struggled financially when he gave up Wall Street to become a restoration carpenter in Tinker's Cove, and she remembered the hard choices they'd had to make. Groceries instead of a new winter coat, heating oil instead of Christmas presents, and paying Doc Ryder five or ten dollars a month against the balance he patiently carried for years before they finally got caught up.

They had been fortunate. A generous check from Bill's parents had helped them through that terrible first winter, and Bill's business gradually became successful. Not that they hadn't had lean years since, but they'd always managed. They even had a tidy sum put away for the kids' college expenses and maybe, someday, if anything was left, retirement. So even though she wasn't exactly pleased that Elizabeth might lose her RA position, it wasn't the end of the world. She had money to pay the additional expenses.

But what if she didn't? What if the college refused to grant credit for Elizabeth's course work because she owed money? They could even withhold her degree! What would happen then? Instead of starting on a satisfying career, Elizabeth might have to take a low-level survival job. Instead of hanging out with upwardly mobile young professionals, she might start dating some loser drug addict type. Lucy could picture it, a tragic spiral downward into poverty, drug addiction, perhaps even crime. She knew she was being a bit melodramatic, but the sad truth was that she had seen too many local kids bottom out on drugs.

"What are you thinking about?" demanded Pam. "You look like you're about to cry."

"Nothing." Lucy laughed. "My imagination was running away with me."

"Look at that house with its thatched roof. Isn't it adorable?"

It was, and so was the town of Salisbury, where tiny old houses lined the twisting, ancient streets. The cathedral, in contrast, was located inside a spacious walled "close," which included a large, grassy lawn and scattered houses for clergy and their families. Lucy thought the church was amazing, especially when you considered it was built over 750 years ago.

Lucy knew a bit about construction and the difficulties Bill encountered in his work, but she was awestruck at the labor and skill of the builders who had constructed the massive cathedral with its soaring spire using only the simplest of techniques. Merely hoisting the stones up to the top of that fantastic spire without the use of a modern crane seemed an incredible feat.

Inside, she discovered that this church was not simply a monument to the past but also had kept pace with changing times. A distinctly modern baptismal font was the first thing she noticed; it had been installed for the cathedral's 750th anniversary to mixed reviews. Quentin sneeringly called it a "saucer," but Lucy rather liked its simple shape and moving water. Wandering farther into the huge interior, she found a kindergarten class set up on child-sized chairs and tables in one of the side aisles, working on a project with crayons and paper.

The children were dressed in navy blue school uniforms. Most seemed to have blond hair and rosy cheeks. They were completely comfortable in the impressive structure, chattering away with each other as they exchanged crayons and displayed their work.

Quentin led them to the transept, where they stood beneath the spire and pointed out how the weight of the tower had bowed the supporting pillars. "Don't worry," he advised them. "If you look through those windows, you can see the bracing that was added to support the spire."

Lucy looked and she supposed it was all safe enough; it had stood for three-quarters of a millennium, but she knew that Bill wouldn't approve of anything that wasn't straight and true.

Advising the group that Bath was still some distance away, Quentin suggested they take a quick look at the Magna Carta and then purchase sandwiches and drinks in the café to eat on the bus. Only a few members of the group followed Quentin into the dimly lit display room, where the ancient charter was displayed in a lighted case.

"Kind of an anticlimax," said Dr. Cope. "It's just a piece of parchment."

"A piece of parchment that changed history," said Quentin. "It was the beginning of democracy; the nobles forced the king to share power."

"So instead of one white male running the show, you got a bunch," said Rachel. "I'm not sure that's a big improvement."

Quentin was standing close to Lucy; she could feel his breath on her neck. She would have liked to move away, but the gallery was small and they were crowded together in front of the Magna Carta. "What do you think, Lucy?" he asked in a teasing voice. "Are you a feminist like Rachel?"

"I guess I'm a humanist," said Lucy, seeing a gap and moving toward the door, ready to find some lunch. "A hungry humanist."

Other visitors had the same idea, as the little café was crowded. Lucy and Will approached the cashier at the same time, and he stepped back with a graceful sweep of his arm and a courtly bow. "After you, m'lady."

Lucy smiled despite herself. "Thank you, m'lord," she said, putting down her food on the counter and fumbling for her wallet. The kid was so full of life and so charming it was easy to sweep aside her suspicions about him. But, of course, she reminded herself as she accepted the change from her ten-pound note, charm was one of the characteristics associated with sociopaths. She resolved to keep an eye on him as they explored Bath. She certainly didn't want a repeat accident, one that might have more dire consequences than a twisted ankle.

Back on the bus, Lucy sipped her tea and chewed her ploughman's cheese and pickle sandwich. "These sandwiches are so good," said Lucy. "I don't know why we can't have sandwiches like these at home."

"There's a rule, I think," said Pam. "Packaged sandwiches must be soggy and horrible." She was unscrewing the cap on her bottle of apple juice. "I couldn't help noticing that Quentin was standing awfully close to you."

"It was crowded." Lucy took another bite of sandwich.

"Not that crowded." Pam was unwrapping her sandwich.

"I thought he'd given up on me and was going after Autumn and Jennifer, but now he seems to be back after me. I like him; he's fun. I had a good time hanging out with him in Brighton. But I'm a married woman. Happily married. I'm not interested in any extracurricular activities." She took another bite of sandwich. "What's his reputation on campus?"

"Oh, everybody knows he's a lech." Pam had smoothed out the cellophane wrapper and had set the sandwich on it, in her lap. She picked up one half and took a bite. "He's kind of a legend in that department. They say some years he works his way through all the girls in the freshman class."

Lucy was skeptical. "That seems like an exaggeration."

"I'm sure it is, but the truth is that his reputation has hurt him. He's been passed over several times for a professorship. The word is the college wants to be able to fire him in case there's a scandal." She took a sip of juice. "It makes sense. It's almost impossible to get rid of a professor. I guess that's why they were considering Temple to take old Crighton's chair when he retires."

"It's too bad," said Lucy, draining her tea and crumpling the cellophane into a ball. "He's a gifted teacher."

Pam chuckled. "From what I hear, that's not all he's gifted at."

"Well, as tempting as you make him sound, I'm sticking with Bill."

"Smart move."

The bus dropped them off in front of Bath Abbey, which Quentin informed them was definitely worth a look. "The Roman baths are just yonder," he said, pointing the way. "Follow me."

A few minutes later, he'd distributed admission tickets and told everyone to be back at the Abbey at four o'clock; until then, they were on their own, free to explore the city.

"I couldn't help noticing there seems to be a lot of shops," said Sue. "And we'll have time for an early tea in the Pump Room."

"We need to stay together." Lucy didn't want a repeat of yesterday.

"And we need to remember that Pam may not be up to much walking." Rachel had given Pam her arm for the walk across the uneven cobblestones of the square.

"Don't worry about me—I'll be fine." Pam was waving her ticket to the baths. "I've always wanted to see this. I remember seeing pictures in *National Geographic,* and now I'm here."

Once inside, they discovered the baths were larger and more complex than they'd imagined. They listened to audioguides that explained different aspects as they made their way down ramps and across uneven, timeworn paving stones, past displays picturing ancient Roman life, the sweat room, and the East Bath. Finally they found themselves standing in an open courtyard with a large rectangular pool in the center filled with bright green water.

"Yuck!" declared Sue. "You couldn't pay me to dip my toe in that."

Lucy was about to say something about the water's high mineral content when she noticed Pam wasn't with them. "Where's Pam?" she asked in a panicked voice.

"I thought she was with you," said Sue, turning to Rachel.

"We were together—she was hanging on to my arm—but then she said the paving was so uneven she'd do better on her own." Rachel reproached herself. "I got so caught up in the audioguide . . ."

"Never mind." Lucy was already retracing her path through the ruins. "We have to find her."

Lucy had to dodge past a group of German tourists who were blocking her way, pointing out the various statues that stood atop the arcade that enclosed the pool. Then she was weaving her way through the East Baths, cursing the stagy dramatic lighting that kept the corners in darkness while making the tank of water glow. Farther on, she darted into the sweat rooms, a massive space that was also dramatically lit to highlight the rows of square pillars that had once supported the floor. Standing on the walkway, Lucy peered down at the mazelike area, where numerous shadows offered plenty of places to conceal a body.

A body! What was she thinking? This was a crowded tourist attraction; it was hardly the place you'd expect an assault to take place. Except that it wasn't very crowded today, and there was that weird lighting that created contrasting patches of light and dark. For a public place, it sure had a lot of nooks and crannies, spaces tucked behind displays of stone carvings, ancient coins, and other artifacts.

"Any sign of her?" Rachel and Sue had caught up with Lucy in the sweat room.

Lucy shook her head.

"Come on, let's finish the tour. Maybe she went on ahead of us," said Sue.

"With that bad ankle?" Lucy was wondering if it would be possible to slip off the observation deck and explore the far corners of the sweat room.

"Maybe. She might have stuck to the ramps and walkways."

"Or she might have fallen behind and been attacked," said Lucy. "What if she's down there somewhere, bleeding or concussed? And how come there are no security guards here? What kind of place is this?"

Sue was holding her arm. "I have a feeling you'll find out if you venture off this viewing platform. I'll bet you fifty pounds they've got closed-circuit surveillance cameras."

"And if anything happened to Pam, they would have seen it," said Rachel. "Come on. We've checked back here and now we have to continue on."

"Okay," grumbled Lucy, following her friends back past the large open pool and on to the Sacred Spring, where water gushed from an underground source. The Germans Lucy had so rudely brushed past were there, listening to their audioguides and blocking the exit. This time, she could tell from their expressions that she wasn't going to get past them.

It seemed to take them forever to listen to the recording, and then they had to discuss what they'd heard; at least that's what Lucy thought they were doing. Maybe they were talking about rude Americans. She didn't understand German, and she was beginning to think she didn't much like these particular German people either. Then one very large-hipped lady turned, and Lucy was able to slip past, into the hall outside the restrooms and gift shop. And there, sitting on a bench, was Pam.

"What took you guys so long?" she asked.

Chapter Eighteen

"Well, actually, we were looking for you." Lucy sounded rather annoyed. "That's what took so long."

"It's my fault," admitted Pam. "I got separated from you guys. I figured this was the best place to catch up with you." She tilted her head toward the door of the ladies' room.

"Good thinking. In fact, I think I'll . . ."

"Go ahead. I'm not moving," said Pam, catching sight of Sue and Rachel emerging from the exhibit and giving them a wave.

When they'd all used the facilities and gathered again in the lobby outside the gift shop, Sue suggested they go on to the Pump Room. "Our ticket to the baths entitles us to a free glass of Bath water. . . ."

"My mother told me not to drink the bathwater," quipped Pam.

Sue gave her a look. "And we can have tea. A real afternoon tea."

"I'm not really very hungry," protested Lucy.

"This may be our only chance," warned Sue. "We can't go back home without having a real English tea."

"If you say so." Rachel shrugged. "I could use a reviving cup of tea, and I guess I could nibble on a scone."

"Perhaps we could share one," suggested Pam. "Just to get a taste."

But after working their way through the gift shop and emerging outside the Pump Room, they found themselves blocked once again by the German tourists—and a long line of others.

Sue scowled. "Where did they all come from?"

"All over. It's a famous tourist attraction." Rachel was pulling out her guidebook. "There's lots to see: the Royal Crescent, Regency architecture, a covered market, the guild hall. . . ."

"And the shops." Sue was brightening.

"I'm not really up for a lot of walking," said Pam. "But you all should go ahead. I'll go sit in the Abbey and read my book."

Lucy wasn't about to leave Pam on her own. "I'll go with you," she said. "I love old churches."

Sue gave her a quizzical look. "You do?"

Lucy nodded. "I never knew, until I got here. I like the way they, uh, smell."

"If you say so." Rachel was doubtful. "Come on, Sue. I see a National Trust gift shop across the way."

"You know where to find us," said Lucy, watching them depart.

"You don't have to do this, Lucy," protested Pam. "I'm fine on my own, and I feel guilty keeping you from seeing the city."

"Don't be silly." Lucy took her arm. "Bath Abbey is the Lantern of the West, and I don't want to miss it."

Inside, the Lantern of the West definitely had that musty old church smell and seemed a bit shabby. At least that's what Lucy thought after she installed Pam in a pew and began to look around. Maybe, she decided, it was simply that those famous windows let in more light than the smaller windows in the other churches they'd seen. And that light revealed the effects of age, just like a sunny day coming after a rainy spell illuminated unnoticed dust and cobwebs in the house. Or maybe it was the fact that history hadn't treated the Abbey well: It had been stripped when Henry VIII dissolved the monasteries and left to fall into disrepair. Various restoration projects had been undertaken through the years, but it was once again damaged by German bombs in World War II.

Still, it was a beautiful and active church, as the brochure describing its architectural features took pains to point out. Lucy was walking along the side aisles, studying the enormous windows and the graceful vaulted ceiling, when she noticed Laura Barfield, bent in prayer. She didn't wish to disturb her and continued on her way, but Laura called out to her.

"Lucy! Are you on your own?"

"My friends wanted to shop, but I'm out of money," she said. "And besides, Pam can't do much walking because of her ankle. She's sitting in the back."

"It's a beautiful place to spend a quiet hour."

"They call it Perpendicular Gothic," said Lucy.

"Whatever they call it, it's good for the soul." Laura cocked her head. "Are you a person of faith?"

"Not really." Lucy slipped into the pew beside Laura; maybe she could turn the conversation toward Will. Most mothers were eager to talk about their kids. "How about you? Are you a churchgoing family?"

"Not so much the family, but I am." She raised her eyes to the intricately decorated ceiling high above them. "Church is the only place I find peace."

Lucy was all sympathy. "Tell me about it. My daughter, she's in college, is driving me crazy. And I've got two more at home. They say boys are tough to raise, but I think girls are worse."

"Oh, I'm not troubled about Will. Boys will be boys—that's what my husband says. He'll sow his wild oats and settle down."

This attitude surprised Lucy. From what Quentin had told her, the college considered him to be at risk; that's why he was in the special support program. She had expected Laura to be eager to discuss her son's problems, but now it didn't seem she thought he had any. Lucy wasn't quite sure how to continue when Laura solved the problem for her.

"No," she said with a sad smile, "it's not Will that troubles me. It's my mother."

"Mothers and daughters," said Lucy cautiously, feeling her way. "It's a special relationship."

"I adored my mother."

Lucy was pretty sure her daughters didn't adore her, especially Elizabeth. But they seemed to get along most of the time, which was a big improvement over the relationship she had with her own mother. Lucy had been a Daddy's girl, and her mother hadn't appreciated her daughter's claim on her husband's affection. "My mother died some years ago," was the best Lucy could come up with. "Alzheimer's."

Laura turned to her, her eyes brimming with tears. "Mine, too. It was awful. Early onset."

"Hard for the family," said Lucy, remembering her mother wandering around a posh assisted-living facility in a happy haze, imagining herself the lady of the manor. "My mother didn't know what she was missing."

"I didn't want to put her away—I tried to care for Mom at home."

"That would be difficult."

"It was impossible, especially after I got pregnant with Will. I had to put her in a, you know, one of those places." This was a wound that hadn't healed; tears were trickling down Laura's cheeks.

"You shouldn't blame yourself. I found that my mother was much happier at Wonderstrand Manor than she would have been with me. They had special programs, wonderful meals. And she was safe there. They kept the doors locked so the residents couldn't wander off." Lucy hadn't thought about this in a long time and found her resentments had lessened; she was remembering her mother fondly. She smiled. "She loved the sing-alongs, all those old songs like 'How Much Is that Doggie in the Window?' and 'Wunderbar.' "

"That place sounds wonderful." Laura had placed her hand on Lucy's arm. "We couldn't afford anything like that. We had to depend on Medicare."

"But even so . . ." protested Lucy.

"No. This was almost twenty years ago. Things were different then. This was a Medicare mill. The patients were kept strapped in their beds; they got minimal care. It was terrible."

"I'm so sorry." Lucy knew her father had provided well for her mother; there had even been a modest inheritance left for her after her mother's sudden death from a stroke.

"The worst part is that Mom had money." Laura's chin vibrated. "She should have been in a place like Wonderful Manor, whatever it was called. But Dad trusted an old friend with his investments. . . ." Laura stopped suddenly. "It was that savings and loan crisis. Maybe you remember?"

Lucy remembered. "My father believed in T-bills."

"Smart man."

Now Lucy felt tears pricking her eyes. She'd never really had a chance to say good-bye to her father, never had a chance to tell him how much she loved him. He'd survived a massive heart attack and was convalescing when he suddenly developed pneumonia. Her mother had been caring for him at home. She'd discouraged Lucy even from visiting and had disregarded his symptoms. Lucy had often felt she should have insisted on visiting; she should have realized her mother was already suffering from Alzheimer's, which she'd tried to hide.

"We have to remember that hindsight is twenty-twenty," she told Laura. "Of course we should have and could have, if we'd only known, but we didn't. We have to forgive ourselves."

Laura's eyes were huge and she cast them upward. "That's what I pray for, all the time: forgiveness. But I don't think He does forgive me."

Lucy was no theologian, but she had attended church enough to pick up the general gist. "Of course He does."

Laura shook her head. "No. I saw my mother's body—the undertaker showed me. He was so upset, said he'd never seen anything like it. Bruises and bedsores and marks from the restraints, her skin rubbed raw. She looked as if she'd been tortured."

"Did you report the nursing home to the authorities?"

Laura's eyes widened. "I was so ashamed—I didn't say a word." She sobbed. "But I can't forget. I'm haunted. Whenever I close my eyes, that's what I see."

Lucy was beginning to feel out of her depth. She furrowed her brow and patted Laura's hand. "Maybe you should talk this over with a professional."

"That's what my husband says. He keeps saying how lucky we are, how Will has grown up to be so fine and he goes to a great college and we have a nice house and no money worries. He says I should get over it and enjoy life."

"That's easier said than done—but he does have a point. You can't change the past, only the future."

Laura brushed away her tears with the backs of her hands and then clasped Lucy's hands with both of hers. "Oh, Lucy, thank you. You've made me feel so much better."

"I'm glad I could help," said Lucy, standing up and looking back toward the pew where Pam was sitting, absorbed in her book.

"Really," insisted Laura. "I think you have a calling. Have you considered the ministry?"

Lucy was chuckling, about to admit the thought had never crossed her mind, when she jumped, hearing a sudden enormous crash. Her first thought was for Pam, but Pam was fine, looking about curiously for the source of the noise. Turning the other way, she saw Will in the center aisle, bending down to replace a kneeling stool.

"That boy is so clumsy," said Laura, giggling as her son advanced down the aisle toward them.

"Aren't they all?" said Lucy, deciding to head back to Pam.

"But don't you want to see the museum?" asked Laura.

"Thanks, but I need to get back to my friend."

"Oh, well, now that Will's here, I can go with him. He loves old things and museums. Isn't that right, Will?"

"Sure, Mom."

Will was smiling agreeably enough, but Lucy wasn't convinced. Her experience had taught her that teens could be less than honest when they were engaged in achieving their own ends. They pleaded for permission to spend the night at a friend's house, declaring that "of course her parents are going to be home," and you got a call from the cops at one in the morning advising you to pick up your kid at the police station because neighbors had called complaining of a drunken party. Or you found a charge on your cable bill for an adult movie that your teenage son swore must be a mistake because he'd never do anything like that. Never. Not ever. And fools that we are, thought Lucy, watching Laura and Will going off together, parents want to believe their children are telling the truth.

"What was that all about?" asked Pam when Lucy joined her on her pew. "It looked intense."

"You can say that again. She's guilt-stricken over her mother's death. She feels she didn't do enough for her."

Pam sighed. "I guess we all feel that way when our parents pass on."

"Not like this. Laura really feels guilty. She needs help."

"I hope she gets it," said Pam, a mischievous glint in her eye. "You know, I believe I spotted an ice-cream place in the plaza outside."

"I believe you're right," said Lucy.

"And I think I could just about manage to hobble over there."

"Well, let's go," said Lucy, taking her arm. "I've had it with churches."

"You said you loved them."

"I've changed my mind," said Lucy, stepping through the door and taking a deep breath of fresh air.

Chapter Nineteen

After finishing their ice-cream cones, Lucy and Pam made their way back to the pickup point in front of the Abbey. They were the first ones there and perched themselves on some concrete bollards to wait for the others to gather.

Predictably, Dr. Cope and Jennifer were the first to arrive. Dr. Cope greeted them with his usual courtesy. "Did you enjoy Bath? I'd have to say this has been my favorite day of the tour. The Roman baths were really something to see. And to think, the Romans appreciated the healthful benefits of regular bathing and had the engineers to create these baths thousands of years before modern man."

Jennifer smiled. "I read somewhere that Queen Elizabeth—the first, that is—took a bath once a month."

"Whether she needed it or not," added Pam, smiling. "And I imagine she did."

"They say the Native Americans in Maine could smell the European ships from shore and were pretty disgusted by the new arrivals' poor hygiene," volunteered Lucy.

"I've heard that, too," said Quentin, sidling up to Jennifer. "Indoor plumbing is one of civilization's finest achievements." His gaze drifted over her figure, lingering at her bust. "Which do you prefer: a shower or a bath?"

Dr. Cope gave him a stony look and wrapped a protective arm around his granddaughter's shoulders. "That's rather personal, isn't it?"

Quentin shrugged, regarding Jennifer with a certain sparkle in his eye. "I just wondered, because the hotel has only showers. I'm looking forward to a nice long soak when I get home."

"Me too," said Lucy. "And I'm awfully glad the water in Tinker's Cove isn't bright green."

"Point taken," laughed Quentin. "Did any of you sample the water in the Pump Room?"

Jennifer wrinkled her nose. "It was disgusting. I couldn't finish the glass."

"A pity." Dr. Cope's tone was serious. "They say it's full of healthful minerals."

"We tried it." Ann Smith joined the group, along with her husband and daughter. "I wouldn't recommend it."

"Absolutely foul," agreed Tom.

"But the food was very good." Caroline actually smiled, seeming relaxed and comfortable for the first time since the incident in Brighton. "That Devonshire cream stuff is awfully good."

"The prices were ridiculous, however," said Ann.

"It was a treat—nothing wrong with a treat now and then," replied Tom.

Listening, Lucy thought this was a conversation the Smiths repeated from time to time, with Ann arguing for restraint while Tom pushed for small extravagances. She suspected there was absolutely nothing he wouldn't do for Caroline, who reminded her a bit of a baby cowbird. The mother cowbird was a heedless creature who laid her eggs in another bird's nest, replacing the natural parents' eggs with her own. When the baby cowbirds hatched, they were usually much larger than the surrogate parents, who struggled to keep up with the growing chicks' enormous appetites.

Across the street, Lucy spotted Sue and Rachel, both toting a couple of shopping bags.

"Golly gee, I was worried we were late and had missed the bus." Sue was a bit out of breath. "The shopping was fabulous."

"The Jane Austen house was lovely," added Rachel.

"It was a fake," protested Sue. "They admitted she never actually lived there."

"It was typical of the period." Rachel smiled. "I think I may have been a Regency lady in a previous life."

"More likely a scullery maid," said Lucy, catching Quentin's eye. "We all think we'd be lords and ladies, but the truth is our ancestors were probably peasants. I'm sure mine were."

"Not me," insisted Rachel. "I'm sure I was to the manor born." She opened her shopping bag and showed off a mug with the words *Her Ladyship* painted on it. "See? It was waiting for me at the National Trust gift shop. And I got one that says 'His Lordship' for Bob."

Sue rolled her eyes and glanced at Lucy. "Actually, I did, too. In fact, I bought tea towels and cocktail glasses as well. For me and Sid. We're officially Lord and Lady Finch."

"I wonder if there's time . . ." Laura Barfield had arrived, looking a bit wan and out of breath. "Where is that shop?"

"Too late," said Quentin. "There's the bus."

"Oh, dear," Laura fretted. "I'm afraid I've lost track of Will."

"I suppose you mean Sir Will," suggested Dr. Cope in a somewhat sarcastic tone.

The sarcasm was lost on Laura, who'd spotted her son rounding the corner of the Abbey, along with Autumn. "He's my prince," she chirped, giving him a wave that he ignored.

"Some prince," muttered Tom Smith, glaring at Will and stepping protectively in front of Caroline.

"Princes aren't perfect," said Jennifer. "Prince Harry seems to get in a lot of trouble."

"He sets a poor example to be sure," said Dr. Cope.

They had all gathered in a little group—only the Smiths were standing apart—waiting expectantly for the minibus to pull up when a huge tour bus slid to a stop in front of them, braking with a loud hiss. The doors opened and a large group began to disembark, chattering noisily and shoving them aside as they maneuvered to snap photos of each other in front of the Abbey.

"Germans," muttered Tom Smith. "This is how they took Poland."

"Shhh," cautioned his wife. "They might hear you. A lot of them speak English, you know."

"I hope they do hear me." Tom lowered his brows. "People are too quick to forgive." He turned to Quentin. "And since I'm mouthing off, how come we're backtracking to Stonehenge? I was talking to the bus driver, just happened to run into him on the plaza there, and he said we're doing things backward."

Quentin nodded, watching as the Germans formed ranks behind their leader and the bus pulled away, allowing the minibus to take its place. "You're right—I juggled things a bit so we'd be able to walk among the stones at Stonehenge. Unless you make arrangements for a special tour, after hours, you can only walk around the perimeter of the henge." He paused as the door opened. "Trust me, this will be much nicer—and we'll be there at sunset."

There was little conversation as the minibus driver retraced the route from Salisbury and on to Stonehenge. It had already been a long day, and Lucy suspected most of the older folks were tired. She sure was, and she was looking forward to getting back home to Bill and the girls and the familiar surroundings of Tinker's Cove. She was surprised to discover that she missed her house: her bed with the pillows that were just right, her roomy rolltop bathtub, even Libby the dog's musty odor that clung to the old sofa in the family room where she liked to nap. But as she gazed out the window at the green fields and rolling hills, she was very glad she'd taken the trip.

They'd certainly got off to a rocky start, with George Temple's death, but now that event, dreadful as it was, seemed like ancient history. So much had happened in the week that it was easy to forget the horrible circumstances of his death, especially since she hadn't really known him. These things happened, she supposed, and even though she had her suspicions, she knew it was her nature to question things. That was why she was a good reporter. But she also knew that she tended to make mountains out of molehills, and the truth was that she didn't really have any hard evidence that Temple had been murdered or that Caroline's fall off the Brighton pier was anything but a sign of that poor girl's disturbed mind. As for Pam's slip off the curb, well, it was probably just that. And Autumn and Jennifer's odd relationship? That could be explained by the fact that they were rivals for Will's affection.

Lucy let out a big sigh and relaxed against her seat. It was time, she decided, to turn her thoughts toward home. She was worried about Elizabeth, she wondered how Bill had managed with the girls, and she really missed little Patrick. It would be great to get home, she decided, noticing the sky, especially in the west, was taking on a pinkish hue.

"We're here!" announced Quentin as the bus turned off the highway into a spacious parking area. The last of the day's buses were lined up at the exit, waiting to depart, and only a few cars were parked at the far end, probably belonging to employees. It looked as though the group was going to have Stonehenge to themselves.

Descending from the minibus, Lucy heard the buzz of steady traffic and was surprised to see the ancient site was quite close to a major highway that carried a heavy load of rush-hour traffic.

"Never mind the traffic," advised Quentin as they followed him toward the ticket booth. "Remember, this is a sacred site, a place of great mystery and spirituality. It was also a place of sacrifice—archaeologists have unearthed the skeleton of a small child, it's skull neatly cleaved in two. Clearly a blood sacrifice."

Laura grew pale. "How terrible!"

Quentin shrugged. "It may have been deformed or mentally deficient. . . ."

"Why, that's even worse," protested Ann. "We must protect the weak."

Quentin's smile was patronizing. "A modern concept, I'm afraid. The ancients were more concerned with basic survival and couldn't afford to waste scant resources on the weak and sick. Everyone had to pull their own weight, even children. If not, they went back to the gods." He paused. "At least that's one theory."

The man at the ticket booth didn't seem terribly thrilled to see them. "Aye, here you are," he said in a voice that sounded like a grumble. "I suppose we might as well get started."

When he stepped outside the booth and stood before them, they saw a man of medium height, dressed in shiny brown polyester slacks and a black sweater with the World Heritage Site logo. His gray hair could use a wash, his brows bristled over his horn rims, and a name tag informed them his name was Dick.

"Follow me," Dick said, leading the way along a winding asphalt path that dipped into a tunnel that ran beneath the roadway. "We've got plans to jazz the place up," he told them. "When you come back—that is, if you come back in a couple of years—you'll find the roadway's been rerouted and we're going to have a fine new visitor center." He stopped abruptly in the middle of the tunnel, beneath a fluorescent light that cast deep shadows on his face. "Mind now, we don't want any nonsense. Don't touch the stones; don't even think about carving your initials on them; don't be a joker and try to push 'em over. Got it?"

They nodded and he resumed the march through the tunnel.

"Awright, then, remember, this 'ere site is a source of inspiration and fascination and a place of worship. There's druids gather 'ere every summer, at Midsummer Eve. 'Course, the builders weren't druids; they were Bronze Age folk, lived here some three thousand years ago. Took it into their 'eads to put up these stones, brought 'em some hunnerd and thirty-five miles from Wales.

"How you ask? Well, we think they floated 'em on barges, came through the Bristol Channel and up the river. That makes the most sense. But we don't really know. And we sure don't know why. The stones line up with the rising of the summer solstice and the setting of the winter solstice, so it probably had something to do with that, but like I said, nobody knows."

He stopped at the tunnel opening. "Well, here you are, wander around to yer 'eart's content. I'll be 'ere if you want to ask about something, but I pretty much told you ever'thing we know. And don't forget to stop in our gift shop on your way out. We keep it open late, especially for groups like you, and we have a fine selection of books and gifts."

Emerging into the dying light of day, Lucy took Pam's arm. "How are you doing? Can you manage here?"

Pam's face glowed in the reddish light of the setting sun; she was standing still, awestruck by the sight of the massive circle of golden stones standing on the green and grassy plain. "This is amazing," she said. "I want to see every bit, even if I have to crawl!"

Personally, Lucy didn't get it. The stones were interesting, all right, but they weren't as tall as she expected; in fact, they were rather stumpy. It did seem a massive undertaking—you had to admire the builders' effort—but without knowing why they went to all that trouble, it seemed a bit pointless.

"What a gorgeous sunset," said Rachel as they made their way toward the stones.

The group had spread out, falling into the groupings they'd adopted over the course of the tour. Quentin was leading the way, followed by Dr. Cope and Jennifer. The Smiths were a tight group of three. Laura Barfield walked alone, and Will and Autumn had gone off together ahead of the others. Lucy and her friends were bringing up the rear, walking slowly with Pam until Sue stopped abruptly.

"You know, I didn't bring my sweater and it's awfully chilly. I think I'll go back. . . ."

"She just wants to go to the shop," said Pam.

"Well, I haven't got anything for Geoff," she said, naming her son-in-law. "He's a scientist. They've probably got something he'd like. About rocks or astronomy . . ." She wrinkled up her face. "Don't you think?"

Rachel laughed. "It's okay—you're dismissed."

"No demerits?"

Lucy took Sue's hand and patted it. "Obviously, this is not your thing."

"Wide-open spaces, nature . . . ," chimed in Pam.

"Not a price tag in sight," added Rachel.

"It's okay. We'll catch up with you later."

"What a relief," sighed Sue, scurrying back through the tunnel.

"She's a shopaholic," laughed Rachel as they stepped off the path and crossed the grassy space to the stone circle.

Up close, the stones seemed taller to Lucy, and she stood in front of a pair, looking up at the third enormous stone that formed a crude arch above her head. She found herself giggling, remembering a silly movie in which Chevy Chase had toppled the whole thing. But these stones, she realized, weren't going anywhere. They projected an enormous sense of solidity and enclosure. The circle invited believers to gather in this spot; it was a place of communion. She instinctively reached her hands out, expecting to touch Pam and Rachel, but they were gone.

So much for a communion of souls, she thought, somewhat disgruntled. Looking around, she saw the group had largely scattered, each individual pursuing his or her own thoughts and reactions. The Smiths were the exception, circulating among the stones in their own little orbit.

Making her way to the very center of the double circle, Lucy watched as the rosy sky deepened to a deep, blazing red and shafts of light from the sinking sun pierced the openings between the stones. It was an amazing sight, and she stood, awestruck and silent at the spectacle. She'd seen some pretty fabulous sunsets in Maine, of course, but this was different. The place itself, with its strange formation of stones, almost like something a child might build out of stones on the beach, made it different. And maybe, she thought with a flash of insight, that was what Stonehenge was really about. Maybe it was a grand, exaggerated version of that innate desire to build that children had, the same impulse that made children reach for building blocks and LEGOs and Tinkertoys. She was smiling to herself, musing on this thought, when she heard the scream.

The sound hit her like an electric shock and she went rigid, snapping to attention. She turned, straining, listening for a repeat but no sound came. She started to run, dodging around the stones, trying to find the screamer. Was it a joke? Had Will startled one of the girls? Had Quentin gotten a little too amorous?

No. What she heard was a gut-wrenching scream of terror. She'd heard that cry before and knew it must be heeded. It was as impossible to ignore as a baby's cry. Somebody was in trouble, and every fiber of her being impelled her to do something.

She was breathing heavily now, getting confused as she ran from stone to stone in the steadily dimming light. The sky was violet, and the stones were hulking black shapes casting long shadows. She was beginning to fear she wouldn't be able to find whoever screamed when she caught a flash of white beyond the farthest stone, a single massive pillar that stood alone.

Panting and gasping for breath, she ran as fast as she could across the circle; then, reaching the stone, she stopped and listened. There was nothing, nothing but the brooding black stone. Maybe it was all a mistake; maybe she'd overreacted. She turned, about to return to the lighted tunnel and the gift shop where her friends were probably waiting for her, when she heard a muffled moan.

Without thinking, running on adrenaline, she charged around the stone and found three dark figures. At first, it wasn't clear what was going on. Then her eyes adjusted and she saw Will was holding Pam tight against him, his hand clapped over her mouth. In the fading light, Pam's eyes gleamed, wide with terror, because the third person, Autumn, was waving a knife in front of her nose.

"What's going on?" demanded Lucy.

Autumn lunged toward her, and Lucy, too shocked to move, would have been stabbed except for the sudden arrival of Tom Smith. He barreled in like a rugby player and took Autumn down; the knife went flying and Lucy scrambled to pick it up.

"Enough is enough," declared Tom. "Let her go."

Will stared at him, still holding tight to Pam, who struggled to free herself. "Are you crazy?" he demanded, glaring at Tom. "We have to get rid of them. They know all about it. I saw the e-mails. Do you really want to go to jail for life?"

"Yeah." Tom pulled himself up to his full five feet six inches and stuck out his barrel chest. "Yeah. I'll go to jail. If somebody has to take the rap, I'm ready. I'll do it. I killed Temple and you know what? I'd do it again!"

Chapter Twenty

Will reluctantly released Pam, and she collapsed into Lucy's arms. Pam was trembling, her teeth chattering, and Lucy held her close. Lucy was cold, too, and still wary. The three could turn on them at any minute, and she was relieved when Quentin came striding toward them.

"It's getting cold and the staff are eager to lock up for the night," he said, apparently so intent on rounding up the group that he ignored the fact that Autumn was sprawled on the ground and Pam was tearfully clinging to Lucy. "Let's go back to the minivan."

"Not so fast," protested Lucy. "Will and Autumn attacked Pam," she said, showing him the knife. "And Tom's confessed to killing Temple. We need to call the authorities. I insist on it."

Lucy didn't get the shocked reaction she expected. "No one was hurt, were they?" asked Quentin, watching as Will bent over Autumn and helped her to her feet. "We'll sort this all out in comfort, in the van. Let's go." He pointed the pair toward the exit and waited for them to take the lead before starting off himself.

Tom fell into step beside Quentin. "Like I said before, I'll take the rap for Temple. It's the only way to end this thing."

"I don't think that will be necessary," said Quentin, slapping him on the back. "But I certainly appreciate the gesture."

Lucy and Pam brought up the rear, saying little. Pam still clung to Lucy, who found herself increasingly furious with Quentin. Her friend had been attacked, and Quentin seemed more concerned with keeping the tour on schedule than doing the right thing and reporting the incident to the authorities. Will and Autumn were out of control and had to be stopped. It was outrageous, and she was determined to get justice for Pam—and Temple, too. Because the more she thought about it, the less she believed Tom Smith's confession. Of the group, he seemed the least likely to be involved, and she suspected his confession was nothing more than a clumsy attempt to protect somebody else. Caroline? His wife? Both were obviously troubled, but neither seemed a likely murder suspect.

Finally reaching the van, Lucy hesitated a moment before climbing aboard the van. What were she and Pam getting into? But the interior lights were on and Sue and Rachel were there, as well as the driver. She looked back over her shoulder, but the windows were already dark in the gift shop and ticket area. The parking lot was now deserted except for the minivan, and she could see the red taillights of the departing employees' cars. Still holding tight to Pam's hand, she clambered up the steps.

"What took you so long?" asked Rachel. "Were you enchanted by the mystery of Stonehenge?"

"Not exactly," muttered Lucy, glaring at Quentin. "I think we're owed an explanation."

The driver cast a questioning look at Quentin. "We're getting late here, sir."

"Yes, yes, we must get going," replied Quentin.

The driver dimmed the lights and the minibus began to move; Quentin seated himself sideways with his legs in the aisle in order to face the group.

"Lucy is right," he said. "There was an altercation involving two Winchester students. . . ."

"*Altercation* isn't the right word," insisted Lucy. "Will and Autumn attacked Pam."

Rachel gasped and Sue reached her hand over the seat to pat Pam on the shoulder.

"This has gone too far," said Dr. Cope. "I—"

Quentin cut him off. "Before you say anything more, let me continue. Obviously there is no excuse whatsoever for violence, but Autumn and Will were acting under the mistaken assumption that Pam was not satisfied that George Temple died of natural causes and had begun an investigation. They were fearful they would be implicated in some way."

"She was asking questions—I saw the e-mails!" declared Will.

Quentin chuckled and shook his head. "One of the things I always warn my students about is their tendency to jump to conclusions. There is no substitute for solid research, and I think Will and Autumn were a bit too impetuous—that is, of course, one of the hallmarks of youth, perhaps complicated in this case by certain emotional and social deficiencies, which the college is working to address in a supportive group setting." He looked at Lucy. "You can be sure this incident will be reported and dealt with by the college, but I'm sure we don't want to expose our young travelers to the vagaries of the British justice system."

Lucy rolled her eyes. "I don't like this, but it's really up to Pam."

"I'm fine with it," said Pam. "But I will hold you to your word. If you don't report them, I will." She paused. "But what about Tom's confession?"

Ann Smith's voice was shaky. "What confession? What did you do, Tom?"

Quentin spoke quickly, before Tom could answer. "This trip has been stressful, and I think Tom was . . . well, I guess you could say he cracked for a minute there, and, well, this is a psychological phenomenon related to stress. It's not all that uncommon actually, where an individual reacts to a traumatic situation by coming to believe he caused the situation. In other words"—Quentin gave a little chuckle—"as preposterous as this may seem, Tom actually confessed to killing George Temple."

"That's ridiculous!" Ann's voice was high-pitched, almost hysterical as she defended her husband. "He's no more guilty than the rest of us!"

"Exactly," said Quentin quickly. "And we all know that the British authorities, including Scotland Yard, conducted a thorough inquiry following George Temple's untimely and tragic death and concluded it was the unfortunate result of an extreme asthma attack."

The van swerved and Quentin grabbed the armrest to avoid being thrown out of his seat. Lucy noticed his teeth gleaming in an embarrassed grimace as he regained his equilibrium. "So I think now the best thing is for us to relax and enjoy the rest of the trip back to London."

There was a general sigh of relief in the bus as everyone settled in for the ride. Lucy, however, wasn't satisfied. She couldn't forget the terrible look on Temple's face as he struggled for breath. The group members' actions at the airport and on the plane seemed normal enough, but if you thought about it another way, those actions seemed part of a carefully choreographed dance of death.

"That's quite a story you've concocted," she said, her voice small but firm in the darkness, "but it doesn't add up. I was at the airport. I was right next to George Temple on the plane. I saw what happened. There was a series of small events that seemed innocent enough by themselves but were actually designed to cause his death, and I think you were all part of it in one way or another."

"But why would we do such a thing?" protested Laura. "What would bring us all together to do such a terrible thing?"

"George Temple was an investment advisor who defrauded his clients," said Lucy. "And from what you've told me yourselves in the course of this trip, I suspect you were all victims of his scheme." Lucy's voice dropped a few notes. "Laura, you told me your mother died because of the poor care she received in a second-rate nursing home. Was that all you could afford because Temple swindled you? Or perhaps your mother?"

"That's terrible," said Rachel, her voice rich with sympathy, "and I can understand that you might very well want revenge. But, Lucy, think a minute. Even if all these people were victimized by George Temple, how did they manage to find each other?"

"Through the kids: Autumn, Will, Jennifer, and Caroline. They're all in this support group Quentin was talking about. They all heard each other's stories and put two and two together and realized their families had all suffered because of George Temple."

"Temple deserved to die." It was Dr. Cope, sounding like the voice of doom. "I have no regrets about what we did. He was every bit as evil as a mass murderer. He toyed with his victims. He ruined them—he caused untold suffering. My son-in-law couldn't face the shame when he learned he'd lost everything, and he killed himself, plunging my daughter into despair. She never recovered—she's dependent on psychotropic drugs. She lives in a fog. George Temple took their lives and deprived my granddaughter of her parents' love and support."

"He got off with a rap on the knuckles," Tom hissed. "Two years was all he got. It took Ann longer than that to recover after the accident, and we lost our baby boy. It wouldn't have happened if we'd had the money to repair the car, to keep it up. We were driving a wreck, didn't have a cent to our names. I was a fool. I trusted him with all our savings. He said it was stupid to put money in the bank when you could do so much better in the stock market. But he never invested it. He just used my money to pay other investors, pretending they were making fabulous returns. It was a classic Ponzi scheme and it all fell apart." He paused, clenching his fists. "I'd do it again. If somebody has to be punished, I'd be honored to plead guilty to killing that weasel."

"You shouldn't take the blame. We were all part of it," said Dr. Cope.

"It started with me," said Tom. "I slipped the toy gun in his pocket so he'd be searched by airport security."

"But I was the one who hung around the airport, pretending to be late, just to upset him," declared Will.

"And I kept fretting to add to the tension," admitted Laura, a note of pride in her voice.

"You did a great job," offered Ann, "but I wrapped him up in a mildewed old scarf to get his asthma going."

"I stole the bottle of allergy medicine out of his carry-on bag." Caroline's voice was confident. Lucy noticed she was sitting alone, apart from her parents.

Jennifer chimed in: "I opened the peanuts, knowing he was allergic, and waved the packet under his nose."

Autumn was rubbing her elbow, sore from her fall. "I knocked his rescue inhaler into his drink. . . ."

"It all went off like clockwork," said Dr. Cope, congratulating the group.

Lucy stared from one to the other, hardly believing what she was hearing. They'd conspired to kill a man. They'd acted in cold blood without a shred of compassion, and they seemed proud of what they'd done. She'd been right next to Temple. She'd seen him struggling for breath and was convinced that nobody, no matter what they'd done, should have to suffer like that. She believed in her heart that his killers must be punished.

Dr. Cope was speaking slowly and clearly; he might have been instructing a patient on how to take his medicine. "When they called for a doctor, I used a spent EpiPen, guaranteeing Temple's death. My crime was the worst—I violated my Hippocratic oath. By withholding the epinephrine, I caused his death." He straightened his back, rising a bit in his seat. "I'm the one who should be punished." He turned to Lucy. "Tomorrow, I'll go with you to Scotland Yard and turn myself in."

"But you didn't go to Scotland Yard. What changed your mind?" asked Sue.

Lucy and her three friends were seated in a window table at the Wolseley, a posh Piccadilly restaurant, waiting for the server to deliver their afternoon tea. It was the last day of the trip; they would be flying home first thing the next day.

Lucy glanced around at the sleek art deco dining room, then looked down at the black and silver place mat, the heavy pieces of silverware. She picked up the silky starched linen napkin and spread it on her lap, smoothing it while she gathered her thoughts.

"It was their stories. What happened to the Smiths was terrible—their baby son died because they couldn't afford to get the brakes fixed on their car. And Laura's mother suffered horribly in that nursing home—she actually died from bedsores!"

"Too dreadful," murmured Sue. "And Jennifer's father committed suicide. Families never recover from a thing like that. There's always the feeling that you could have done something to prevent it."

"But the worst was Autumn," said Pam. "Her family became homeless. The bank foreclosed on their house, and they lived in their car for a while, but when her father began drinking, that became impossible for them. Her mother went to a homeless shelter with Autumn, thinking it would be safer, but she was raped there."

"Autumn, too," said Lucy, soothing herself by stroking a spoon that felt pleasantly solid in her hand. "And then her mother got hooked on drugs, and Autumn went into foster care." She put the spoon down as a small parade of waiters approached. "What a nightmare!"

Conversation stopped as the first waiter presented a silver cake stand laden with sandwiches, scones, and cakes and placed it in the center of the table with a flourish. "The scones are cranberry today," he announced. "The sandwiches are egg and cress on tomato bread, salmon on wholemeal bread, *jambon* on cheese bread, and chicken salad on white bread."

They listened attentively as he pointed out the tiny triangles that were so artfully arranged. Lucy was starving and her mouth was watering.

"Also, we have an assortment of cakes: mini éclairs, gateau au chocolat, tartes des fruits, and lemon cupcakes. Enjoy!"

"I'm sure we will," said Rachel, somewhat dazed.

"Earl Grey for you, madam?" Another waiter was at Lucy's elbow, filling her cup with fragrant, steaming tea and then leaving the silver pot on the table for her. The others, in turn, received their Lapsang Souchong, Assam, and Darjeeling. Then the servers vanished and they were confronted with the problem of where to start.

"I say we go for the cakes first," said Sue. "Why fill up on the other stuff?"

Rachel adopted her nanny face. "We can't begin with cake—the sandwiches are the most nourishing."

"Let's compromise and start with the scones," suggested Pam. "Just look at that Devonshire cream."

It took some time to properly assemble the scones and cream, as well as the strawberry jam, on their plates, and Lucy became thoughtful. "These are really good," she said, biting into the warm, buttery, slightly crisp scone that was a perfect foil for the luscious toppings.

"I know," said Sue. "These are amazingly delicious—so delicious, in fact, that I'm going to pretend they don't have any calories at all."

"Me too!" declared Pam.

They sat in silence, savoring their treat, until Sue raised her finger, indicating a thought had occurred to her. "Have you heard from Elizabeth, Lucy? I just wondered because, frankly, I could use something a little stronger than tea, and they do have champagne." Her face brightened at the prospect, then adopted a more serious expression. "But if you're strapped, we can certainly stick to the tea."

Lucy shifted her head, mentally changing gears. "You won't believe this. The dean actually thanked her for showing her how important the school's traditions are to the students. She nominated her for the school spirit award."

Pam was grinning. "Maybe it's just me, but school spirit and Elizabeth don't seem like terms I would use in the same sentence."

Lucy shrugged and raised her hand, signaling the waiter. "We'd like champagne all 'round, please."

The waiter nodded, serious in his penguin suit. "Excellent choice, madam."

Chapter Twenty-One

On the flight home, Lucy and her friends were seated separately, scattered throughout the cabin. Lucy, now a seasoned flyer, was flipping through the flight magazine while other passengers were still boarding. It looked to be another crowded flight, and the overhead compartments were filling up fast. Lucy, who was seated once again on the aisle, had to duck when somebody's bag tumbled out and landed in her lap.

"I'm so sorry," said an older gentleman, retrieving his briefcase.

"No damage done," said Lucy, glancing at him and receiving a shock. For a moment, she thought he was George Temple, come back from the grave.

There was a click as the overhead compartment was closed, and he took the seat directly opposite her, on the other side of the aisle. Déjà vu all over again, she thought, stealing another look. The man didn't really look like George, she realized, although he did have gray hair and was wearing a similar jacket.

"I know I'm showing my age but I miss the days when flying was an adventure," he said, smiling at her. "My goodness, they used to treat us like royalty, and the stewardesses were all young and beautiful."

"I guess we were all younger," said Lucy, smiling back. "This is my first overseas trip."

"Did you have a good time?" he asked.

Lucy thought a moment. "It wasn't what I expected," she said finally.

"Well," he replied, opening the packet containing earphones, "I hope we have a pleasant flight."

"Me too," said Lucy, turning back to her magazine.

Takeoff went smoothly and Lucy tried to interest herself in a movie, but her thoughts kept returning to George Temple. She understood that he'd done a terrible thing; she could still hear Tom Smith declaring, "Temple wasn't any better than a serial killer. What's the difference? Bobby died because of George, because of what he did. He never apologized; he never admitted he'd done anything wrong. He thought, right up until the moment he died, that he was better than everybody else. My only regret is that I didn't get to tell him why he was dying, that he was being punished for what he did to us."

Lucy understood his anger, at least she thought she did, but she wasn't at all sure that it was okay for people to take the law into their own hands. Temple was tried; he served jail time. Maybe it wasn't the justice system's shining moment, but in the years she'd covered various trials as a reporter, she'd learned that judges' decisions rarely satisfied everybody. In fact, one lawyer told her that a good decision was one that didn't make either party completely happy.

She squinted at the little screen. Matt Damon sure wasn't happy, and neither was Leonardo DiCaprio, and that Mark Wahlberg guy had a really foul mouth. She decided to try the BBC news instead, but there were floods in China and violence in Africa and the world seemed to be in a dreadful state. Hearing the tinkle of the drinks cart, she smiled, thinking that Sue would be pleased. Be honest, she chided herself. She was looking forward to that white wine, too.

She was finishing up her lunch, tucking the empty wrappers into a plastic cup that had held spring water, when a thought struck her. The meal had many components: a plastic plate and cutlery, a salad, a foil packet containing salad dressing, a paper napkin, and some sort of pasta with sauce, all of which came from different suppliers. But, she thought in an *aha* moment, somebody had put it all together. Somebody in the British Airways corporation had chosen these products and arranged for them to be assembled and distributed to passengers.

Nothing got done without an organizer, she thought. Not a bake sale, not a school play, and not a murder. The tour group hadn't all woken up one morning and decided to murder George Temple; somebody had to put the idea into their heads. Somebody had organized the killing and assigned the parts; somebody had convinced the others to share the blame.

"May I take your tray?" asked the stewardess.

Lucy handed it over, and then opened her book, but she wasn't reading. She was thinking that she knew exactly who had orchestrated Temple's death . . . but could she prove it?

Her suspicions grew even stronger two months later, when she was covering the commencement ceremony at Winchester College. President Chapman announced that Professor Crighton was now emeritus and that Professor Quentin Rea would henceforward occupy the English Literature chair. She sat there, jaw dropping, as Quentin stepped forward to receive his stole, to enthusiastic applause. The applause, she realized, had less to do with Quentin himself than the high spirits of the crowd, who had gathered to congratulate and support their kids. The applause from the section where the faculty was seated was merely polite, but it was difficult to know if that was simply because they had attended so many commencement ceremonies that they were bored or if they believed Quentin unworthy of the honor.

Her mind was in a whirl, but she had to concentrate on getting down President Chapman's speech, all about the impressive work Professor Rea had done through the years, the way he'd reached out to students, especially those having trouble adjusting to college life, and something about the new priorities in which teaching was taking precedence over publishing. Lucy had no idea if this was actually a trend in higher education or a defense against criticism that Quentin hadn't published much.

When all the speeches had been delivered and the diplomas awarded, after the graduates had tossed their caps into the air and were gathered with family members for the traditional photos, she fell into step beside Fred Rumford. Rumford was a history professor, and she'd occasionally interviewed him in the past, most recently when a scuba diver discovered an eighteenth-century shipwreck off the coast.

"Are you looking forward to summer vacation?" she asked.

"Not me," he replied, shaking his head. He'd taken off his black robe and was carrying it over his arm. He'd forgotten his cap, however. It was a rather large beret and gave him a clownish look. "Summer school starts next week. There's no rest for the wicked."

"Too bad." She smiled. "Though I don't imagine it's actually a grueling schedule."

"No." He laughed, pulling off the cap. "Shame on me. It's just one class, but it meets daily for six weeks."

"Then you're free?"

"Yup. I'm heading for Greece, spending August cruising the Greek islands on my friend's schooner." He gave the cap a twirl on his finger.

Lucy pictured sparkling blue water, rocky shores, and dazzling white houses and was sick with envy. "Sounds divine," she said.

He shrugged. "I'm crew. My friend hires the boat out to paying customers. I expect I'll have to do a lot of kowtowing."

Lucy laughed. "That's life." She paused. "Listen, what's up with Quentin Rea? I didn't know he was being considered for a chair."

Rumford grimaced. "It's all about the money. These are tough times—the board of directors can't afford top talent. I heard they were going to give the chair to George Temple, on the cheap. He, at least, has published a few things that were well received. But when he died, they held their noses and voted for Rea."

"I thought he plays kind of fast and loose with the female students. . . ."

"I'm pretty sure Chapman read him the riot act, told him she expected him to behave in a professional manner." He grinned wickedly. "Besides, he is getting older. I think even his tremendous libido may be weakening. And face it, he isn't as attractive as he used to be."

"But I thought that professors were virtually untouchable."

Rumford shook his head. "The world is changing, Lucy. I wouldn't be surprised if she made him sign some sort of contract, with stiff penalties for misconduct."

"Would he sign something like that?"

"In a minute. He was always ambitious, always wanted to be a professor, and I'm sure he realized this was his last chance." Rumford nodded. "Remember, he didn't have a chance in hell of getting the job until Temple died."

"That's what I thought," said Lucy as they came to a fork in the pathway. One way led to the cafeteria, where a reception was in full swing; the other led to the parking lot. "I guess you're expected at the party."

"Punch and cookies," he said. "Used to be we could count on Quentin to spike the punch but now . . ." He trailed off, raising a skeptical eyebrow.

Lucy laughed. "If I don't see you before you leave, have a great time in Greece."

"You, too, Lucy. Have a good summer."

Lucy continued on toward the parking lot, mulling over what Rumford had told her. He'd confirmed her suspicion that Quentin had a strong motive for getting Temple out of the way, a motive that had nothing to do with righting old wrongs or getting revenge. And he could have learned about Temple's past from one of the students he was so friendly with.

Lucy stopped in her tracks, in the middle of the concrete path, and turned around. It was a slim chance—most of the undergraduates had left already—but maybe she could find one of the kids from the tour. Freshmen, she knew, were assigned housing in two dorms, ugly brick boxes that had originally been built to accommodate returning GIs after World War II. One was called Patton and the other Eisenhower.

Patton was the closest. The doors were normally locked and could only be opened by using a special ID card, but practicality had trumped security as students struggled to move out their possessions. Or maybe it was just end-of-term partying; the plain steel door was propped open with a beer keg.

Lucy shook her head at this evidence of underage drinking and entered a dim hallway paved with gray vinyl tiles and lined with doors. She wandered along, peeking from time to time into the abandoned rooms with their stripped beds and open dresser drawers. Here and there, a poster still hung on the painted concrete block walls. She climbed the stairs to the second and third floors, but nobody was there. All the rooms were empty, which puzzled her, because Fred had told her a summer school session was planned. Surely some of the freshmen would be staying on to make up a course or perhaps pick up some extra credits. The answer was in a notice posted on a bulletin board: Patton would be closed for renovations; summer students would have to move to Eisenhower.

Crossing the quad, Lucy found a different atmosphere in the other dorm. The door was also propped open, this time with a lacrosse stick, and most of the rooms were empty, but here and there she found signs of occupation, although the dorm seemed temporarily deserted. It was a nice May day, after all, and those who weren't attending the ceremony were probably out enjoying the weather.

Many of the students had put signs with their names on the doors, and she looked for Caroline, Jennifer, Will, or Autumn but didn't find them. She was about to give up when she heard voices and went to investigate. Maybe she could ask them, whoever they were, if any of the kids from the tour were still on campus.

But as she drew closer, she realized the voices were engaged in an argument.

"Let me go," growled a male voice. "They expect me at the reception."

"No!" The voice was female, young. "Not until you promise."

"You're being ridiculous." The male was losing patience.

"No, I'm not. You said you loved me."

Lucy stopped. Maybe this wasn't the time to strike up a conversation with these two. She had turned around and was heading back to the stairs when she heard something that made her reconsider.

"Autumn, of course I love you."

It was Quentin, she realized. Quentin and Autumn.

"Then why won't you marry me?"

There was a long pause. Lucy found she was holding her breath, waiting for the answer.

"I haven't said I won't marry you."

Lucy's eyebrows went up.

"It's just that marriage is a big step. We should take our time."

"I don't have time. I'm pregnant."

Lucy's jaw dropped.

"It's almost three months. We have to make a decision soon if I'm going to get an abortion."

"I'm aware of that and I'll take care of you, I promise. And the child. But that's not a reason to get married. Not anymore. There's no stigma about being a single mother anymore. . . ."

"Look. I don't want to have the baby unless you're going to marry me."

"How come you weren't on the Pill? Pretty irresponsible if you ask me."

"Right. Like I should poison my body with that stuff. How come you didn't get a vasectomy?"

"Look, I have to get to that reception. We'll talk later."

"NO!" Autumn's voice was a hysterical cry.

"Calm down." Quentin was firm. "I have to go now. We'll talk about this later. We've got plenty of time to discuss this rationally, but this is not the time. I have to make an appearance at the reception."

"Okay, I'll go, too."

"No, you won't." Quentin's voice was threatening and Lucy felt uneasy. "Meet me at my apartment. In an hour."

"No. I'm going to go to the reception and make a big announcement."

Lucy heard a sharp slap, the sound of a hand meeting a cheek, and heard a shriek. She darted into the nearest room and hid behind the door as angry footsteps pounded down the hall. When she heard Quentin start down the stairs, she returned to the hallway, where she heard sobs.

Looking out the window at the end of the hall, she saw Quentin hurrying across the quad, his black gown flapping behind him. She stood watching for a minute, then came to a decision. She could still hear Autumn sobbing as she walked back to the door decorated with nothing but the original computer card the college used to assign rooms. The door was ajar, so she gave a perfunctory knock and pushed it open.

Autumn was sitting on the edge of the bed, grabbing tissues by the fistful and wiping her eyes. "Wha-what are you doing here?" she demanded, eyes flashing.

"I was looking for you, actually." Lucy noticed Autumn had a new tattoo, a Gothic-style Q on her arm.

"Well, you found me." Autumn blew her nose. "How much did you hear?"

"Just about everything," said Lucy. She seated herself on the single bed next to the girl. "I know it doesn't seem like it right now, but this isn't the end of the world. Whatever you decide, there's help. You'll get through this."

Autumn pounded her fist on her knee. "It's all his fault. If it wasn't for him, I wouldn't be in this mess."

"You have a point." Lucy gave Autumn a quick hug. "But trust me, that kind of thinking is not productive." She paused. "The most you're going to get out of him is money for an abortion."

"I don't want an abortion. I just said that. And I don't want to be a single mom. My mom was a single mom and I know what that's like. And I'm sure not giving up my kid for adoption. I've been a foster kid and it's no fun." She pressed her lips together. "Nope, I'm gonna make him marry me."

Lucy felt her stomach tighten. The girl was playing with fire and didn't know it. "Even if you can blackmail him into marrying you, what sort of start would that be? What kind of marriage would you have?"

Autumn gave her a sweet smile, and Lucy caught a glimpse of the sweet, vulnerable kid underneath the tattoos and piercings and fierce hair. "He said he loved me, and I love him. Love will see us through."

"You threatened to expose him." Lucy was dead serious. "He's a dangerous man. Look how he planned Temple's murder. He used all of you. He exploited your hurt and desire for revenge for his own advancement."

Autumn's eyes were wide. "How do you know about that?"

Lucy sighed. "It's obvious. He wanted Temple out of the way so he'd get Crighton's job." She slumped, as if a huge weight were pressing on her. "And it's also obvious that he isn't going to marry you."

Autumn's temper flared. "You're just jealous. He told me you two had a fling, years ago."

Lucy felt as if she'd been slapped. "I almost made the biggest mistake of my life, but I was smart enough to stop before I went too far." Lucy's voice was low, her tone serious. She'd been a reporter long enough to know that young women were very vulnerable. A summer rarely passed without some poor girl's body turning up swollen in a pond, or decomposed and ravaged by animals in the woods. Sometimes they just disappeared entirely. "You better think this over very carefully. He's a dangerous man, and there's a tried-and-true remedy for girls who cause trouble: They get killed."

Autumn snorted. "Now you're really being ridiculous. He loves me. You'll see. He just needs some time to calm down and think it over." She smiled a ravishing, confident smile. "I'm going to wear black for the wedding."

"Good thinking," said Lucy, standing up and smoothing out her pants. "Because it will also work for your funeral."

Chapter Twenty-Two

"Don't forget your boots." Lucy held up a pair of duck boots she'd found in the back of Elizabeth's closet.

Her oldest daughter rolled her eyes. "I won't need them."

"They have rain in Florida."

"I'm not going to wear those, not ever again."

Lucy put the boots back neatly in the corner. "We'll save them for when you come home to visit."

She knew she was going out on a limb here; she was pretty sure Elizabeth was a lot more interested in getting away from home than coming back for visits. After graduating magna cum laude from Chamberlain College, she'd spent a discontented summer working as a chambermaid at the Queen Victoria Inn and looking for a real job. She'd sent out hundreds of résumés to all parts of the country except New England—an omission that had not gone unnoticed by her mother. Now, after a grueling series of interviews, she'd been hired by the Cavendish Hotel chain and was headed for a training session at their flagship hotel in Palm Beach. They were packing a box of clothes to send ahead so she would only need a carry-on for the flight.

"Yeah," said Elizabeth, pulling a bulky sweater out of the huge duffel bag she was packing with clothes, "that's a good idea. I'll leave the warm clothes here."

"Better take a few things. They have cold snaps, you know. They sometimes have to light fires in the groves so the oranges don't freeze on the trees."

Elizabeth looked at her as if she were crazy. "Where do you get these ideas?"

"The news. I've seen it on the TV news." Lucy's cell phone was playing her song, and she pulled it out of her pocket. "Lots of times," she said, flipping it open and seeing her boss, Ted's, number. "What's up?" she asked.

Ted's voice was apologetic. "I'm sorry to do this to you, but I've got this wedding, Pam's niece. I'm actually in Connecticut."

"No problem. I was just helping Elizabeth pack, but I'm pretty sure she thinks I'm getting in the way."

Elizabeth shook her head but it was a weak protest.

"State police called. They found a body and they're having a press conference. They need help identifying it. Just get the basics—we'll run one of those gray-scale photos with a big question mark. *Who was she?* Heaven knows we don't have much else this week—talk about the dog days of August."

"There's a hurricane off the coast," said Lucy. "They say we might get it."

Ted perked up. "By Wednesday?"

Wednesday was deadline day. "Next weekend, maybe."

"Damn. We'll just have to go with the body. The press conference is two p.m. at the barracks in Shiloh."

At two o'clock Lucy was seated, along with a handful of reporters and camera crews from the Boston and Portland TV stations, in a basement room used for press conferences. A podium had been set up, backed with an American flag and the Maine state flag, and they billowed gently in the breeze created by a standing fan in the corner. Upstairs was air-conditioned, but thrifty Maine planners had reasoned the basement would be naturally cool. It wasn't. Lucy lifted her shirt off her sweaty shoulders and fanned herself with her reporter's notebook.

"They always turn up in August," said the guy next to her, a stringer for the *Boston Globe.* "I guess they start to smell in the heat. I heard a dog found this one."

Lucy nodded. "You're way ahead of me. Where'd they find it? It's a woman, right?"

"This is unofficial, but I heard some women talking at the gas station. They said it's a girl. She was stuffed in a plastic bag and dumped in the Metinnicut River. The bag snagged on some rocks or logs or something, and when the water level went down, like it does in summer—"

"I get the picture," said Lucy.

There was a small commotion as a group of officials were heard coming down the stairs and entering the room. Lucy recognized Strom Kipfer, the Shiloh police chief; Detective Horowitz from the state police, dressed as usual in a rumpled gray suit; and the county DA, Phil Aucoin. Aucoin took the podium while the others arranged themselves behind him in a row.

"Thanks for coming," he said, fingering a folded piece of paper. "First let me introduce everybody." He worked his way down the row, spelling names and giving each person's title. When he finished, he sighed and began reading a prepared statement.

"Early yesterday morning, a woman walking her dog along the bed of the Metinnicut River, which is quite low this year, discovered a large construction-grade plastic bag snagged on a log. The dog pawed the bag, ripping it and revealing a human foot. The woman called nine-one-one and local police responded, determining that the bag contained the body of a woman. Because of the method of disposal, they assumed the woman was the victim of a murder.

"The body was removed by the medical examiner at nine thirty-three a.m. and subsequently examined. There was some decomposition but the cool water temperature and the plastic bag protected the body, and he was able to determine that she was killed by a single blow to the head. She was about twenty years of age, five feet six inches tall, one hundred fifteen pounds, and in good health apart from the fact that she needed dental care. She had short dark hair and numerous piercings."

Lucy's head snapped up. *Oh, no,* she thought.

"She was dressed in black leggings, a short skirt, and a black T-shirt."

Lucy was scribbling it all down. *Let it be somebody else.*

"The victim was approximately ten weeks pregnant."

Lucy's stomach tied itself into a knot and she felt sick.

"Decomposition was too far advanced to allow for a photograph of the face, but we were able to photograph a tattoo on the woman's body, and we're going to distribute that today and ask that you publish it, bearing in mind that some news outlets may have individual policies that prohibit the publication of such potentially offensive material."

Lucy was holding her breath when the officer handed her a color photo. She exhaled slowly, then forced herself to look. The tattoo was a single letter in Gothic script: a *Q*.

The DA asked for questions but Lucy wasn't listening. She was picturing Autumn, remembering how she'd smiled, imagining herself in a black wedding dress. She'd never got to wear it; in fact, it seemed she had died in the same outfit she was wearing that day in May when they'd talked in the dorm. The day Lucy had warned her that Quentin was a dangerous man. Probably the day she died.

The conference was over. The officials were shaking hands here and there, making small talk with the reporters who were packing up to leave. Lucy was sitting there, her notebook in her lap, her pen in one hand and the photo in the other.

"Is everything all right?" It was her sometime friend Detective Horowitz. Their jobs tended to make them adversaries; as a reporter, she usually wanted more information than he wanted to share. But they were also both aware that they needed each other and had developed a respectful collegiality. As always, he looked tired, and today he seemed unusually concerned.

"Can I talk to you privately?" she asked.

"Sure."

Lucy got up, dropping the notebook on the floor and wavering unsteadily on her feet. He took her elbow, leading her to a side door that opened into a storage area. She was still clutching the photo in one hand and the pen in the other. "I know who this is," she said, tears springing to her eyes. She sobbed. "And I know who killed her."

* * *

Two weeks later, Lucy was surprised when Detective Horowitz called her at the office. She'd just sat down, fresh from the airport where she'd waved a brave good-bye to Elizabeth. Truth was, she felt rather down. Elizabeth had never been an easy child, but this summer they'd somehow avoided conflicts, at least most of the time. Lucy had really enjoyed having her eldest daughter home, and she knew she was going to miss her.

Horowitz got right to the point. "Everything you told me checked out," he said.

"So you've arrested him?" asked Lucy. It would be a relief to know Quentin was off the street and behind bars, unable to strike again.

"No."

Lucy couldn't believe it. "Why not?"

"That's why I'm calling you. I need your help."

"I think I've done enough—I gave you the whole case on a platter."

"I know. I've questioned him several times and I'm convinced he did it."

"So what's the problem?"

"It's all circumstantial. He denies everything. Well, he admits he had an affair with the girl but insists he didn't kill her. Which is smart because he knows we can do a DNA test. But even if the kid is his, it's not proof that he killed her."

"But there must be other evidence. Blood? Hair? Fibers?"

"Most likely, but we haven't been able to get a search warrant. The judge turned us down flat—he's a big believer in academic freedom. He says it would 'set a terrible precedent if police were allowed to invade college campuses like storm troopers and upset the peaceful and systematic pursuit of knowledge.' I'm quoting here."

"That's unbelievable."

"Yeah." There was a long pause. "That's why the DA asked me to get in touch with you." Another pause. "Well, actually, it was my idea. Your name came up in the course of the investigation as being someone he'd had a relationship with."

Lucy was quick to defend herself. "That's not true. I took a course from him, years ago, and I spent some time with him on the trip to England, but I wouldn't say we had a relationship. We were friendly, and that's really an exaggeration."

Horowitz's voice was conciliatory. "Look, I'm not making judgments or anything. I'm just asking for some help—and it would make a good story for your paper."

The man was a devil. Lucy knew when she was beat. If she said no, he'd just call Ted. "What do you want me to do?"

"Wear a wire."

The female trooper who helped Lucy with the wire apparatus was enthusiastic. "These things have really been improved," she said, displaying a compact plastic case. "They used to be so bulky, but you can just tuck this baby into your bra. He won't suspect a thing. It's even got GPS, but I don't think we'll need that today." They were in the ladies' room outside the coffeehouse Winchester College had recently added to the student union building. "Professor Rea teaches an eight a.m. class on Mondays, Wednesdays, and Fridays, and he always comes here afterward for coffee. You can pretend you're here on a story and strike up a conversation."

"And somehow, in the course of chatting about whether he likes mocha or hazelnut better, I'm supposed to get him to confess he's a murderer? How am I supposed to do that?"

She shrugged. "You'll think of something. Horowitz says if anybody can, it's you. He says you're really . . ." She stopped suddenly, her neck reddening.

"Go on. I can take it. What did he say?"

She smiled in apology. "He said you can be a real pain in the butt, that he'd confess just to get rid of you." She suddenly turned her attention to the earpiece she was wearing. "He's here. It's showtime. And remember," she added, giving Lucy a shove toward the door, "you've got plenty of backup. You're perfectly safe."

Lucy's heart was racing when she stepped out of the ladies' room and crossed the cozy space with orange walls and a distressed wood floor, past the scattered tables and comfy armchairs, to get in line at the counter behind Quentin. She didn't say anything and pretended to be going over some notes in her notebook while he ordered. When he turned, coffee in hand, she looked up.

"Hi!" she exclaimed with a big smile.

"Well, hi yourself. What brings you here?"

"Work." She turned to the kid at the counter, who was probably a student. "I'll have a small cappuccino."

"That'll be three-fifty," said the kid.

Lucy reached for her wallet but Quentin was quicker. "Let me treat."

Lucy gave him her best, what she hoped was an absolutely ravishing, smile. "Thanks."

There was a bit of an awkward pause while they waited for the kid to make the cappuccino. The machine was hissing and sputtering; the air was filled with the delicious scent of coffee. "If only it tasted as good as it smells," mused Lucy. She made her eyes big. "By the way, congratulations. I hear you're a professor now."

"Yeah," he said with a crooked smile as the kid passed over a cup topped with milky white froth. Lucy took it and followed him to a corner table flanked with French-style leather armchairs. They sat and Lucy's eyes met his as she took a sip of her cappuccino, making sure plenty of froth stuck to her lip. As she expected, he leaned forward and wiped it away with a finger, which he licked, his eyes never leaving hers. She smiled, a Mona Lisa smile this time. Things were going well—but she felt like throwing up.

"So what's the big story?" he asked.

"Oh, the body," she said as coolly as she could.

Quentin seemed to flinch but quickly recovered. He leaned forward, stroking her hand with his finger. "What body? I haven't heard anything—"

"It's an old story. They found the body of this girl in the river. It was in the news about two weeks ago. *Mystery girl?* You didn't see it?"

Quentin was all innocence. "No."

"Dumped in the river in a plastic bag, no identification. Lady walking her dog discovered it."

"I'm glad I don't have a dog," said Quentin, attempting a joke.

"Yeah." Lucy laughed. "It's dangerous—they're always finding the most unspeakable stuff. My dog came home with half a dead rabbit the other day. So gross."

"So, why did you come here?" Quentin couldn't resist asking. "Do they think this girl was a student here?"

Lucy took another sip of cappuccino and licked her lip, slowly. "You know Ted. He's always looking for an angle. He sent me over to ask if any students were missing."

Quentin leaned back, a study in casual ease. "And was anybody missing?"

"Actually, yes. Somebody was. Or is."

"Really?"

Lucy knew she had to drag this out; she had to play with him and make him tense if she was ever going to get anything out of him. "You know her, and so do I."

Quentin narrowed his eyes. "I think you're playing with me."

"Me? Don't be silly." She licked her lips again and raised her eyes flirtatiously. "Autumn Mackie. Remember? From the London trip?"

"Sure." He crossed his legs. "To tell the truth, that doesn't surprise me. She wasn't college material. She probably realized it and dropped out."

"The registrar said she didn't file a withdrawal or anything."

"Her type never do. They just go on their merry way." He paused. "She probably got mixed up with the wrong sort of guy."

"I'm a little surprised at your attitude. I thought you two had something going on during the trip."

"She may have had a bit of a crush on me," said Quentin in a disapproving tone. "These girls today. They're very forward. I'm afraid I had to discourage her."

"You know, the more I think about it, the more it seems that the girl in the river fits Autumn's description." Lucy looked down at the table. "I hope it isn't her. I hope you're right, that she went on her merry way somewhere."

"I'm sure that's the case." Quentin's eyes were drifting toward the door, and Lucy sensed he was thinking of leaving. She had to do something, fast.

"The girl in the river was pregnant," she said.

Quentin clucked his tongue. "Oh, my."

"Perhaps you could offer to take a look at the body? You would know if it's Autumn."

"Why me? Why not you?"

Lucy fixed her eyes on his. "Because the dead girl has a tattoo of a *Q*, not an *L*."

Quentin shrugged. "Okay, I admit it. I knew about the girl. The cops even interviewed me. I guess they did a computer search for everybody in the area whose name begins with *Q*—which is admittedly a rather small number. But I couldn't help them. I didn't recognize the girl—and I don't know how she got in the river."

Lucy pushed the cup and saucer away. "It is Autumn—they identified her from her dental records."

She was watching Quentin closely, looking for some reaction. "That is terrible," he said. "How awful for her family."

"She didn't have any family, thanks to George Temple, and you know it."

He glanced at his watch. "You know, I think I ought to be going. It was great seeing you, Lucy."

Lucy felt crushed, watching him leave. She was a complete failure. She hadn't got anything out of him. She sat there at the table, replaying the whole conversation in her mind and wondering what she could have said that would have made a difference, when Horowitz materialized and took the other chair.

"I'm sorry," she said.

"It was a long shot." Horowitz sighed. "He's smart—too smart for us. Don't feel bad. You did your best."

"Yeah." Lucy pushed her chair back. "Well, I've got a deadline." She was on her feet and out the door, eager to forget the whole thing. It left a bad taste in her mouth. She didn't like it that a young girl was dead. She thought Quentin was appalling, disgusting, lower than low. She wanted him to pay for what he'd done, but she didn't like being a snitch either.

She blinked, stepping out into the bright September sun, and made her way toward the parking lot. It was hot, a real scorcher. The asphalt had been soaking up heat for weeks, and the air above it was wavery, making her feel disoriented. She'd parked in the shade, thank heavens. The car was tucked beneath a large old maple that was just beginning to turn color, anticipating fall. The leaves were part green, part yellow, she noticed, clicking the button on the key that unlocked the door. She stepped into the shade, feeling the cooler temperature as she reached for the car door, and that's when something tightened around her neck, yanking her backward.

She didn't even get a chance to yell for help, managing only a startled cry, before she was overpowered. She had no air. She struggled, kicked, and tried to grab her assailant's hair, his ear, gouge his eyes with her keys, but she was at a disadvantage. He was behind her and she knew her blows were weak. She was beginning to lose consciousness; black was blocking out the dazzling sunshine, and in one last, desperate effort, she grabbed below his belt, squeezing as hard as she could.

Then, suddenly, the pressure on her neck eased and she was thrown forward, onto her hands and knees.

"Stop! Police!" The voice was female, clear and sharp. "Raise your hands!"

Lucy pushed herself up and saw Detective Horowitz and a couple of uniformed cops thudding across the parking lot, guns drawn. The female state trooper was also holding a gun, legs spread apart, and she had Quentin firmly in her sights.

He was doubled over, clutching himself.

"You have the right to remain silent . . ." she began reciting the Miranda warning as Horowitz applied the cuffs.

"Are you all right?" One of the troopers was helping Lucy to her feet.

"I'm okay," said Lucy, her hand at her neck. "How did you . . . ?"

"The wire. You were still wearing the wire."

Lucy's head was clearing. "GPS," she said, glaring at Horowitz. "GPS! You used me! You knew he'd try to kill me! That was the plan all along."

"Don't be ridiculous. That would be strictly against agency policy," said Horowitz, sounding rather insincere. "Besides, you were never in any danger. We had you covered the entire time." He glanced at the professor. "Anyway, he's in a lot worse shape than you."

"Somehow that's not making me feel all warm and fuzzy," said Lucy.

"Think positively," said Horowitz as a cruiser pulled up. The handcuffed professor was pushed inside, still crouching in pain. "You've got a hell of a story. Ted's gonna love it."

Lucy saw red. "Ted was in on this?"

Horowitz consulted his watch. "You've got just over an hour before deadline."

He was right, realized Lucy, hurrying to get behind the wheel. She was stiff and sore, her throat was ragged, and her hands were trembling as she started the car. But she had one hell of a story. Maybe Ted would even hold the paper for an hour. She found her phone and called him, popping two aspirin as she navigated the parking lot. "Hey, Ted," she began, when he interrupted.

"Lucy! Are you all right? I've been so worried. . . ."

"Yeah, yeah, yeah. Now listen. Start typing. 'This morning, state police arrested . . .' "

Epilogue

It was about a month later when Lucy received a call from DA Phil Aucoin.

"I need to clear up a few things," he said. "Can you come in today around three?"

Lucy understood that while the time of the conversation might be negotiable, there was no way she was going to get out of the meeting. She knew she would have to testify about the attack, and Aucoin would want to make sure he knew what she was going to say; he wouldn't want any surprises in the courtroom. She wasn't eager to relive the fear she'd felt when that necktie had tightened around her throat but figured she might as well get it over with as soon as possible. "Sure," she said.

Aucoin's office was in the county complex in Gilead, a small boxy brick building dwarfed by the massive jail, with its razor-wire fence, and the stately nineteenth-century courthouse built of gleaming white granite. He didn't look up from his cluttered desk when she entered, so she took the one available chair and looked around. Every surface in the small room, including the floor, was covered with stacks of paper. The one window had a fine view of the Civil War memorial that stood on the green lawn in front of the courthouse, but she couldn't see it because of the pile of thick manila folders that threatened to slip off the sill any minute.

"Just a mo'," he muttered, reaching for the phone. He listened a few minutes, then spoke. "Best I can do is six months served and two years probation," he said.

Lucy could hear the outraged protest coming from the other end of the line.

Aucoin shook his head and rolled his eyes. "Your client assaulted an eighty-two-year-old woman who was on her way to a nursing home to visit her one-hundred-and-one-year-old mother, just like she does every Sunday after church. You wanna go to court with that and take your chances with a jury?"

The sound effects continued, and Aucoin rolled his eyes again. "I'm well aware that your client ended up with a concussion, but believe me, juries love that stuff. Little old ladies who fight back—trust me, we've got an aging population. Most of the jurors are going to be on the far side of forty, and they don't like young punks."

The outraged squawks ceased, Aucoin nodded a few times, said, "Okay," and ended the call. He looked at Lucy. "One down," he said, making a notation on the folder, closing the file and reaching for another, much thicker one. "Quentin Rea wants a deal," he said, locking eyes with her. "He's alleging that the members of a Winchester College tour to England last spring conspired to kill the tour leader, a professor named George Temple. He says you can corroborate the whole story."

Lucy's first reaction was outrage. What a worm! But the more she thought about it, the more typical it seemed. If Quentin Rea was going down, he wasn't going down alone. Biting her lip, attempting to control her emotions, she studied Aucoin's face: the deep grooves that ran from his nose to his mouth, the bags under his eyes, the wiry hair that refused to be tamed and shot up from his forehead in an unruly, oversized pompadour. He was a man who knew only too well that people were capable of doing terrible things to each other; nothing surprised him anymore.

"What exactly is he saying?" asked Lucy.

Aucoin began reading from five or six pages that were clipped together. "He says he was approached in his office last December by a student named Caroline Smith who was in a special support group for freshmen who were having trouble adjusting to college life. She'd figured out that three other students, and herself, had all come from families that had been defrauded by George Temple in the 1990s. These students were the late Autumn Mackie, who Rea is presently under indictment for killing; William Barfield; and Jennifer Fain. Apparently they'd all recounted their tales of woe during the group discussions, and Caroline recognized certain elements that led her to conclude they'd all been wronged by this George Temple, who was now an instructor at the college. She was able to confirm this in subsequent private discussions."

Lucy listened, thinking this might well be true. Caroline's parents, Tom and Ann Smith, had probably talked about Temple a lot through the years, making it quite clear to their surviving child that he was the source of all their troubles. Tom, she knew, had nursed his anger toward Temple. Of the four, Caroline probably was the one who was most aware of Temple's crime. And if she had initiated the plot, she might well have felt guilty enough to try to kill herself by jumping off the Brighton Pier.

Aucoin continued. "George Temple was convicted of fraud, served time, got hired by Winchester thanks to some social connections. Stayed clean."

Lucy nodded. "I understand he was quite a success at the college. Popular with students and faculty. He was even being considered for a tenure position."

Aucoin made a note. "Not according to our boy, Quentin. He says Temple was unqualified, called him an 'academic bottom-feeder.' But even so, he says he was shocked when this Caroline said she and the others wanted his help in getting back at Temple. He says he absolutely refused to get involved in any way."

"That would be the proper thing to do," said Lucy, who was willing to bet that Rea had chosen to do the exact opposite. He would never pass up an opportunity to get rid of his rival, especially when someone else was willing to do the dirty work.

"However, Rea says he was troubled that the four might go ahead without him and kept an eye on the situation," continued Aucoin.

That was clever of him, thought Lucy. It gave him a reason for knowing about the plot without admitting any responsibility for Temple's murder.

"He claims the four kids and their families got together at a tailgate party at the Polar Bowl on New Year's Day and worked out a plan to kill Temple."

"Over the bratwurst?" asked Lucy.

Aucoin smiled, enjoying her little joke. "He didn't say. I guess he wasn't keeping that close an eye on things. He claims he just happened to see them in the parking lot."

Right, thought Lucy. Like Rea hadn't organized the meeting himself, probably cooked the bratwurst and mulled the cider and sent out the invitations. "Temple died on the plane," she said. "I was sitting across the aisle from him. It was an allergy attack."

"That's what Rea says. The kids knew he had severe allergies, and one of the parents, a Dr. Cope, figured out how they could set off an attack."

"Grandparent," corrected Lucy. "Dr. Cope is Jennifer's grandfather."

Aucoin made another notation, then resumed his narrative. "To make a long story short, they all signed up for Temple's trip to England, took turns waving around mildewed scarves and peanut trail mix, and when he started wheezing, this doctor rushed forward with a fake EpiPen and finished him off."

"That would be a violation of his Hippocratic oath," said Lucy. "I happen to know that Dr. Cope took that very seriously. We talked about it in St. Paul's. He told me he wished he could have saved Temple." She pressed her lips together, remembering the rest of the story, how Dr. Cope had later told her his son-in-law had committed suicide when he learned Temple had impoverished him and that his grief-stricken daughter had turned to drugs for consolation, leaving him to raise Jennifer. She thought of the Smith family, who trusted Temple to invest all their money and when he'd ruined them, lost their precious baby boy in a car accident. An accident they believed could have been avoided if they'd been able to afford new brakes. She remembered sitting in Bath Abbey and listening to Laura Barfield tell how her mother had suffered in that dreadful nursing home, because it was the best she could afford after Temple had lost all her money. She thought of Laura's all-enveloping guilt that she wore like one of those suffocating black chadors Muslim women wrapped themselves in. And then there was Autumn, who'd survived the loss of her home and her parents and years in foster care only to be murdered by Quentin Rea when she posed a threat to his professorship. She came to a decision. She was certainly not going to cause these people any more grief. But she didn't want to lie to Aucoin either. She was going to have to be very careful about what she said.

"It seems to me," she said slowly, "that if anybody wanted Temple dead, it was Quentin Rea. He had the most to gain. Temple was going to get the professorship that Quentin wanted, that he'd worked for his entire life."

Aucoin narrowed his eyes. "Do you think Rea was behind this plot to kill Temple?"

Lucy shrugged, hopefully indicating she didn't have the faintest idea. "I know a little bit about asthma allergies—my oldest daughter is allergic. The hardest thing about being allergic is the unpredictability. Elizabeth knows what her triggers are, but sometimes she forgets and uses a feather pillow, something like that. She might have an attack, but she might not. It all depends on whether she's been taking her medicine, how old the feather pillow is, a whole bunch of factors."

"So you're saying it would be pretty hard to kill someone by triggering an allergic attack?"

"I think it would be close to impossible," said Lucy. She decided to mention something she'd been suspecting, even though it was little more than a wild guess. "You know Rea is an English professor, right? I wouldn't be at all surprised if he has an unpublished manuscript or two in a drawer."

Aucoin's eyes widened. "Actually, we found two. *Death in Florence: An Elizabeth Barrett Browning Mystery* and *Murder on Flight 214: An Homage to Agatha Christie.* Also about twenty rejection slips."

Lucy resisted the impulse to let out a long sigh of relief. "Well, there you have it," she said. "He couldn't sell his little story to a publisher but figured he'd see if you'd buy it and cut him a deal for a reduced sentence."

"I think you're right," said Aucoin, leaning back in his chair. "I'm glad we had this little talk. Some of what he said had the ring of truth. . . ."

"The best lies always do," said Lucy.

Aucoin nodded. "But even if he was telling the truth, I'd never get a jury to believe it."

"The media would love it," said Lucy, putting the final nail in Rea's coffin. "I can see the headlines now: 'The Big Sneeze: Allergy Trial Goes to Jury.' "

Aucoin looked like a man who'd driven to the edge of a cliff and braked just in time, saving himself from a fall down a deadly precipice. He snapped the file shut and pounded it with a rubber stamp. "No deals. We go to trial on what we've got. The murder of Autumn Mackie and the attempted murder of Lucy Stone. I expect we'll put him away for life."

Lucy stood up and smiled. "See you in court."

BRITISH MANOR MURDER

For Stella Rose

Chapter One

"If only they'd send a ransom note," wailed Lucy Stone, pulling her old gray cardigan tighter across her chest. "Then at least we'd have a chance of getting Patrick back."

Looking out the kitchen window this early March morning she saw the same wintry scene she'd been staring at since Christmas: an endless expanse of snow several feet deep, punctuated here and there with bare black branches. There was a complete absence of color, just like her life since her five-year-old grandson Patrick had been snatched away from her.

"He wasn't kidnapped, Lucy," reminded her husband Bill. "He's with his parents."

"In Alaska," replied Lucy, making it sound as if Alaska was located on the moon.

Actually, she thought to herself, the moon might be closer to the little Maine town of Tinker's Cove than Alaska, which seemed impossibly far away.

"Toby's building his career," said Bill, referring to his son, Patrick's father. "He has to go where there's work and this was too good to pass up—a full-time government job in fisheries management . . . with excellent benefits."

Lucy gazed at Bill, her husband of more than twenty years. He looked the same as always, tall and fit, dressed in the working man's winter uniform of plaid flannel shirt, lined jeans, and sturdy work boots, but now his beard was frosted with gray. As usual, he was being entirely reasonable.

"I know," she admitted, "but I don't see why they had to take Patrick. They left him with us when they went to Haiti," she said, getting to the crux of the problem. Patrick had lived with his grandparents for nearly four months before Christmas, while his parents, Toby and Molly, had gone to Haiti where Toby completed a graduate-level study of fish farming practices. Lucy had adored spending time with her only grandchild, reliving the days when she was a young mother herself.

"Alaska is not Haiti," said Bill.

"It's practically the frontier," grumbled Lucy. "And all this moving around is very disruptive for a child. Kids need stability. They need to be in one place."

"He's in the right place. With his parents."

Lucy did not like hearing this, even if it was the truth, and was quick to retaliate. "They're not Patriots fans in Alaska," she said, naming New England's beloved football team. "Patrick's probably a Seahawks fan by now."

Bill looked stunned, hearing this heresy spoken. "Toby would never let that happen."

Lucy raised her eyebrows. "It's hard to resist group pressure. He's probably already got a Seahawks hat or jersey." She paused, then went for the jugular. Invoking the name of the Patriots' quarterback, she said, "He probably doesn't even remember Tom Brady."

This didn't get the reaction from Bill that Lucy expected. Instead of fussing and fuming, he sat down opposite her at the round golden oak table. "I know you're joking, Lucy, but the truth is you really haven't been yourself since Patrick left." He reached across the table and took her hands in his. "This can't go on, Lucy. You've got to pull yourself together. You've got to think of Sara and Zoe," he said, naming their two daughters who were still at home. Their oldest daughter, Elizabeth, like her brother Toby, had already flown the nest; she was living in Paris and working at the tony Cavendish Hotel there.

Lucy thought guiltily of Zoe, who was in her senior year of high school, and was waiting anxiously for the college acceptance—or rejection—letters that should arrive any day now. Zoe prided herself on being independent and had written the essays all by herself, refusing help from her parents, but Lucy wondered uneasily if she should have insisted on getting more involved. The truth was that she took Zoe at her word that it was all under control, simply because she hadn't felt like arguing after working all day as a reporter for the local weekly newspaper, the *Pennysaver*.

As for Sara, who was a student at nearby Winchester College, well, Lucy had to admit she didn't even know what courses Sara was taking this term or if she was still dating Hank, someone she had met at the college dive club. She was rarely home these days. Lucy assumed she was deeply involved in college life, but she hadn't taken the trouble to find that out, either.

Lucy was uneasily aware that she hadn't been much of a mother lately or even much of a wife, and the worst of it was that she didn't care. She was operating on automatic. She dragged herself out of bed in the morning when the alarm rang, drank her coffee, and ate her oatmeal. Then she drove to work, where she dutifully put in her time but found the work she used to enjoy so much as a part-time reporter and feature writer had become merely tedious. The worst part of the day came later, after she went home and cooked supper, cleaned up the kitchen, and sat herself down in front of the TV. The shows came and went, but she couldn't say what she was watching. She was only waiting until it was time to go to bed, and bedtime seemed to come a bit earlier every night.

"I'm sorry," she said, brushing away a tear. "I'm just so sad. I miss Patrick."

"Don't cry," said Bill. "There's been enough crying. Too much crying."

"I'm sorry," sobbed Lucy as he slid the tissue box across the table to her. She pulled out a handful and wiped her face, giving him a weak smile. "I'm going to try harder. I really am."

"Good," said Bill, exhaling a big sigh and standing up. "Don't forget. It's coffee-klatch Thursday."

Lucy propped her chin on her hand. "I don't know . . ." she began, thinking that she'd have to comb her hair and get dressed and put on some lipstick. Then there were the boots and jacket and scarf and hat and gloves she'd have to wear. And she'd have to brush the two or three inches of new snow that had fallen during the night off the car. It all seemed so hard. She had the morning off because Thursday was the day the *Pennysaver* came out. Since she wasn't needed at the office she could go back to bed, which was what she was planning to do as soon as Bill left for work.

"C'mon, Lucy. You promised to try harder," he said, reading her mind. "I'm not leaving until I see you washed and dressed and in the car. You better hurry or you'll be late," he added, glancing at the clock. "I'll clear the snow off your car while you get ready. Is that a deal?"

Lucy glowered at him, then pressed her hands on the table and stood up. "Deal," she muttered, narrowing her eyes.

Lucy was late but only by a few minutes when she got to Jake's Donut Shack and found her three friends already seated at their usual table. They had first met as young mothers, bumping into each other frequently at school and sports events, but as their kids grew older and those encounters became fewer, they agreed to meet every Thursday for breakfast. They'd kept up the tradition for years, celebrating the good times and supporting each other through the bad.

"Hi, Lucy," said Pam Stillings, welcoming her. Pam had not only retained the ponytail and colorful poncho she'd worn as a teen, but she'd also retained the enthusiasm and positive outlook she'd exhibited as a college cheerleader. It was her unshakable optimism that helped explain her success as the wife of a small town newspaper editor in a time of rising expenses, dwindling subscribers, and increased competition for advertisers. Her husband, Ted, was Lucy's boss.

"How are you doing?" asked Rachel Goodman as Lucy sat down but neglected to remove her parka. Rachel's dark eyes were full of concern as she put one hand on Lucy's shoulder and with the other gave Lucy's zipper a tug; she was a psych major in college and never got over it. Her husband Bob had a busy law practice in town.

Taking the hint, Lucy unzipped her parka and removed her hat and gloves, dropping them on the table.

"They're still having winter clearance sales at the outlet mall," said Sue Finch, eyeing Lucy's tired winter gear. "I saw some cute hats and scarves at fifty percent off in that ski shop." Sue was the group's fashionista, always smartly turned out despite her occasional stints as a substitute teacher at Little Prodigies, the child-care center she owned in partnership with Chris Cashman. Sue's husband, Sid, owned a custom closet company, which he claimed he'd had to do just to keep up with Sue's ever-expanding wardrobe.

"I'm doing okay," said Lucy. "We Skyped last night and Patrick was so cute. He said—" She stopped abruptly, choking up.

"What did he say?" asked Rachel as the three friends exchanged concerned glances.

Lucy sniffed. Taking the tissue Sue offered, she wiped her eyes. "He said he missed reading stories with me."

"Skype is so amazing," said Pam. "You could read stories to him on it."

"It's not the same without the physical contact," said Lucy. "I really miss snuggling with him. Who knows? Next time I see him he may be too big for cuddles. They grow up so fast."

"Let's order," said Sue, waving over Norine, the waitress. "I'm beginning to get the shakes."

"What do you mean? The shakes? You never eat anything," said Pam.

"I need more coffee," said Sue, indicating her empty mug.

"The usual for everybody?" inquired Norine, filling their mugs. "Black coffee for Sue, granola and yogurt for Pam, a sunshine muffin for Rachel, and hash and eggs for Lucy."

"Just coffee for me," said Lucy, reversing years of Thursday breakfast choices with a sigh. "I can't face a big plate of eggs this morning."

Norine cocked her head. "You sure?"

"Maybe some toast," said Lucy.

"Okay," said Norine, sounding rather doubtful.

When she'd gone, Rachel glanced at the others and, getting encouraging nods, plunged right in. "Lucy, we know how much you miss Patrick, but we really think you need to get some . . . um . . . help."

Somewhat stunned, Lucy realized this was something her friends had discussed and agreed upon.

"We think you're in danger of slipping into a serious depression," continued Rachel.

"Just because I don't want a greasy meal this morning doesn't mean I'm depressed," said Lucy, protesting. "Maybe I'm not hungry."

"You haven't been yourself lately," said Pam. "Even Ted has noticed."

"She's right," said Sue, chiming in. "When was the last time you washed and styled your hair? Or put on a lick of lipstick?"

"I guess I forgot this morning," said Lucy. "I was tired. Really tired."

"Tiredness is a symptom of depression," said Rachel.

"Or of being busy," countered Lucy.

"You don't need to get defensive," said Rachel. "We want to help you."

"You can beat this," said Pam. "For one thing, you could try my yoga class. We work to realign our chakras and restore the proper mind-body-spirit connection. A lot of people find it very helpful and I have some openings in my six a.m. Monday-Wednesday-Friday class."

"I don't think so," said Lucy. "I'm not very coordinated."

"You don't have to be athletic to enjoy yoga," insisted Pam. "It's not competitive. That is not the point at all. The poses are very adaptable. I have quite a few students with physical handicaps. That's the great thing about yoga—you do what you're comfortable with. You get to know your body."

"My body likes to lie down," said Lucy, getting a chuckle from the group.

"We do that!" exclaimed Pam. "At the end of the session, there's breathing. Everybody lies on their mats and some people even fall asleep."

"I don't think I need a class to fall asleep," said Lucy with a big yawn. "I can do that all on my own."

"Yoga is definitely one approach you can use to combat depression," said Rachel, "but based on what you're saying, especially about being tired all the time and wanting to sleep so much, I think you could really do with some therapy."

"Therapy?" exclaimed Lucy. "You think I'm crazy?"

"Crazy is such a loaded word," said Rachel. "Think of mental health as a sort of spectrum. One end is bright and sunny and happy and the other end is dark and disorganized and troubled, with lots of various shades in between. We all travel back and forth along this spectrum during our lifetimes, depending on many factors. The teens, for example, tend to be rather a difficult time for most, and oddly enough, recent research seems to show that old age is actually a pretty happy time for most."

"So give me a few more years," said Lucy, looking up as Norine arrived with their orders.

"Normally, I'd say there's nothing wrong with Lucy that some shopping wouldn't cure," said Sue, taking a sip of coffee, "but this time I think something rather more drastic is called for."

"Not a makeover," said Lucy, frowning at the plate of buttery toast triangles that Norine had plopped down in front of her.

"They won't bite," said Norine, adding a big sniff for emphasis.

"Not a makeover," said Sue, giving her a once over. "But come to think of it, that's not a bad idea. No, I have something else in mind. A change of scene. Big time."

"Not Florida," said Lucy, naming the usual winter break destination. She picked up one of the toast triangles and took a small bite.

"Why not?" asked Pam. "Florida is great. It's warm and sunny and there are all those theme parks and spring training baseball games."

"One word," said Lucy. "Alligators."

"Ah, interesting," said Rachel, sounding like a comical impersonation of a Freudian analyst. "Alligators can summon up primal fears from the subconscious, reminding us of the monsters we feared in childhood."

"Except the monsters weren't real and alligators are," said Lucy, opening the little plastic packet of marmalade and spreading it on her toast.

"Well there are no alligators where I'm going," said Sue. "I've been invited by Perry—"

"That guy you met in London at the V and A?" asked Pam, recalling an incident that took place a few years earlier when the four friends had taken a trip together to England. "The one with the hats?"

"Righto," said Sue. "As you may remember, the Victoria and Albert Museum had a special exhibit of hats that year and that's where I met Perry and discovered a shared enthusiasm. He is the Earl of Wickham and has invited Sid and me to come visit him at his ancestral home, Moreton Manor. He's putting on a big exhibition of his hat collection and asked me to donate a few pieces. I inherited a couple of Lily Dache originals from my grandma, you know. So to make a long story short, he's invited me to bring my hats and my husband. Sid doesn't want to go so I asked his lordship if I could bring a friend and he said, 'Why ever not? We've got a hundred and twenty rooms.' So there it is, Lucy. You know how much you loved England when we went there a couple years ago."

"It's the opportunity of a lifetime," said Pam with a sigh. "Imagine staying in a stately home and hanging out with nobility."

"A change of scene can have a positive impact on the psyche," said Rachel. "New places, new people, new ideas—they can be very stimulating. However," she added, in a warning tone, "the effect can be quite short-lived. For real change, I still think Lucy needs to talk to a qualified therapist."

"Stuff and nonsense," snapped Sue. "There's nothing the matter with Lucy that a cream tea and a breath of spring won't cure. You know spring comes earlier in England than it does here. Remember the daffodils?"

Lucy took the last bite of her marmalade-covered toast and thought of the hundreds, maybe thousands, of naturalized daffodils with their nodding blooms she'd seen overrunning acres and acres of woodland at Hampton Court. "I'll go," she said, surprising her friends and even herself as the words flew out of her mouth, apparently of their own accord.

But that wasn't really true; deep down, she knew she'd been looking for something that would help her break out of this depression. She was ashamed that she was unhappy, even miserable, and she didn't want to go on like this. It wasn't fair to the kids who'd grown up hearing her repeat her mother's favorite adage that "you can find sympathy in the dictionary" all too often. Whenever she'd suspected they were feeling sorry for themselves, she had advised them to count their blessings, and though she'd tried to follow her own advice, it hadn't worked. Even worse, she felt that it wasn't fair to Bill to have a mopey wife who neglected him. But most of all, it wasn't fair to herself. This was her one life. It wasn't a dress rehearsal, it was showtime and she needed to take center stage. Maybe a trip, a change of scene, was just what she needed to perk herself up. "When do we leave?" she asked.

Chapter Two

"The show opens May eighth, but Perry wants us to have a nice visit, so he suggests we come a week or two before," said Sue as Norine stopped by their table to present their checks.

"Bluebells might be in bloom then," said Lucy, who remembered seeing a photograph of an English bluebell walk in a travel magazine she'd read in the dentist's waiting room. The photo showed a woodland where the ground was covered in a gorgeous carpet of blue blooms.

"Jo Malone's Bluebell was Princess Diana's favorite scent." Sue was an avid magazine reader and knew about such things.

"Wouldn't it be wonderful to smell bluebells," said Lucy, checking the tab and putting down a five dollar bill.

"Maybe we will." Sue stood up and was buttoning the luxurious shearling coat Sid had given her for Christmas.

"I'm sure there'll be bluebells," said Pam, digging into her enormous African basket purse in search of her wallet. "Be sure to take a photo and send it to us."

"We'll want to hear all about it," said Rachel, wrapping her plum-colored pashmina scarf around her neck.

"Do you think you'll meet royalty?" asked Pam as they made their way through the café to the door. "Maybe Perry is friends with Prince Charles or somebody."

"Oh!" exclaimed Lucy. Assailed by second thoughts, she stopped at the door. "I wouldn't know what to do!"

"I think you curtsey," said Pam, opening the door.

"I know you're not supposed to touch royalty unless they touch you first," said Rachel as they gathered in a little circle on the sidewalk. "Some basketball player got in trouble for hugging Princess Kate, didn't he? In Brooklyn."

"What was Princess Kate doing in Brooklyn?" asked Pam.

"Hanging out with Beyoncé and JayZ," said Rachel. "I read it in the *New York Times.*"

"Face it. They're the closest thing we Americans have to royalty," said Sue, adding a wistful sigh. "We're hardly in that category so I doubt very much that we'll be meeting any royals, but what if we do?" She smoothed her brown leather gloves. "They're just people and I'm sure our natural good manners will see us through. After all, we're Americans. We're not subjects and we don't have to bow and scrape and tug our forelocks. That was the whole point of that little revolution we had in 1776."

"I don't know," said Lucy as dark clouds of doubt started to build in her mind. "What if they dress for dinner like at *Downton Abbey*, and there's all those forks and knives and snooty footmen who sneer when you pick up the wrong utensil?" She shivered and stuffed her gloved hands into her pockets.

"*Downton Abbey* is a TV show and it all takes place a long time ago. They're in the roaring twenties now, which is almost a hundred years ago. The women are all wearing those awful chemises and ugly cloches, which I don't think flatter anybody," declared Sue, flipping up her fuzzy collar. "I think we can assume that a lot has changed since then."

"I wouldn't be so sure, if I were you," cautioned Rachel, fingering her car keys. "If Perry has this big ancestral house, you have to assume he's rather well-off. I don't think they're going to be living like we do. You know, clipping detergent coupons and taking out the garbage."

Lucy knew she hadn't even had the energy to clip a coupon or take out the garbage lately.

"It's probably more like *Lifestyles of the Rich and Famous* than

Downton Abbey," said Pam, adjusting her hand-knit mittens and hoisting her bag over her shoulder. "I've got to run. I've got to teach a yoga class." Turning and hurrying off down the street, she passed the neat row of storefronts. "See you next week!" she called over her shoulder.

Rich and famous certainly didn't describe her lifestyle, thought Lucy, giving Pam a little wave and stamping her feet. She'd unthinkingly put on running shoes instead of winter boots, and her feet were beginning to freeze. "I don't know what to pack." She hated packing—all the worry about whether toothpaste could go in a carry-on bag or had to be carried separately in a clear baggie. She was sure she'd feel completely out of place in a stately home and thought it might be better to skip the trip altogether.

"I'm going to pack like I always do," said Sue, who prided herself on having the appropriate outfit for every occasion. "Mostly casual sportswear, comfortable shoes suitable for sightseeing, and one evening outfit. I have that long black skirt that I can dress up with a lacy top or a tuxedo shirt."

"I'll help you pack. I've got a TSA pamphlet at home," offered Rachel, sensing Lucy's hesitation and giving her a reassuring hug. "See you next Thursday, if not before." She tossed Sue a quick air kiss before crossing the sidewalk to her car and driving off.

"You've got those nice black pants. They will certainly do in candlelight," said Sue as they walked down the street. "Especially if you wear heels and something a little sparkly." They stopped by Sue's parked SUV, where she hesitated, then ventured a little joke. "And when I say sparkly, I don't mean your Christmas sweatshirt with the rhinestones and sequins."

At first, Lucy felt stung by the comment, but seeing Sue's suppressed smile she realized her friend was teasing her. "Darn! You must have read my mind," replied Lucy, revealing the first flash of humor her friend had seen in a long time.

"I think this trip is a good idea," said Sue, beaming at her and giving her a parting embrace before climbing into the enormous Navigator. Settling herself behind the steering wheel, she lowered the window. "And don't forget to bring your good jewelry," she advised, before shifting into DRIVE and zooming off.

* * *

Seven weeks later, Lucy found herself following Sue in a straggling procession of freshly disembarked British Air passengers who were making their way through a maze of stainless steel and glass corridors at Heathrow, hoping eventually to reach Immigration and be admitted to the United Kingdom. As Sue had advised, she'd carefully packed a small leatherette case containing her good jewelry—a modest diamond and platinum lavaliere she'd inherited from her grandmother and a pair of cultured pearl earrings that Bill had given her—in her purse. She had disregarded the rest of Sue's advice, however, and had neglected to pack anything dressy in the carry-on-sized roller suitcase she was towing behind herself. There hadn't been room after she'd thrown together a pile of comfortable jeans and favorite sweaters, plus a couple of guide books and a mystery novel or two.

Finally reaching the glass booths inhabited by immigration officers, Lucy patiently waited her turn, grateful for the rest from the rushed march through the terminal. She watched with amusement as Sue flirted with the rather good-looking young fellow who was smiling as he examined her passport. Sue could never resist a man in uniform.

Getting the nod from a rather less attractive officer whose neck rolls spilled over his tight collar, Lucy stepped forward and presented her passport along with the little slip of paper she'd been told to fill out on the airplane. It provided the details of her visit in England, including lodgings.

"Moreton Manor, eh?" he said, scowling at the paper. "Is that a hotel?"

"It's a house," said Lucy, smiling in what she hoped was a friendly manner.

"And what's your business there?" he demanded, fixing his rather small, pale blue eyes on her.

"I'm a houseguest," said Lucy.

"And who is your host?" he asked, turning to his computer screen.

"The Earl of Wickham," said Lucy, somehow feeling this wasn't going to work in her favor.

"And how exactly do you happen to know the earl?" The officer seemed to have developed a rather strong Cockney accent and was studying her bright pink all-weather jacket with some skepticism.

"My friend"—she nodded toward Sue, who was waiting for her beyond the barrier—"met the earl at a hat exhibit a few years ago. They both collect hats, you see, and there's going to be a show of the earl's hats at Moreton Manor. He invited Sue and her husband, but Sid didn't want to go, so I got invited." Lucy paused. "I've been a bit down in the dumps lately and everyone thought the trip would do me good."

The officer took a long look at her passport, then folded it closed and handed it to her. "I'm sure it will, luv, and be sure to give my regards to his lordship."

"Oh, I will," said Lucy, suspecting he was being rather sarcastic but not quite willing to risk joking with a person in authority.

"What was that all about?" asked Sue when Lucy finally joined her. "They couldn't have thought you were a terrorist or a smuggler, though that jacket does look like something a desperate refugee might wear."

"I like this jacket. It's bright and cheerful," said Lucy. "I saw someone wearing one just like it on the British version of *Antiques Roadshow*. I've been watching a lot of PBS, boning up for the trip." She nodded. "And I got it for practically nothing in a thrift shop."

"Why am I not surprised," said Sue with a resigned sigh. "We don't havc anything to declare so we can skip customs, but we have to get the bag of hats. It's on to the baggage claim."

After collecting Sue's big roller case that contained her hats, they proceeded to the ARRIVALS hall, toting all the bags on a wheeled trolley. There, they joined a small group of travelers studying a large yellow sign with arrows pointing to various transport options.

"We're supposed to catch a bus to Oxford," said Sue, checking her smartphone for the instructions Perry had sent.

"That way," Lucy said, pointing in the direction indicated by the sign.

"It's still quite early in the morning. Do you want to stop for a coffee or something? I couldn't drink that stuff on the plane."

"Sounds good." Lucy could never sleep on a plane and was feeling even more tired than usual. "I need something to perk me up."

The two perched on stools at a little snack bar and ordered extra-large coffees. After a few reviving sips, Sue again consulted her smartphone. "The busses to Oxford run quite frequently. We can catch one in an hour."

"You've got the schedule?" asked Lucy, somewhat amazed.

"Perry sent it. And once we're on board, I'm supposed to call and he's going to have someone meet us."

"In a limo?" asked Lucy. "A Bentley or a Rolls-Royce?"

Sue licked her lips and smiled. "I imagine so. Don't you?"

When the bus rolled into the Gloucester Green bus station in Oxford, a fortyish man in a dark green Barbour barn coat, green Wellies, and a tweed cap stepped forward and greeted them. "Mrs. Finch and Mrs. Stone?" he asked, tipping his hat.

"That's us," replied Sue with a big smile. "But I'm Sue and this is Lucy."

"Harold Quimby," he said, introducing himself. "Pleased to meet you ladies. Now if you'll just come this way . . ." He deftly relieved them of the giant bag and led the way past the busses' docking station to the parking lot where he stopped beside a huge and very muddy, very aged Land Rover. He opened the rear hatch and stowed their bags amid a collection of umbrellas, boots, blankets, flashlights, and assorted tools, including a small hatchet. "I hope you don't mind a few stops."

Lucy was doing her best to restrain a case of the giggles and not succeeding, despite a stern glance from Sue.

"Is it a long drive to the manor?" asked Sue.

"Not at all." Harold opened the rear door for them and removed a wire dog crate from the backseat. "I bet you were expecting a fancy car, weren't you?" he asked with an amused smile.

"We were," admitted Lucy.

"The Bentley's in the shop. Besides, I had to come this way anyway, so I said I'd meet you at the station."

"We're really very grateful," said Sue, climbing into the backseat and sliding over to make room for Lucy.

"We certainly are," agreed Lucy, joining her.

"I'll have you at the manor in two shakes of a lamb's tail," promised Harold, shutting the door. He went around to the rear of the car where he collapsed the crate and added it to the jumble in the rear, then slammed the hatch and hopped into the driver's seat on the wrong side of the car.

"It seems odd to have you sitting there on the right," said Lucy.

"I tried driving in the States once," said Harold, "and I kept slipping into the wrong lane. I even went around a roundabout the wrong way."

"Then I'm glad we're here, where you're used to the roads," said Sue.

"Aye, I could drive around here with my eyes closed," he said, turning to give them a wink. "But for your sake I won't."

Leaning back in the comfortable seat, Lucy gazed curiously out the window, watching as the densely packed, narrow streets of the old university town gave way to wider, more spacious modern roadways, dotted here and there with gas stations and shopping malls. Those eventually disappeared and they were in the countryside. Hedges lined the road, occasionally revealing thatched cottages and fields where sheep often grazed.

Reaching a small village where a pub and a few stores clustered together, Harold turned into a fenced yard filled with sheds, dog houses, mowers, and tractors. A sign on a large stone building announced in gold letters on a black ground that this establishment was GALBRAITH AND SONS, LTD. Beneath it, a smaller sign bore the words FARM STORE.

Harold hopped out and was greeted by a stout man wearing an apron, who clapped him on the back and led him inside. Lucy and Sue waited in the Land Rover. A couple of young assistants, also in aprons, barely acknowledged them as they began loading various and sundry products into the car. First, several bags of smelly fertilizer were tucked in next to Sue's suitcases. An enormous bag of chicken feed was arranged on top of Lucy's suitcase, and a huge bale of wood shavings wrapped in plastic was added to the pile. The final items were two boxes of adorable fuzzy yellow, chirping chicks, which Lucy and Sue were requested to hold in their laps.

"Everybody comfortable?" asked Harold, taking his seat behind the wheel.

"We're okay," said Lucy, uncomfortably aware of the bale of wood chips right behind her head.

"I meant the chicks," said Harold.

Sue lifted a flap, peered into the box, and studied the tiny balls of yellow fluff. "They seem to be all right," she said somewhat skeptically. "They've kind of hunkered down. I think they're sleeping."

"That's good," said Harold as the Land Rover lurched forward and crossed the yard to the gate. He suddenly slammed on the brakes when confronted with a delivery truck attempting to enter. The bale of wood chips slid forward, knocking Lucy in the head before bursting open and showering them all. The jolt wakened the chicks, who were all peeping frantically.

"The chicks!" exclaimed Harold, backing up to let the truck enter.

Lucy and Sue checked, discovering no harm had been done to the baby birds, who were flapping their tiny little winglets and settling themselves.

"They're fine," said Sue.

Lucy was tilting her head from side to side, stretching her neck to check for whiplash.

"No harm done, then," said Harold, shifting into drive and exiting through the gateway.

Lucy and Sue were still picking wood chips out of their hair when he turned through a pair of massive stone piers, each topped with a carved stone lion.

"Moreton Manor," announced Harold as they proceeded along a drive lined with leafy trees.

In the rather long grass beneath the trees, Lucy noticed dots of blue flowers. "Are those bluebells?"

"Indeed they are," said Harold. "Moreton is famous for its bluebells. People come from miles around."

"I can't wait to see them," said Lucy.

The Land Rover suddenly swerved round a bend, continued past a circular lawn with a fountain, and came to a halt in front of a massive stone building. "Welcome to Moreton," said Harold, hopping out.

Lucy gazed at the enormous stately home, which loomed high above them like a castle from a fairy tale. Dotted with ferocious gargoyles, the stone walls were punctuated with numerous arched and many-paned windows, including an ornate conservatory. In the morning sunlight, the stone walls took on a golden glow. The steep slate roof was topped with several pointed towers, each ending in a massive spike that threatened to pierce the clouds.

Lucy and Sue carefully set the boxes of chicks on the car seat, then stepped out of the car onto the graveled area in front of the stately home. They found themselves confronted with an impressive stone staircase that led to a rather forbidding set of double doors studded with black iron nail heads and strapped with elaborately curved hinges. Two crenellated towers stood on either side of the staircase.

While they stared in awe at the huge castle, Harold busied himself extracting their suitcases from beneath the heavy sacks of feed and fertilizer. Finally setting the baggage beside them, he said a quick farewell and drove off, leaving them wondering what to do. Should they climb the staircase to that forbidding door? Was there some other, more accessible entrance?

"I see only one doorway." Sue started up the steps, awkwardly pulling the oversized roller bag that contained her precious hats.

"There must be a doorbell or something up there," said Lucy. Pulling both of the smaller carry-on bags up the steps made her rather out of breath.

"I hope so," said Sue. "I wonder where Perry is."

"I'm down here!"

They turned and looked down to the bottom of the stairs where the earl was standing, hands on hips, looking up at them. He was dressed casually in a sweater and jeans, and his rather long hair was loosely combed behind his ears.

Taking in his slim build, rather like Mick Jagger's, Lucy thought of the adage that you couldn't be too rich or too thin.

"Come on down!" he yelled, grinning and sounding like a game-show host.

Getting down the stairs proved somewhat more difficult than going up, and Perry scampered up the stairs to help them with the suitcases. When they were all safe on the ground, he escorted them around the side of the staircase where a narrow opening led to a ground-level entrance beneath the stairs. "This is the easiest way in when you've got luggage," he explained.

When Lucy's eyes got used to the darkness, she noticed the entrance was dimly lit by an ancient filament lightbulb.

They followed Perry down a short ramp to a door, which he held open for them, allowing them to step inside. There, they found themselves in a narrow passage with a worn linoleum floor. The hallway was lined with doors and lit with a series of pendant fixtures that looked as if they were the latest technology in 1910.

"This is beneath the main house, which is open to the public," said Perry, doing a neat little dance in the tight space to get around them and their suitcases. "We live in an outbuilding we've had modernized. It's all connected by this underground tunnel. If I take this big boy, can you manage your cases and follow me?"

"No problem," said Lucy.

"I must apologize, but the staff these days are mostly involved with the visitors. My grandfather had a staff of eighty and never had to carry a suitcase or even get a cup of tea. We have over three hundred, but there's never anybody around when we need a hand."

"Lucy and I are used to fending for ourselves," said Sue as she trotted along behind Perry. "I do want to thank you for inviting us."

"Me, too," said Lucy. "This is a real treat."

"I do hope so," said Perry. "I'm so glad you could come."

"I wouldn't miss your hat show for the world," said Sue.

"I'm especially eager to see those Lily Dache hats you've brought—"

"Perry! Perry! The general's fallen!" called a woman, suddenly interrupting.

They all stopped in their tracks and turned around to face the woman who was running along the passage toward them, frantically hailing the earl.

"Is he hurt?" he asked as she drew closer.

"I'm afraid so," said the woman. "I think he may be beyond help."

Chapter Three

"Oh d-d-dear," stammered Perry, whose face had gone quite white. "Not the general. This is terrible, and what bad timing. . . ."

"I really need you to come," said the woman, who Lucy thought bore a strong resemblance to Perry. She was obviously upset and seemed to be physically struggling against the desire to grab Perry and drag him away.

"Of course, of course." Perry was once again doing his little dance around Lucy and Sue and the suitcases. "Duty calls," he told them, "but if you continue on just a little way, through that door, you'll find yourselves in the family kitchen. Sally should be there and she can show you to your rooms. I must apologize."

"No need," said Sue. "This is an emergency and you're needed elsewhere."

"I'll get back to you as soon as I can," he promised, before dashing away along the passage and following the woman.

"That sounded bad," said Lucy, fearing the worst as they resumed their trek. "I hope the general's all right."

"They did seem awfully upset," said Sue.

"I wonder if the general is a relative, perhaps an elderly uncle or something."

"Old people do tend to fall a lot."

"And they break their hips," added Lucy. "Wouldn't that be an awful beginning to our visit?"

"Definitely not optimal," agreed Sue as they reached the door at the end of the corridor. She reached for the knob, which turned easily, and opened it, blinking a bit at the bright sunshine that was a sudden contrast to the dimly lit hallway.

The two friends stepped inside and looked around, discovering a room that a shelter magazine would label a great room—a combination dream kitchen and cozy family room. The cabinets were obviously custom, the stainless-steel refrigerator had double doors and was at least six-feet wide, the countertops were marble, the floor was stone, and a huge cream-colored Aga stove stood in a repurposed fireplace. Noticing the large pine dresser crammed with blue and white china, Lucy practically swooned.

Beyond the kitchen area was a comfortable seating area where two large sofas and several easy chairs covered in flowery chintz were arranged so that sitters could choose to view the fireplace, the flat-screen TV, or the paved terrace outside the large French doors. A number of throws and assorted pillows were arranged on the furniture, promising complete ease and relaxation. Two large labs, one black and one yellow, were sprawled on the sofas, taking full advantage of the arrangement.

"Wow," said Sue. "I didn't expect this."

"We're not at Downton Abbey, that's for sure," said Lucy. "Mrs. Patmore would kill for this kitchen."

"There's no Mrs. Patmore, and not even poor overworked little Daisy," said Sue. "Or Sally, for that matter."

Waking from their naps, the dogs yawned then set their eyes on the two intruders. Eager to pet them, Lucy approached the nearest, the yellow dog, but stopped in her tracks when the dog fixed his eyes on her and began growling.

"Not friendly," she said, retreating a few steps. When the black Lab also curled up its lip and growled, she decided discretion was the better part of valor and scurried over to the kitchen area where she joined Sue behind the large island. "What should we do?"

"Those dogs are making me nervous," said Sue, who was not an animal lover.

"I don't like the look of them, either. We can't stay here." Lucy was beginning to think the trip was a mistake.

"Maybe we can help Perry with the general," said Sue.

"What can we do? How can we help?" asked Lucy.

"Well, I just took a CPR course," said Sue.

"Good to know," muttered Lucy as they left the kitchen and retraced their steps along the passageway.

"I bet this was the downstairs where the servants toiled away," said Lucy, thinking how horrible it would be to work all day in the poorly lit subterranean tunnel.

"Did you notice the bells in the kitchen?" asked Sue. "They were over the doorway. There were a bunch of them, all labeled. DRAWING ROOM, HIS LORDSHIP, HER LADYSHIP, NURSERY, and lots more." She stopped walking and squeezed Lucy's arm. "Can you believe it, Lucy? Here we are in an English country house, honored guests, for all the world like Lady Susan and Lady Lucy. It makes me wish for a big hat with plumes and a skirt with a bustle."

"I suspect that back then we'd be wearing black dresses and white aprons," said Lucy, glumly realistic. "And the plumes would be on our feather dusters instead of our hats."

"You're probably right," admitted Sue, resuming the hike along the passage. "But a girl can dream."

After passing through the door to the passage beneath the manor house, they continued on a short distance to a cellar where they encountered a utilitarian stone staircase with a plain black metal railing.

"Shall we?" asked Sue.

"Nothing ventured, nothing gained," grumbled Lucy, mounting the stairs.

Reaching the door at the top of the stairs, they paused to read the framed notice listing rules for servants, which were printed in black boldface on paper card that had yellowed with age.

KEEP OUTER DOOR LOCKED AT ALL TIMES.

ONLY THE BUTLER MAY ANSWER THE BELL. BE PUNCTUAL.

NO GAMBLING OR OATHS OR ABUSIVE LANGAGE ALLOWED.

NO SERVANT IS TO RECEIVE VISITORS IN THE HOUSE.

ANY MAID FOUND FRATERNISING WITH A MEMBER OF THE OPPOSITE SEX WILL BE DISMISSED IMMEDIATELY WITHOUT A HEARING.

THE HALL DOOR IS TO BE CLOSED AT HALF PAST TEN O'CLOCK EVERY NIGHT.

THE SERVANTS' HALL IS TO BE CLEARED AND CLOSED AT HALF PAST TEN O'CLOCK EVERY NIGHT.

ANY BREAKAGES OR DAMAGES TO THE HOUSE WILL BE DEDUCTED FROM WAGES.

"I imagine they've kept this as a sort of joke," said Sue.

"I hope so. Otherwise it would be very hard to retain staff these days," said Lucy, pushing open the door and revealing a space so large and grand that it caused them to gasp in awe. Craning their necks, they saw, high above them, a blue sky dotted with puffy clouds upon which perched numerous scantily clad pink-fleshed ladies and gentlemen of ample girth. Around them fluttered dozens of plump little cherubs, some playing musical instruments and others equipped with bows and arrows.

"I'd like to do something like this in my bathroom," quipped Sue, waving a hand toward the ceiling.

"I'm thinking of upgrading my back stairway," said Lucy, comparing the cramped little flight of wooden steps in her kitchen to the enormous marble staircase that dominated the magnificent hall. She continued to let her gaze wander around the huge room, which she decided must be the reception area approached by the massive flight of stone stairs they'd attempted to climb when they were dropped off outside the manor. This was the room that would greet visitors to the great house. Its grandiose size and luxurious furnishings were intended to impress. Huge bronze consoles with colorful marble tops stood on either side of the doorway and an assortment of polished white marble statues and busts were arranged along the paneled walls. Hanging behind the statues were many large, full-length portraits of gorgeously gowned women and bewigged men in satin knee breeches, often wearing crimson and ermine robes.

One of these portraits had fallen and was being examined by Perry and the woman who'd summoned him earlier. The painting was easily ten or more feet tall with a massive carved gilt frame, which was smashed to bits. The canvas was also torn, but the figure of a bewigged gentleman in a red coat astride a prancing white horse was undamaged.

"This is going to cost a mint," said the woman, shaking her head and sounding very glum.

"That's the least of it. We've got to get this all cleared up before the house opens at ten," said Perry, scratching his chin. He looked up and caught sight of Lucy and Sue. "Oh, do forgive me," he exclaimed. "I've neglected you. Let me introduce you to my sister, Lady Philippa Maddox. These are my friends from New England, Sue Finch and Lucy Stone."

"We've been expecting you," said Lady Philippa. She looked like a smaller, feminine version of Perry, with frizzy blond hair and bright blue eyes. She was dressed in beige slacks, a much-washed blue cashmere sweater, and a string of pearls. On her feet, she was sporting a pair of bright neon-green running shoes. "Do call me Poppy. Everyone does."

"So this is the general?" asked Lucy.

"Yes," said Poppy. "Rather like Humpty Dumpty. he took a great fall and it's going to take an awful lot of money to put him together again."

"We were worried he was a person, perhaps even a relative," said Sue. "I took a CPR course and we thought perhaps we could help."

"Only if CPR is short for art restorer," said Perry.

"I'm afraid not," admitted Sue. "Who is he? An ancestor?"

"No, he was a gift, presented to the eighth earl by the subject himself, General Horatio Hoare," said Poppy.

"A horrible fellow, by all accounts. He was killed in Canada in the Seven Years War and they sent his body home in a barrel of rum," said Perry. "People at the time said he came home in much better spirits than he left."

"But he was terribly fond of the eighth earl," said Poppy.

"Extremely fond, they say," said Perry, with a raised eyebrow. "He promised that so long as his painting was on the wall no harm would come to Moreton Manor."

"Or you could say he jinxed the place," said Poppy. "Take down my picture and I'll make you sorry. Now that it's fallen, I guess we can expect a run of bad luck."

"That's just a lot of nonsense. An old wives' tale," said Perry.

"Remember what happened the last time it came down?" said Poppy gloomily.

"Never mind about that," replied Perry. "It was a long time ago."

"Well, I'd better make arrangements to have the staff tidy up. We can't have the visitors stepping over bits of frame." Poppy bit her lip. "I wish I could be as confident as you are," she said to Perry. "I have a rather bad feeling about this."

"What happened the last time the general fell down?" asked Lucy as they all retraced their steps on the long passage to the kitchen. The servants must have done this dozens of times every day, she thought, noticing the worn linoleum.

"The ninth earl's countess was found dead at the bottom of that big staircase in the hall," said Perry.

"That would be a terrible fall," said Lucy.

"It was never determined if it was an accident or suicide or foul play," said Perry. "There were lots of rumors, of course."

"The earl married his mistress in what was considered at the time to be indecent haste," said Poppy. "The king banned the earl from court for several years."

"But there was no trial or investigation?" asked Lucy.

"Not back then," scoffed Perry. "He was an earl and only the king had any power to touch him."

"Even the king had to be careful of upsetting the nobles," said Poppy. "Think of Magna Carta."

"And Charles I," volunteered Lucy.

"Point taken, but I think it was actually Parliament that beheaded him, though to be fair, back in those days even the Commons was mostly titled gentlemen," said Perry. "His son Charles II stayed here for a night or two on his way to safe haven in the Scilly Islands, you know."

"It must be wonderful living in a house with so much history," said Sue.

"It's more like living in a museum now that the house is open to the public. We're the exhibits," said Perry. "Somewhat tarnished relics of England's glorious past, now on our last legs and forced to display our aristocratic heritage for ten pounds a head."

"Don't listen to him," advised Poppy. "The Heads Up! Hat Festival was his idea to attract more visitors to the house."

"Plagued by guilt, Poppy dear. You've been working so hard, managing this three-ring circus."

"It's a business, Perry. Just a business like any other."

"And you do have a terrific head for business," said Perry as they finally reached the door to the kitchen. He opened the door and held it for them, adding a little bow and a flourish.

They entered, discovering Sally was in place, hanging towels on a wooden drying rack in front of the Aga stove. The rack was suspended on a system of ropes and pulleys and could be lowered for easy access, then raised up to the high ceiling where it would be out of the way.

"What is that fabulous thing?" asked Lucy, who wanted one for her kitchen.

"A Sheila-Maid." Sally had curly red hair and lots of freckles. She was not wearing a servant's uniform but was sporting a tight pair of jeans and an equally tight striped pullover with a scoop neck that revealed a rose tattoo on her left breast.

"I wonder if I can get a Sheila-Maid in the States," said Lucy.

"You can get just about anything on the Internet, but I inherited my hats from Gramma. Do you want to see them?" Sue asked, indicating her enormous suitcase, which she'd left beside the door.

"Oh, yes!" enthused Perry, bounding across the room.

She unzipped the case entirely filled with two hatboxes, one large and one small. She opened the smaller one first and lifted out a cloche entirely covered with pink silk flowers, green velvet leaves, and the occasional crystal dewdrop.

"Heaven!" exclaimed Perry, taking it carefully in his hands and admiring it. "Roaring Twenties?"

"No. The swinging sixties. It's one of Lily Dache's last designs. I have photos of Gramma wearing it to church on Easter Sunday, along with a stunning Givenchy-style suit she sewed herself from a Vogue pattern."

"What else have you got?" asked Perry, returning the hat.

"I guess this would be a fascinator," said Sue. From the same hatbox, she produced a black velvet headband topped with a black rose and a froth of veil. "The sort of thing women wore to church when times were changing and hats were no longer fashionable, but they weren't quite ready to give them up entirely."

"Heresy!" exclaimed Perry. "Hats not fashionable!"

"Not in the US," said Lucy.

"We've clung to them," said Poppy. "I wouldn't dream of going to a wedding without a hat."

"And the royal family are doing their part to maintain the tradition," said Lucy.

"Bless the dears," said Perry, peering into the suitcase curiously. "What do you have in the other hatbox?"

Sue reached into the second, larger hatbox and produced a creamy straw number with a small, rounded crown and a huge brim, at least eight inches wide all around. A length of matching chiffon was wound around the crown and ended in long streamers that tied beneath the chin. "Voilà!" she exclaimed proudly.

"Is that?" asked Perry, eyebrows raised.

"The very same," said Sue, presenting it to Perry. "Katharine Hepburn wore it in *The Philadelphia Story.*"

Perry held the hat reverently. "How did you ever?"

"It came up on eBay and I couldn't resist."

"It must have cost you a fortune."

"I wanted to wow you," said Sue.

"Well, you certainly have," he said, returning the hat, which Sue carefully replaced in the box.

"Perry, I know how exciting this is for you, but don't you think you should let your guests settle in?" Poppy turned to Lucy and Sue. "You must be exhausted after the red-eye flight."

"I wouldn't mind freshening up," said Lucy.

"You've even got time for a little nap before lunch," said Poppy. "Sally will show you the way."

Sue left the hat box in Perry's care, then she and Lucy grabbed their bags and followed Sally out of the kitchen to another set of stairs, wooden and covered with a striped runner. They began climbing, continuing up one flight after another until they reached the former servants' quarters on the top floor.

"Don't worry," said Sally. "They've been fixed up. None of the old servants would recognize their rooms."

"At this point, I'd take a folding cot and an Army blanket," said Lucy, panting from the climb.

"That won't be necessary," said Sally, leading them down a spacious carpeted hallway to their rooms, which were joined by a shared bath.

Both guest rooms had sloping attic ceilings, and the walls were papered with Laura Ashley flowers. They each had a mirrored vanity table, a dresser, and a bench for their suitcases; the beds were covered with plump duvets that matched the wallpaper, as did the curtains on the casement windows.

"I'll leave you now," said Sally. "Don't be afraid to nap, if you want. I'll make sure you don't miss lunch."

"Thanks," said Lucy, closing the door behind her and joining Sue at the window, where she seemed transfixed.

"It's gorgeous," said Sue with a wave of her hand.

Looking into the distance, Lucy saw a seemingly endless expanse of rolling hills and fields that eventually met a series of distant bluish mountains. Somewhat closer to the house, a road wound its way through farmland, eventually turning through the gateway and the tree-lined drive. From this lofty vantage, they could see that a spur branched off from the main drive and led to an enormous parking lot already half-full of cars and busses. Hundreds of tiny little figures, mostly in pairs or small groups, were moving from the vehicles and making their way to a ticket booth. A long line of people were following a leader holding a closed umbrella aloft like a pennant.

"Moreton Manor is open for business," said Lucy. "Here come the hoi polloi, Lady Sue."

"Yes, Lady Lucy. It's the little people, here for a glimpse of the good life."

"From up here, they sure do look little," said Lucy, yawning. "I think I will retire to my chamber and rest my eyes."

"Just don't snore," said Sue, who was hoisting her suitcase onto the bench.

Once in her own room, Lucy discovered the view was quite different. Instead of the view across the park, all she saw out her window was a stone wall punctuated by windows. It was the manor, she realized. She was in a separate building connected to the main house by the underground corridor.

A charming framed watercolor on the wall beside the window gave the overview she needed, providing a bird's-eye view of the stately home separated from a smaller building on the right by a walled garden. Assuming the smaller building was the family's quarters, and comparing the view from the window to the painting, Lucy looked down and found the walled garden, a delightful square containing neat beds of plants centered by a sundial. What she couldn't see from the window but was pictured in the painting, was a row of outbuildings along the right side of the manor that created one side of a large walled area she surmised was originally a stable yard.

The whole arrangement was quite clever, she decided. The walled areas of garden and stable yard provided privacy for the family from the visiting public, which still had acres of manicured gardens and walking trails open to them.

Turning away from the window, she was drawn to the bed, with its puffy duvet and plump pillows. She slipped off her shoes and slid under the duvet. Feeling the hard case of her cell phone in her rear pocket, she decided she'd better call home before she fell asleep.

Bill answered on the first ring. "How was the flight? I saw it landed on time," he said, a slight note of reproach in his tone.

"I should have called sooner," she admitted. "It's been busy. Catching the bus, getting a ride to the manor—"

"Did they meet you in a Rolls?" he asked.

"Not quite," said Lucy, plucking a wood chip from her hair. "It was a Land Rover and there were baby chicks and fertilizer."

"Real country then. But I don't suppose the landed gentry actually get their hands dirty."

Lucy thought of Perry, with his enthusiastic love of hats, and doubted very much that he had anything to do with the farming aspect of the manor. "It's not like we expected. The manor is really a museum and the family live in a separate building. I guess it was once the kitchen and work area for the big house. The two are connected by a tunnel that's—"

"Like Monticello?" asked Bill, interrupting.

"Yeah, kind of," said Lucy, remembering a family vacation. "But this smaller house has been completely renovated. It's really like a McMansion. You wouldn't believe the kitchen. It's like something out of *House Beautiful*. The guest rooms used to be servant's quarters, but they've been fancied up."

"So you're feeling better and having a good time?" he asked, getting to the point.

The concern in his voice struck her and she felt tears filling her eyes. "So far, so good, but I am tired." She blinked furiously, quickly adding, "Jet lag. How's everybody?"

"Sara's studying for finals. Zoe's excited about the prom . . ."

That was too much for Lucy, who was suddenly guilt-stricken. "Be sure to take pictures for me," she begged, sniffling.

"I will," he promised.

"Any news from Alaska?" she asked, feeling as if she was picking at a scab she really ought to leave alone if she wanted the wound to heal.

"No, but no news is good news, right?" He paused. "A guy stopped by, said he saw my truck, and asked about Toby. He said they were friends in college but lost touch. He wanted to know what Toby was up to."

"Did you get his name?" asked Lucy.

"Doug something. Fitzpatrick, maybe?"

"I don't remember Toby mentioning him."

"You know how it is. They have their own lives."

"I know," said Lucy, remembering how shocked she'd been

when four-year-old Toby was greeted by a strange woman in the supermarket who turned out to be the mother of one of the kids in his preschool. All of a sudden she was thinking of Patrick and felt the familiar tug of sadness, which threatened to overwhelm her. No longer able to fight the tears, she said she was really tired.

Bill let her go. "Love you. Have a great time."

"I'm trying," she said, ending the call and reaching for the box of tissues on the nightstand.

Chapter Four

Putting the phone on the bedside table and pressing her face into the pillows, Lucy was afraid that she wouldn't be able to sleep. Oddly enough, even though she felt exhausted much of the time, when she got to bed, sleep would elude her and her mind would run in circles, imagining the dangers little Patrick faced in Alaska. She fretted about possible tragedies such as encounters with polar bears, falls into icy streams, and snowmobile accidents; knowing her fears were unfounded didn't matter and she would lie under the covers, wakeful and trembling with terror. That had been the usual scenario lately.

She was quite surprised when a knock on the door woke her up two hours later. "Mmmph?" was all she managed to say, feeling rather groggy.

It was enough for Sally, who poked her head around the door. "Perry sent me up to tell you and your friend that lunch is almost ready."

"Thank you," said Lucy, wishing she could sink back into the very comfortable pillows.

That wish must have become reality, because next thing she knew Sue was shaking her shoulder. "Rise and shine, sleeping beauty. Up and at 'em, onward and upward. You know the drill."

Lucy glared at her friend, who was impeccably turned out. Sue was always beautifully dressed. She was doing the country house look with a gray cashmere sweater, charcoal tweed slacks, the shiny new hunter green Wellies she'd worn on the plane, and a string of pearls. Her makeup had been freshly applied and her hair was shiny from brushing.

"How long have you been up?" inquired Lucy, suspecting she looked rather the worse for wear.

"About half an hour. Just since Sally called me." She gave Lucy a stern look. "You had better hurry or we'll miss lunch."

Lucy groaned and hauled herself out of bed with great effort. Once in the bathroom, a glance at the mirror over the sink proved her suspicion was correct—she looked awful. Her hair was sticking up every which way and a long, angry red pillow-crease crossed her face. She dampened a washcloth with cool water and used it to wipe her face, then quickly washed her hands and applied a quick slick of lipstick. Back in her room, she made a stab at taming her hair, which seemed hopeless until Sue grabbed her hairbrush and with a few deft swipes created order out of chaos.

"Thanks," said Lucy, studying her improved reflection with amazement.

"Is that what you're wearing?" asked Sue in a rather disapproving tone.

Lucy regarded her image in the mirror. She was wearing the same turtleneck sweater and jeans she'd worn on the plane, as well as her usual athletic shoes. "I just have more of the same in my suitcase." She got an eye roll from Sue.

"You can take the girl out of Maine, but you can't take the Maine out of the girl," complained Sue, opening the door.

Following an appetizing scent redolent of meat and herbs, they made their way together down the stairs to the family kitchen. There, they found Perry standing at the Aga stove stirring a bright red casserole with a wooden spoon. The two dogs were sitting on their haunches beside him, apparently hoping there might be a slip twixt the spoon and the lip as he raised the spoon for a taste.

"What is that? It smells delicious," exclaimed Sue.

"Venison stew. We try to live off the estate as much as we can," he said, putting the spoon down and adding a few grinds of pepper.

Discouraged, the dogs turned their attention to Lucy and Sue, approaching them with wagging tails.

"Ah, so now you like us," said Lucy, scratching the nearest Lab, which happened to be the black one, behind its ears. "I have a dog at home just like you."

"Did they bother you?" asked Poppy, entering through the doorway that led to the service corridor. She was carrying a couple needlepoint throw pillows and a somewhat dented silver ewer, all of which she dropped on a chair.

"They didn't seem to appreciate our presence earlier," said Sue, nervously eyeing the yellow Lab that was leaning its shoulder against her leg. "They were sleeping on the sofas and growled at us."

"They were just worried you'd make them give up their comfortable perches," said Poppy. "The trick with dogs is to be firm. Isn't that right, Monty?"

Hearing his name, the yellow Lab trotted over to Poppy and sat down in front of her, one paw raised.

"Good boy." She pointed to one of the two dog beds that were arranged in a corner. "Now go lie down. You, too, Churchy."

The dogs obeyed, but not without reproachful glances and sighs.

"They're such actors," said Perry. "They could go on stage."

Poppy set a big bowl on the center island and began pulling salad greens out of the fridge, which prompted Lucy to offer to help.

"Thanks," said Poppy, handing her a head of lettuce.

After giving her hands a quick wash, Lucy began tearing the lettuce into bite-size pieces and adding them to the bowl. The butter lettuce was lovely, crisp and silky to her touch, much nicer than anything she had grown in her Maine garden, and she said so.

"That's one of the advantages of having professional gardeners on staff," said Poppy.

"Perry was saying most of your food comes from the estate," said Sue.

"We have quite a farm, and there's game, too," said Poppy as a rather stocky man dressed in Wellies and an aged Barbour jacket came in through the French doors. "Ah, here's my husband, Gerald. He manages the estate farm. Gerald, meet Perry's friends, Lucy and Sue. They've come for the hat show."

"Very good," he said, nodding affably as he removed his jacket and hung it on one of the hooks on the wall next to the door. Several other pieces of clothing were already hanging there, and a neat row of boots stood at attention beneath them. He paused for a moment, rubbing his hands and studying Sue and Lucy, almost as if he were sizing up a pair of fillies offered for sale at an agricultural show. Then he cocked an eyebrow and turned to his wife. "Since we have company, shall we open a bottle of wine?"

Lucy was quick to speak up. "None for me."

Gerald turned to Sue and, detecting a hint of interest, gave a chuckle. "I bet Sue here wouldn't mind a drop. Am I right?"

"I wouldn't mind, but don't open a bottle on my account."

"I'll have a glass," said Perry.

"And Gerald will have several," said Poppy with a disapproving expression.

"Just being sociable, m'dear." Gerald disappeared through a doorway, returning a few moments later with two dusty bottles.

"Not the Margaux, I hope," said Perry, casting a suspicious glance at the bottles.

"Just a nice old claret," said Gerald.

"I see I'm just in time. Dad's got the plonk out," said a young man, who had also come in through the French doors. He was smiling.

Lucy noticed he had an air of confidence and physical ease that seemed quite remarkable. With his blond hair, high cheekbones, and cleft chin, he could have been a model, she thought, or an actor. He was dressed stylishly in a dark pea coat and had a Burberry plaid scarf wrapped around his neck.

"Desi!" exclaimed Poppy. "You made good time!"

"Just sailed along on the M40," he replied, giving his mother a peck on the cheek.

Poppy introduced Lucy and Sue, explaining that Desi was her son and he was visiting, taking a break before taking up a position as a soloist at the Royal Ballet.

"Congratulations," said Sue, accepting a glass of wine from Gerald. "That's quite an achievement."

"Just luck," he said modestly as his father handed him a glass of wine. "I brought Flo with me, but she wanted to see the new chicks before coming in."

"Having a smoke, you mean," said Poppy.

"I hope she's not smoking in the chicken house," said Gerald.

"She wouldn't do that," said Desi. "She knows better."

"Who knows what she knows these days," grumbled Gerald. "I don't understand what's going on with that girl."

"That means we're seven for lunch," said Perry, counting out a stack of plates and handing them to Sue. "Would you mind setting the table?"

"Not at all," replied Sue.

"No sense setting a place for Flora. She won't eat anything," said Gerald.

"Don't be ridiculous," snapped Poppy, who had opened a drawer and was counting out cutlery.

"You know I'm right," insisted Gerald, refilling his glass. "Fine family we've got. Desi prancing about like Tinker Bell and Flora looking like she's come straight out of a concentration camp."

"Shhh! She's coming," cautioned Poppy as a faint shadow appeared at the French door.

Desi hurried to open the door, admitting the thinnest woman Lucy had ever seen. With enormous eyes and cheekbones that matched her brother's, Flora would have been pretty, but her dark hair was limp and lifeless, her skin dull and ashy.

She entered the room tentatively, as if entering a cage of wild animals.

"I see you have company," she said, turning to go.

"Just some friends of Perry's," said Poppy, hurrying across the room to greet her daughter and giving her a big hug. "Come and meet Lucy and Sue."

Flora seemed to shrink, becoming even smaller under her mother's embrace.

Her mother quickly released her. "Give me your coat, dear," she said in a coaxing tone.

For a moment it seemed as if Flora would bolt and run out the door, then she seemed to settle and began unzipping her puffy black jacket. After the zipper was undone, she let her arms fall to her side and Poppy slipped off the jacket and hung it up.

"We're ready," said Perry, removing a fragrant loaf of bread from an oven and setting it on a round bread board he carried to the table.

Lucy brought the bowl of salad, Desi donned oven mitts to convey the heavy casserole from the Aga, and they all seated themselves at the large scrubbed pine table.

"I didn't know you were interested in cooking," said Sue as Perry began dishing up the stew.

"Necessity is the mother of invention," he replied. "Poppy runs the show, y'see. I do my best to earn my keep so she doesn't chuck me out."

"Nonsense," said Poppy, passing the salad bowl. "I'd never do that."

"You couldn't, even if you wanted to," said Gerald, busying himself opening the second bottle of wine. "He's the earl. The place belongs to him."

"Not exactly," said Perry, arranging the merest dab of stew on the last plate and passing it to Flora. "The corporation actually owns the trust. Poppy and I are officers, as are your children, Gerald."

"Fat lot of good it's ever going to do them," muttered Gerald, topping off his glass before sending the bottle around the table for everyone to serve themselves. Only Sue and Desi added more wine to their glasses.

"It's the family birthright," said Poppy. "It's a privilege and a responsibility. Lord knows, I've done my best to make them aware of their heritage." She paused. "Has everyone got salad?"

"I for one am very glad to be such a lucky boy," said Desi, accepting the bowl that his mother passed to him. "It's good to know I've got a job waiting for me when my legs give out."

"Can't be soon enough for me," grumbled Gerald.

"Oh, Dad," moaned Flora, "you're such a cliché. Ballet is tough. Desi works hard. I bet he's in better shape than those rugby players you admire so much."

Gerald set down his stemmed glass with a thud. "Rugby is a man's sport," he declared. "Ballet is for prissies."

Lucy and Sue shared a glance; it was a terribly embarrassing situation.

"Why do you have to be such a Neanderthal, Dad?" demanded Flora, who had leaped to her feet, leaving the food on her plate untouched.

"It's okay, Flo. He's just teasing," said Desi, tugging her hand. "Sit back down and eat some lunch."

Flora sat back down and even picked up her fork, using it to push the food around on her plate.

There was an uncomfortable silence.

Sue tactfully broke it by changing the subject. "How's the hat show going?" she asked, turning to Perry. "Is everything ready?"

"Almost," said Perry. "We're setting it up in the long gallery, and I'm pairing the hats with paintings and other artifacts from the house."

"That's a clever idea," said Lucy.

"Perhaps a bit too clever," admitted Perry with a rueful grin. "Sometimes I think I may have overreached. It's quite a lot of work."

"Whenever he takes something, we have to put up a notice, explaining its absence, or find something similar to put in its place," said Poppy. "It would be easier if things were properly catalogued. We've hired a curator, Winifred Wynn, but she's only about halfway through."

"Things are always so much more complicated than you expect," said Lucy.

"Damned nuisance, these English Heritage chaps," muttered Gerald, causing Desi to suppress a smile.

"Did you know the general fell?" Poppy was not so much asking as explaining the arrival of Harold Quimby, the driver who'd met Lucy and Sue at the bus station. He was standing outside the French doors and Poppy waved him in.

"When did this happen?" asked Desi.

"Just this morning. The old fellow came down with a big crash," said Perry.

"What's the news?" asked Poppy. "Harold, you know everyone here, right?"

"Indeed I do," he answered with a nod to Sue and Lucy. "I hope you ladies are enjoying your stay?"

"Very much. Thank you," said Lucy.

"How are the chicks?" asked Sue. "Are they settling in?"

"I presume so," said Harold. "I was only delivering them to the farm."

"Harold is our facilities manager. He's responsible for maintaining this old pile," said Poppy. "Have you had a chance to investigate the general's accident?"

Harold pulled out a chair and seated himself at the table. "I have and I'm afraid I have bad news."

"Have you eaten?" asked Perry with a nod at the stew.

"I have, thanks," replied Harold. "There's no easy way to say this. We've got dry rot. The general fell because the wall gave way. There's nothing but powder behind that paneling."

Poppy's face had gone white and she was wringing her hands. Perry was biting his bottom lip. Gerald poured himself some more wine, and Flora dropped her fork with a clatter.

Desi was the only one who spoke. "Can you give us an estimate of the cost?"

"Ruinous," moaned Poppy. "We'll have to hire experts to investigate and then we'll have to do the repairs, and that's just the wall. We also have to find an art expert to evaluate the damage to the painting."

"Don't forget the frame," said Flora, speaking in a quiet voice.

"She's absolutely right," said Harold. "The frame is every bit as important as the picture. Maybe even more so."

"Good to know she's learning something at university," grumbled Gerald. "Something besides texting and taking drugs."

"Right, Dad," said Flora, adding an eye roll. "You forgot bonking. That's what I do the most."

"Enough," said Poppy. "We need to focus on the current crisis. Harold, do you have any idea what this will cost?"

"Not at the moment, but I'm getting estimates. We should probably go with Titmarsh and Fox. They've done work here before and they're familiar with the property. As for the painting, I consulted with Winifred and she's got a call in to the National Gallery."

"Lord help us," said Poppy, raising her eyes to the ceiling.

"Well, you know how it is," said Harold. "There's never just a little dry rot."

"And how did it get this far?" demanded Gerald in an accusatory tone. "You're supposed to be on top of these things."

"Oh, believe me, I'll be on to the roofers about this," said Harold in a somber tone as the phone began ringing. "They didn't report any problems when they did that section a few years ago. We may be able to get some satisfaction from them or their insurance company."

"Very good then," said Gerald, nodding and humphing.

"I'll get it," said Desi, leaving the table and crossing the room to answer the phone.

"I told you," said Poppy with a resigned smile. "The general has cursed us and it's just beginning."

"Oh, you don't believe in that old tale," protested Gerald.

"Trouble always comes in threes," offered Flora, who was studying a piece of carrot she'd speared on her fork.

"It won't bite." Desi had finished the call and was returning to the table, where he sat down heavily.

"More bad news?" asked Perry.

"Afraid so," Desi replied with a sigh. "That was Aunt Millicent. She's coming for the hat show."

"Bugger," said Perry. "And when will the old bat arrive?"

"Tomorrow."

"Double bugger," said Perry.

Chapter Five

"Don't mind Perry," said Poppy with a smile. "He's actually quite fond of Aunt Millicent."

"I wouldn't go quite that far," protested Perry. "But this must all be horribly boring for you," he said, addressing Lucy and Sue. "Never fear, I have arranged for our resident historian, Maurice Willoughby, to give you a tour of the manor." He checked his watch. "He should be in the library about now, if that's all right with you?"

"Fine with me," said Sue. "Lead on."

Once again Lucy found herself following Perry through the subterranean passage and then climbing up yet another narrow, twisty staircase until they emerged into a spacious, carpeted hallway where a set of open double doors revealed an enormous library.

"Ah, you must be the Americans," said the only occupant, looking up from a rather cluttered desk.

"Let me introduce Maurice Willoughby," said Perry. "These are my friends Sue Finch and Lucy Stone."

Maurice quickly rose and came around the desk, where he clasped Lucy's and Sue's hands in turn with his rather pudgy, rather damp one. He had the soft, bottom-heavy build of a man who spent too much time sitting, and the doughy complexion that came from being indoors. His straight, black hair was slicked down and his smile revealed a mouth full of extremely crooked teeth.

"I'm terribly pleased to make your acquaintance," he said quickly in a dismissive tone as he sidled up to Perry. "If you have a moment, m'lord." He picked up an aged piece of parchment bedecked with wax seals and stained, crumpled red ribbons. "I have found some interesting information about the third earl."

"Later, I think, Maurice," said Perry, scratching his chin. "I was hoping you'd give the ladies a tour of the old pile. Poppy and I have all this dry rot business to deal with and, well, when you get right down to it, you know far more about the place than I ever will."

"Of course, m'lord," Maurice replied, clearly disappointed. "Your wish is my command," he added with a little giggle.

"Maurice, as you well know, there's no need for all this m'lord nonsense. Just call me Perry, okay?"

"Sorry. It's just these surroundings," said Maurice, waving his hand at the beautifully appointed room.

The walls were lined with wooden shelves holding hundreds, perhaps thousands, of gilded, leather-bound volumes. A dozen large blue and white Chinese vases were lined up on top of the bookcases. Persian carpets covered the floor, numerous sofas and chairs were arranged in various comfortable groupings, and the ceiling boasted complicated plaster work that imitated twisting vines. The windows were made of old, wavy glass held in place by lead strips and set into stone casements. A peek outside revealed the moat below, the manicured lawns of the estate park, and the rolling countryside beyond.

"It's all so fabulously feudal, it can go to a fellow's head. Especially if that fellow went to a bricks and mortar university as I did." Maurice grinned.

Perry laughed. "Well, I can't say that Oxford did much for me," he admitted. "I didn't make it past my first term. And I may be the lord of the manor but we know who's really in charge, don't we? I better not keep Poppy waiting . . . so I trust I'm leaving my friends in good hands?"

"Absolutely," promised Maurice with a nod that shook the

loose skin beneath his chin. "I think we'll start with the hall. This way, ladies." He indicated the double doors with a little bow and a flourish.

Once in the corridor, he led them past a couple portraits of ancestors and then popped open a concealed jib door. "I'm afraid we'll have to deal with the madding crowd, the marauding masses, the hoi polloi," he said, indicating a narrow staircase, "but this will give us a bit of an advantage."

Lucy and Sue followed him down the twists and turns of the staircase, eventually emerging in the huge hall filled with visitors. Behind ropes, they were confined to a walkway of heavy-duty industrial carpet. The damaged portrait of the general was propped against one wall and the area was cordoned off with yellow caution tape.

"Rather like a crime scene," observed Lucy.

"I'm afraid this poor ancestor took a tumble," explained a guide, a pleasantly plump woman wearing an official green blazer with the Moreton Manor emblem embroidered in gold thread on the breast pocket.

"Not an ancestor at all," said Maurice, correcting her in a rather sharp tone as he unsnapped a segment of rope, allowing Lucy and Sue to join the throng of visitors gathered on the trail of carpet. "The victim of this rather unfortunate accident is General Horatio Hoare, a friend of the third earl, and you"—he paused to check the guide's name tag—"Marjorie, ought to know that. I suggest you review your Facts and Fancies of Moreton Manor this evening."

"Oh, yes, Mr. Willoughby, I will certainly do that," said Marjorie, clearly embarrassed by the scolding which took place in front of numerous visitors. "I do hope the curse is just an old wives' tale," she added in an effort to regain some credibility.

"The only curse I know of," said Maurice, giving her a baleful glance, "is the unemployment that befalls unprepared guides."

Lucy decided it was time to stop Maurice's bullying and tossed the poor woman a lifeline. "The curse is real enough. The earl mentioned it himself this morning, when they discovered the painting had fallen. It's supposed to keep the manor safe as long as it's on the wall. The last time it came down a countess had a fatal accident."

This declaration caused a little buzz among the visitors, who were clearly impressed by this bit of inside information.

Maurice, however, reacted defensively. "Well, as it happens," he said, puffing himself up, "there are various viewpoints on that particular incident. Shall we continue?"

"Yes, please," said Sue. "Can you tell us who painted the ceiling?"

"Ah, yes. The ceiling was commissioned by the fifth earl after his grand tour of the continent, which was of course the custom of the time. Young gentlemen were expected to travel abroad to attain the refinement expected of the aristocracy. He hired an Italian by the name of Giardino, not well known, but I think we can agree he did a fine job."

Lucy and Sue, as well as the gathered visitors, gazed upward at the cavorting gods and goddesses perched on their sturdy clouds.

"Amazing," said one woman.

"Moving along," said Maurice, "I believe the next room is the salon, the manor's main reception room."

Lucy and Sue marched along, following him through one enormous room after another, all filled with tapestries and paintings and elaborately carved furniture.

The enormous dining table was set with forty places for a formal dinner, complete with a massive silver centerpiece depicting Nelson's victory at Trafalgar. Maurice took great pleasure in demonstrating how the cannons on the silver battleships could actually be fired to produce a gentle popping sound and a puff of smoke. The conservatory they'd viewed from outside was filled with lush tropical foliage plants and gorgeous blooming orchids. The morning room, which Maurice explained was traditionally the bailiwick of the countess, contained charming French furniture upholstered with pale blue silk brocade. Continuing up the stairs, they passed through several richly appointed guest rooms and then came to the earl's and countess's bedrooms located on either side of a roomy hallway.

"Absolutely gorgeous," observed Sue, glancing at the huge four-poster bed with crewel hangings. Set on a raised platform, it dominated the countess's chamber. "I could get used to this," she added, glancing at the vanity table covered with a froth of lace that occupied the space in front of the bay window.

The earl's bedroom was even grander. Red brocade covered the walls and an enormous dressing stand encrusted with gilt and crystal fittings stood nearby. His bed was larger, the platform higher, the paintings more numerous.

"Hey, Perce, we could do with something like this, couldn't we? Plenty of room for a bit of slap and tickle," exclaimed one woman.

Perce winked at his companion. "We could even invite the neighbors in."

"Ooh, for shame, Perce," chided the woman, growing a bit flushed.

Hearing this exchange, Lucy gave Sue an amused smile, but her thoughts were rather different. She was thinking of her bedroom at home, where a handmade quilt she'd picked up at an estate sale covered the bed and the dresser tops were always filled with clutter—change and keys, photos and bits of jewelry, appointment cards—that they were too busy or too lazy to put away properly. And she thought of the cozy kitchen that was the center of Perry and Poppy's life. "I wonder if Perry and Poppy mind giving up all this grandeur for what seems to be a rather simple lifestyle," she wondered aloud.

"If you ask me," replied Maurice with a bit of a Cockney accent creeping into his tone, "they're just doing what their kind have always done, and that is taking advantage of those less fortunate. This place was built on the labor of mill workers and miners and tenant farmers and now they charge those same folk ten pounds a head to come and see what they did with all the money they sweated out of their grandparents. They've still got 'em coming and going, working up a bit of an appetite after touring the house, so they buy lunch or a cream tea in the café. And nobody goes home without a tea towel or a souvenir magnet."

"I disagree," said Sue. "I think most people come because they want to imagine being the lord and lady, if only for an hour or two."

"But what did they do with themselves all day, when they had all those servants to do everything for them?" asked Lucy. "It must have been a rather empty life, all for show. They didn't even bring up their own children. I'd rather do things for myself. I take satisfaction in cooking supper and digging the garden, I even enjoyed changing the kids' diapers."

"Different strokes for different folks," said Sue.

Maurice delivered them to the exit, which he was quick to point out conveniently led to the café and gift shop, as well as the garden.

"Thank you so much for the tour," said Sue. "I really enjoyed it."

"Me too," added Lucy. "Can we visit the garden, too?"

"Absolutely," said Maurice. "Don't miss the maze.'

"I bet it's amazing," said Lucy, getting a groan from Sue.

He pointed the way and they parted, Maurice presumably returning to his work in the library and Lucy and Sue heading down the brick path to the walled garden.

Lucy gasped as they stepped through the gateway and discovered the wealth of blooms in the garden. Neat beds of flowering bulbs were defined by boxwood borders and filled with rows of bedding plants including petunias and geraniums as well as alliums and tulips. Arbors covered with climbing vines promised a profusion of roses in a few weeks, green shoots in the perennial borders were harbingers of the blooms to come. The two friends wandered along the winding paths, exclaiming over the rare forms and colors, and the sheer magnitude of the plantings.

"You know," admitted Lucy, "I buy ten of these and ten of those. Sometimes the packages—like alliums—contain only three or four bulbs. Look at all these. It's mind boggling."

"I'm beginning to think Maurice is on to something," said Sue. "This represents a lot of money."

"And a lot of digging," said Lucy.

"But I suppose"—Sue nodded at some of the visitors who were also admiring the garden—"if you're going to charge ten pounds a head, you've got to give them something to see."

"What's that?" asked Lucy, pointing to a small stone building perched on a distant knoll.

"A folly, I imagine," said Sue.

"Let's go take a look," urged Lucy. "I need to stretch my legs after sitting on that plane."

"This doesn't sound like you," said Sue. "You're supposed to be depressed."

"I'm feeling a lot better," admitted Lucy. "I want to breathe deeply and get my circulation going. Put some pink in my cheeks."

"That's what they invented blush for," complained Sue.

"Come on. It'll do you good. You'll sleep like a baby tonight."

"I'm pretty sure that won't be a problem," said Sue with a sigh. They stepped through an opening in the wall and found themselves following a winding path covered with wood chips that led through a small woodland. Coming to a fork in the path, they observed a neat sign with arrows pointing the way to DIANA'S TEMPLE, THE MAZE, MANOR VILLAGE, MORETON CARAVAN CAMPGROUND, and MORETON ESTATE FARM.

"The maze is one way, the folly another," observed Sue. "Which way shall we go?"

"We can't miss the maze," said Lucy. "It's famous."

"But the folly is closer," said Sue, starting up the path.

"I hope there's a good view at the top of this hill. Was I the one who wanted to stretch my legs?" complained Lucy, growing out of breath.

"You were, and there's no backing out now," insisted Sue, trudging up the incline and pointing out an ersatz Greek temple. "See! We're almost there."

The temple was a round structure with a domed roof and a porch entirely circled with columns. As they drew closer, they saw there was a round little room in the center of the temple, but it was completely enclosed apart from a single door and a pair of barred and shuttered windows.

"Wouldn't you think they'd want to enjoy the view?" asked Lucy in a puzzled tone.

"Maybe it's just for storage," said Sue as the door suddenly opened and a tall, leggy blonde popped out.

"Hi!" exclaimed Lucy, somewhat surprised.

The blonde didn't reply, but merely tossed her long, professionally highlighted hair over her shoulder and hoisted a huge shoulder bag into place under her arm before striding off on her very high heels.

"Not exactly country clothes," observed Sue. "She was wearing Louboutins."

"Loulouwhats?" asked Lucy, seating herself on the stone steps of the folly and gazing into the distance.

"Louboutins. Very expensive shoes. I recognized the red soles," said Sue, sitting beside her.

"You're looking at shoes. I'm looking at the view. Have you ever seen anything lovelier?"

Sue nodded, admiring the nearby pasture dotted with cows, the neat fields enclosed by hedges, the fringe of woodland, and the blue hills beyond. "God must be an Englishman," she said.

"So I've heard," agreed Lucy, leaning her shoulder against a pillar. She was stretching her neck when a sudden "humph" startled her and she turned to see that Gerald was standing behind them.

"Marvelous view, eh?" he said, pocketing a set of keys.

"Absolutely," said Sue.

"We've just been admiring the temple," said Lucy. "What's it used for, if you don't mind my asking?"

"Uh, storage—chairs and cushions, that sort of thing."

"Can we see?" asked Lucy.

"Sorry, but no can do. Don't have the key."

"No matter," said Sue, giving Lucy a reproving glance. "We ought to be heading back to the manor."

"Good idea, good idea," he said, sputtering like a walrus, "but be careful of the ha-ha. Wouldn't want to tumble into a cow pat would you?"

"We'll be careful," said Lucy.

Gerald lumbered awkwardly down the steps, then turned to face them. "It's never a good idea to go looking for trouble," he said before marching off.

Chapter Six

"What was that all about?" asked Lucy, pulling herself to her feet and finding the maneuver rather painful.

"He's obviously having an affair with the blonde," said Sue, "and doesn't want us to mention seeing them."

"Gerald? With that gorgeous girl?"

"Yes, Lucy. Older rich guy, ambitious young woman. It's a tale as old as time."

"Poor Poppy," said Lucy. "She seems so nice."

"Nice isn't any help at all when a man decides to stray," said Sue as they walked together along the path.

Lucy was silent for a while, then spoke up. "No wonder he was so defensive when I asked to see inside the folly."

"He's probably got a little love nest in there."

"How horrible. There are probably spiders." Lucy disliked dark, dank spaces. "It was obvious he had the keys, even though he said he didn't."

"You're a regular Sherlock Holmes." Sue stepped aside to let some visitors pass. "Shall we investigate the amazing maze?"

The way to the maze was clearly marked and took them past rolling lawns dotted with trees and bluebells. There was no attendant at the maze entrance, which was simply a gap in a tall wall of privet hedge.

Lucy hesitated. "What if we can't find our way out?"

"Don't be silly," said Sue." How hard can it be?"

"At this point, I don't think I could do a connect-the-dots," said Lucy with a sigh.

"Well, I think we have to try it. What will the folks back home think?"

"How would they even know?" grumbled Lucy, following Sue as she stepped boldly into the maze.

At the first intersection, she insisted on turning right. "There's always a key to these things, and it's usually to keep turning the same way, so we'll go right."

"Why right?" asked Lucy.

"Why not?" replied Sue, confident as ever. Nevertheless, they followed the narrow mowed paths lined on either side with twelve-foot tall hedges and kept turning right at every intersection until they encountered the same statue of a cupid that they'd seen before.

"Uh-oh," said Lucy. "I'm afraid we're just going in circles."

"Maybe there's two of these little guys," said Sue.

"I doubt it, Sue, and I'm really tired," said Lucy, pulling her cell phone out of her pocket. "I think we should call for help."

"Not yet," protested Sue. "Let's try going left."

"Which way is left?" asked Lucy.

"I don't know," admitted Sue. "I thought I had a good sense of direction, but I'm all turned around."

"That settles it," said Lucy. "I'm calling."

Perry took the call with some amusement and promised to send someone to lead them out.

True to his word, it was only a matter of minutes before a gardener showed up. He was a good-looking, muscular young man with sun-bleached blond hair, and was wearing an unbuttoned plaid shirt over a tight wife-beater shirt and jeans.

"This is so embarrassing," said Sue, greeting him with a rueful smile.

"Not to worry," said the gardener. "It happens more than you might think."

"Is there a trick to it?" asked Sue, who was unable to resist twisting a bit of hair flirtatiously around her finger. "You found us very quickly."

"It's pretty simple, really. Do you want to go to the center of the maze, where there is a charming bit of sculpture clearly designed to promote a bit of dalliance or would you rather go directly to the exit?"

Lucy began, "It is getting rather late—"

"Oh, I think we want to see the naughty sculpture," interrupted Sue with a definite twinkle in her eye.

"Righto," he said, leading the way. "It's left, right, left and so on until you reach the center and then it's right, left, right until you come to the exit."

"That's rather a lot to keep straight," said Lucy, who was finding the narrow pathways rather claustrophobic. "I don't know what we'd do if you hadn't come to our rescue."

"I was double-digging a flower bed, so it's you who came to my rescue," said the young fellow.

"We really appreciate your help," said Sue. "By the way, what's your name?"

"Geoff. Just Geoff will do." He stepped aside with a flourish so they could enter the center of the maze. "Meet Diana, Goddess of the Hunt," he said, indicating the statue that was the centerpiece of the outdoor room.

It wasn't the nude sculpture that caught their attention, however, but the prone body of a young man lying at her feet.

"Oy! What's this?" exclaimed Geoff in a take-charge voice. He strode across the neatly clipped grass and bent over the young man, shaking his shoulder.

Lucy stood next to Sue, trying to understand this unexpected and shocking situation. She studied the man on the ground, observing that he was young and was wearing tight jeans and a black T-shirt; he had a shaved head and his arms were covered with tattoos. She thought he must have passed out, perhaps from a diabetic coma or a drug overdose.

"Shall we go for help?" she asked before realizing the question was foolish.

Geoff pulled a cell phone from his pocket. "I think it may be too late." He raised the phone to his ear and spoke into it then turned to Lucy and Sue. "It seems you're going to have to stay and give a statement, so you might as well make yourselves comfortable," he said, indicating a stone bench some distance from the body.

"Is he dead?" asked Sue, who had begun to tremble.

Lucy took her hand and led her to the bench, where they both sat down.

"I'm afraid so," said Geoff. "I've called the office and they will call the authorities and arrange for the maze to be closed to visitors. I'm to stay with you until—" Hearing laughter he broke off and went to head off the visitors.

They could hear him explaining that there had been an accident and the maze would have to be closed to visitors today and then giving them directions to the exit.

"This is so horrible," said Sue, who was unable to take her eyes off the corpse.

Lucy wrapped an arm around her friend's shoulder and patted her hand in that automatic way people do when they're trying to offer comfort. All the while, she was wondering how this person came to die in the maze at a stately home.

"He doesn't look like your typical visitor," she said, turning to Geoff. "Does he work here?"

"Not that I know of. I've never seen him before."

"Do you think he had one of those heart problems you hear about? Everything's okay until you drop dead?" asked Sue.

"Maybe he got scared and stressed by being in the maze," said Lucy.

"No, I think it was a drug overdose," said Geoff. "There's a syringe on the ground, next to the body."

"But why would anybody pay ten pounds admission to shoot up in the Moreton Manor maze?" wondered Lucy. "It doesn't make sense."

"It's beyond me," said Geoff, looking up as two uniformed police officers arrived. They were both men, one was black and the other white, and they went straight to the body.

"Naloxone?" inquired one.

"Too late," said the other. "Better call for the medical examiner."

While the black officer busied himself with his radio, the white officer introduced himself as he withdrew a leather-covered notebook from his pocket. "I'm PC Floyd. That's my colleague PC Lahiri. Can you identify the victim?"

"Afraid not," said Geoff. "These ladies got lost in the maze, called for help, and I was sent to lead them out. I called the office as soon as we discovered the body."

"And when was that?"

"About ten minutes ago," said Geoff.

"I'll need your names and addresses," said PC Floyd, opening the notebook and making a notation. After he'd taken down their information, he fixed his eye on Geoff. "Are you sure you do not know the victim?"

"Never seen him before," said Geoff rather quickly.

"Absolutely not," said Sue.

"Same here," said Lucy as a fortyish woman in a white jumpsuit arrived, accompanied by Harold Quimby.

"Thanks for showing me the way," she said, dismissing him and turning to PC Lahiri. "So what's the story?"

"Unidentified corpse, discovered twenty minutes ago," he said.

Quimby was speaking with PC Floyd. "May I take these ladies back to the manor? They're guests of the earl and I'm sure this has been very upsetting for them."

"No problem," replied the officer.

"Will there be an investigation?" asked Quimby.

PC Floyd shook his head. "Most unlikely. We don't have the manpower to investigate every victim of an overdose and that's the truth. All we can do is identify him and notify his next of kin so they can claim the body."

"Well, if you have any questions you know where to find us," said Quimby, turning to Lucy and Sue. "I am so sorry about this. Let's get you back to the house. The kettle's on the hob for tea . . . or perhaps you'd like something stronger?"

"Something stronger," said Sue, whose voice was still shaky.

There was no tea nor cocktails on offer in the kitchen when they returned and found Perry standing over the stove, cooking up a thick vegetable stew. He did offer glasses of wine, however, and they settled themselves with their drinks on the comfy sofa, dislodging the dogs who rather grudgingly rearranged themselves on the rug in front of the fireplace. It being warm there was no fire, but the delicious scent of the ribollita filled the air.

"I am so sorry you had to be involved in this sordid episode," said Perry, replacing the lid on the casserole before joining them and seating himself next to Sue. "That's the problem with opening your home to the public—people don't always behave very well."

"I suppose not," said Sue. "Have you had many people dying on your doorstep?"

Perry gave a rueful smile. "Not really. A few through the years. Mostly quite elderly. They get carried away a bit in the garden and overdo. The distances can be quite deceiving."

"This fellow didn't seem like a typical stately home visitor," said Lucy. "He was quite young and dressed in jeans and a T-shirt. He had tattoos. . . ."

"Who had tattoos?" Flora had wandered in from the garden. As usual, she was dressed in a long flowing dress. Combined with her unkempt, stringy hair she looked rather like Ophelia after she'd drowned herself in the pond.

"A young man who was found dead in the maze," said Perry. "Sue and Lucy actually found him."

"Along with a gardener named Geoff," said Lucy.

"Thank goodness Geoff was there," said Sue.

"Someone was found dead in the maze?" asked Flora, wide-eyed. "Who was it?"

"They don't know," said Perry.

"Well, what did he look like?" asked Flora.

"Young, shaved head, tattoos on his arms," said Lucy.

"They said it was an overdose," offered Sue, but Flora was already leaving the room. Only her heavy perfume lingered, leaving any sign that she had been there.

"Do you think she knows him?" asked Lucy. "Maybe he was a friend."

"I hope not. He doesn't sound like the sort of person Flora ought to be friends with," Perry said. Rising and crossing the room to the stove, he lifted the lid on the pot and checked the progress of the ribollita. "So, apart from finding a body, did you enjoy the tour?"

"Oh, yes," exclaimed Sue, eager to change the subject. "We have nothing like this in America. There are grand houses, of course, but they were built by robber barons in the nineteenth century. We have nothing with such a long history."

"Willoughby's quite the historian," said Perry. "He's working on revising the guidebook for us."

"He's certainly a stickler for accuracy," said Lucy, recalling the way the historian corrected poor Marjorie.

"Is that Willoughby you're talking about?" inquired Desi. He'd paused at the island to pour himself a glass of wine before seating himself on the second sofa.

"He can be a bit overbearing at times," said Perry, "but he's certainly a hard worker. And that guidebook was last revised when Gram and Gramps were living here."

"It must have been wonderful when you had the whole place," said Sue with a sigh.

"Wonderful and scary," said Perry. "When I was a kid, they had a butler, Chivers was his name, who absolutely terrified me. He even frightened Gram. 'Whatever you do,' she used to say in this very serious voice, 'please don't upset Chivers.'"

"That was before my time," said Desi. "I used to love coming here when I was a kid. Of course, things were rather falling apart by then. Gramps had died and Uncle Wilfred followed soon after. Money was running short and there were no servants to speak of anymore. Flo and I were city kids so we loved the freedom here, having all this space to run around and ride ponies." He paused and took a sip of wine. "Rainy days were the best, though. Then we'd go exploring in the far reaches of the house, going from room to room and opening drawers and finding all sorts of trash and sometimes, real treasures."

"That's right," said Perry. "Remember when you found that sixteenth century inventory? It had been used to wrap up some jelly glasses."

"So typical, using a priceless antique document to protect some worthless jelly glasses," said Desi with a chuckle. "And there was that fabulous Chinese porcelain—a monkey, I think it was—used as a doorstop."

"We're still trying to sort things out. I don't know what we'd do without our curator," said Poppy, arriving with an armful of papers and a thick wad of upholstery fabric samples, all of which she dropped on an armchair where they joined the cushions and dented silver ewer she'd previously put there. "What a day." She sighed as she sank into another chair. "I am so sorry you were involved in the recent unpleasantness," she said, speaking to Lucy and Sue. "All I can do is offer my sincere apologies and assure you that this sort of thing is the exception rather than the rule." She turned to her son and deftly changed the subject. "Is this that good cab you brought, Desi?"

"Yup. My friend Henri grows it at the family domaine."

Sue caught Lucy's eye and winked, as if to say, "Look at us! Hanging out with people who know people who own vineyards."

"Delicious," said Poppy, savoring a sip before joining her son on the sofa. She looked up as an attractive young woman dressed in the countrywoman's uniform of cashmere sweater and tweed skirt entered the room. "Oh, Winifred, let me introduce our friends from America," she said, naming Sue and Lucy. "Winifred Wynn is our curator and a gift from God."

"I don't know about that," said Winifred, smiling. "I just came by to let you know that the art restorer from the National Gallery is coming tomorrow to check out the damage to the general."

"Thanks for the update." Poppy dismissed her by adding, "Have a good evening."

When Winifred was gone, Poppy took a big swallow of wine. "Tomorrow is going to be a busy day. Don't forget Aunt Millicent is coming, along with that dragon Harrison."

"Harrison is Aunt Millicent's lady's maid," said Perry. "She's almost as bad as Chivers."

"Worse, I think," said Poppy. "We could hide from Chivers, especially in his later years when he took to drinking Gramps' port. Harrison is relentless. She won't take no for an answer. Aunt wants to sleep in the countess's bedroom—"

"That's impossible," said Perry. "It has to remain open to the public."

"I know, but that doesn't seem to matter to Aunt."

Perry frowned. "She can have the Chinese room. It's closed anyway while the bed curtains are restored."

"She's not going to like that," said Desi. "Can't you offer some treat to placate the old thing?"

"Have some folks in for dinner? Let her play the grande dame," suggested Perry. "We could use the big dining room, if we timed it right. The house closes at six and we could eat at eight. That would give the staff time to clear away the ropes and carpet savers, and reset the table with the second-best china."

"That's a good idea. She detests eating here in the kitchen," said Poppy. "I'll invite the vicar and his wife. They're always available on short notice. We've got Lucy and Sue, and there's Willoughby and Winifred." Poppy counted people on her fingers. "I need one more man."

"Quimby!" exclaimed Perry.

"And we'll get a couple gardeners to play footmen for the night."

"Oh," chimed in Sue, "we met the nicest fellow today, by the name of Geoff. We got lost in the maze and he came to help us. When we found the body, he took over."

"Dishy Geoff," said Poppy, determined to steer clear of any topic as disagreeable as the discovery of a body. "Hearts were broken throughout the county when his engagement was announced. With a wedding coming, I'm sure he'll be glad for a bit of extra cash."

Lucy was struck by Poppy's smooth direction of the conversation and wondered if she was simply determined to limit the discussion to amusing topics or whether she knew more about the dead man than she wished to reveal. Certain that Flora had recognized the description of the young man, Lucy suspected that Perry thought so, too.

"Will we have to dress?" asked Desi.

"Dinner jacket will do," said Poppy, getting a groan from Desi.

"This will be a treat," said Sue. "Dressing up for a formal dinner at Moreton Manor."

Not so much, thought Lucy, biting her lip. She didn't have anything to wear, and she wasn't at all sure she wanted to stay with people who regarded a young man's death as nothing more than an awkward inconvenience.

"Do you have plans for tomorrow?" asked Perry. "I'm afraid I'm going to have to neglect you, as I'm rather involved with the exhibition."

"Never fear," said Sue. "Lucy and I are perfectly capable of amusing ourselves. In fact, I was thinking of exploring Oxford. It's not far, is it?"

"Not at all far, twenty minutes or so," said Poppy. "We can have someone drive you. Just give a call when you're ready to come back."

"Great," said Lucy, who had noticed Perry placing a basket of bread on the kitchen island. "Shall I set the table?"

"I think I'll just set the grub here on the island, buffet style, if that's okay with everyone?"

"Fine with me," said Sue.

Desi was opening a cupboard and counting out plates. "Shall I call Flo?"

"She'll come if she wants to," said Poppy with a sigh. "It's better not to force the issue. At least, that's what the therapists tell me. Flora knows when we eat dinner." Poppy looked up as Gerald arrived, stomping his muddy feet on the doormat. "Did you have a rumbly in your tumbly, dear?"

Lucy was tempted to say he'd had a bit of a *tumbly* in the *rumbly*, but thought better of it and bit her tongue. Sue, however, caught her eye and gave a mischievous smile and Lucy found herself giggling.

"Something funny?" demanded Gerald, who had advanced to the island and was emptying the wine bottle into his glass.

"It's just the way you English people have with words," said Lucy. "I feel as if I'm in a Winnie the Pooh book."

"It's more like a fairy tale," said Sue. "This beautiful house, the garden, the folly—it's all so magical."

Lucy stared into her wineglass where the surface of the wine reflected light from the downlights in the ceiling. Sue was right, she thought. Moreton Manor was like a castle in a fairy tale, and fairy tales were full of wicked witches, evil queens, nasty trolls, and big, bad wolves.

Gerald glared briefly at Sue, then downed half his glass of wine. "Is there any more of this plonk?" he demanded.

"It's not plonk," protested Desi. "It's 2013 cabernet from Henri Le Vec's vineyard in France. It's rather special. It's the wine the family reserves for itself."

"Well, whatever it is, it's all gone and we're going to need another bottle," said Gerald. "Are you going down to the cellar or shall I?"

"I'll go," said Desi, promptly disappearing through a door.

"I think we can start. Desi will be back in a minute," said Perry, setting the tureen on the island and handing a plate to Sue.

Lucy's mood improved as everyone gathered around the island and helped themselves to generous servings of Perry's delicious ribollita. The vegetables were fresh from the garden and bursting with flavor, the whole grain bread had a crunchy crust, and the wine was plentiful. Even the butter was marvelously flavorful, tasting of sunshine and sweet meadow grass.

"This isn't at all what I expected," said Sue. "I have to say it's a pleasant surprise."

"Did you expect *Downton Abbey*?" asked Poppy.

"I guess I did, a little bit," confessed Sue, who was fetching second helpings for herself.

Lucy watched in amazement. In all the years she had known her, she had rarely seen Sue finish her firsts, much less go back for seconds.

"Well, you'll get plenty of *Downton Abbey* tomorrow when Aunt Millicent arrives," said Desi.

"I didn't bring any dressy clothes," admitted Lucy, getting an eye roll from Sue. "Can you recommend any shops in Oxford?"

"I'm afraid I'm no help. I haven't bought anything from a shop in years. Most of my clothes were bought at agricultural fairs," admitted Poppy.

"We'll put that question to Flo," said Desi. "She's certain to have some ideas."

"Great," said Lucy, rising to help Poppy clear the table for dessert.

"Rhubarb and custard," said Perry. "I hope you like rhubarb."

"Love it," declared Lucy, thinking of the huge plant in her garden at home. That led to thoughts of Bill and Patrick and the girls and she was suddenly stricken with a huge wave of sadness and longing for home.

"Coffee, Lucy?" asked Perry, sounding concerned.

"Better not," she said, quickly rallying. "Jet lag, you know."

"I don't think even coffee will keep me awake," said Sue, accepting a cup. But even she turned down a second cup when it was offered. "I think Lucy and I need an early night."

"Of course," said Poppy. "You've had a difficult day. We'll see you in the morning. Sleep well."

Lucy and Sue started up the stairs to their guest rooms, Sue pausing midway to give her nose a good blow. "Dogs," she said by way of explanation. "I think I'm allergic."

They had reached the first landing when an odd sound caught their attention. Lucy pushed open the doorway. Leaning into the corridor that contained the family's bedrooms, they clearly heard someone sobbing.

"That must be Flora," said Lucy. "I bet she's crying over the fellow in the maze."

"Do you think she knew him?" asked Sue.

"She seemed to recognize his description. She ran out of the room."

"The others didn't seem to know him," said Sue thoughtfully. "I guess he really wasn't the sort of fellow you'd bring home to meet the family."

"I guess this is the side of Moreton Manor that the day-trippers don't see."

"It's not all strawberries and cream."

"It's not even rhubarb and custard," said Lucy.

Chapter Seven

Once in her room, Lucy decided to call home. The discovery of the tattooed young man's body had upset her, and she couldn't erase the picture from her mind. Who was he? Why had he come to Moreton Manor? And most disturbing of all, what had caused him to turn to drugs? Such a waste of a young life troubled her, but she was also upset by the family's determination to ignore the situation. She'd heard the term *stiff upper lip* before, but she hadn't realized what it actually meant. She didn't know if they were also troubled by the discovery of the body and were repressing an emotional response or if they simply didn't care. Flora was the only one who seemed upset, and Lucy wasn't sure if that was because she had some sort of relationship with the young man or if her reaction was a symptom of her obviously fragile mental state.

Lucy felt anxious. Dark clouds were building in her mind and she knew she needed to touch base with those she loved; she needed to reassure herself that everyone at home was safe and things were going well. She wanted to hear Bill's voice and needed to know that he was there for her, even if they were separated by thousands of miles of ocean. But when she punched in his cell phone number, he didn't answer, so she tried the land line in the house and got Zoe.

"How's it going?" she asked her daughter, making a determined effort to lighten her voice. "Are you all ready for the prom?"

"I think so. It'll be okay if I do my hair myself, don't you think? And I got a tube of self-tanner. I don't want to spend the money for a professional spray tan."

Hearing this, Lucy was puzzled. "But you had the appointments. I left checks for you to use."

"I know, Mom, but we got the reply from Strethmore . . ." Zoe desperately wanted to attend Strethmore College, and she'd been accepted, but the financial aid package had not been very generous. The family had appealed the award, explaining the need for more funds, and the answer had apparently arrived.

"How much did they come up with?" asked Lucy.

"Ten thousand and Dad says it's not enough, so that's why I'm trying to save money."

Lucy was impressed by her daughter's reaction, but thought it was misguided. "Look, sweetie, skipping a salon appointment and a fake tan session isn't going to make much difference in the big picture. We'll figure it out when I get back."

"Well, Pop is meeting some guy, some friend of Toby's who's a financial planner. He says this guy has some ideas about maximizing investments or something."

Lucy thought of the modest balance that remained in the education fund that had been depleted by the older kids' college expenses and wondered what sort of investment could increase it substantially in the short time they had before it was needed for their youngest child. "Is this that Doug fellow?"

"I didn't get his name," said Zoe.

"Well listen, I think you should get your hair done and get the spray tan. You'll be even more gorgeous than you usually are and you'll have a wonderful time at the prom. I want to see lots of pictures."

"Okay, Mom," said Zoe, sounding pleased. "And how's your trip?"

"Well, it's not quite what I expected," said Lucy, choosing her words carefully.

"Life's full of surprises, isn't it?" said Zoe.

"It sure is," said Lucy. "Take care, sweetie. I love you."

"Love you, too, Mom."

Poppy was already at the big table, studying a spread sheet while she ate her boiled egg and toast, when Lucy and Sue came into the kitchen early the next morning. She looked up and greeted them with a smile. "Coffee's ready, help yourselves to whatever you want," she invited with a nod at the various offerings awaiting them on the island. "By the way, I got a call from the police late last night and it seems they've identified the young man. He's from London and it's a bit of puzzle what he was doing here at Moreton, but they're satisfied his death was due to an accidental overdose. Case closed."

"Did they tell you his name?" asked Lucy, slipping a couple crumpets into the toaster.

"They did, but I forgot," said Poppy, turning over a page of the spreadsheet. "Maybe it was Eric something or other."

Sue filled her mug with coffee and joined Poppy at the table. Lucy soon followed with her coffee and crumpets. They all looked up in surprise when Flora arrived, as she habitually skipped breakfast. Whatever had reduced her to tears in the night seemed to have been resolved as she was clearly in a much calmer mood and even helped herself to a small bowl of yogurt topped with three strawberries.

When she politely inquired if Lucy and Sue had any plans for the day and learned they intended to go to Oxford, she quickly offered to drive them and give them a tour.

"Hope you don't mind going in the Mini," she said an hour or so later, leading the way to the stable yard where an assortment of vehicles were parked, including an ancient MiniCooper.

"Not at all," said Lucy, who knew that she would have to sit in the back because that was simply the way the universe was ordered. Not that she minded, but it would be nice if just once Sue would at least offer her the front seat.

The Mini had no suspension to speak of, and the three women bounced along down the drive and along country roads bounded by tall hedges. It was a lovely spring morning, warm and sunny and not at all like spring in coastal Maine, which was always a rather chilly affair due to breezes blowing in over the cool ocean water. There were lots of flowers in bloom, including bluebells, and the birds were tweeting and trilling to beat the band. It wasn't long at all before they spotted the "dreaming spires" of Oxford in the distance.

Flora knew her way around and drove confidently down the narrow streets and past numerous bicyclists, taking them right under the quaint Hertford Bridge. Supposedly inspired by the Bridge of Sighs in Venice, it extended over a narrow street and connected two buildings.

"Ooh, look!" exclaimed Lucy, "I've seen that on TV."

"In the Inspector Morse mysteries," said Flora. "They've managed to use the whole city in one episode or another. It's kind of a local industry."

"Things do seem very familiar," admitted Lucy, who was a fan of the original TV show as well as the recent spinoffs. "It's kind of like déjà vu."

Flora zipped around the famous Radcliffe Camera, with its unusual circular design, and past the ancient stone colleges, whose walls were often plastered with announcements for concerts, sales, and other events. She soon popped out on an extremely busy main street, explaining that the Botanic Garden and Magdalen Bridge were at one end, the Ashmolean Museum was at the other end, and there was shopping in between.

"Oh, let's go to the museum," begged Lucy, recalling the description in her guide book. "It has Guy Fawkes' lantern."

"And the Alfred Jewel," added Flora.

Sue was not enthused. "On one condition. We'll take a quick peek, eat an early lunch, and spend the rest of the day shopping."

"The Eagle and Child is a famous pub. Tolkien hung out there with his writer friends, the Inklings. It's quite near the museum," said Flora.

"We must go there so I can send pictures to Toby—he loves Tolkien—and then we can shop till we drop," said Lucy, surprising her friend. "I do need to buy something to wear to dinner tonight." She leaned forward in her seat. "Flora, are there any shops you would recommend? That aren't too expensive."

"I usually go to one of the resale places," admitted Flora. "You can even take the dress back after you're done with it. I like Secondhand Rose. It's next to Marks and Spencer. You can't miss it."

"Lucy!" protested Sue. "Why didn't you pack something?"

"I really don't have anything I thought would do," admitted Lucy.

"Well, here we are," said Flora, suddenly taking a U-turn and pulling up in front of a very ancient gray stone church with a tall tower. "I'll let you two explore while I, well, I have a bunch of boring stuff that I can't put off," she said, adding an exaggerated eye roll. "I have to meet my tutor."

"Oh, sure," said Sue, somewhat hesitantly. Lucy figured that, like herself, Sue was surprised by this sudden dismissal, but didn't want to seem unappreciative of the trouble Flora had taken.

"If you want a ride back, meet me here at three," Flora said.

"Three it is. See you then," said Lucy, beginning the process of extricating herself from the tiny car. Then the two friends stood on the sidewalk and watched as Flora zoomed off.

"I wonder . . ." began Lucy.

"She's a student, Lucy," said Sue. "She has to meet her tutor. That's how they do it here. More like independent study when we were in college."

"Funny sort of tutorial," insisted Lucy. "There was no sign of a book or a notebook or a laptop in that car. And why does a little rich girl like Flora buy her clothes at a secondhand shop?"

"Vintage is all the rage with young people," said Sue. "Give it up, Lucy. You're not Inspector Morse. I don't know about you, but I can't say I'm very excited about this Guy Fawkes." She gave Lucy a serious look. "You may not know this, Lucy, but he was a very bad sort. He tried to blow up Parliament."

"I do know," said Lucy. "They remember him with bonfires every fifth of November on Guy Fawkes Day."

"Well," sniffed Sue, "there's no accounting for tastes. As for that Alfred Jewel, it's nothing at all you could wear. I saw a photo and it's really a very ugly lumpish sort of thing."

"I take it you don't want to visit the museum," said Lucy.

"No, and I don't care about the musty old pub either. Eagles and children don't go together very well." She looked longingly at a sign pointing to the Covered Market. "I want to go shopping."

"Okay," agreed Lucy. "On one condition. We visit the Botanic Garden."

"It seems rather far to walk," began Sue, only to be silenced with a look from Lucy. "Okay. Okay."

"Good," said Lucy, who really didn't mind skipping the museum. She was eager to find something to wear to the formal dinner and was grateful for Flora's advice.

Secondhand Rose was just where Flora had said it was, and Lucy found an affordable long black skirt and a creamy lace top that Sue pronounced acceptable.

After visiting most of the shops, which offered designs aimed at college-aged girls, even Sue admitted defeat. She was able to satisfy her need to spend at a Boots drugstore, where she found a tempting array of bath and beauty products not available in the US, so the morning was not a complete loss for her.

They grabbed a quick lunch at a noisy pub mainly patronized by students, where Lucy ordered a sandwich and Sue opted for a liquid lunch of Guinness stout.

"It's only got ninety calories and it's awfully good for you," she insisted, but Lucy wasn't convinced.

Thus fortified, they made their way toward the Magdalen Bridge and the Botanic Garden, which Lucy found extremely familiar.

"I swear, half of those Morse episodes are filmed here," she said as they strolled along a wide path that ran along the river. Eventually finding a bench, they sat down and took in the busy scene on the Cherwell River filled with boaters floating along in punts they'd rented from the boat hire on the other side of the Magdalen Bridge.

The sun was warm and they were both feeling tired after their long walk. It was quite delightful to simply sit and rest and soak up the sunshine. They dozed off.

Lucy woke with a start. Checking her watch, she found it was twenty to three. "Sue, Sue, wake up!" she cried, jumping to her feet.

"Wha', wha'? I wasn't sleeping," protested Sue.

"Never mind. We have to go. It's almost three."

"Flora will wait for us," said Sue, gathering her things together and strolling in the direction of the garden's gift shop.

"I'm not sure she will. She might think we've made other plans," said Lucy, more to herself than Sue.

Inside the shop, Lucy confronted the array of tempting garden merchandise and paused to examine a pair of rose gloves said to be thorn-proof.

Suddenly, it was Sue who was in a hurry. "Come, come, Lucy. You can get those at home, you know."

Lucy reluctantly replaced the gloves. "I know."

They exited the garden together, and Lucy insisted on taking a quick look at the famous Magdalen Bridge, which irritated Sue.

"I don't want to have to hire a taxi or rent a car to get back," she said.

"Look, it's not that far to the tower," said Lucy. "We have to cross the road anyway so we might as well do it here."

The road narrowed at the bridge, which was very much in use and carried a constant stream of traffic. They were able to dart between the slowed vehicles without too much trouble. Then they took a quick peek at the river below where people were lined up and waiting to rent punts. Turning around, they headed back up the busy High Street toward the agreed upon meeting place at the tower. Lucy looked back across the bridge for one last view of the river. It was then that she caught a glimpse of Flora on the opposite side of the bridge, standing and staring down at the river water below.

Something in the way she was standing and the way her attention was so fixed on the river worried Lucy. It was hard to believe the young woman who looked like a homeless person, with her shoulder blades clearly delineated beneath her oversized shirt and her unkempt hair, was a member of one of England's most aristocratic families. "Look!" she told Sue, pointing through the traffic toward Flora. "We have to get over there."

"Hold on, Lucy," cautioned Sue. "We don't want to embarrass her."

"She might do something . . . desperate," said Lucy, spotting a break in the traffic and dashing recklessly back across the roadway, getting a chorus of honks from angry drivers.

By the time she reached the sidewalk, she discovered Flora had moved on and was already some distance ahead of her, making her way toward the tower with her loose clothing flapping about her skeletal frame. Lucy continued along on the left side of the street, with Sue on the other, until she was able to safely cross over once again and join her.

"That was foolish, Lucy," chided Sue. "You could have been killed."

"There was just something in the way she was standing," said Lucy. "It scared me. I was afraid she'd jump or something."

Sue took her hand and squeezed it. "I know. I thought the same thing."

"She knew that boy—the one who died. I'm sure of it," said Lucy.

"Do you think she's doing drugs?" asked Sue, thinking aloud. "It would explain a lot."

"In addition to not eating. She's definitely a troubled soul."

"Poor Poppy is worried about her."

"Maybe instead of worrying, she ought to do something," suggested Lucy.

"I'm sure she tries," said Sue. "It must be a terribly difficult situation."

They were both relieved when they reached the tower and saw Flora waiting for them. She greeted them with a big smile and politely asked if they'd enjoyed their day in town then led them through narrow, winding streets to the parking lot where she'd left the Mini. Once they were in the car, however, she fell silent and seemed preoccupied with her thoughts, actually sailing through a red light.

"Watch out!" exclaimed Sue as they swerved around an approaching van and nearly collided with a bicyclist who twisted her front wheel sharply, causing her bike to tip over. She saved herself by hopping along on one foot until she was able to right her bike and continue on her way while raising a middle finger and shaking it at Flora.

"You could have killed that poor girl," said Lucy, impressed by the cyclist's coordination.

"If I had, they'd probably give me a medal," declared Flora angrily. "Everyone agrees these cyclists are a menace. They're always knocking over pedestrians."

Neither Lucy nor Sue responded and they made the return drive in an uncomfortable silence. Lucy wondered if Flora's outburst was due to embarrassment, but when she caught a glimpse of her expression in the rearview mirror she thought Flora looked terribly sad. When they finally arrived at the manor, Flora didn't bother to park the Mini in the garage but left it in the middle of the stable yard. She hopped out and ran into one of the connected outbuildings, abandoning them without a word.

"Well, that was interesting," said Lucy as they gathered their bags and got out of the car.

"You have to admit she had a point about those cyclists. We almost got run down a few times today."

"I know," agreed Lucy, "but that cyclist had the right-of-way and Flora wasn't paying attention. That girl's got something on her mind, and it's not good."

When they went inside, Sally told them they were just in time for the obligatory afternoon tea with Aunt Millicent and sent them upstairs to the family's private living room. Lucy had expected Aunt Millicent to be a tall and forbidding Maggie Smith type, so she was surprised when they joined Perry and Poppy in the attractively furnished room and were introduced to a very short, very stout woman whose georgette dress smelled of moth balls. Her black, frizzy hair was obviously dyed and was thinning on top. Her Florentine gold necklace was much too tight for her plump neck.

"Since you're Americans, you won't know the proper way to address me, so I better tell you," she said, helping herself to a piece of cake from the plate Perry was passing around. "I'm Lady Wickham, but," she added, as if conferring a special privilege, "you may call me Your Ladyship."

"It's lovely to meet you, Lady Wickham," said Sue, accepting a cup of tea from Poppy.

"I hope you had a pleasant journey," said Lucy, taking a seat among the plump pillows scattered on a Chesterfield sofa. "Did you come far?"

"Not far, but it certainly wasn't pleasant," said Lady Wickham. "Everyone drives so terribly fast these days."

"Flora gave us a lovely tour of Oxford," said Sue, sitting down next to Lucy.

"I hope you didn't have to ride in that ridiculous Mini," said Lady Wickham, raising her eyebrows.

"It was tons of fun," said Lucy. "We had a fine day."

"More cake, Aunt?" offered Perry.

"Oh, all right," said Lady Wickham, taking a second piece. "Of course this walnut cake is nothing like it used to be when I was a girl. Then, we thought we'd died and gone to heaven if there was Fullers walnut cake for tea."

"Fullers has been out of business for quite a while," said Poppy.

"Times change, and not for the better, I find," said Lady Wickham with a dismissive glance at the tea tray loaded with an abundant assortment of cakes, sandwiches, and scones, as well as Devonshire cream, butter, and various jams. "Take this marmalade, for instance. Store bought." She sighed. "We always used to make our own with Lyle's golden syrup."

"I find Cooper's does it better than I can," said Perry.

"And why are you doing the cooking?" demanded Lady Wickham. "Can't you afford a cook?"

"I enjoy it. It's simple as that," said Perry.

"And I suppose you enjoy accommodating your American guests in the servants' quarters instead of proper guest rooms, and putting me in that dreadful Chinese torture chamber with writhing dragons climbing all over the walls."

"Aunt," began Poppy in a deliberately soothing tone, "you know that wallpaper is quite special. Art students come here to study it."

"The countess's bedroom is a feature of the house tour," said Perry. "Our visitors expect to see it. That suite of furniture is quite remarkable."

"You wouldn't want to wake up in the morning with a crowd of people staring at you, would you?" asked Flora.

"Certainly not," declared Lady Wickham, plucking a couple sandwiches from the tea tray. "If it were up to me, Moreton Manor would remain a private home, like my very own Fairleigh."

"You're very fortunate to be able to maintain Fairleigh," said Perry. "We have to cope with roof repairs and death duties and all sorts of enormous expenses."

"We consider ourselves fortunate to be able to keep Moreton from rack and ruin, and to share it with our visitors," said Poppy, looking up as Winifred arrived, along with another woman. "And tonight we're eating in the dining room. It will be quite like old times."

"I'm sorry to interrupt," began Winifred. "But Jane and I did want to have a word with you about the damaged painting."

Lady Wickham pounced on this bit of information. "Damage? What painting?"

"The general," said Perry. "He fell off the wall."

"My goodness! How could that happen?"

"An accident, Aunt," said Poppy. "Let me introduce Winifred Wynn, our curator, and her colleague Jane Sliptoe, who is here as a consultant from the National Gallery. She's here to examine the damage and help us plan a course of action."

"And since you're here, would you care for some tea?" offered Perry.

"I would love a cup," said Jane, who was dressed professionally in a crisp white shirt and black pantsuit. "Milk, no sugar."

"Just a slice of lemon for me," said Winifred.

Perry poured while the two women seated themselves.

Winifred accepted her cup, took a sip, and followed it with a deep breath, as if she were about to plunge into a deep pool. "Do you want the good news first or the bad?"

"Is the general done for?" asked Perry.

"No, no. The general can be fixed, and it won't be too expensive, either. A bit of glue ought to do it."

Poppy let out a great breath. "That is good news. What a relief."

"So what is the bad news?" asked Perry.

"Well," began Jane, "Winifred asked me to take a look around the gallery where you're having the hat show. She was particularly interested in several Italian paintings attributed to Veronese and Titian."

"Attributed?" asked Poppy suspiciously.

"Wrongly, I'm afraid," said Jane. "They're copies. The sort of thing a young nobleman would collect on a grand tour. Actually quite a good example of that sort of stuff. Very high quality . . ."

"But not originals," said Poppy with a sigh.

"I took a look 'round the chapel, too," said Winifred, setting her cup and saucer on the coffee table. "There's a very good gold reliquary in there. I suspect it's a Bonnanotte and quite a nice one."

"I could use it in the hat show," exclaimed Perry. "It would go terribly well with that bishop's miter."

"Or we could sell it to pay for those, um, other repairs," said Poppy.

"What repairs?" demanded Lady Wickham, her eyebrows shooting up.

"Oh dear. Just look at the time," said Perry, pointing to his watch.

"Yes!" exclaimed Poppy. "It is getting late and we have to dress for dinner."

That was the signal that afternoon tea was over. The others went their separate ways, but Lucy and Sue stayed to help Perry collect the cups and saucers and load them into the dishwasher before they went to their rooms to change into their finery for the formal dinner in the manor's grand dining room.

In general, Lucy was skeptical of enterprises that required new clothes, but when she caught a glimpse of herself in a mirror as she descended the magnificent staircase in the hall, she decided this was a lifestyle she could definitely get used to. She felt as if she were in a movie when she stepped into the salon she'd seen earlier on the tour with Maurice and accepted a glass of sherry from Dishy Geoff togged out in crisp white shirt and black jacket with tails. She paused for a moment, taking sips of sherry and admiring the spacious room, which felt rather like an enormous tent because the ceiling was draped with yards and yards of rich, red, paisley fabric. The parquet floor was dotted with Persian rugs and the furniture was largely French, with curved legs and plenty of gilding.

She looked for Sue, who had gone ahead, and found her standing in front of an embossed leather screen, talking with Perry. Poppy was helping her elderly aunt adjust her shawl, a process that seemed to be hopelessly complicated, and Gerald was in a corner with the leggy blonde she'd seen at the folly. She was wearing a strapless red number that showed a great deal of bosom that rose and fell with every breath.

"Lucy, I don't think you know Vickie Prior-Keyes," said Flora, grabbing her by the arm and dragging her across the room. She was dressed head to toe in black, which made her look rather like Morticia Addams . . . if Morticia had been on a starvation diet. "Vickie is a buddy of mine from school."

Gerald didn't seem particularly pleased by the interruption and neither did Vickie.

"Delighted, I'm sure," she said with an expression that belied her words. "Now, Flora, I've been telling your dad that heritage is a valuable tool for image makers, and you have heritage to spare."

"What do you mean?" asked Quimby, who had joined the group and was clearly enthralled by Vickie's décolletage.

"Corporate sponsors, of course," said Vickie.

"Corporate sponsors?" asked Poppy, taking her husband's arm in a possessive way. "Like who?"

"Anyone, really. Take the tea you serve in the café. Whatever it is."

"Twining's, I believe," said Poppy.

"Well, I would suggest approaching them to see if they will pay for the right to mention that in an ad—Twining's, the tea served at Moreton Manor."

"Rather weak tea, I think," said Poppy with a chuckle. "Since they've got a royal warrant."

"Well, perhaps that wasn't the best example," said Vickie, allowing her breasts to rise and fall rather dramatically. "It's the idea of the thing. Ketchup or mustard or carpet cleaner—there are numerous possibilities."

"In my day," declared Lady Wickham from the throne-like chair where she was holding court with Maurice and Winifred, "commerce was never discussed at the dinner table."

Maurice, ever the sycophant, was beaming with pleasure, apparently thrilled to be talking with a countess, but Winifred seemed to be looking for an escape route. It came in the form of a black man in a clerical collar, who was entering the room holding hands with a white woman.

"Exactly. We should save talk of business for tomorrow," said Poppy in the unusual position of agreeing with her aunt. "I do hope everyone knows everyone. Aunt, I don't know if you've met our new vicar, Robert Goodenough, and his wife, Sarah."

Sarah, who had curly blond hair and was wearing a dazzling African print dress, gave everyone a big smile. "We're so pleased to be here."

"I suppose this is quite an improvement from Africa," said Lady Wickham. "What with that ebony virus and those Loko Harem terrorists."

"Actually, we're from Hoxton," said Robert with a smile.

"And it's *Ebola* virus and *Boko* Haram," said Flora, rolling her eyes.

"And the children?" inquired Poppy. "Are they settling in?"

"Very well," said Sarah. "They like their new school very much, and I've been enjoying the garden. I'm growing lettuce and all sorts of lovely vegetables."

"I love gardening," said Lucy. "Coming from chilly New England, I'm terribly jealous of your gentle English climate."

"You must come and see my garden," invited Sarah. "Are you free tomorrow? For high tea?"

"High tea. A workingman's meal," sniffed Lady Wickham. "Beans on toast, I suppose."

"I'll do you better than that," said Sarah with a tolerant smile toward Lady Wickham.

"I've heard such lovely things about your house, Your Ladyship," said Maurice as Dishy Geoff made another pass with the tray containing glasses of sherry. "Can you tell me about it?"

"It's nothing very fancy," said Lady Wickham, accepting a fresh glass. "Just a simple Georgian, but I do think that's the nicest sort of house."

"I quite agree," said Maurice. "Lovely proportions."

"And I do have some rather nice bits and pieces from my family," she continued.

"Do tell," urged Maurice, before savoring a sip of sherry.

"Well, this ring you see," she said, presenting him with a rather plump, unmanicured hand. "I'm told it's a rather good emerald."

Maurice took her hand and bent his head to take a better look. "It's magnificent. Such clarity."

"Don't swallow the damn thing," advised Gerald, draining his glass of sherry and reaching for another.

"Maurice is revising the manor's guidebook," said Poppy. "He's discovered a wealth of information—"

"Costing a damned fortune, too," grumbled Gerald.

"These old houses are so rich in history," said Sue.

"Well, of course. You have no history to speak of in America," said Lady Wickham.

"Our town was settled in the sixteen hundreds by people who left England," said Lucy, who was finding Her Ladyship's condescension rather irritating. "They must have been very unhappy to risk their lives on a treacherous sea voyage and to struggle in a new land."

"Probably thieves or pirates," sniffed Lady Wickham.

"Do tell us about your upcoming show, Desi," said Poppy, eager to change the subject.

"It's *Sleeping Beauty*. One of my favorites," said Desi.

"Are you the prince?" asked Sarah.

"Prince! That's a good one," scoffed Gerald. "He's a prancing priss."

Lady Wickham shrieked with laughter. "He's a prance, get it? Not a prince. A prance!"

The sudden noise startled Dishy Geoff and he dropped the tray full of empty glasses, smashing several of the precious crystal wine glasses.

"No matter," said Poppy, determinedly calm.

"I'm terribly sorry," said Geoff, stooping to gather up the broken bits.

"It wasn't his fault," said Desi, defending Geoff.

"I think we should go in to dinner," said Poppy.

Lucy turned to Sue, who was now standing beside her. "How many courses?" she asked, under her breath.

"Probably far too many," replied Sue.

Chapter Eight

Lucy groaned and rolled over in her sleep.

Someone was running a chain saw in her bedroom and another crazed lumberjack was driving a wood-splitting maul into her skull. She wanted to call for help, but her mouth was filled with cotton. She was gagged. This was bad, very bad indeed. She had to find a way to save herself! But that would require opening her eyes and she could tell . . . right through her closed eyelids . . . that the light was intensely bright. So bright that it would hurt.

The chainsaw noise stopped, which was a mercy, but was immediately replaced by the cheerful ringing tones of "Frère Jacques"—her cell phone's ring tone. If only she could answer it, she could call for help!

She woke with a start and lifted her head from the pillow. Immediately, she felt nauseous, so she let it fall back and groped the nightstand with one hand. Realizing her hands were mercifully not tied, she gave a grunt. She wasn't a captive after all.

Finding the phone, she held it in front of her face and peeped at it through slitted eyes, making out a familiar shape.

Bill! It was Bill calling. He would rescue her.

She swiped at the phone with a clumsy gesture and heard his voice. "Lucy! Lucy!!"

She wanted to speak, to tell him about the maul in her head, but her mouth was so dry that all she could manage was another groan.

"Are you all right?" he asked. "What's the matter?"

"Hung . . . hunggg . . ."

"You have a hangover?" he asked.

"Unnnh!" she replied.

"That's too bad, but all you need, sweetheart, is the hair of the dog. That'll cure you."

The very thought made her nauseous. She waited for the feeling to pass then ran a fuzzy tongue over her lips. "Unh," she replied.

"Well, since you're monosyllabic, I'll do the talking," said Bill, his voice brimming with enthusiasm and energy. "Remember that friend of Toby's, Doug Fitzpatrick? Well, I ran into him at the pub. I just got home, actually. I was headed to bed and then I remembered the time difference and figured you'd be up since you're such an early riser. This news is too good to keep. Anyway, we got talking, Doug and I, and he's building a deck and said he wasn't sure if he should use treated wood or mahogany or that AZEK stuff and I gave him some ideas. Anyway, it turns out that he's a financial planner and he said since I'd been so generous with my knowledge about decks, well, he had a really good tip for me.

"We know that Zoe's four years at Strethmore will cost in the neighborhood of two hundred forty thousand bucks, and they're giving her ten a year so that brings it down to two hundred thou. There's seventy thousand left in the college fund and that's only enough to send her to the state university . . . which she really doesn't want to do. Anyway, this Doug told me he has this amazing opportunity that would double the seventy thousand in three months, so with a hundred and forty thousand, we'd only have to come up with fifteen thousand a year. We could use the home equity line for that, which is much smarter than taking out those education loans. The interest is much lower. So what do you think?"

"Mmmm," replied Lucy, who hadn't really been listening after he started rattling off numbers.

"I know. You probably think it's too good to be true. That's what I thought at first, but Luce, you know, ever since I left Wall Street, I've missed wheeling and dealing and making real money.

This is the sort of thing that the big guys, the insiders, do all the time. This is my chance to get back in the game."

The maul was still stuck in her head, but Lucy figured she could live with it. She let out a big sigh and sank into sleep, the phone slipping from her fingers.

When she woke up a couple hours later, she still had a headache, but it wasn't nearly as bad. She still felt horrible, but her mind was clear enough to recall the lavish formal dinner of the night before. How anyone could manage to consume eight courses accompanied by six different wines, followed by coffee and liqueurs was a mystery to her, but the rest of the company seemed to have no difficulty.

Her Ladyship, for one, had chomped her way through every course, leaving nary a crumb on her plate. It was no surprise that Gerald drank heavily, but he wasn't the only one. Quimby had kept pace with him, and Vickie and Sue hadn't been far behind. Even Robert Goodenough drank rather more than she would expect of a man of the cloth, but perhaps she was simply reflecting the Puritan attitudes that lingered in New England. She certainly felt a nagging sense of guilt and considered her headache was well deserved, but that didn't stop her from downing a couple Advil. She thought she might have actually spoken to Bill on the phone, but she wasn't sure, and resolved to call him later when she felt a bit better.

Lucy assumed Sue was sleeping off the effects of the booze. When she cracked open the door to Sue's room from the connecting bathroom, she found her bed was empty and neatly made. Returning to her own room, Lucy got dressed slowly and attempted to tidy up the clothes she'd tossed every which way the night before but found that bending down to gather the stockings and underwear strewn on the floor was really too painful. Maybe later, she decided, heading downstairs for some coffee.

Much to her surprise, Sue was already in the kitchen, looking remarkably perky as she sat at the scrubbed pine table with her mug of coffee. Perry was toasting up crumpets, which Poppy was buttering, and a woman Lucy had not seen before was getting in their way. She was tall and thin, with very short and badly cut hair, and was wearing an extremely plain gray dress topped with a faded black cardigan that did nothing for her pasty complexion. It was hard to guess her age, but Lucy thought she was probably younger than she looked, since it was clear she wasn't interested in her appearance. She moved surely and quickly, however, which probably meant she was in her early sixties.

"M'lady must have her tea," she was saying. "Where would I find a tray? And why is it taking the kettle so long to boil, may I ask?"

"We prefer coffee in the morning so the kettle's not on," said Perry. "You have to plug it in."

"What sort of house doesn't have a kettle on the boil in the morning, I ask you," fumed the woman, lifting the pot and finding it empty. She rolled her eyes dramatically before taking it over to the sink and filling it. "M'lady had a terrible night, you know. There's an awful pong in her room. It's very noticeable." She sniffed. "Not at all the sort of thing you expect in a grand house like this, but then again, I told her, things aren't what they used to be."

"Lucy," said Perry, "I don't think you've met Harrison, Aunt's, um, companion."

Lucy had seated herself beside Sue at the table and was trying hard not to look as awful as she felt.

Harrison tightened her lips and glared at Perry. "I am not a companion. I am a lady's maid."

"Probably the last of a noble breed," said Poppy. "Coffee, Lucy?"

Lucy managed a nod and a grateful smile.

"They ought to put her on the endangered list," cracked Perry with a mischievous grin.

"Enough of that," chided Harrison with a sniff. "I will need tea and a pot, a cup and saucer, cream and sugar, toast and silverware, a pot of jam."

"And you know exactly where to find all of those things since you've been here many times and know this kitchen as well as you know your own," said Poppy, filling a mug with coffee and bringing it over to Lucy.

"Humph," said Harrison, setting a small teapot on a tray with a thump. She continued collecting the items she needed for Lady Wickham's breakfast tray, constantly crossing Perry and Poppy and even tangling with the dogs. "Blasted beasts," she finally declared, kicking Churchy, who yelped before slouching off to his bed in the corner.

Poppy protested. "There's no need for that."

But she was speaking to Harrison's back as she disappeared through the doorway, bearing the breakfast tray. When she turned to push the swinging door open with her bottom, Lucy noticed a strange bulge in the sweater beneath one of her arms and wondered, fleetingly, if she had some sort of tumor.

"Awful woman," muttered Perry, setting a platter on the table. "Crumpets, anyone?"

"Yummy," declared Sue, eagerly reaching for a couple crumpets and surprising Lucy, who had never known her friend to actually eat breakfast.

"Maybe later," said Lucy with a sigh, staring into her coffee cup.

"Oh, dear," said Poppy in a sympathetic tone. "I think Lucy has a case of the Irish flu."

"Oh, dear. You're undoubtedly suffering the wrath of grapes," said Perry.

"My mother, who knew a thing or two about the horrors, used to rely on a Prairie Oyster. You take an egg and break it into a glass of beer," suggested Sue.

"I don't think so," said Lucy, feeling a surge of nausea. She rose quickly from the table and pointed in the direction of the downstairs loo, making it just in time to throw up in the toilet. She was horribly embarrassed and wanted nothing more than to slink back to bed, but neither Sue nor Perry and Poppy seemed to disapprove of her condition.

"What you need," said Perry in a bright tone, "is fresh air." He glanced to the windows where sunshine was streaming in. "It's a perfect day for a picnic in the bluebell woods. What say you all?"

"That would be delightful," said Sue. "Do you think you could manage a picnic, Lucy?"

"Actually," said Lucy, finding herself taking an interest in her coffee, "I'm feeling much better."

"Terrific," said Perry. "I will start packing the picnic basket."

"Hold on," protested Poppy. "It's all very well and good for you to go chasing after bluebells and butterflies and rainbows, but I have to meet with Quimby. He had the builders in yesterday and I suspect he has bad news for us."

"How can I help?" asked Perry, raising an eyebrow. "Do you want me to hold your hand?"

"That would be ever so nice," said Poppy.

"Quimby will be gentle, I'm sure," said Perry, rising from the table and disappearing into a pantry, from which he returned carrying a vintage picnic basket.

"You're a rat," said Poppy with a smile.

"No, I'm more like Toad," said Perry. "I think that's why I've always loved *The Wind in the Willows.*"

"It's all right. You go and tear around the countryside, just like Toad. I'll make you pay when you come home."

"Speaking of paying," said Perry, staring into the open refrigerator. "I could have sworn we had a couple bottles of May wine in here."

"We do," said Poppy.

"No. We only have one."

"Perhaps Flora or Desi had a late-night party," suggested Poppy.

Or perhaps, thought Lucy, remembering the mysterious bulge under Harrison's arm, the lady's maid was planning an early-morning tipple.

Lucy felt much improved after drinking the coffee, so she headed back upstairs to tidy up the clothes still scattered on the floor. She didn't have much energy, though, and after gathering everything into a heap, she threw it onto the closet floor, sat down with her phone, and called Bill. The call went to voice mail, however, so she left a message for him to call her back. Then she brushed her teeth, grabbed her jacket, and went into Sue's room to see if her friend was ready.

Sue was studying her limited wardrobe and trying to decide whether to stay in the tailored slacks she'd worn to breakfast or to change into jeans.

Lucy knew it could take quite a while, so she decided to go on without her. When she reached the big family kitchen, she found the picnic basket sitting on a table, ready to go, but there was no sign of Perry or anyone else. She added her jacket to the pile of neatly folded blankets and, at a bit of a loss for something to do, decided to explore the main house. She had been wondering what the rooms that were not included on the tour were like, so she made her way through the underground tunnel to the manor. Reaching the utilitarian flight of stairs, she continued on up past the first floor with its enormous hall and followed the twists and turns of the staircase until she reached the next landing.

When she stepped through the doorway, she found herself in a wide, carpeted hall where the doorways to various rooms were interspersed with antique chests, tables, chairs, and lots of paintings. There were numerous bouquets of garden flowers, and the window at the end of the hallway was open, but the air was not fresh. Harrison was right; there was an undeniable stink in the air. Lucy, who lived in an antique house in the country was familiar with the smell and put it down to an animal that had died inside a wall. She knew from experience that the corpse of a tiny little house mouse could give off a fearful stench.

Fortunately, she also knew from experience that it didn't last long and in a day or two the smell would certainly be gone. She returned to the stairway and descended to the bottom, where she met Sally in the tunnel.

She was marching along, pushing an upright vacuum cleaner and muttering to herself. "Hares, hares, hares."

"Hares?" asked Lucy.

"It's the last day of April, so I'm saying *hares*," she answered.

"Whatever for?" asked Lucy.

"Good luck. Between you and me, they could do with a bit of luck around here." She rolled her eyes. "D'you know there was a body in the maze? You'd think people would have the decency to die in their own backyards, wouldn't you? I don't know what the world's coming to, I tell you. So I'm doing what I can and tomorrow, the first of May, I'll say *rabbits*."

"Well, with any luck that awful smell will be gone. Probably a mouse or something."

"Oh, yes," said Sally, grimacing. "Lady Wickham has been on about it, that's for sure. And that Harrison has probably gone through several cans of air freshener, which just makes everything smell worse." She paused, thinking. "Do you and your friend have any special plans for today? I was just wondering because I'd like to hoover those rooms."

"Perry is taking us on a picnic in the bluebell woods," Lucy said.

"Well, better wear your raincoat."

Lucy glanced out the window, where the sun was brightly shining. "Really?"

"This is England," said Sally. "It rains a lot."

"Thanks for the advice," said Lucy, holding the swinging door open so Sally could push the vacuum through and into the kitchen.

The picnic basket and other things, including her jacket, were gone so Lucy hurried on outside. The others were in the stable courtyard where Perry was loading the picnic things into the Land Rover and Sue was already sitting in the front passenger seat. Lucy climbed in the back, where Church and Monty greeted her happily, wagging their tails and smiling doggy smiles, regaling her with doggy breath.

"Don't mind them," said Perry, slamming the hatch shut and climbing behind the wheel.

"I don't," said Lucy, who really did as each dog had claimed a window, leaving her to make do in the middle of the seat.

"I just love dogs," said Sue, who had never owned a dog, or even a cat, in her life.

"I can't imagine life without at least one," said Perry. "The more the merrier. Right, Lucy?"

"I have a Lab," said Lucy, thinking of Libby back home in Maine. "She's getting old and sleeps a lot."

"These fellas are only a year old. They're brothers," said Perry. "They're rambunctious now but they'll calm down."

"They're lucky dogs, having all this," said Sue, indicating the manor's extensive grounds with a wave of her hand.

"They just get to enjoy it," said Perry. "They don't have to fret and worry about making payroll and keeping the house in good repair, like Poppy and I do. It's a real challenge and it seems to get harder every year."

Lucy was finding it hard to sympathize. For one thing, Monty and Churchy were jumping around in the backseat, walking all over her and occasionally smacking her with their powerful tails. When that happened, they seemed to realize apologies were due, which meant giving her a sloppy lick on the face.

Putting the annoying dogs aside and gazing out the car windows at the passing scene, she thought that Perry was very lucky indeed to live in such beautiful countryside. "Is all this part of the estate?"

"Oh, yes, we've got thousands of acres."

Amazing, she thought. Back home in Maine nobody but the timber companies owned thousands of acres; most of the land had been carved into small farms hundreds of years ago, and even those had been shrinking as bits were sold off for houses and shopping malls.

"Well, here we are," announced Perry, turning off the road onto a narrow track that wound through a sparse woodland where the ground was covered with a sea of blue flowers.

Lucy had never seen anything like it. There were hundreds, thousands of the blooms, and the color was so intense that it seemed to radiate blueness. The very air seemed to vibrate with it, like heat waves rising from an asphalt road on a hot summer day. A sweet fragrance filled the air.

"Wow," said Sue, taking it all in. "This is gorgeous."

Lucy was already out of the car, examining the plants, which she decided were like the wood hyacinths in her garden at home. Except that where those sort of popped up scattershot, and came in different colors, the bluebells had grown together in a mass, crowding out everything except the trees, creating an incredible expanse of vibrant blue.

"How do you do this?" asked Lucy, watching as the dogs bounded off through the flowers. "Did you plant them? Do you fertilize them? Cut them down after they bloom?"

"No," said Perry, opening the hatch. "They just grow like this.

It's been this way for as long as I can remember." He handed Lucy a folded plaid blanket. "We usually set the picnic out under that big old beech tree," he said, with a nod. "Just follow the path."

When she reached the spot Perry had indicated, Lucy found the vast tree with its elephantine gray trunk had created a sheltering, tent-like environment beneath its massive branches, some of which grew downward, even meeting the ground. She and Sue spread out the blankets and cushions they had brought, making themselves comfortable while Perry got a portable CD player going with some soft rock. Sting was singing about golden fields of barley, and Lucy was humming along, thinking of azure fields of bluebells when Monty bounded up, proudly displaying something furry he had clamped in his mouth.

"Give!" ordered Perry and the dog very reluctantly dropped the furry object right in front of Lucy on the blanket.

"It's a baby bunny, and it's still alive," she exclaimed, eager to save the poor little thing. "We should take it to a vet."

"Don't be ridiculous," said Perry, scooping up the little creature and deftly snapping its neck before tossing it aside, where it disappeared beneath the bluebells. Both dogs chased after it as if it were a tennis ball.

Seeing Lucy's shocked expression, Perry offered an explanation. "Rabbits are pests. They cause a lot of damage."

"Even Peter got in trouble with Mr. McGregor," said Sue with a sad smile. "And Mrs. McGregor baked his father into a pie."

"We don't have pie. We have Cornish pasties and Scotch eggs and lovely strawberries, but first I think we should celebrate this beautiful day with a glass of May wine," said Perry, busying himself with a corkscrew.

Soon, the unfortunate baby bunny was forgotten as they sipped the sweet woodruff-flavored wine and nibbled on the delicious foods Perry had brought. Scenting the food, the dogs joined them, settling down on the blankets and falling asleep. They played a casual, hilarious game of Charades, and they laughed at Monty, who was continuing to chase rabbits in his dreams. Eventually they found themselves yawning and drifting off, lulled by the soothing music, the warm breezes, and the heady May wine.

They were wakened by a spring shower, proving Sally's prediction correct as they quickly gathered up the picnic things and ran to the car.

"Oh bugger!" exclaimed Perry. "I'm late! I'm supposed to meet some art students who are donating works for the show."

The dogs jumped in, settling on either side of Lucy as before, and they were off, bouncing down the unpaved track until they reached the road, then Perry drove much too fast on the twisting country roads. Lucy tried closing her eyes, afraid to see what might be coming around a corner, but that made her feel carsick. She concentrated instead on praying for their safe return to the manor, and her prayers were answered when Perry turned into the stable yard and braked.

The dogs were thrown off the seat, the jumbled picnic things crashed in the way back and Lucy and Sue were very glad they were wearing seatbelts. Perry hopped out of the car and hurried inside, calling his apologies to them.

When they had gotten out of the car, and realized they and the dogs were still in one piece, Sue announced she was in need of an allergy pill. "Maybe it's the dogs, maybe the flowers, but I'm feeling miserable," she said, giving her nose a good blow.

"Go on," said Lucy, "I'll take the picnic basket back to the kitchen."

When she and the dogs arrived in the kitchen, they found Poppy sitting at the scrubbed pine table, looking rather dejected.

"What's the matter?" asked Lucy.

Poppy drained her mug of tea, set it back down on the table, and refilled it from a brown crockery pot. She stared into the mug for rather a long time before speaking. "Quimby says the dry rot is everywhere," she said, dabbing at her eyes with a tissue. "He says they have to check the roof, too, as water must have gotten in somehow. We just had the roof done a couple years ago." She sighed. "It's going to cost millions, maybe billions. I don't know how we're going to afford it."

"I'm sure you'll find a way," said Lucy. It was the sort of thing you were supposed to say in such circumstances. She was unpacking the picnic basket, storing the leftovers in the refrigerator and putting the dirty crockery in the dishwasher.

"It's all the general's fault," muttered Poppy. "He had no business falling off that wall. There's Aunt Millicent's horrible smell and now this! It's really too much."

"But this is the end of the trouble," said Lucy, closing the dishwasher door. "Trouble comes in threes and you've had three catastrophes: the general, the dry rot, and the body in the maze. Now you're done with trouble."

Poppy stared at her. "I hope you're right, but somehow I have a feeling that the worst is yet to come."

Chapter Nine

"So, Lucy, are you feeling better and enjoying yourself?" asked Sue. The two friends were walking along a footpath that led through the estate to the village where they were going to have high tea at the vicarage with the Goodenoughs.

"I am. I really am," said Lucy, realizing with surprise that it was true. The black mood that had dogged her for so long was definitely losing its grip. "Everything here is so different, it's like being on another planet."

"I'm glad the change is doing you good," said Sue.

"How about you?" asked Lucy. "Are you having a good time?"

"I am, mostly, but I have to say I'm glad we're getting out this evening. There seems to be quite a gloomy atmosphere at the manor, and it makes me feel guilty about enjoying myself."

"Poppy does seem to take things rather hard," said Lucy. "And they really have had a run of bad luck."

"Well, being married to Gerald would make anyone gloomy," observed Sue.

"And then there's Aunt Millicent—"

"And the awful Harrison!" exclaimed Sue, finishing Lucy's sentence.

"Let's not think about any of that," said Lucy as they reached a vantage point from which to view the village and paused to admire the handful of thatched stone cottages clustered around the ancient stone church. The vicarage was a newer addition, built of red brick in neo-Gothic style with pointy windows and set in a large garden.

Lucy and Sue continued to follow the path, which descended gently and brought them to the vicarage garden gate. Two little boys, twins about eight years old, were chasing a soccer ball around the lawn. One gave the ball a ferocious kick and sent it soaring right over Lucy and Sue's heads and out of the garden. Lucy chased it a little ways down the path and retrieved it, bringing it back and handing it to one of the boys as she and Sue entered the garden. He took it and ran off, only to be stopped by his mother, Sarah.

"Matthew! What do you say to our visitors?"

The little boy stopped in his tracks and turned to face them, a puzzled expression on his round brown face. Lucy thought he looked quite adorable dressed in a school uniform of navy blue shorts with a white shirt that had come untucked. A loosened striped necktie hung around his open collar.

After a moment's thought he said, "Very pleased to meet you."

Lucy and Sue smiled, but Sarah was not pleased. "I think you forgot to thank Lucy for fetching your ball."

"Oh, that's right," said Matthew. "Thank you very much."

"You're very welcome," said Lucy.

"And Mark, I think you also have something to say, since you are the one who almost hit our friends with the ball."

"I'm very sorry," said Mark, whose high socks had slipped down to his ankles. "I didn't mean for the ball to go so high."

"No matter," said Sue. "No one was hurt."

"Well, back to your game, boys. I want to show our guests my Bible garden," said Sarah, leading the way through a hedge. "We haven't been here long, so it's just starting," she explained, waving a hand at a neatly organized flower bed. "There are over one hundred twenty-five plants mentioned in the Bible. I used box for an edging. It's mentioned in Isaiah."

"I see roses from the Song of Solomon," said Lucy, naming one of the few Biblical references she was familiar with.

"That's right," said Sarah with an approving nod. "I know you mentioned that you love to garden, but are you also a person of faith?"

Sue found this question extremely amusing and Lucy was forced to make a confession.

"I spend a lot more time in my garden than in church," she admitted, "and I mostly grow vegetables."

"What's this plant?" asked Sue, pointing to a handsome specimen with oval, rather bumpy leaves.

"That's sage. It's mentioned in Exodus."

"I didn't know you could grow it," said Sue. "Mine always came in jars."

"It's easy," said Lucy. "You can keep it in a pot in the kitchen."

"You could add parsley and basil and you'd have a little kitchen herb garden," said Sarah. "That's what I did when we lived in London and I had to content myself with house plants. It's been such a joy to me to have a real garden."

"The house in Hoxton was full of plants," said Robert, joining them and giving his wife a kiss on the cheek. "Sarah can make anything grow"—he beamed with pride—"even those two little rapscallions."

"Well, come on, everyone. I think I hear the kettle singing."

"Matthew, Mark! Tea!" called Robert, and the boys came running.

The kitchen table was already set with blue and white dishes in a flowery pattern arranged on a red and white striped oilcloth. Sarah busied herself filling a big brown teapot while Robert supervised the boys, making sure they actually washed their hands.

"Sometimes they just rinse them and dry them on the towel," said Sarah. "They're always mystified that I can tell. I say it's my super mother sense."

"But it's just the dirt they leave on the towel," said Lucy, taking a seat.

"Exactly," said Sarah, placing a large salad topped with ham and hard boiled eggs in the middle of the table, and adding a basket of bread. "I hope you don't mind a simple supper."

"It looks delicious," said Sue.

"And a welcome change from that enormous formal dinner last night," added Lucy.

Robert and the boys soon joined them and, after bowing their heads for a quick grace, they all tucked in to the lovely salad. Lucy found herself exclaiming over the lettuce and the early peas, which came from the Goodenoughs' garden, as well as the crusty bread from the village bakery and the sweet butter from the estate farm.

"The eggs came from there, too," said Robert.

"Just some of the advantages of living in the country," said Sarah. "And there's rhubarb custard for dessert."

"Rhubarb!" exclaimed Lucy. "My favorite."

When they had finished eating, Sarah set the boys to clearing the table, and Robert suggested they might like a tour of the church. He led the way, taking them in through a side door. "It's quite old. Parts date from the thirteenth century, or so I'm told," he said proudly.

Lucy and Sue followed as he led them past stained-glass windows and around carved inscriptions in the stone floor that marked tombs. Numerous brasses were hung on the walls, mostly memorializing fallen soldiers from the British Empire's numerous wars. A single candle burned behind the altar, which was covered with a white cloth embroidered with gold thread.

"I've heard that church attendance has been dropping steadily in Europe," said Lucy. "Is that the case here?"

"Not if I can help it," said Robert with a hearty chuckle. "I can't do it alone, of course, but there is a solid core of members who are working hard to keep the church a vital part of the community. We have evensong on Sunday afternoons. We have musical programs, speakers, yoga classes, all sorts of activities. Sarah also does a lot, especially with the mums and babies."

"It's very peaceful," said Sue, and Lucy realized it was true. There wasn't a sound to be heard, except the twilight twittering of the birds.

"I think I could stay here forever," Sue added, surprising Lucy.

Robert nodded his head. "Things can be a bit complicated up at the manor."

"They have so many problems," said Sue. "They've discovered dry rot, for one thing. I guess it's going to be terribly expensive."

"It is," said Robert. "They had some here, before my time.

Some of the older members told me about it. It was a crisis for the congregation."

"You see the photos of these beautiful old country houses and they seem like something out of a fairy tale," said Lucy. "But the reality is quite different."

"Robert, you mustn't keep these ladies cooped up in this musty old church," said Sarah, joining them. "It's lovely outside, and I have a bottle of dandelion wine."

"What about the boys?" asked Robert as they stepped through the doorway.

"They're doing their school work," said Sarah. "They'll be busy for quite a while."

After they'd settled themselves in chairs on the lawn and been provided with glasses of homemade wine, the conversation drifted once again to the manor and the people who lived there.

"I was saying to Robert that life in a grand house like the manor seems enviable, but I really prefer a simpler lifestyle," said Lucy.

"I really admire Poppy and Perry for undertaking the work of maintaining the manor," said Robert. "It's a national treasure. It's part of our country's heritage and it should be preserved."

"If you ask me," said Sarah, "I think they're struggling to maintain a way of life that really wasn't very nice and is pretty much over and done with. I marvel at it sometimes, the way people will happily spend their hard-earned money to see these monstrous houses that were built on the backs of their ancestors. Where do they think the wealth came from? It came from mills and mines and railways, and from conquered people in the so-called Empire, from oppressed and overworked people who had no choice but to please their masters if they wished to survive."

"We decided that the visitors see themselves as the lord and lady for the day, not as the scullery maid or footman," said Sue.

"I think you're right," said Robert. "And in their vision, the lord and lady lead fairy-tale lives, with no problems at all."

"Unlike Poppy and Perry, who seem beset by trouble," said Sue, who was on her third glass of wine. "And it's not just the manor. They have family troubles, too. Gerald doesn't approve of Desi and Flora is wasting away."

"I think we can all agree that wealth and status do not guarantee happiness," said Robert. "In fact, sometimes I think it's quite the opposite. Some of the happiest people I know are quite content with very little. They trust in the Lord."

"Ah, Robert," sighed Sarah. "He loves the parables—the widow's mite, the loaves and fishes, the lilies of the field."

"And that we should not judge lest we be judged," said Robert.

"That's all very well and good, Robert," said Sarah, "but don't we have a responsibility to stand up against injustice and demand what's right? If Poppy and Gerald and their sort had their way, there would still be fox hunting. And children like ours wouldn't stand a chance of getting into a good grammar school, much less university."

"I have to admit I was a bit shocked today," said Lucy, "when the dogs brought Perry a baby rabbit and he just snapped its neck and tossed it aside. And then there was the poor young fellow who overdosed in the maze. . . ."

"We heard about that," said Robert. "Any idea who he was?"

"Poppy said the police told her his name but she forgot it," said Lucy, a note of outrage in her voice. "She thought it might have been Eric something."

"Well, I'm not surprised," said Sarah, giving her husband a look. "It's typical, cold-blooded country squire behavior. They simply turn a blind eye to anything disagreeable."

"I will be sure to pray for the poor young man's soul on Sunday," promised Robert.

"I think you should pray for the dogs to behave themselves," said Sarah with a smile. "They are awful and nobody even tries to control them. Perry and Poppy wouldn't think of leashing them. I can't tell you how many times I've had to shoo them out of my garden." Sarah paused. "They dug up my hollyhocks, you know."

"It's worth your life to move one off a sofa," said Sue.

"Now, now," said Robert. "I think you're forgetting all the good that they do. The manor employs hundreds of people. It's the biggest employer in the county."

"Robert can always find something good to say about everyone," said Sarah. "Even when we lived in Hoxton, not the fashionable south side but the north where there were some pretty desperate characters, he would insist that we should love our neighbors. That's a tall order when the neighbors are drug dealers and pimps, mind you."

"I'll say," said Lucy. "I found it impossible to love my neighbor when he ran a leaf blower for three hours on a Sunday afternoon."

"Well, some things are inexcusable," said Robert with a smile. "I firmly believe that God considers leaf blowers to be instruments of the devil."

Believing it was always preferable to leave on a light note, and not wishing to walk home in the dark, Sue and Lucy thanked their hosts for a lovely evening and headed back to the manor. Dusk was falling but it was still light enough to see without difficulty, although the trees and bushes were merely dark shapes—here a row of evergreens pruned into neat cones, there a massive century-old beech tree. An owl swooped over them in soundless flight, and bats flapped this way and that, darting after insect meals.

"Sarah told me that they have bats in the vicarage, and they can't do anything about it because they're protected," said Sue. "They have to leave an attic window open for them."

"You know," mused Lucy as they approached the manor, "you think a country like Britain is pretty much the same as the US except they speak with funny accents, but that's not true. It's very different, isn't it? I mean, you couldn't expect Americans to tolerate bats in their attics, much less leave windows open for them."

"You can say that again," said Sue as the door leading to the stable yard flew open and Vickie tottered out on her ridiculously high heels and fell at their feet.

"Oh, my," exclaimed Lucy, falling to her knees and cradling the fallen woman's head. She was sprawled on her back, legs and arms spread wide, and her giggles were interspersed with hiccups. "Are you all right?"

"She's more than all right," said Gerald, stepping through the door. "She's blotto. Stinking drunk."

"What should we do with her?" asked Sue. "We can't leave her here."

"Come on, dearie," said Gerald, grabbing her by her hands. "Upsy-daisy."

Lucy and Sue each took a shoulder and together the three managed to get Vickie on her feet, then Gerald took over, wrapping his arm around her waist and supporting her as they made their way to the kitchen door. There, Poppy took one long, cool look at the situation and immediately left the room.

"I guess I'll be sleeping in my dressing room tonight," grumbled Gerald as he deposited Vickie in a big armchair.

She giggled a few more times, then passed out.

"We can't leave her like this," said Sue. "Someone should stay with her."

"Well, it can't be me," said Gerald. "I'm in enough trouble as it is."

"I guess it's us," said Lucy. "I'll go up and get some blankets and pillows."

When she returned with the bedding, Vickie was snoring loudly. Lucy and Sue quickly made up beds on the sofas for themselves, then took turns climbing back upstairs to wash up and change into pajamas. Once she was tucked in, Lucy found the sofa quite comfortable, but wasn't really able to sleep. She feared Vickie would be sick and there was the possibility she could choke on her vomit. Sue didn't seem to share Lucy's anxiety; she fell asleep as soon as her head hit the pillow. Lucy dozed off from time to time, only to waken with a start then be reassured by Vickie's regular snores,

Soon after the grandfather clock chimed four times, she did finally fall asleep, only to be wakened around six by Harrison.

"My word," the maid was exclaiming, "this is a pretty kettle of fish." She was standing with arms akimbo, surveying the unusual scene. After she'd taken it all in, she sniffed. "Don't tell me that dreadful pong is over here now."

"Not that I know of," said Lucy. "We were worried about her"—she nodded toward Vickie slumped in the chair with a blanket balled up in her lap. "She was a bit under the weather."

"Humph," said Harrison. "It's none of my affair. I've got to get her ladyship her morning tea." She filled the kettle from the sink, then set it on the Aga with a clatter. "Her ladyship didn't get a wink last night, the smell was that bad."

Lucy stood up, considered folding up her bedding and decided instead to head upstairs to the bathroom for a much-needed pee. She certainly didn't want to waste the climb, however, so she gathered up the sheets and blanket and pillow in her arms. After she'd completed her original mission, she remade the stripped bed, then washed up and dressed, before going back downstairs to make some coffee.

Her curiosity got the better of her while she waited for the coffee to be ready. She decided to investigate and made her way through the underground tunnel to the manor house and up the stairs to the landing. When she opened the door to the hallway, a noticeable stench greeted her. It wasn't as strong as the smell Harrison had described so she proceeded down the hallway, discovering the offensive odor grew stronger with every step. When she reached the midpoint, she found she really couldn't go on. The evil stench was so overpowering she feared she would vomit. She turned and fled back to the fresher air in the stairway.

Definitely not a mouse, she decided, but something much larger.

Chapter Ten

When Lucy returned to the kitchen, the coffeepot was full of aromatic, freshly brewed coffee and there was no trace of the previous night's events. Vickie was gone, as was the bedding Sue had used. Sue herself was dressed and made up to her usual perfection. Perry was setting out boxes of cereal and bowls, along with fresh strawberries and a pitcher of milk.

"Help yourselves, ladies," he said, inviting them to partake. "I've got to run. I've got to put the finishing touches on the hat exhibit." He paused and wrinkled his nose. "But first I've got to deal with the pong. It's become quite atrocious and we've had to close the manor to the public."

"It sure is. I got a whiff and it made me feel quite sick," said Lucy.

"What is it with you?" asked Sue, who was filling her mug. "Have you got a tummy bug?"

"I don't think so," said Lucy, who was eying the strawberries. "I'm okay now. I'm even hungry."

"It's enough to make anyone sick," said Perry. "I have got to get rid of it before tomorrow. Poppy thinks we can get away with one day without attracting unwanted attention, but if we have to close it for longer, we'll end up on the evening news." He was standing at the island, sipping coffee from a mug. "Speaking of pleasanter things, I was working with the art students yesterday, you know, and I've got to say, even though I shouldn't, that the hat show is really quite fantastic."

"I can't wait to see it," said Sue.

"Well, do drop in anytime and tell me what you think," said Perry, stashing his mug in the dishwasher. "I would really appreciate your input, as they say."

"Okay," said Sue, who was filling her mug. "I'll go take a look."

"As for me, 'it is a far, far better thing that I do . . .'" he said, quoting Dickens and wrapping a handkerchief across his face, bandit-style. "'All in the valley of death rode the six hundred,'" he continued, moving on to Tennyson and grabbing an umbrella from the stand. For dramatic effect, he flourished it like a sword.

"Such a fuss," said Sue, smiling indulgently.

"It is truly dreadful," he said, loosening the handkerchief and letting it hang around his neck. "I don't blame Aunt for complaining, but I've looked and looked in her room and can't find anything."

"Perhaps there's a secret chamber," said Sue.

"I rather doubt it, since nobody's ever mentioned one and it would be rather an attraction if we had one. We don't even have a ghost, which a lot of our visitors find disappointing. They simply love the idea of Katherine Howard's ghost shrieking her innocence at Hampton Court, apparently wandering about with her head tucked under her arm. I've asked Willoughby to do some research, but he hasn't come up with anything along those lines." He sighed and replaced the handkerchief over his nose. "'Into the jaws of death, Into the mouth of hell,'" he declared, marching out of the room.

Sue had only coffee for breakfast, but Lucy was used to eating a hearty breakfast so she busied herself filling her bowl with several Weetabix biscuits, topped them with a couple scoops of luscious berries, and drowned it all in deliciously rich double cream.

"That cream is twice as rich as heavy cream," said Sue, watching with a raised eyebrow.

"Tastes like it, too," said Lucy, licking her spoon.

"A minute on the lips, a year on the hips," Sue added, then left to view the exhibit, taking her coffee mug with her.

Finding herself alone in the kitchen and noticing the sunlight flooding through the windows, Lucy decided to take her breakfast out to the terrace. She seated herself at a glass-topped table, savoring both her delicious breakfast and the incredible beauty of the manor house. She gazed at the ancient stone building while she ate, taking note of the intricate stone carvings and marveling at the work of the medieval stone carvers and masons who'd created them. There were gargoyles and pointy little turrets topped with graceful finials, and each window had an elaborately worked casing with rosettes at each corner. The stair tower, she decided, was especially fine with its neat oriel windows which rose in a spiral fashion, winding around the tower. A lacy band of carved stonework emphasized the unusual window placement, and ended at a huge round clock face with carved roman numerals and single massive black iron hand. The clock, a sixteenth-century masterpiece, was still keeping time and ringing out the hours. It was no wonder that the stair tower had been chosen as a symbol to represent the manor and appeared on the admission tickets, most of the gift shop merchandise like mugs and tea towels, as well as all the promotional material.

As she studied the beautiful stair tower, she found something was bothering her. Something wasn't quite right, but she couldn't figure it out. In her mind, she climbed the stairs, retracing the climb she'd made on that first day when Willoughby gave her and Sue a tour. They'd progressed up the spiraling flights of shallow steps, designed, Willoughby had said, so that ladies in long skirts could glide gracefully up and down. The oriel windows followed the line of the stairs, set aslant, and offering impressionistic views of the estate park through wavy old glass. Each landing offered a window seat in case the climber should grow tired and need a rest . . . or perhaps a perch for a quick dalliance.

She was still gazing at the elaborate staircase and spooning up the last bit of strawberries and cream when Sue appeared. She was carrying her jacket and tote bag on her arm and was ready to go out for the day.

"Don't tell me you're still eating?" she exclaimed. "Our driver is here and time's a-wasting."

"No problem," said Lucy, remembering that she and Sue had

planned to spend the day touring Windsor Castle. "I'll just take the breakfast things in and grab my bag. I won't be a moment."

Hurrying into the kitchen, she was happy to see that Sally was at the sink loading the dishwasher. "I've got a few more for you," Lucy said, handing off the tray. Then she bounded up the stairs, pausing in her room only to grab her bag and a light jacket, and to slap on some lipstick. She dashed down, quick as a bunny, and met Sue on the terrace.

They had a different driver, a young fellow they hadn't met before. "I'm Justin Quimby," he said, introducing himself. He looked like a younger version of Harold, albeit with sun-bleached hair and a muscular build.

"Are you related to Harold?" asked Sue.

"I'm his son," he said, opening the car doors for them.

"And you work here, too?" asked Lucy, as Sue grabbed the front passenger seat and she climbed in the back.

"Only part-time. I'm at university."

"Which university?" asked Sue as he got behind the wheel of the Land Rover.

"Cambridge," he said, shifting into gear and taking off down the drive. He drove much faster than his father.

"And what are you studying?" asked Lucy.

"Physics."

"Oh," said Lucy, realizing she'd gone as far as she could on that line of conversation. "And what do you do for fun?"

"I'm kind of a keen climber," he admitted, swerving to avoid a bus full of day-trippers.

"Mountains?" asked Sue. "Like Mount Everest?"

"No, that sort of thing isn't for me. All that packing and planning. I like to go freestyle, without equipment. I see something interesting and I climb it. Most of my climbs are about twenty or thirty minutes."

"What can you climb in twenty minutes?" asked Lucy.

"Oh, say, church towers, cliffs, all sorts of things."

"Isn't it dangerous?" asked Sue.

"Especially if you don't use ropes and stuff," added Lucy.

"Well, that's the point, isn't it?" asked Justin, zooming onto the highway between two large trucks.

"We'd actually prefer to get to Windsor in one piece," said Lucy as Justin wove his way through traffic, seizing the tiniest openings to pass slower cars and trucks.

"Relax, Lucy. Justin is a very good driver," said Sue, giving him her most flirtatious smile.

"It's my tummy again," said Lucy, who never got carsick or seasick or airsick, but would say anything to get Justin to drive more carefully. "I'm feeling . . ."

Justin, she was happy to see, took the hint and eased up on the gas.

Sue, however, wasn't pleased. "You shouldn't have eaten such a rich breakfast," she said, admonishing Lucy.

"I know that now," said Lucy, relaxing her hold on the grab bar. Her fingers were quite stiff, she realized, massaging them briefly until Justin made another sharp swerve around a poky van and she had to hang on for dear life.

They made it to Windsor, much to Lucy's amazement, and Justin dropped them off at the entrance to the castle, arranging to meet them at the train station at four o'clock. After paying the hefty entrance fee, they entered the walled castle enclosure and were amazed at the size of the complex, which included numerous buildings around the old round tower. They dutifully trooped through amazing rooms, including the magnificent banquet hall that had been restored after a devastating fire.

Sue was impressed by Henry VIII's enormous suit of armor, which she said with a meaningful glance in Lucy's direction, was an excellent example of the effect of an untamed appetite. Lucy preferred the Queen's Dolls House, a replica of Buckingham Palace that had been made as a present for Queen Mary and featured tiny versions of the castle's contents contributed by British manufacturers. Saint George's Chapel, where Henry VIII and his favorite wife, Jane Seymour, were buried was the last stop on the tour.

"It's a fine example of perpendicular architecture," said Sue, reading from the guide. She looked up at the lofty ceiling and added, "I guess that means it's quite tall."

"It's spooky," said Lucy, gazing at the stone tablets marking the royal graves. "Henry VIII was a terrible man. If you ask me, six wives is five too many."

"I guess being able to have and do whatever you want, including having your wives beheaded, probably isn't good for your character. And if that suit of armor is an accurate indication, he must have been a glutton," said Sue, adding a little moue of distaste.

She pointed to the little balcony in one corner. It hung beneath the ceiling and was completely enclosed with wood paneling except for a small window. "That's called the queen's closet. It's where the queen and her ladies sat, able to watch without being watched."

Lucy gazed at the odd little feature, imagining what it was like to be a queen in the sixteenth century and concluding that despite her humble status, she was much better off as an ordinary middle-class woman in the twenty-first century.

"On to the gift shop," declared Sue, snapping the guidebook shut.

Lucy dutifully followed her friend to the shop, where she wondered if her friends at home would really appreciate Windsor Castle refrigerator magnets. She was browsing through the assorted wares when she spotted some lovely tapestry pillows she found hard to resist. She was wondering what she could sacrifice in order to fit the pillows in her small carry-on suitcase when one of the sales clerks caught her eye.

"You can just buy the covers," she said with a smile.

Lucy picked up one of the pillows, which was done in rich reds and blues, and realized it was exactly like a pillow she'd seen at the manor. There were actually three of them in a row on the window seat in the second-floor landing—one each beneath a narrow lancet window.

That was it, she realized. The second landing had three windows but the other landings in the staircase had four. And now that she came to think of it, that second-floor landing was smaller than the ground floor landing and the one above it.

"Do you want to eat here? I'm sure there's a café somewhere," said Sue, studying her guidebook.

"Not really. As a matter of fact, I'd like to go back to the manor. There's something I want to check out."

Sue did not like that idea at all. "Don't be silly, Lucy. This is probably our one time to be in Windsor and the book says the town is worth exploring—lots of shops and restaurants. There's also Eton College and you know you want to see that. Besides, we arranged for Justin to pick us up at four. I'm sure he has other responsibilities to attend to."

"I'm really not all that keen," confessed Lucy. "These old buildings are all starting to look alike to me. We could call him and ask if it would be convenient . . ."

Sue placed a hand on Lucy's forehead, checking to see if she had a fever. "That doesn't sound like you at all, Mrs. Can't Miss a Museum. And besides, these English people are so polite that he'd never admit it wasn't convenient to pick us up early."

"I know. You're right, but I've been thinking about the manor and I think I know where your secret chamber is located."

"It was just a notion," said Sue as they walked down the hill to the town. "Perry says there's no secret chamber. Besides, I'm awfully hungry, I had only coffee for breakfast. I want to eat something."

This was such an unusual admission from Sue that Lucy decided her exploration of the staircase could wait a few hours. Besides, she told herself, Sue was probably right and the secret chamber would turn out to be a bathroom or a closet added when the manor was modernized. She was hungry, too, and she had to admit that the town was charming, with ancient buildings lining narrow winding streets, and there were plenty of restaurants to choose from. They settled on a sleek, modern café that featured soups and salads, then continued exploring the town after they'd eaten. Following the path of least resistance, they strolled downhill toward the River Thames, where they paused on a bridge to admire a handsome flock of swans. Then they found themselves at Eton College, the famous establishment prep school, where they spotted a couple students in their distinctive uniforms with long black jackets and waistcoats.

"We're probably looking at a future prime minister," said Sue.

"Which one?" asked Lucy.

"I'm sure it doesn't matter," said Sue with a naughty grin. "They look to me to be cut from the same cloth—privileged, upper class, spoiled rotten little one per centers."

Lucy was surprised by her friend's attitude. "Well, since when did you become a rabble-rouser?"

"I guess it's seeing all this stuff, not just here in Windsor Castle but even at Moreton. Accumulating all these things represents centuries of excess."

"But there's art and amazing examples of craftsmanship, and history, and beauty," said Lucy. "And you're a collector yourself. Your house is full of lovely things."

"Too full," said Sue with a righteous little nod. "I'm going to give most of it away when I get home. I'm going to become a minimalist."

"Good luck with that," said Lucy as they began the climb back up the hill. She thought they'd done enough sightseeing for the day and was eager to get back to the manor. "Shall we head to the train station? It's after three."

"Not yet," said Sue, spotting a shop sign. "It's a Barbour store. You know, those fabulous waxed jackets that Perry and Poppy and everybody wear. Let's check it out."

"So much for minimalism," said Lucy.

But Sue was true to her word. After she bought herself a classic Barbour barn coat, she made a point of dropping off her old DKNY jacket at a nearby Oxfam shop. Lucy was unable to resist the thrift shop prices there and bought some gently read Puffin books for Patrick. Only then, did they head to the train station for their ride to the manor.

They reached Moreton Manor just in time for a late tea.

"We don't usually bother with afternoon tea," said a rather harried Poppy, setting a plate of freshly baked scones on the kitchen table, "but Aunt Millicent insists."

"Well, I think it's a jolly good tradition," said Perry, biting into a chocolate digestive biscuit.

"I think it's a lot of bother," said Poppy as Lady Wickham sailed into the kitchen from the garden.

"What's a lot of bother?" asked Lady Wickham, settling her plump little self on a chair and accepting a cup of tea.

"Dead-heading the tulips," said Perry, adroitly changing the subject.

"Well, I suppose that's the price you pay for all those fabulous blooms," said Lucy, gamely joining the conversation. "My flowers in Maine are never as lovely as yours."

"We English are known for our gardens," said her ladyship complacently. She took a sip of tea, then set her cup and saucer down on the table and tented her fingers. "But I have to say, Poppy, that something has to be done about the smell. It's really quite unbearable."

"I agree," said Gerald, entering from the tunnel connecting the family's quarters with the manor house. "It seems to be coming from behind a wall in her room, as far as I can tell." He paused to blow his nose. "After a bit, it kind of overcomes you and it's hard to tell if it's stronger in one area than another."

"Well, we have to get to the bottom of it. We can't keep the manor closed to guests indefinitely. In the meantime, Aunt, perhaps you should move up to the guest level here with us," said Poppy. "There's plenty of room up there."

"The servants' quarters!" exclaimed Lady Wickham. "Well, I never thought the day would come when my own relations would consign me to the servants' quarters."

"There are no servants now, Aunt," said Perry.

"Our rooms are really very lovely," said Sue.

"It was quite a job doing them up," said Gerald, pouring himself a cup of tea and sitting down heavily at the table. "Just getting the plumbing in was quite a challenge, I can tell you."

"I suppose you have to cut out little bits and pieces where you can," said Lucy, adding a dollop of jam to the Devonshire cream she'd spread on her scone. "Like you did in the stairway."

"What do you mean?" asked Gerald. "What stairway?"

"Why, on the landing in the stair tower. The one that only has three windows instead of four. I thought you must have added a bath in that space."

"No," said Poppy. "We have so many extra rooms, we just remodeled dressing rooms or even bedrooms. That's what we did in the old servant's quarters."

"My bath is on the other side of the room," said her ladyship. "It's away from the stair landing."

"Well, why are there only three windows?" asked Lucy. "All the other landings have four. And from the outside, you can see four windows."

"A priest's hole?" suggested Sue.

"Very well could be," said Perry, "but if so, it's lost in the mists of time. I have no idea how to get into it."

"But there's a window," said Poppy. "We could get in through the window."

"Too narrow," said Gerald, speaking through a mouthful of scone. "But we should look and see what's what."

"How do you propose to do that?" asked Perry. "It's at least thirty, maybe forty feet up. We don't have a ladder that big."

"What about those gizmos construction fellas have?" said Gerald. "Those trucks with the little buckets that go up. You know."

"I do know what you mean, and I don't happen to know any construction fellas," said Perry.

"Why not ask Justin Quimby to take a look?" suggested Sue. "He was telling us he likes to climb things."

"Free climbing, he called it. It's his hobby," said Lucy.

A few disappointed visitors who'd been unable to tour the manor because of the smell, but had been given free passes to the garden, were just leaving when Justin arrived to take a look at the proposed climb up the stair tower.

"Looks pretty easy to me," he said, "so long as the stone-work is sound."

"We-e-ll, maybe," said Perry, sounding dubious. "I wouldn't want to bet on it."

"It should be all right," said Gerald. "After all, it's been standing for eight hundred years."

"My point exactly," said Perry.

"Well, I'll give it a try," said Justin. "If it's no good, I won't continue. I'll just come down."

"We have plenty of rope. You could lower yourself from the top," urged Poppy.

"Too much trouble," said Justin, who was seated on the ground, changing out of his heavy work boots and putting on a pair of light and flexible rock climbing shoes. He stood up, flexed his fingers, and stretched out his arms, then grabbed a hold of a knob of stone on the tower and literally sprang off the ground and began working his way up the tower toward the window.

Word of Justin's attempted climb had spread quickly and the entire family and a number of employees had gathered in the stable yard to watch. Most were holding their breaths as they watched the daring feat. When Justin reached the relative safety of the window sill there was a collective sigh of relief.

"Well, what do you see?" demanded Gerald.

"I see . . . I see legs," said Justin, peering through the window. "Somebody's in there! There's a body on the floor!"

"Oooh," moaned Poppy, swaying on her feet before collapsing to the paving in a dead faint.

Chapter Eleven

"It must be some Romish priest, probably been in there for centuries," declared Lady Wickham, adding a disapproving sniff.

"I rather doubt that, considering the stink," said Gerald. He was bent over his wife and flapping a newspaper rather halfheartedly in an effort to give her more air.

Desi was on his knees, rubbing his mother's hands and urging her to come to.

Perry was already on the phone, calling the police. "I'm afraid we have a bit of a situation here at the manor," he was saying. "It seems there's a body stuffed inside a wall." There was a long pause, then he continued. "No, no, it's not an old body. It's pretty fresh. Well, not actually fresh. It's quite gone off, but definitely recent. Within the last week or so, I'd say."

Hearing this, Flora went quite ashen and Justin urged her to sit down on the paving and shoved her head between her knees.

"This is no place for you, m'lady," Harrison was saying, urging her elderly mistress to leave the scene.

Lady Wickham was having none of that, however, and was clearly enjoying this shocking new development. "Don't be silly, Harrison," she said in a snappish tone. "I've been through much worse than this. Remember that trouble with the Irish. You never knew when they were going to blow the Ritz to bits!"

"Well, I'll just get you a wrap," Harrison replied, hurrying off.

Sue was watching Lucy, who was watching everyone else. "C'mon, Lucy," she hissed, pulling her friend away from the group. "Stop staring. I know what you're thinking."

"No, you don't."

"You're thinking that if there's a body in a wall it didn't get there by itself, which means somebody put it there, and that somebody is probably a murderer."

"Well, that's pretty obvious, isn't it? And don't forget . . . this is the second body that's turned up in a week."

"And you're thinking there's a serial killer on the loose and you're looking at everybody here, wondering if one of them is a murderous psychopath."

"Don't be ridiculous," said Lucy. "I don't think that at all. I'm just fascinated by this human drama and the way everyone is reacting. Poor Poppy, for example. Do you think she's got a sensitive nature? Or perhaps all this has revived memories of some traumatic event?"

"I think it's the straw that broke the camel's back," murmured Sue. "I don't think she wants to deal with this on top of everything else."

"She certainly didn't expect to have a dead body on her hands, much less two," said Lucy.

"But I'm not so sure about Gerald," said Sue.

"Now who's looking for suspects!" exclaimed Lucy.

"Not I and not you," said Sue as the *woo-wah* of a police siren was heard in the distance. "We," she said, making eye contact with Lucy, "we are going to leave this to the police. Remember Paris? They considered us suspects and they took our passports. This time we are not going to get involved."

"Absolutely right," agreed Lucy as the police car rolled through the gate and drew to a halt in the stable yard.

Everyone turned and watched as a middle-aged man with graying temples and a stocky build got out of the passenger side and a rather plain young woman extricated herself from the driver side.

"DI George Hennessy," said the man, briefly flashing his identification. He was sporting a beautiful Harris tweed jacket and a crisply ironed shirt topped with a striped tie. "And Detective Sergeant Isabel Matthews," he continued, "of the Thames Valley Police."

Sgt. Matthews's straight dark hair was fastened in a skimpy ponytail and she was wearing black polyester slacks and a blazer jacket that almost but didn't quite match, over a roomy beige cotton turtleneck.

"You reported a body?" DI Hennessy arched an eyebrow, rather as if he thought people who reported bodies ought to have the courtesy to provide them in an obvious location.

"Yes," said Perry, stepping forward to introduce himself. "I'm Peregrine Pryce-West—"

"I know who you are," said Hennessy, cutting him off. "And don't think the fact that you're an earl will have any impact on this investigation whatsoever, your lordship."

"None whatsoever," added Sgt. Matthews, chiming in.

"Of course. I certainly don't expect any sort of special treatment," said Perry. "Now the body, well, it's in a wall." He pointed up to the window in the stair tower. "It's behind that window, the second row up."

"Let's take a look-see," said Hennessy, indicating that Perry should lead the way.

"It's not that simple," said Perry. "The area behind the window has been walled off."

"There's no jib door, no bookcase that swings around if you tap three times?" asked Hennessy.

"Not that we know of," said Perry.

"Sounds like a job for the crime scene officers, sir," said Sgt. Matthews.

"You get on with that," said Hennessy, instructing the sergeant. "I'll get the lay of the land." He turned to Perry. "So who are all these folks?" he asked, indicating the small group of observers.

"Just family, staff, and two visitors from America," said Perry. "Shall I introduce you?"

"Sergeant Matthews will get everyone's details," said Hennessy.

"How about giving me a look 'round, while we wait for the CSOs." He paused. "I understand you've got some long borders here designed by Gertrude Jekyll."

"Indeed we do," said Perry, sounding relieved by the distraction. "And I think this is the best time to see them when the flowers are just beginning to bloom. Would you like to take a look?"

"Wouldn't mind," admitted the inspector.

The two strolled off, chatting amiably about various types of fertilizers and agreeing that aged horse manure was by far the best, while Sgt. Matthews got her notebook out and started jotting down names and addresses. She started with her ladyship.

"For your information, I am the Countess of Wickham," she said, emphasizing the word *countess*. She clearly would have preferred to look down her nose at the police officer, but since Sgt. Matthews was quite tall, she had to express her haughty attitude with her voice while looking up her nose.

Sgt. Matthews wasn't impressed. "I presume you have a name as well as a title?" she asked.

"Millicent Pryce-West," admitted the countess.

"And do you live here at the manor?" Matthews asked.

"Of course not," snapped her ladyship. "Everyone knows I live at Fairleigh in Hazelton. The house was in my husband's family, y'see."

"And is your husband here with you?"

"Don't be ridiculous. I am the Dowager Countess."

"So sorry," said Sgt. Matthews in the polite way normal in such circumstances.

"Well, don't be," replied Lady Wickham. "Wilfred was really rather horrid and it was quite a while ago."

"I see," said the sergeant.

"I doubt it, but it's no matter," said Lady Wickham. "Are you quite finished with me?"

"Almost," responded the officer, raising a cautionary finger. "I gather you're a guest here?"

"I'm a member of the family," the countess declared, raising her eyebrows. "Lord Wickham is my nephew."

Sgt. Matthews was beginning to run out of patience. "What

I'm trying to establish is whether you will be staying on here for some time, or whether you'll be returning to Fairleigh. In other words, how can we contact you, if need be?"

"What need would there possibly be?" demanded the old woman. "And how would I know whether my niece and nephew will need me here or whether it would be better for me to go? And in that case I might very well visit a friend. I have many friends, you see, as well as numerous relations, and they all beg me to come and visit. I simply don't know what I'm going to do. As it happens, I've been evicted from the Chinese bedroom because of the smell and they want me to stay in one of the old servants' rooms. Can you imagine?"

The sergeant didn't seem too troubled by Lady Wickham's predicament. "Well," she said, closing her notebook, "in that case you had better stay here until Inspector Hennessy notifies you otherwise."

"Well, I never," said her ladyship, drawing herself up to her full five feet. "If you persist in this nonsense, I shall have to call my dear friend the commissioner."

Sgt. Matthews had moved on and was methodically moving from one person to another, jotting down their names and details. When she reached Sue and Lucy, and learned they were Americans, she warned them they might need to provide their passports.

"Will we have to surrender them?" asked Lucy, mindful of Sue's warning.

"That will depend on how the investigation develops. Inspector Hennessy will make that determination," Sgt. Matthews said. "As I've been telling everyone, no one is going anywhere unless the inspector gives permission."

"I understand," said Lucy, noticing that Perry and the inspector had returned just as a white police van arrived, delivering several officers who began suiting up in white crime scene overalls.

Perry led them inside, along with Sgt. Matthews and DI Hennessy, leaving everyone else standing in the stable yard.

Lucy felt rather deflated and suspected that the others did, too.

"Well," said Poppy, letting out a big sigh, "we have to keep body and soul together. Rather a lot of bodies and souls," she added as more police vehicles arrived and the officers began unloading numerous cases containing equipment. "I could use some help making tea and sandwiches."

In no time at all, with her usual efficiency, Poppy set everyone except Aunt Millicent to work in the kitchen. Her ladyship considered herself far above such mundane chores and withdrew to a sofa where she began reading the latest *Country Life* magazine.

Lucy and Sue were setting out cups and saucers on trays when Robert Goodenough arrived to offer priestly support, having heard there was trouble at the manor.

"That's putting it mildly," said Poppy. "We've got a body in the wall."

"How dreadful," said Robert.

"The police are talking about using jackhammers to get it out." She shook her head. "What a mess! Just think of the damage . . ."

"To the manor, of course," said Robert in a thoughtful tone, as if switching gears. "I had thought it might be a friend or relation, perhaps an employee."

"We have no idea who it is," said Poppy. "Nobody is missing, that's for certain. I rather do resent people coming and dying here at Moreton. One was bad enough, but two is excessive. I think it's most inconsiderate."

"Perhaps I should go and lend a hand. See if there's anything I can do," offered Robert.

"They're up there," said Poppy, indicating the manor house on the opposite side of the terrace. "You can cross through the tunnel and take the stairs up to the second landing. Tell them there's tea and sandwiches down here."

"Splendid," said Robert, gratified to have a mission. He marched off, only to return a few minutes later.

"Good news," he reported. "No jackhammers, at least not yet. They've gone to see Willoughby in the library. They're looking for old plans to the manor, hoping to find the entry point. It was Winifred's idea."

"God bless Winifred," said Poppy, breathing a sigh of relief.

"Yes, indeed," said Robert, "and all His creatures here on earth."

"Perhaps I should cover the sandwiches and save them for later?"

asked Poppy, offering a plate of assorted sandwiches. "We've got ploughman's, roast beef, and chicken. I don't want them to dry out."

"I can take them along to the library, if that's all right," offered Robert. "Research is hungry work."

Seizing the opportunity, Lucy grabbed a tray filled with mugs of tea and followed him. "They'll need something to drink," she said, trying to sound helpful.

"I've got the cream and sugar," said Sue, refusing to be left behind.

"It's a mission of mercy," said Robert, smiling as they left the kitchen and made their way to the library.

They found the inspector and Perry consulting with Willoughby and Winifred; all four were bent over a table filled with maps and various documents. Some were clearly ancient with ribbons and dangling wax seals, others were modern architectural renderings. The estate manager Quimby and several crime scene officers were standing slightly apart, ready to assist if needed.

"We've brought food and drink!" exclaimed Robert, holding the plate of sandwiches aloft as if presenting a suckling pig at a banquet.

"How thoughtful. Thank you," said Perry, absorbed in the plan he was studying and taking no interest in the refreshments.

There was an awkward moment as some of the officers eyed the food hungrily, not sure if they should partake. Willoughby settled the matter and broke the ice, declaring a cuppa was just the thing to clear the mind.

Lucy thought *cuppa* was an odd term for the librarian to use, but she remembered he was not to the manor born, and had attended what he called a bricks and mortar university and not Cambridge or Oxford.

"I'll have milk and two sugars," he told Sue, accepting a cup of tea and perching on a sofa with the mug in one hand and a sandwich in the other. Soon everyone was eating, except for Winifred and Perry, who continued to pore over the plans.

When Hennessy finished his tea, he came to a decision. "We'll have to open the wall," he said. "I know you don't want to damage the fabric of the manor, but it has to be done. We can't wait."

"If the body got in there, there must be some sort of opening," argued Winifred.

Perry turned to the historian. "Willoughby, you've been studying this building for months. Have you found any reference to walling off the window?"

"I'm afraid not," said Willoughby, moving on to his second sandwich.

"Then I guess we have no choice," said Perry with a sigh. "Poppy will be devastated."

The police officers trooped off to begin the process of dismantling the wall and uncovering the body. Perry went to inform Poppy, and Lucy and Sue began collecting empty tea mugs and crumpled napkins.

"I can't believe there's no record of such a significant alteration," said Winifred, furrowing her brow and searching through the pile of documents.

"I'm sure you're right, but I haven't found it yet," said Willoughby. "You know how it is with these places," he added with a shrug. "They've never had an organized, systematic scholarship—what we professionals would consider standard operating procedure. In times past, they wrote it all down and tucked it away in a chest or someplace they thought would keep important papers safe. Two or three generations later, somebody decided that old chest was an eyesore and banished it to the attic or a pantry. Think of that inventory they found at Burghley. Used to wrap china, wasn't it?"

"I suppose you're right," said Winifred. "And I imagine they'll find the secret entrance once they've got inside."

"Mystery solved," said Willoughby.

"Well, one mystery, anyway. There's still the question of the corpse's identity."

"Of course," said Willoughby, busy rolling up the documents and replacing them in their glass case.

Lucy and Sue departed with their loaded trays and returned to the kitchen. They found Lady Wickham dozing on the sofa, and Robert and Poppy sitting at the kitchen table. The vicar was doing his best to console Poppy.

"You must think me awful," said Poppy, wiping her eyes with a tissue. "After all, a person is more important than a building, right? Instead of worrying about the wall, I should be thinking of this poor corpse and the people he left behind."

"It's completely understandable," replied Robert, covering her hand with his. "The manor is part of your heritage. It's like a member of your family."

"You're so understanding," said Poppy, giving Robert a long look before lowering her eyes.

As Lucy and Sue loaded the mugs into the dishwasher, they were aware of the demolition work taking place in the ancient building. Through the windows, they saw the crime scene officers moving back and forth, carrying equipment. They could even hear the faint whine of power tools grinding through the thick stone wall, as well as bangs and crashes, and occasional grunts and exclamations. A sudden cessation of noise indicated the barrier had been breached, which was followed by an ear-piercing shriek.

Lady Wickham started, suddenly awake, and raised her head. Robert and Poppy came to attention at the table. Lucy and Sue were frozen in place at the sink.

The silence was broken when Sgt. Matthews brought an ashen-faced Harrison into the kitchen. "We need some strong tea with lots of sugar. She's had a shock."

"Why, Harrison, I wondered where you'd got to," said Lady Wickham, looking up from her magazine.

"I am sorry, m'lady," said Harrison, quickly wiping her eyes and tucking the tissue into a pocket. "I was gathering up your things. We had to move you, of course, because of the work. Them taking down the wall, you see."

"Very well," said her ladyship in a rare exhibit of cooperation.

"Well, to make a long story short, I saw the body and it gave me quite a turn," continued the lady's maid.

"Quite natural, I'm sure," said Lady Wickham.

"It was me son, Cyril, you see," said Harrison, waving away the cup of tea that Lucy had prepared for her.

"Your son?" inquired the elderly countess, whose face had gone quite white. Then she quickly added, "I had no idea you had a son."

"Oh, how awful!" exclaimed Poppy, full of sympathy.

"I'm so sorry!" added Sue.

"What a dreadful shock that must have been," said Lucy, proffering the tea once again.

"Do sit down," urged Poppy. She glanced at the vicar. "Perhaps a prayer?"

"No, no," insisted Harrison, waving them all away. "It's time I got her ladyship settled in her new room"—she paused and added with a disdainful sniff—"such as it is."

Poppy turned to Sgt. Matthews. "May Harrison take my aunt to her room?"

"Of course," replied the sergeant, writing in her notebook.

"I shouldn't think I need permission to move about in my nephew's house," snapped Lady Wickham, accepting a helping hand from Harrison to rise from the sofa. Leaning heavily on her maid's arm, she was led away from the kitchen.

"My goodness," said Poppy after they'd gone. "You'd think it was Aunt Millicent who lost her son, instead of the other way around."

"Grief takes people differently," said Robert. "Poor Harrison is most likely in denial, clinging to her routine duties as a way of avoiding the dreadful truth."

"That doesn't change the fact that Aunt Millicent is a monster," said Poppy, looking up as DI Hennessy entered the kitchen, followed by Perry and Quimby.

"We have made a preliminary identification of the body, one Cyril Harrison," said Hennessy. "Considering the identity of the victim and his relationship to a member of the household, not to mention the location of the body, I will require a complete list of employees and family members and will be conducting interviews over the next few days."

"We are prepared to offer every cooperation," said Poppy. "Will it be possible to keep the house open for the visitors?"

"What about the hat show?" asked Perry. "Can it open as scheduled?"

"If I may," began the vicar in a reproachful tone. "Might I suggest a prayer?"

Somewhat chastened, they all fell silent and bowed their heads.

"O God, we give you thanks and praise for your goodness and pray that you may give to the departed eternal rest and let light perpetual shine upon them, and most especially on Cyril."

They all joined in the final amen, but Lucy knew that while Cyril might or might not find perpetual light and eternal rest, there would certainly be no rest for those left behind at Moreton Manor.

Chapter Twelve

"Now, if you'll show me the way, I would like to offer some support to the lady's maid, the victim's mother," requested the vicar.

"Do you really think that's a good idea?" asked Desi. "She didn't seem to want any sympathy."

"I won't press the issue," replied Robert, "but I do want to let her know that the church is there for her if she should find a need for support and consolation."

"Well, it's your funeral," said Poppy with a sigh. "Aunt Millicent's been moved upstairs here in the family wing. Desi can show you the way."

They left and Poppy collapsed in a chair at the big kitchen table, her chin propped on one arm. "I suppose we ought to do something about dinner," she said with a distinct lack of enthusiasm.

"I don't think anyone's very hungry," volunteered Flora. "I know I'm not."

Lucy didn't like the way this was going, not one bit. She was starving, although somewhat ashamed to admit it. "Aunt Millicent will certainly expect something," she said in an effort to divert blame.

"There's an Indian take-out place in the village, isn't there?" suggested Sue. "Lucy and I could pick up some supper there."

"What a good idea," said Perry. "I haven't had Indian in ages."

"I simply adore chicken korma," volunteered Vickie, who had just arrived in the kitchen with Gerald. She seemed to have made a full recovery from last night's binge, although she had substituted a pair of nubby-soled flat driving shoes for the perilously high-heeled Louboutins.

"What about Lady Wickham? Will she be okay with Indian?" asked Lucy.

"Absolutely," said Desi, returning to the kitchen. "It reminds her of the glory days of the Raj."

"But only if we put it on a Crown Derby plate," said Poppy with a laugh that was verging on the hysterical.

"I'll go dust one off," said Perry, handing a set of keys to Sue. "You can take the Ford. That's probably the most familiar to you. Before you leave, you better check with the inspector and make sure it's all right."

"Maybe they'll want some food, too," said Sue.

When Sue and Lucy found the inspector in the stable yard, he was deep in conversation with a scene-of-crime officer and wasn't interested in Indian food. "No, no, none for us. We'll fend for ourselves, but thank you for asking."

"It's all right for us to leave the estate, then?" asked Sue.

"Just don't try to leave the country," he advised.

"Wouldn't dream of it," said Lucy, speaking more honestly than the inspector imagined. She was finding the whole situation absolutely fascinating, and her reporter's blood was up, keen to discover the story behind the murder. "Do you have any leads so far?"

"Early days, early days," said the inspector, dismissing them.

When they reached the garage, actually converted from part of the stable, they found Sgt. Matthews busy checking out the vehicles parked there. In addition to Perry's Ford Focus, there were several Land Rovers, Flora's Mini Cooper, and a sporty MG convertible.

"Quite a collection," said Lucy.

"Never ceases to amaze me," said Sgt. Matthews, "how some people have so much and others have so very little."

"We're supposed to take the Ford to go get Indian food," said Sue. "The inspector said it was all right."

"I'm just getting the registration information," said the sergeant. "Routine."

"Any leads so far?" inquired Lucy. "It seems like one of those locked room mysteries. Something Agatha Christie might write."

"I've seen some pretty weird stuff and this one is right up there," said Sgt. Matthews. "Did you happen to notice anything out of the usual in recent days?"

"Only the awful smell," said Sue.

"Well, there was the body in the maze," offered Lucy.

"The OD," said Sgt. Matthews with a nod.

"There might be a connection," said Lucy.

"Perhaps," admitted Sgt. Matthews. "We'll be looking into it."

"We're only visitors," continued Lucy, responding to the sergeant's dismissive tone, "but it does seem to me that there's quite a bit of tension in the household."

"How so?" asked the sergeant.

"I think it's just the unexpected arrival of Lady Wickham," said Sue, giving Lucy a warning look. "She's rather difficult and demanding."

"It's more than that," said Lucy, disregarding Sue. "Poppy and Gerald don't seem to be getting along, Flora's anorexic, Gerald disapproves of Desi being a dancer, and I think there may be money problems"

"Money problems?" asked Sgt. Matthews, somewhat incredulous.

"Poppy frets about money all the time. There's a lot of expense running a place like this and there's dry rot and paintings falling off the walls. Things are not as perfect as they seem," said Lucy.

"They never are," said Sue in a cautionary tone. "But Lucy's one of those glass-half-empty people. On the other hand, there's a lot of excitement about Perry's hat show. It's due to open in a few days and it's already generating quite a buzz."

"I don't suppose you knew the victim, this Cyril Harrison?" asked the sergeant.

"How could we?" replied Lucy. "We've only been here a few days."

"People get around," countered Sgt. Matthews. "I understand you live near Boston, which is quite popular with British travelers."

"Sorry," said Sue. "Never met the man—not here and not in the US."

"Perhaps you heard some mention of him here?" asked Sgt. Matthews. "Or Eric Starkey?"

"That's the man in the maze?" asked Lucy.

"Right."

"Not at all," said Sue. "I never heard either of those names until now."

"I don't think they even knew of Cyril," volunteered Lucy. "Even Lady Wickham seemed surprised to learn that her maid had a son." But even as she spoke, Lucy wondered if Lady Wickham had been telling the truth when she claimed she didn't know Harrison had a son.

"Now that doesn't surprise me," said the sergeant, "since the upper classes tend to think only of themselves." She paused, then shrugged. "Somebody knew Cyril, that's for sure, and you know what else? They didn't like him."

"For sure," said Sue, unlocking the door to the Ford. "We better get going. People are starving."

"Death has that effect on some people," said Sgt. Matthews with a dismissive wave.

Sue started the car and Lucy hopped in, feeling slightly disoriented to be sitting on the left-hand side as a passenger. "Can you do this? Drive on the wrong side of the road?"

"Not sure," said Sue, carefully backing the car out of the stable and driving toward the gateway. "We'll find out."

After Sue had successfully negotiated the gateway and was proceeding at a stately pace along the drive, Lucy spoke up. "You know Sergeant Matthews was questioning us, don't you? At first, I thought she was just chatting us up, being friendly, but then I realized that we're suspects, too."

"Was it when she asked you if you'd ever met Cyril in Boston?" asked Sue in a rather sarcastic tone.

"That was a definite clue," admitted Lucy, "but I think it has to be an inside job. Somebody here at the manor killed Cyril."

"I'm putting my money on Vickie," said Sue. "She's an outsider, and so was Cyril."

"You just don't like her," said Lucy.

"True, but you have to admit, she's the one who was most likely to have known Cyril. She's a party girl. She's a networker and could have run into him anywhere. I betcha she knew Eric. In fact, I wouldn't be surprised if her little binge last night was a reaction to his death."

"You might be on to something," admitted Lucy. "But what about Cyril? We don't know anything about him. Why do you think he was going to parties and networking?"

"I don't have a clue about Cyril, true, but I do think Vickie's the sort of girl who gets around, who isn't above a bit of slumming," said Sue, attempting to make a left turn onto the wrong side of the road and causing some other drivers to honk at them. "Oops," she said, correcting her course.

"Do you want me to drive?" suggested Lucy.

"No, no, I'm getting the hang of it," insisted Sue as the car strayed over the line toward the opposite lane. "Do you have a favorite suspect?" she asked, swerving back into the proper lane.

"Willoughby," said Lucy, keeping a nervous eye on the oncoming traffic.

"The librarian?" exclaimed Sue. "Mr. Milquetoast?"

"Appearances can be deceiving," said Lucy, "and he's the one most likely to know about the secret room."

"But he insisted he didn't know about it," insisted Sue.

"He could have been lying," said Lucy.

"A librarian wouldn't do that," said Sue. "Think of Miss Tilley back home."

"Willoughby is nothing like Miss Tilley," said Lucy, who was very fond of the elderly, retired librarian. " I can't help feeling there's something a bit off about him." She fell silent for a moment, studying a green field dotted with white sheep. "If it's not Willoughby, I think it's probably Gerald."

"There's more to Gerald than meets the eye," agreed Sue, signaling left and turning right at a stop sign, much to the surprise of an approaching driver. "I don't trust him."

"So we're agreed?" asked Lucy as Sue pulled into the parking area in front of the Indian restaurant.

"Agreed. Chicken korma, assorted curries, jasmine rice, samosas, and plenty of naan bread, right?"

Lucy chuckled at this abrupt change of subject. "Right."

It was getting on to eight o'clock when they returned with the take-out food and appetites had definitely improved in the interim. There was great interest as Lucy and Sue unpacked the food and set it out on the kitchen island. Poppy added a pile of plates and a handful of silverware, Flora produced a stack of paper napkins, and Gerald, after considerable thought, decided that a Riesling was the perfect wine to accompany Indian food.

"Grub's ready," declared Perry, inviting everyone to partake.

Vickie was the first to grab a plate and was just about to add a dollop of chicken korma when Harrison sailed in, grabbed a plate and shoved her aside. "Her ladyship specially requested chicken korma," she said, scooping up spoonful after spoonful of the stuff until it was all gone, then topped it with a small mountain of jasmine rice.

She set the plate on a tray, then added a huge piece of naan bread, a wineglass, a few pieces of silverware and a napkin. Then, tucking one of the bottles of Riesling under her arm, she lifted the tray and carried it out of the kitchen.

"Well, I'll be gobsmacked," said Vickie. "She took every last bit of chicken korma."

"There wasn't all that much," said Sue. "They were running out at the Curry Palace and they gave us all they had."

"Well, I guess it's curry for me."

Soon everyone had filled their plates and settled at the big scrubbed pine table. There was little conversation as they all focused on eating.

It was Desi who finally said what they all were thinking. "Did we know that Harrison had a son?"

"I certainly didn't," said Poppy. "And we've known Aunt Millicent our whole lives. She was our mother's favorite sister-in-law. And Harrison, too. She's been with Aunt forever. If we visited Fairleigh, she was there; if Aunt came to visit us, so did Harrison. They were—they are—like Siamese twins."

"But Cyril was never mentioned?" asked Lucy.

"Never," said Perry. "I mean, we used to call Harrison terrible names. The Miserable Maid. The Spiteful Spinster. The Woeful Wonder. Remember?"

"I still call her names," admitted Gerald. "To myself, o' course. Wicked Witchy Bitch comes to mind."

"Now I feel rather awful about it," said Poppy.

"I don't," said Gerald, refilling his glass. "The woman's awful—and ugly to boot."

"She's certainly devoted to Aunt," offered Flora.

"Apparently to the exclusion of her own son," said Sue.

"I wonder if he came here to do one of those birth mother reunion things," speculated Lucy. "I mean, maybe she'd put him out for adoption so she could keep working. Maybe that's why nobody knew about him."

"I doubt it very much," said Desi. "I suspect he was up to no good."

"Probably right," agreed Gerald. "Who would want the Wicked Witchy Bitch for a mother?"

A short rasping sound caught their attention and everyone turned around to see Harrison standing in the doorway, tray in hand. "I'm just after a bit of the Major Grey's for m'lady. She does like a little bit of chutney with her chicken korma," she said, approaching the table. "I do hope I'm not intruding."

"No, no," said Poppy, hopping up and plucking the jar of chutney off the table. "Take this. We have more in the pantry."

"And if you don't mind, her ladyship would appreciate another bit of that funny flat bread."

"The naan, of course," said Poppy, producing the last piece. "Anything else? Or will that be all?"

"That will be all," said Harrison, turning rather smartly on her heel and leaving.

Once the door had closed behind her Flora and Vickie exploded in nervous giggles, which earned them a disapproving look from Poppy. The others, however, were embarrassed and finished the meal in silence.

Lucy felt a sense of relief when she finally got back to her room and closed the door, shutting out everyone and being by herself.

Me time they called it in the magazines and she was finding that it was something she really needed. Maybe it was all those years spent satisfying the needs of Bill and the kids, not to mention the demands of her boss, Ted, and even the constant calls for "something for the bake sale" or "just an hour or two" selling raffle tickets on Saturday morning at the IGA.

It was too early to go to bed, so she decided to settle herself on the chaise by the window for an hour or so with P. D. James's fascinating Inspector Dalgliesh, and was just opening the book when her cell phone rang. She was tempted to ignore it and let the call go to voice mail but then panicked, thinking something might be wrong at home.

"Is everything all right?" she asked, fearing the worst.

"More than all right, everything's great," said Bill. "I just want to double-check and make sure it's okay with you if I close out the college fund and invest the money with Doug Fitzpatrick."

"Who?" asked Lucy as alarm bells went off in her head. "What?"

"Don't tell me you don't remember," said Bill. "I told you all about it the other day. He says he can double our money in three months."

Lucy didn't remember that conversation, but she did remember Zoe's concerns about the investment advisor her father was spending so much time with.

"That's crazy, Bill," said Lucy. "There's no investment on earth that yields that sort of return."

"Now that's where you're wrong, Lucy. When I was on Wall Street, I saw some amazing deals go down, but I was never in on them. It was all insider stuff. Now I've got a chance to be on the inside."

"It sounds to me that you're letting your emotions cloud your good sense," said Lucy.

"You're a fine one to say that," snapped Bill. "I watched you wallow in a cloud of negativity all winter, and frankly, I'm worried that you're sinking into depression again. You're definitely drinking too much. That was quite a hangover you had."

"I am not depressed and that hangover was a one-time thing, after a big dinner," countered Lucy, who had a dim recollection of talking to Bill on the phone when she was hungover. "I just think that if something seems too good to be true, it probably is."

"See! That's what I would call negative thinking. You need to snap out of it and think positively."

Lucy couldn't believe what she was hearing. "Bill, I'm not depressed, honest," she said, deciding to take a different approach, "and I know how much you want to make it possible for Zoe to go to the college of her choice. For all I know, maybe this is the deal of the century. I'm no financial wizard; I can't even balance the checkbook. All I ask is that you check this guy out, and take a real close look at this deal. If it's as good as it seems, if you're really convinced we won't lose it all, then I guess we should do it."

"Aw, Lucy, I knew you'd come around," crowed Bill.

"Promise you'll at least call Toby, see if he remembers this guy," said Lucy with a sinking feeling.

"Good idea. I'd like to check in with him anyway. I haven't heard from them lately."

Lucy had a sudden vision of avalanches, tidal waves, and earthquakes; she saw the entire state of Alaska drifting off from Canada and floating in an iceberg strewn sea. It was nonsense, all nonsense, she decided, firmly banishing the nightmarish images. "No news is good news."

"That's my Lucy," said Bill, ending the call.

The tense atmosphere didn't improve much the next morning as Sue and Lucy discovered when they came down for breakfast.

"The police have set up an incident room in the stable and they're going to be interviewing us all," said Perry, "so don't plan on going anywhere today."

"They want to interview us?" asked Sue, pouring herself a cup of coffee.

"Hennessey said everyone, so I assume that includes you and Lucy."

"At least they've set up in the stable," said Poppy, emerging from the pantry with a box of Weetabix. "They're letting us open to the public, but the scene-of-crime people will be working on the hidey-hole. They still haven't figured out how the killer got Cyril's body in there."

An awful thought occurred to Lucy. "You don't think he was alive? That someone locked him in there and left him to die?"

Poppy and Perry exchanged glances.

"I suppose anything is possible," said Perry with a grimace.

"They're doing an autopsy, of course," said Poppy. "I guess we'll know more then."

"Right now, they're not telling us anything."

"Police procedure," said Lucy, who'd found official silence extremely frustrating as a reporter in Tinker's Cove. "They don't give out information because it helps them in the investigation."

"Aha," said Perry with a smile. "The one who says the victim was wearing blue nail polish is obviously the murderer."

"Right," said Lucy, pouring a generous helping of cream on her Weetabix.

After helping clear up the breakfast dishes, Lucy and Sue found themselves alone in the kitchen and settled themselves on the sofas with the dogs. Sue leafed through the well-thumbed pile of *Country Life* magazines, while Lucy curled up with her mystery.

If only Inspector Hennessy was more like Dalgliesh, she thought, admitting to herself that while a sensitive nature was a definite plus for a fictional detective, it would probably be a detriment to a real life detective.

Gerald, fresh from his session with Hennessy, seemed to agree with her. "Bugger the blasted fella," he declared, marching into the kitchen and heading straight for the drinks tray, where he poured himself a couple fingers of whiskey.

"So the questioning didn't go well," offered Sue.

"Damned impertinent. Wanted to know, well, things that are none of his damned business."

"Was there a drift to the questions?" asked Lucy. "Could you tell if he's got a theory about the murder?"

"Damned if I could tell what the fella's thinking," said Gerald, draining the crystal tumbler. "Fella didn't seem to know a thing about life in the country, that's for certain. Didn't know this time o' year you've got to keep an eye on the sheep." He set the empty glass on the counter next to the sink, grabbed a stout walking stick that was propped by the door, and marched out, apparently intending to keep an eye on the sheep.

"I thought he was keeping an eye on Vickie," said Sue after he'd gone.

Flora wandered in soon after her father had gone, opened the refrigerator door, and stood there for quite a while, staring at the contents.

"You remind me of my girls back in Maine," said Lucy. "They do the same thing, hoping the yogurt and mini carrots will morph into chocolate."

"I'm not really hungry," said Flora, plucking a strawberry from the bowl sitting on the kitchen island. "Just bored, I guess."

"And stressed, I imagine," said Lucy, noticing the blue shadows under Flora's eyes, and her twitchy fingers.

Flora bit into the strawberry and chewed thoughtfully. "I don't have anything to hide."

"Of course not," said Sue. "Still, it's not nice to be questioned by the police."

"It certainly isn't," said Poppy, arriving with a trug full of freshly cut flowers. She set the trug on the counter and produced a large vase from a cabinet, then began filling it with water. "I know I shouldn't say this, but murder is terribly inconvenient. I wish they would just solve the darn thing and move on."

"Are visitors staying away now that news of the murder is out?" asked Sue.

"Quite the contrary," said Perry, hurrying in. "They're coming in droves, attracted by the gruesome crime. So many, in fact, that we're running low on tickets. Do you know where they're stored, Pops?"

"Try the gift shop," advised Poppy, and Perry hurried off just as Vickie and Desi came in, faces flushed and dressed in riding clothes.

"Wonderful morning for a ride," said Desi, taking a bottle of orange juice out of the fridge and filling two glasses. "Mist on the moors and all that."

"It was beautiful!" exclaimed Vickie. "You are so lucky to have all this. Imagine riding for an hour at least and never leaving your land."

"It's not really all ours. It's . . . well, it's complicated," said Desi, draining his glass.

"Would you like a bit more?" offered Vickie, picking up the juice bottle and preparing to refill his glass.

"No, that was plenty," said Desi, holding up a hand as if to signal a stop. "Got to watch my weight, for the dancing you know."

"Oh, Desi, you're so fit and trim. You don't need to worry about that."

"Tell that to the ballet master," he said with a wink. "Now I understand I have a date with a copper."

"Perhaps later you can show me the folly?" suggested Vickie, cocking her head invitingly.

"Per'aps," said Desi, making a quick exit, much to the amusement of his mother.

Looking for elevenses, Winifred and Maurice arrived as Flora was leaving.

"I'll put on the kettle," offered Winifred, "and, Maurice, why don't you see if you can find some biscuits." She turned to Lucy and Sue. "Will you be wanting tea, too? Poppy?"

"None for me," said Poppy, snipping the stem of a tulip and slipping it into the vase.

"No thanks," said Sue.

"Love some," said Lucy, eager to take advantage of the opportunity to question Willoughby, who she considered a prime suspect. "I'll get the mugs."

Soon she was sitting at the table with the two experts, nibbling on chocolate digestives and sipping tea. "Have the police figured out how poor Cyril got put in the secret room?" she asked, trying to keep her tone light and casual.

"If they have, they're not saying," said Willoughby, his mouth full of biscuit.

"I suppose you haven't found anything in those old plans?" asked Poppy.

"Not so far," said Willoughby with a shrug. "I did find plans for the memorial for that little girl—the one they pickled."

"Her portrait is in the east hall," offered Winifred. "If you'd care for a look, I'd be happy to show it to you."

"They pickled a little girl?" asked Sue, wide-eyed.

"She was dead. Died at sea," said Willoughby.

"Her father, the sixth earl, I believe, couldn't bear to have her buried at sea so he had them stuff her into a barrel of rum, just like they did to the General, old Horatio. It was the only way to preserve a body at the time. He brought her back home to the family burial plot," said Poppy. "A lot of visitors like to visit her grave. They leave little tokens."

"A touching story, I'm sure," said Harrison with a sniff. She was carrying a large plastic basket overflowing with dirty laundry. "I hope you don't mind if I use the washer? For milady's smalls?"

Poppy glanced at the huge basket and repressed a smile. "Not at all," she said, stripping the leaves off a lilac branch.

Chapter Thirteen

"So, how did it go?" asked Lucy when Sue emerged from her interview with DI Hennessy. Lucy was sitting on the terrace outside the family room, trying to enjoy the sunshine and abundant vines that clambered up the lichen-spotted stone wall of the manor, but finding instead that her mind kept returning to the murder.

"Okay, I guess," said Sue, seating herself on a teak garden bench. "There really wasn't much I could tell them." She paused. "Well, that's not exactly true. I could tell Sergeant Izzy quite a bit about how she could improve her appearance." She examined her fingernails, which were painted with pale pink polish. "Honestly, polyester should be banned, done away with. It's a crime against humanity."

"It is practical for a working woman," said Lucy.

"It's ugly," said Sue. "The sergeant has great bone structure. She just needs a little touch of concealer and bronzer, a bit of mascara, and a slick of lip gloss. It would only take a few minutes in the morning and she'd look so much better." Sue paused for emphasis as if she was going to deliver earthshaking news. "I actually don't mind the ponytail. It works for her."

"I'm sure she'd be thrilled to know that you approve," said Lucy in a sarcastic tone.

Sue sighed and looked around, planting her hands on her thighs. "So what can we do today? We can't go anywhere until they interview you, right?"

"Right," said Lucy, watching with interest as Lady Wickham stepped through the French doors and crossed the terrace on her way to the stable for her interview.

As her voluminous skirts billowed around her, it was rather like watching a clipper ship in full sail. She was accompanied by Harrison, of course, who bobbed along behind her like an oversized dinghy attached to the mother ship.

"This ought to be interesting," said Lucy, rising from her chair and intending to follow the pair through the gate in the wall that led to the adjacent stable yard.

"What do you think you're doing?" asked Sue.

"Stretching my legs," said Lucy innocently. "We can't leave. There's nothing to do so I'm going to take a bit of exercise and walk about."

"You're hoping to eavesdrop, that's what you're doing," said Sue.

"Nonsense!" declared Lucy. "I would never do such a thing."

"I think I'll take a bit of exercise myself," said Sue, getting up.

"Good idea," said Lucy, smiling. "It will do you good."

As Lucy had expected, the dowager countess was not at all hesitant about making known her displeasure at the situation. Her strident voice could be clearly heard through the open window and was booming through the walled courtyard.

"This is outrageous!" she announced in ringing tones. "My father was a marquess. I was married to an earl. I am a member of one of England's most venerable noble families. We date back to 1066 I'll have you know, and I am not accustomed to being treated as if I were some common person of no account."

Sue and Lucy could not hear Sgt. Hennessy's reply, but they could figure it out from Lady Wickham's next remark.

"There is no question of Harrison leaving my side! I might well find this trying situation too much due to my delicate condition. I might even faint and would need my maid's assistance with my smelling salts."

This argument apparently did not sway the inspector, as Harrison promptly emerged from the stable, clutching an ancient, cracked leather handbag. "Oh, shame on you!" she scolded, waving a knobby finger at Lucy and Sue. "Eavesdropping, were you?"

Taking a page from Lady Wickham's book, Sue pulled herself up to her full height and glared at the lady's maid. "How dare you say such a thing!"

"We're simply getting a bit of exercise," said Lucy.

"Don't be getting all hoity-toity with me," replied Harrison, narrowing her eyes. "I know quality when I see it and you're not it." Having delivered that sally, she marched off, her back ramrod straight beneath her black dress, shiny from being ironed too much.

"Well, I guess she told us," said Lucy as the open window of the interview room was slammed down, cutting off her ladyship's further remarks.

"Is Harrison for real?" asked Sue, musing aloud as they returned to the seating area on the terrace. "The woman lost her son, but she doesn't seem the least bit troubled by it, not to say moved or distressed."

"Maybe they were estranged. Perhaps she didn't even know him," said Lucy. "A lot of girls who found themselves pregnant gave their babies up for adoption. Sometimes they never even saw them."

"I know and thank goodness those days are over," said Sue. "Rachel would probably say that Harrison is compensating for her loss by substituting Lady Wickham for the child she lost."

"She's devoted to the countess. The horrid old woman is everything to her," said Lucy.

"Well, I don't approve," declared Sue. "It's twisted and unnatural."

"What's unnatural?" asked Perry, who was crossing the terrace, car keys in hand.

"We just encountered Harrison," explained Sue, "and were struck that she doesn't seem to be at all grief-stricken by her son's death."

Perry smiled and shrugged. "She's always been a bit of a puzzle," he said in a dismissive tone that seemed to Lucy to be yet another example of upper-class disdain for those who served them.

"I'm headed into the village to the printers. Care to join me for a pub lunch?"

"Thanks, but I'm waiting to be interviewed," said Lucy. "Sue can go, though."

"Are you sure you don't mind?" asked Sue. "I hate to desert you."

"Go," said Lucy. "I'll be fine."

"Well, if you're sure . . ."

"I'm sure," said Lucy as Sgt. Matthews appeared in the stable yard gate, beckoning her.

Giving Sue and Perry a little wave, Lucy followed the sergeant into the borrowed interview room.

She found the inspector sitting at a card table with legs that folded away for storage. He was surrounded by shelves loaded with miscellaneous crockery, dusty old saddles piled on sawhorses, and cracked leather bridles and riding whips hanging from hooks.

"Do sit down," he said, indicating an aged Windsor chair that was missing a few of the spindles from its back.

"Thank you," said Lucy, seating herself and discovering the chair wobbled a bit on the uneven flagstone flooring.

"For the record, will you please confirm that you are Lucy Stone from Tinker's Cove, Maine in the USA and that you are a houseguest here at the manor."

"That's right. I came with my friend, Sue Finch, for the hat show."

"You have a shared interest in hats?" asked the inspector.

"Not really. I just came along for the trip."

"Have you any knowledge of the victim, Cyril Harrison?" he asked.

"None at all."

"And previous to your arrival at the manor, did you have any acquaintance with any of the other people here at the manor?"

"Only Perry, the earl. Sue met him in the cafeteria at the Victoria and Albert Museum a few years ago. I was introduced to him then."

"And what is your impression of the family at the manor?" the inspector asked, leaning back so his chair tilted on its rear legs and propping one argyle-socked ankle on the other knee as if settling in for a good old gossip.

"Oh, goodness, I don't know," said Lucy, unwilling to speak ill of her host family. "They seem pretty typical of any family, despite their wealth and titles."

"In what way?" persisted the inspector, leaning forward, which caused the chair to land with a thump.

"Just normal," said Lucy. "But I can't help wondering how that poor man got into that hidey-hole. Have they found the entrance? And what was he doing here, getting himself killed?"

"That is exactly what we are trying to discover, Mrs. Stone," said the inspector with an amused smile.

"I am a reporter back in Maine," said Lucy, finding the inspector's relaxed attitude encouraging. "I have covered the occasional serious crime. I've even helped solve a few."

"Well, I can assure you that the Thames Valley Police force is quite capable and will not require your assistance," he said, swiftly putting her down.

"I didn't mean to imply," she began, backtracking.

"Of course not," said the inspector. "But it would be wise for you to bear in mind that you are on unfamiliar territory here and we are dealing with a ruthless and cunning murderer." He paused, glancing around at the accumulated clutter that represented decades, if not centuries, of aristocratic country life, and leaned back once again in his chair, which creaked under the strain. "Mind you, these people are different from you and me, and it's best not to cross them. I'll be glad when this case is over and done." Then he seemed to collect himself and told her she could go. "Best be careful for the remainder of your stay," he said as she rose to leave.

Lucy didn't mind being left to her own devices while Sue lunched with Perry. She spent the rest of the morning admiring the manor's famous gardens, even chatting with a couple of gardeners about the famous fig tree that was two centuries old. Then she had a sandwich in the kitchen with Sally, who much to her disappointment had nothing at all to say about the family or the murder, preferring instead to dwell on the reproductive potential of the Duchess of Cambridge. "I reeelly don't think she'll go for a third, now that they've got an heir and a spare," she opined. "Especially since she has such dreadful morning sickness. Poor thing. Now I myself was never bothered much by that, but I did have dreadful swollen ankles with my fourth."

Fearing more obstetrical confessions from Sally, Lucy made her excuses and settled herself in her favorite teak chaise on the terrace where she planned to spend a quiet afternoon with the intriguing Inspector Dalgliesh, who always solved the murder.

Sue and Perry returned around three and Lucy joined them in a sneak peek at the hat show in the long gallery, which was almost ready for the gala opening.

"We're just waiting for a few last minute arrivals from the royals," said Perry, his eyes sparkling with excitement. "Camilla is sending the feather fascinator she wore at her wedding to Prince Charles, and we're also getting the toilet bowl hat Princess Beatrice wore at Wills and Kate's wedding. Bea doesn't own it anymore. She donated it to charity and it was auctioned off. I don't mind saying it was a bit of a struggle getting the name of the anonymous buyer and then tracking him down, but believe it or not, Poppy came to the rescue." He paused. "She can be quite persuasive when she wants to be. I think she promised to let the poor soul sleep in the Chinese bedroom after paying for the new curtains or something."

Lucy didn't share Sue's passion for fashion, but she had to admit the display of headgear was fascinating from a sociological perspective. It was amazing what people would put on their heads—anything from boxy Tudor headdresses that looked like cages for thought to Native American feather warbonnets. There was even a hideous, pleated, plastic rain hat that folded flat for storage in its own little plastic envelope, designed to be carried in a lady's purse, ready to protect her 1960s bouffant hairdo in case of a sudden shower. The exhibit was extremely well done, and many of the hats were shown with works of art that depicted similar designs.

"Did you curate this yourself?" asked Lucy, impressed by the broad knowledge and expertise needed to create such an exhibition.

"Well, I had a little help from Winifred," admitted Perry, "but I did most of it myself."

"It must have been an enormous amount of work," said Sue.

"Well, you know what they say about work. When you love what you're doing, it's not work at all. It was fun." He gave a wry smile. "I only hope the critics appreciate what I've done. They can be so cruel. They really savaged that Lucian Freud retrospective."

"Well, Lucian Freud is rather an acquired taste," said Sue, leaving Lucy to wonder who and what she was talking about.

"He's good enough for the Duchess of Devonshire. She's had him paint her several times, so he's good enough for me. But I say, enough of this idle chitchat. It must be time for cocktails." Perry checked his watch. "Oh, well, rather early," he admitted, "but it must be six somewhere, right?"

When they arrived in the great room, they discovered other family members had the same thought. Gerald was wielding a corkscrew and opening a second bottle of wine, the first already having been emptied to fill his own glass, as well as those of Poppy, Desi, Vickie, and Flora.

"You must've heard the cork pop," teased Poppy.

"It's been a long day," said Perry, "beginning with my interview with Inspector Hennessy at the ridiculous hour of eight o'clock." He accepted a glass of wine from Gerald, sniffing it appreciatively. "I suppose the early hour was necessary," he admitted after swishing that first mouthful and swallowing. "They do say that crime never sleeps."

"Do you really think they'll ever solve it?" asked Vickie in a doubtful tone. "All they asked me was pretty much my name and address, and what I do for a living."

"And what exactly do you do, if I might ask?" asked Poppy in a rather snarky tone.

"She's a marketing consultant," snapped Gerald, glaring at his wife. "You know that perfectly well."

Poppy was not to be deterred. "I rather thought she did something else," she insisted, giving Gerald a knowing look.

"Nonsense." Gerald drained his glass and promptly refilled it. "Stuff's rather thin, if you ask me. Goes down like water."

"I think we're all a bit on edge," said Desi in a soothing tone.

"Well, it's not at all pleasant having police in the house," declared Lady Wickham, sailing in and casting a rather disapproving eye on the group. "I believe it's teatime."

"I'll put the kettle on," said Poppy with a marked lack of enthusiasm.

"Oh, let me," said Lucy. "You must be exhausted."

"I am, rather," admitted Poppy. "I can't think why. I didn't really do much today."

"It's stress, Mummy," said Flora. "It wears you out."

"Nonsense," declared Lady Wickham, plunking herself down in the middle of a sofa and leaving no room for anyone else to sit. "When I was a girl, there was no such thing as stress and I do think that nowadays it's simply an excuse for all sorts of bad behavior. 'I would have replied to your invitation, but I was simply too stressed.' That sort of—" she dropped her thought, observing Quimby entering through the French doors.

"I'm sorry to interrupt," he began.

"Well, you should be," said the dowager. "You're intruding."

"I have something rather important to tell you," he said, looking at Poppy.

"Well, go on," said her ladyship, impatiently.

"It's bad news, I'm afraid." He paused a moment, allowing everyone to prepare themselves.

"Well, don't keep us hanging," ordered Lady Wickham. "If it's bad, it certainly won't improve with keeping. Best to tell it and get it over with."

"The police have taken the vicar in for questioning," he said as the kettle began to shriek and Poppy got up to make the tea.

"The vicar!" exclaimed Perry. "That's preposterous."

"I can't believe it," said Desi.

"Well, I think it's high time," declared her ladyship. "I always thought there was something suspicious about him."

"The only thing you found suspicious about him is his skin color," said Flora.

"I simply don't trust black people. It's as simple as that," said Lady Wickham, accepting a cup of tea from Poppy. After examining it she handed it back. "I do hate to be a bother, Poppy dear, but I do think this milk is a bit off."

"You're the one who's a bit off," continued Flora. "I can't believe you've decided Robert is a criminal simply because he's black."

"He hasn't been arrested or charged," said Quimby. "It's as they say . . . he's helping the police with their enquiries."

"I think we all know what that means," said Flora, implying something worse.

Poppy busied herself opening a fresh bottle of milk and fixing a second cup of tea for her aunt, but she gave her daughter a warning look. "The police have information that we don't have."

Flora reacted angrily. "You're just as bad as Aunt. Robert's been so good to us. It's as if he's a member of the family."

"Oh, heavens," moaned Lady Wickham. "Perish the thought."

"Well, I do not believe in deserting my friends," said Flora. "I'm going over to the vicarage to see Sarah. She must be beside herself with worry. She might even need someone to stay with the boys."

"And you're going to be the child-minder?" inquired Gerald. "That would be a first."

"Your father has a point," said Poppy. "Sarah doesn't need visitors now. You'd merely be a complication. I think you should stay home."

"Why must you all be so horrible?" demanded Flora, putting on her jacket. "I'm going, and if I'm not needed, I'll come home."

Lucy found that she agreed with Poppy, but for a different reason. She remembered the inspector's warning that a dangerous murderer was at large. "I don't think you should go," she said. "It might not be safe."

"I refuse to be afraid in my own back yard," declared Flora.

"Well, then," said Lucy, "I'll go with you. You shouldn't go alone."

"Oh, all right!" snapped Flora as Lucy grabbed one of the waxed jackets off its hook and followed her out the door.

Chapter Fourteen

Lucy felt extremely awkward, tagging along with Flora who didn't even deign to acknowledge her presence as she marched purposefully along the path to the vicarage.

"It's so pleasant here," said Lucy, hoping to strike up some sort of conversation. "And the garden is so lovely. You're very lucky to live in such a beautiful place."

"I guess," muttered Flora.

"I don't really know them, but the Goodenoughs seem to be such a lovely couple. This must be terrible for them," continued Lucy as they passed the maze. "Do you know them well?"

"Kind of," said Flora, keeping her head down, studying the path.

"When Sue and I had tea at the vicarage—" Lucy tripped on a root and nearly fell, but managed to save herself by executing a series of awkward maneuvers.

"Look," said Flora, turning to face her. "I'm really fine on my own. I know every bump and twist on these paths. There's no need for you to come, too."

Lucy was not impressed by Flora's bravado. The girl looked so frail that it hardly seemed possible she could make it to the vicarage, much less fight off an attacker.

"There is a murderer on the loose," said Lucy, in her mother-knows-best tone of voice. "I don't think it's wise for anyone to be wandering about alone." She gave an uneasy glance in the direction of the afternoon sun covered with clouds. "Especially in the rain."

"I don't know how that man came to get himself killed and stuffed in that priest's hole," said Flora, "but I'm quite sure it has nothing to do with me."

"You can't be sure of that," said Lucy. "We don't know the killer's motive. For all we know, the killer could be some psychopath, some serial killer who simply enjoys killing people and hiding their bodies in unusual places."

Flora almost grinned, finding this amusing. "I suppose that sort of thing happens more in America. . . ."

"No, we go in more for mass shootings of innocent schoolchildren and police killing people they've arrested, especially if they're black," said Lucy, causing Flora to raise her eyebrows in surprise. "You Brits, on the other hand, are much more imaginative, what with your poisons, nooses, and lead pipes."

"Is that what this is to you?" asked Flora, challenging her. "A game of Cluedo?"

"Absolutely not," said Lucy. "I hate violence of any kind, and I also hate seeing an innocent man accused of a crime." She resumed walking. "Of course, we can't be sure that the police are wrong and that Robert is innocent."

"I'm sure," said Flora, falling into step beside her and surprising Lucy as she easily kept up with her brisk pace.

Lucy was struck by Flora's absolute faith in Robert's innocence, but couldn't share it. She was older and, if not wiser, more experienced, and knew that life was sometimes complicated. She could think of any number of reasons why Robert, or anyone, might commit murder and some of them—like self-defense—were completely justified.

When they arrived at the vicarage, the grassy yard was empty except for a soccer ball abandoned by the boys. The kitchen door, however, was ajar and they could see Sarah and the boys sitting at the table, eating their evening meal. Flora tapped on the door.

Sarah jumped up and invited them in. "We're just having tea. Will you join us?" She bit her lip, then added, "Since Robert's not here, there's plenty of food."

"He'll be back in no time, looking for his supper," said Flora in an encouraging tone.

"I wish I could believe that," said Sarah, collecting plates and mugs from the tall kitchen dresser and setting them on the table.

Lucy and Flora were soon tucking in to a delicious shepherd's pie, accompanied by a fresh garden salad and gallons of strong, hot tea. When they'd finished eating and the boys were dismissed to do their homework, Lucy and Flora helped clear the table.

"Do you have any idea why the police think Robert killed Cyril Harrison?" asked Lucy, spreading a piece of cling wrap over the remains of the shepherd's pie.

"Apart from the fact that he's the only black man in the county?" countered Sarah.

"They must have had a better reason than that," insisted Lucy, getting snorts from both Sarah and Flora. "Did he have a history with Cyril?"

"Years ago," admitted Sarah, "when he was a young curate, he was running a boys' and girls' club in Hoxton. He got in a dispute with Cyril over one of the kids, but that was years ago."

"What was it about?" asked Flora, scraping a plate into a container of food scraps intended for the compost heap.

"Wasn't that poor kid who died of an overdose in the maze from Hoxton?" asked Lucy. "Eric something or other?"

"Probably just a coincidence," said Sarah, "but I'm not surprised. Everything in Hoxton was about drugs. Cyril was trying to get one of the regular club boys to sell drugs to the others and Robert, well, I remember he was very upset about it."

"Did he threaten Cyril?" asked Lucy. "Did they fight?"

"I can't remember if it actually came to blows," said Sarah, who was bent over the dishwasher. "In most unchristian terms, he probably just told Cyril where to go."

"So Cyril was a drug dealer," said Lucy.

"Hardly what you'd expect of Harrison's child," said Flora. With a snap, she replaced the lid on the container of compostables.

"I wonder if the kid Eric had some connection to Cyril," mused Lucy.

"Oh, probably," said Sarah. "We like to think that drugs are an urban problem and a lower-class problem confined to council housing, but that's not the reality at all. Opioid addiction is everywhere and it's about time we started treating it like the disease it is, instead of criminalizing it."

Everywhere indeed, thought Lucy, wondering exactly what business had brought Cyril to Moreton Manor. Was it a desire to see his mother or was Eric one of his customers? Or both?

Their chores complete, the three women stood awkwardly in the kitchen. It was time for Lucy and Flora to leave and let Sarah get on with supervising the boys' homework, but they were reluctant to go.

"I'm not terribly worried about Robert," said Sarah in a reassuring tone.

"How so?" asked Lucy.

"Well, once they have established a time of death, it will be easy enough for him to produce an alibi. He is absolutely religious about writing everything down in his calendar, you see, and he's a very busy man." She smiled. "He hasn't had time to commit a murder!"

"That is good news," said Flora.

Lucy wasn't so sure, however. Her experience with criminal investigations had given her some insight into the way police operated, and she knew that a strong alibi was often seen as a red flag. Most people couldn't remember what they did the day before, and innocent people didn't bother to build alibis.

"Thanks for the dinner," said Lucy, remembering her manners. "If you need anything, don't hesitate to call."

"Right," added Flora, pausing at the door.

"Well," said Sarah, "you might mention Robert in your prayers."

Lucy wasn't normally given to praying, but Robert's situation was definitely on her mind as they walked back to the manor, reaching it just as the rain started.

Once in bed, she found it hard to get to sleep. She doubted very much that the police were interested in Robert simply because he was black and she wondered if his dealings with Cyril back in Hoxton had been as straightforward as Sarah had claimed. Lucy had found Robert to be a charming dinner companion, and she admired the warm and easy relationships he had with Sarah and the boys, but she also knew that people could change. Perhaps Robert had some secret that Cyril had threatened to reveal, a secret that could destroy the life he had created since leaving Hoxton. It was possible, she thought, as she finally drifted off.

She woke up later than usual, and when she went downstairs to the great room she found Sue was just leaving, eager to see Camilla's feather fascinator that had finally been delivered. Left to her own devices, Lucy found there was just enough coffee left in the pot to fill her cup, which she took outside to the terrace. She was sitting in the sunshine, savoring the coffee and the fine day when two women came through the gate and seated themselves on the teak garden bench.

"It's quite nice here, isn't it, Madge?" commented the one with badly dyed hair cut in a mannish style. She was dressed in jeans and a sparkly top and was holding one of the maps of the manor given to visitors when they paid admission.

"I'm glad to get off my feet," said her companion, who was similarly dressed but had unwisely chosen to wear a pair of high-heeled boots. "I forgot how these boots pinch my bunion. It hurts something awful, it does."

Lucy was quite sure the two women were day-trippers who had no business being in the part of the garden reserved for the family, but she didn't know how to broach the subject. She wasn't even sure it was her responsibility and wondered if she should call someone.

The matter was decided for her when one of the women addressed her. "Pardon me," began Madge, "but could you tell me where you got that cuppa? I'm parched, I am."

Lucy glanced down at the mug in her hand, noting that it was decorated with the Moreton Manor logo. She realized the woman must think she was sitting in an outdoor café and decided she had to clarify the situation. "I'm afraid you've wandered into a—"

"Ooh, you're not from around here, are you?" interrupted Madge.

"I bet she's from America!" exclaimed her companion.

"I am," admitted Lucy. "I'm from Maine."

"That's near Boston, isn't it? I have a cousin who lives there. Perhaps you know Dennis Maitland? I think he lives in Marblehead."

"I'm afraid I don't," said Lucy. "And I have to tell you that you're actually trespassing on a private area. This garden is reserved for the family and their guests."

"You don't say," said Madge, raising her eyebrows. "It doesn't look like much, if you ask me. I'd expect toffs like them to have a nicer garden, wouldn't you?"

Her companion agreed. "I would. There's really nothing here but that sad climbing rose, and the furniture is pretty much past it."

"It's a shame, really, when you think how nice some of that plastic outdoor furniture is," continued Madge.

"And very reasonable, too," added the companion.

"Well, I guess they put most of their effort into the parts that are open to the public," said Lucy, getting to her feet. "The gate over there will take you back to the public area."

"And how did you come to be here, in this special private area?" asked Madge, narrowing her eyes.

"I'm a guest of the family," said Lucy, feeling rather annoyed at the women's persistence. "I haven't had my breakfast yet. So if you'll just move on . . ."

"Do tell," said the companion, who had gotten up from the bench and was standing next to Lucy. "What does the earl eat for breakfast?"

"If I was rich, I'd have a big fry-up every day," said Madge, who had also gotten up from the bench and was examining the developing buds on the climbing rose.

"I hate to disappoint you," said Lucy, "but it's mostly Weetabix and fruit."

"That's how these rich folk stay so thin, I expect," said the companion, wandering over to join Madge by the rose plant that was clambering up the side of the manor. "What are you looking at, Madge?"

"Aphids. Look here."

"Oooh, you're right."

"Better get the gardener on it right away, dear," said the companion, speaking to Lucy.

"I will," said Lucy, "but you really have to leave. Now. Or I will have to call someone."

"There's no need to get all shirty," said Madge, shifting her carry bag from one arm to the other.

"We're just being friendly, is all," said the companion, taking Madge's arm. "I guess we know where we's not wanted, don't we Madge?'

"Indeed we do," said Madge as the two made their way, in a maddeningly slow fashion, to the gate.

Once they'd finally gone through, Lucy considered latching it, but remembered that various family members and manor employees went through it all the time. There had to be a better way, she thought, considering the ease with which Madge and her friend had entered the private garden.

As she thought about it, Lucy realized the manor had virtually no security system at all. There were no keypads requiring insiders to enter a number code, there were no ID cards with magnetic strips or readers to scan them. The manor relied on the guides and other workers to keep a watchful eye on the visitors. If no one was looking, which seemed to be case this morning, anyone could just walk in and make themselves at home.

Lucy supposed that Cyril, as Harrison's son, had a legitimate reason for being in the manor, but what about his killer? Could it have been an intruder? Someone with absolutely no connection to the manor except the fact that Cyril happened to be there? It was possible but unlikely, she decided as she went inside in search of something to eat. Anybody could have killed Cyril, but that left the problem of the secret room. As upsetting as it was, she had to conclude that the murder was an inside job after all.

Chapter Fifteen

After she'd finished her bowl of Weetabix, Lucy went in search of Sue, figuring she was probably in the long gallery with Perry, making last minute adjustments to the hat show. As she expected, she found them oohing and ahhing over Camilla's feather fascinator.

"Such a smart choice for an older woman," Sue was saying as Perry fussed over the delicate assemblage of feathers. "Flowers would have looked silly and much too young."

"She could have gotten away with an orchid or two," said Perry, "but I agree with you. This was much more sophisticated." He set the hat on the stand awaiting it, which had an enlarged wedding photo of Prince Charles and the Duchess of Cornwall. "Camilla is a very sophisticated lady. Did you know her great-grandmother was Mrs. Keppel, who had a famous long-term affair with Edward VII? She was really a sort of official mistress . . . in the French style. His wife Queen Alexandra even invited her to be present at his death bed."

"I'm afraid I'm too much of a New England puritan to approve of such goings-on," said Lucy, joining them.

"Well, things have certainly become tamer for us nobs, now that we have to work for a living," said Perry, stepping back to admire the fascinator.

"Is it really true that the Edwardians were into wife swapping in a big way?" asked Sue. "I've heard there were little name plates on the guest room doors so adulterous couples could pair up at house parties."

"It's true," said Perry. "Those little brass card holders are still on the doors in the main wing. The day-trippers love them."

"I guess Lady Wickham, old as she is, wasn't around to flirt with Edward VII," said Lucy.

"No, but she was around in the swinging sixties, and there was quite a revival of naughtiness then," said Perry, with a knowing nod. "We have photographs of house parties she attended. There was a lot of nudity, lots of drugs and booze. Rock stars, too. Aunt was quite a looker and rumor has it she had a fling with the Mad Boy."

"The Mad Boy?" asked Sue, eyebrows raised.

"Robert Heber-Percy, but everyone called him the Mad Boy. He was famously bisexual." He paused, pursing his lips. "Came from a fine old family."

"Do you suppose they might have discovered the secret room then? During one of those house parties?" asked Lucy.

"Perhaps playing Sardines," suggested Perry with a smile. "You'd have to ask Aunt, but I wouldn't advise it. She doesn't like to be reminded of her youthful indiscretions, now that she's become such a self-righteous old thing."

"I guess it's not so unusual for people to become more conservative as they get older," said Sue. "Our friend Rachel majored in psychology and she'd have a term for it, I'm sure."

"Damned annoying, that's what I call it," said Perry. "Now, what do you think about the bishop's miter? Should we have it front on to show the embroidery or backwards so people can see the little dangly bits?"

Sue took a long look at the display, examining it this way and that, a process that Lucy found somewhat irritating. "Perhaps a mirror?" Sue finally suggested.

"That way we can have our cake and eat it too!" exclaimed Perry, making a note on his ever-present clipboard.

Lucy decided that she would have to amuse herself since she really didn't share Perry and Sue's passion for millinery. "I'll see you guys at lunch?" she asked by way of a farewell.

"Mmm, yes," murmured Sue, tweaking a silk flower on a hat that had belonged to the Queen Mother.

Lucy was feeling rather sorry for herself as she left the long gallery and made her way along a dimly lighted corridor she hoped led back to the wing reserved for family and guests; she really didn't know what to do with herself. It was no wonder those Edwardians got up to so much mischief, she decided, concluding that there really wasn't much to do in these grand country houses, after all. She would have liked to take a walk in the garden, but a glance out a leaded casement window revealed a steady drizzle had begun to fall. Perhaps she could snag a book from the library and have a little chat with Willoughby, she thought, taking a turn down another long corridor she suspected might lead to the library.

She hadn't gone far when a door opened and out popped Harrison, carrying a rather heavy tray holding the extensive collection of crockery that had contained Lady Wickham's substantial breakfast. As she drew closer, she realized the lady's maid was crying and tears were running down her withered old cheeks.

"Let me take that," said Lucy, reaching for the tray. "Why don't you sit down for a moment," she urged, indicating one of the chairs that lined the corridor. "I'm sure I have a tissue in my pocket."

"No need," said Harrison with a heroic sniff. She was hanging on to the tray for dear life.

"You've had a terrible loss," said Lucy, her voice gentle. "There's no shame in grieving."

"I must get on," insisted Harrison.

"But Cyril was your son. Even if you weren't very close, that's how it is with sons." Lucy continued, thinking of her own Toby. "They make their own lives, of course, but we mothers still love them and they love us. Isn't that right?"

"I wouldn't know, madam," said Harrison, formal as ever. "And now if you don't mind, m'lady is waiting for a fresh pot of tea."

"Of course," said Lucy, stepping aside and letting the maid pass. She watched as the elderly servant made her way down the long hall, bearing the massive mahogany tray. Her back was ramrod straight. Strange, Lucy thought.

Realizing that Harrison was going to the kitchen, she decided to follow her. Unlike herself, Harrison knew her way around the manor.

"I hope you don't mind my following you," Lucy said, eager to explain her behavior. "It's just I'm always getting lost."

"Suit yourself," said Harrison, marching along.

It was quite a hike to the kitchen, and rather awkward, too, since Harrison did not indulge in small talk. Lucy respected her silence, finally concluding that it wasn't all that unreasonable. Harrison was obviously grieving, even if she didn't want to admit it. But Lucy suspected that silence and keeping her thoughts to herself was a form of self-defense for a servant like Harrison. When you were at another's beck and call, without even a home of your own, your only truly private space was your mind. It was no wonder Harrison didn't want to share her personal thoughts in idle chatter.

The kitchen was empty when they arrived, and Harrison got busy loading her ladyship's used breakfast crockery into the dishwasher. Then she set about making a fresh pot of tea, which Lucy hadn't realized was quite such a complicated process involving her ladyship's special loose tea leaves and much rinsing of the china pot with hot water until it was deemed to be the correct temperature. When she'd gone, Lucy fixed herself a mug of tea, using one of the tea bags everybody else used.

Cradling the warm mug in her hands, she settled herself in a huge, rather tattered wing chair arranged with its back to the room, and gazed out the French doors, admiring the sodden lilacs that hung heavily on their stems amid the shiny wet leaves. She was thinking that when she finished her tea she would borrow a pair of Wellies and brave the weather to continue her exploration of the garden, which she expected would be equally beautiful in the refreshing rain.

She was just finishing the last of her tea when Desi and Flora came in and was about to make her presence known when Flora spoke. "Desi, something weird's going on."

Intrigued, Lucy decided to indulge in a bit of eavesdropping.

"Besides a dead body in a secret chamber?" asked Desi.

Flora chuckled. "This isn't quite on that scale, but it's been bothering me."

"Go on," said Desi.

"Well, it's that little statue of Saint Roch and his dog, I just love the way the dog's ear is bent," she began.

"The ceramic one in the library? Is that the one you mean?"

"Yes. That's where it's always been, but it's not there now."

"It's probably been sent for a repair," said Desi. "Check with Winifred. She'd know."

"I did and she said it wasn't sent out or moved."

"Well, then ask Willoughby. The library is his domain, after all. He'd know."

"I don't like to ask. It might make him uncomfortable." She paused. "He might think I'm accusing him of breaking it and hiding it or perhaps even stealing it or—"

"Why would he think that?"

"I don't know. Maybe because I sort of think he might do something like that. I don't quite trust him."

"Why ever not?" asked Desi.

Lucy leaned forward, the better to hear Flora's answer. Unfortunately, that movement dislodged a needlework pillow, which fell to the floor with a thump.

Realizing she'd been discovered, she got to her feet and yawned. "Goodness," she declared, "I must have dozed off."

"It's the weather," said Desi. "Gray days like this make me quite sleepy. Nothing to do but curl up with a good book that I can pretend to read while I doze."

"Good idea," said Lucy, eager to make her escape, "but I think I'll get some fresh air." She excused herself and left hurriedly.

As she had planned, Lucy spent the morning in the garden, tramping along the paths in a pair of borrowed Wellies. As she'd expected, the rainfall had refreshed all the plants and the lawn was a vibrant emerald green. The leaves on the shrubs glistened with damp, and the various hues of the flowers had deepened. She especially admired the little pools of pink and magenta fallen petals beneath some flowering trees. She even climbed the hill to the folly to admire the view.

When she'd finally had enough, she returned to the great room where Poppy was arranging sandwiches on a large platter, which she set on the big scrubbed pine table with a thump. She sat down, a glum expression on her face. Perry and Sue were already sitting at the table, Desi and Flora were adding various condiments, and Gerald was helping himself to a bowl of soup from the pot on the stove.

"It's mulligatawny soup," said Poppy with a huge sigh.

"That will please Aunt no end," said Perry.

"When is the old girl leaving?" asked Gerald, seating himself beside his wife.

"No time soon, I'm afraid," said Poppy. "She announced this morning that her boiler has given up the ghost and has to be replaced. She says she's making arrangements to have it fixed but, according to her, it's practically impossible to find knowledgeable workmen these days."

"Workmen who'll work for ten shillings a week, you mean," said Gerald. "And who know how to fix an old coal burner that was the latest technology in 1910."

"Exactly," agreed Perry, pausing to take a bite of pickle. "Her place at Hazelton is practically falling down, and I suspect she's short of cash to keep it up."

"Nonsense," said Poppy. "The old bird is just cheap."

"Penny wise and pound foolish," said Desi, sitting down with a steaming bowl of soup. "If she fixed the place up, she could rent it and make a fortune."

"Rent Fairleigh? She'd never consider it," exclaimed Poppy.

"Just as well," said Flora. "If she rented it, we'd be stuck with her permanently—and horrible Harrison, too."

"Well," said Poppy with another big sigh, "it looks like they're going to be here for the foreseeable future, so we'll just have to make the best of it."

"You mean the worst of it," said Perry with a mischievous grin.

After lunch, Lucy and Sue agreed that it would be best if they cleared out for the afternoon and gave their hosts, amiable as they'd been, some time to themselves.

"Poor Poppy's been a rock," said Sue as they headed down the drive in the borrowed Ford, "but she's got an awful lot to deal with. There's the murder and the police investigation, Aunt Millicent who looks like she's going to be a permanent guest, which means she's also got to deal with Harrison, and on top of all that, there's the hat show."

"Don't forget the painting of the General and the dry rot," added Lucy.

"And people think it's easy being a lady with a big manor," said Sue. "So where shall we go? Any ideas?"

"I wouldn't mind checking out some antiques shops," said Lucy. "I saw one mentioned in a magazine that's supposed to be around here. It's called The Jugged Hare."

"Do you know where it is?" asked Sue.

"I do. It's on Tinker's Lane—"

"Easy to remember," said Sue with a laugh.

"In a town called Riverdale, which is also easy for me to remember because my grandparents lived in that section of the Bronx."

"Well, it seems fated to be," said Sue. "Put it in the GPS."

Riverdale, it turned out, was actually some distance from the manor, but they had the entire afternoon to fill and enjoyed the drive along winding country roads, past green fields dotted with sheep, quaint thatched farmhouses, and through picturesque little towns.

Reaching Hazelton, Lucy had a sudden brain wave. "I think Lady Wickham's place is in Hazelton. What's it called? Fairmore?"

"Fairleigh," said Sue, pulling off to the side of the road and reaching for a map. She opened it and the two put their heads together, tracing their route. "Here it is," declared Sue with a stab of her finger. "And you're right. Fairleigh is just a bit farther along this road."

"Shall we check it out?" suggested Lucy.

"Absolutely," agreed Sue. "I must say, I'm burning with curiosity. From what she says, it's a fine example of Georgian architecture."

When they arrived at the gates to Fairleigh, they found them closed and locked, and any view of the house was blocked by an imposing stone wall. Driving on, however, they found the imposing stone wall soon became the ordinary wire fencing that enclosed most of the farms in the area. That fence was broken a bit farther on by a utilitarian gate that opened onto a dirt road.

"Shall we?" asked Sue with a nod at the gate.

"Not if it's locked," said Lucy. "If it's open, well, that's as good as an invitation, right?"

"Right," agreed Sue, pulling the Ford onto the verge and braking.

As it happened, the gate was unlocked and the two walked along the dirt road that ran between two large, empty pastures.

"No livestock," said Lucy. "Maybe she sells the hay."

Sue kicked at one of the many weeds growing in the dirt roadway. "I don't think this is used much."

"It doesn't seem like an active farm," said Lucy. "At the manor, tractors and trucks are always coming and going."

"How far should we go?" asked Sue as they began climbing a slight rise.

"Let's just check out that little woods," said Lucy.

As she guessed, a thin strip of woodland marked the edge of the lawn that surrounded the ancient house, and they could clearly see Lady Wickham's home. It was much smaller than Moreton, but still very large, and did have the classic Georgian proportions that her ladyship was so fond of.

"Rather spooky, isn't it?" said Sue.

The dreary weather didn't help, but it was obvious, even from a distance, that the house had seen better days. A large urn, one of a pair that sat on either side of the front door, had fallen from its base and was lying on its side. Brown, dying vines covered the walls, and clumps of grass sprouted in the drive. The place seemed deserted, and no watchman or groundskeeper approached to question their presence.

"No wonder Aunt Millicent is in no hurry to leave Moreton Manor," said Lucy.

"It looks to me as if her ladyship has come on hard times," said Sue as they made their way back to the car.

The Jugged Hare, it turned out, was practically just around the corner in a charming thatched cottage and the two friends enjoyed browsing amongst the bread tins, plate racks, Windsor chairs, and Toby jugs that were displayed for sale. Sue was contemplating buying a Nottingham lace panel when Lucy spotted a charming porcelain figurine of a ragged man accompanied by a little dog with an adorably bent ear that exactly matched the description Flora had given of the missing statuette.

"That's a very fine piece," the shopkeeper told her, noting her interest. "That's Saint Roch. He was driven away by folks because he was a leper. The little dog brought him bread, keeping him alive until he was miraculously healed."

"That's quite a story," said Lucy. "Do you have any idea how old it is?"

"That I can't say," admitted the shopkeeper. A balding man with a very red face, he was dressed in a faded brown cardigan sweater. "It's not from one of the English potteries, y'see. My guess is that it's French. But," he added, lowering his voice, "it's got excellent provenance. It comes from a fine lady, it does, and that's no lie."

"Really?" Lucy suspected she knew who the fine lady was and leaned a bit closer. "Can you tell me who?"

"Now that I can't. Sworn to secrecy. She's a bit short of the ready and is selling off a few bits and pieces." He paused. "If you're interested, I could do a bit better on the price."

Lucy turned the piece over and saw the price written on the little sticker was one hundred pounds. "That is a bit rich for my blood," she admitted, "but I do like the piece very much."

The shopkeeper took the statuette from her and checked the price, then went off to consult his records. "Eighty pounds?" he inquired when he returned from the back room.

"Sold," said Lucy.

Sue watched with amazement as her notoriously thrifty friend forked over four twenty pound notes.

Encouraged by the reduction in price, Sue attempted to bargain for the lace panel. "It's machine made," she said, offering half of the ticketed price of fifty pounds.

"Of course it is," retorted the shopkeeper, indignantly pulling himself up to his full five feet four inches. "That's what Nottingham lace is, and it's very popular these days. I sell a lot of it."

"Forty pounds?" offered Sue.

"Sold," said the shopkeeper.

When they were back in the car, Sue spoke up. "I didn't think china figurines were your thing, and certainly not at that price. It's pounds, not dollars, you know."

"I know," said Lucy, "but I have a hunch about this little guy."

"What sort of hunch?" asked Sue, unfolding the map.

"I think it might be a missing piece from the manor," said Lucy. "I heard Flora saying that a St. Roch figurine had mysteriously disappeared."

"And putting two and two together . . ." prompted Sue.

"Well, it wouldn't be the first time that an impoverished old lady found a way to supplement her meager income by stealing, would it? Maybe it isn't even her ladyship. Maybe it's Harrison."

"I think you're reaching," said Sue. "Harrison seems to be a pillar of respectability."

"It's true that she seems incorruptible, but I think it may simply be a façade. And you've got to admit, she'd do anything Lady Wickham asked her to do. She's insanely devoted to the old woman."

"I think it's more likely that Cyril is the thief," said Sue. "According to Sarah Goodenough, he was hardly a model citizen. Maybe he was at the manor to steal valuables and was discovered and that's why he got himself killed."

"By a member of the family?" asked Lucy, incredulous.

"They're the ones most likely to know about the secret chamber, what with all those games of Sardines," said Sue, barely able to keep a straight face.

"Oh, you're teasing me!" exclaimed Lucy.

"Only to make a point," said Sue in a serious voice. "I think you may be getting too involved. Remember, we're guests and we have no business poking into the private affairs of Perry and his family. No family is perfect."

"Most families don't have dead bodies in their closets," said Lucy.

"Everyone has a skeleton or two, though," said Sue. "And they don't appreciate having their dirty laundry aired publicly, pardon my mixed metaphor."

Lucy smiled, imagining a couple dancing skeletons stuffing dirty clothes in a washing machine. "Well," she said, stroking the little figurine she was holding in her lap, "it will be interesting to see if this really is the missing statuette." And even more interesting, she thought to herself, would be seeing how the various members of the family reacted to her discovery.

Chapter Sixteen

The sun was coming out when they returned to the manor. The day's visitors were drifting along the path to the parking lot where their cars and busses awaited them. Aware that she and Sue attracted some curious glances as they drove through the gateway marked PRIVATE, Lucy couldn't help but feel a bit smug. She had never flown first class, she'd never had front-row seats at the theater, and she didn't have a platinum credit card so it was a rare treat to find herself on the VIP side of the rope.

Looking down at the package in her lap that contained the figurine the shopkeeper had wrapped with great care, she wondered what it was like to be one of the privileged few, like Perry and Poppy and the rest of their family. They came and went from grand houses that were filled with priceless treasures. Did they really take it all for granted? Or did they pause now and then in front of the Renoir painting or the Hepplewhite chair and thank the fates for their extraordinary good fortune?

When she and Sue entered the great room, it was clear that Poppy was not enjoying her exalted position. "We're going to have to go begging to English Heritage," she was saying to Gerald, waving a piece of paper. "There's no way we can afford a million and a half pounds. No way at all."

"It's got to be done," said Gerald, taking the paper from her and studying it. "If we don't stop the dry rot, it will wreck the whole place."

"Just thinking about the paperwork makes me weak," said Poppy, sinking into a chair.

"There is another way, you know," said Gerald. "That Vickie girl has some good ideas, and she's had some interest from Cadbury and Watney's."

"I'd rather fall on my knees in front of that stuck-up English Heritage examiner than use the manor to sell chocolate bars and beer," said Poppy with a sigh.

"Come on, Mum," said Flora, drifting into the room. "Maybe Watney's will brew a special ale for us. Moreton Manor IPA—drink as if you're to the manor born."

"Perish the thought," groaned Poppy, shaking her head. Smiling wanly, she addressed Sue and Lucy. "Sorry to burden you with our problems. How was your day?"

"Interesting," said Lucy, unwrapping the figurine. "I found this darling little piece in an antiques shop. What do you think about it?"

"I think it looks a lot like one of ours," said Poppy, narrowing her eyes.

"It is!" exclaimed Flora, who had picked up the piece and was examining it closely. "See this little chip on the dog's ear? I'd know it anywhere."

"We must reimburse you," said Poppy. "Did you pay a lot for it?"

"Let it be my gift," said Lucy. "A thank-you for your generous hospitality."

"Wherever did you find it?" asked Flora.

"In a shop called The Jugged Hare."

"That place near Aunt Millicent's house? In Hazelton?" asked Flora, exchanging a meaningful look with her mother.

"In Riverdale, I think," said Lucy, unwilling to admit she'd made the connection.

"You know what this means, don't you?" Flora posed the question rhetorically. "It proves what I've thought for some time . . . that things have been disappearing from the house. We need to get to the bottom of this."

The door opened and Harrison entered the kitchen, bearing her usual burden of a tray overloaded with crockery.

Flora continued. "Tomorrow, I'm going to enlist Winifred to check the inventory of the manor's contents, starting with the library."

Lucy watched in horror as Harrison seemed to lose her grip on the tray and various cups and saucers began sliding toward one end. She regained control at the last moment.

"Can I help you with that?" offered Lucy.

"No, thank you, madam," replied Harrison, adding her usual sniff. She set the tray down on the island and turned to Gerald. "Her ladyship asked me to request a dry sherry, if you have one."

"I think we can manage that," he replied, stepping over to the drinks tray and choosing a small stemmed glass.

"She would prefer to have a bottle in her room," said Harrison, busy filling the dishwasher. "She's not feeling up to coming down for meals just yet."

"Of course," said Gerald with an amused smile as he handed over a bottle of Tio Pepe.

Harrison set the bottle on the empty tray and carried it out of the room with an air of great solemnity that was broken as soon as the door closed behind her and everyone erupted into giggles.

"Shame on us all," said Poppy.

"If we didn't laugh, we'd cry," said Gerald, who was opening a bottle of wine. "Rose all right?" he asked, getting nods all round.

After dinner, when Lucy and Sue were climbing the stairs to their rooms, Lucy voiced a revised opinion of Gerald. "You know, at first I couldn't imagine what Poppy sees in Gerald. I even suspected he was carrying on with Vickie."

"If he isn't, I think he'd like to," said Sue. "He does seem sort of a stereotype—a Barbour-wearing, hard-drinking, tweedy snob."

"He is all that," agreed Lucy, "but we got a glimpse of the man beneath the bluster tonight. I suspect he behaves exactly the way Poppy expects him to, the way she thinks all husbands behave, and as a good wife, she turns a blind eye to his failings."

"I think you're right, but I still wouldn't want to find myself alone in a secluded spot with him," said Sue.

"Better safe than sorry, as my mother used to say."

* * *

Next morning, DI Hennessy and Sgt. Matthews were back at the manor for a second round of questioning. The police weren't saying much, but word spread quickly that Robert was no longer a suspect. As Sarah had insisted, he had an unshakeable alibi. He'd been having dinner with the Bishop of Canterbury at the time of Cyril's death, determined to be between six o'clock and midnight on April 27.

DI Hennessy had nothing to say on the subject when he interviewed Lucy, however, and he wasn't very interested in her suspicions about Lady Wickham and Harrison.

"I overheard Flora saying a favorite figurine of hers was missing," said Lucy. "A little ceramic figure of Saint Roch with a little dog. You can imagine how surprised I was when I found a figurine matching her description in an antique shop practically around the corner from Fairleigh, which happens to be the home of Lady Wickham. The shopkeeper said it came from a titled lady who had come on hard times and was selling off some of her things. Except it wasn't Lady Wickham's to sell, after—"

"Actually, Mrs. Stone," the inspector interrupted, "all I really need from you is a statement of your whereabouts on the evening of April twenty-seventh."

"Of course," said Lucy, feeling rather put down. "That was the day we got here. We had dinner with the family and went to bed early. I was pretty wiped out with jet lag."

"You slept alone?" inquired the inspector.

"Of course. My husband is in Maine," responded Lucy. It was only after she'd spoken that she realized her virtue had left her without an alibi. "I certainly didn't spend the evening killing Cyril," she added. "I didn't even know him or anything about the secret room." She watched as the inspector wrote it all down in his notebook. "I gather you've figured out how the secret room works." She hoped he wouldn't be able to resist showing off a successful bit of investigation.

"Trap door. Neatly hidden under the floor and a rug. No sign it was there unless you knew."

"And I suppose whoever knew about it is the killer," said Lucy.

"Not necessarily, but so far nobody is admitting to knowing about it."

Lucy thought of Desi and Flora's youthful explorations of the manor. "Not even—" She stopped, thinking it better to not mention it.

"Yes?" coaxed Hennessy. "You were about to say . . ."

"Nothing, really," said Lucy, "except that with all the research and restoration that's gone on through the years, you'd think it would have been discovered."

"Exactly," said the inspector, leaning forward as if he was going to share a confidence. "I suspect some of the people I've interviewed here at the manor haven't been entirely forthcoming."

"I suppose that's par for the course," said Lucy, smiling.

"Sadly, it is," the inspector said, nodding. "The trick is figuring out who's lying and who's telling the truth."

"Well, I'm going to be helping Flora and Winifred with the inventory of the manor's contents and if anything interesting turns up, I'll let you know."

"That does put my mind at ease," said Hennessy, dismissing her with a wave.

It wasn't until she was outside, in the stable yard, that she realized he was being sarcastic. *Never mind*, she told herself. She hadn't exactly been impressed with his investigation so far, and prospects for a sudden breakthrough seemed slim. Most crimes were never solved and it looked as if that was going to be the case for Cyril's murder, too. Even if the police had someone in mind, it seemed doubtful they could make a case against the murderer. Time wasn't on their side, and neither was the fact that the crime had taken place in a manor owned by one of England's oldest aristocratic families. The law was supposed to apply equally to all, but Lucy knew that was not always the case, not in England and not home in the US, either.

She caught up with Sue in the library where the little figurine of St. Roch was back in its proper place, and asked about her interview with Sgt. Matthews. "Did you tell her about the figurine and our suspicions of Lady Wickham and Harrison?"

"I did," said Sue, "and she seemed quite interested."

"Really? Hennessy just gave me the brush off when I told him."

"Well, that's the difference between men and women," said Sue with a smile. "Women are more open-minded."

"I think you mean they're more willing to think poorly of one another," said Lucy.

"That, too," agreed Sue as Winifred arrived, accompanied by Flora and Willoughby.

Winifred had come armed with copies of the manor's inventory, which she admitted was incomplete but was a starting point.

"You might find items that are not listed, so please jot them down. And if something is missing, we mustn't conclude that it's gone. It might just be in another room. Things do get moved, especially in the rooms that aren't on the tour." She paused. "I'm quite confident about the public rooms, but with over one hundred smaller rooms, it's very difficult to keep track of things."

"I think you will find that the library is in good order," said Willoughby, pursing his lips. "Everything present and accounted for."

"Absolutely," agreed Winifred.

Looking around the huge room, however, Lucy wasn't convinced. Dotted here and there hung oil paintings and the walls were lined with shelves filled with hundreds of leather-bound volumes. A series of blue and white vases were arranged on top of the bookshelves, along with an occasional marble bust. The room also contained numerous couches and chairs, tables holding lamps and assorted bits of decorative china, as well as potted plants and vases of flowers. Even the floor was covered with numerous antique rugs laid over the wall-to-wall carpet. This room alone, she decided, must contain thousands of items and it seemed impossible that any one person could keep track of it all.

In fact, she realized, spotting a jib door that she would never have noticed if it hadn't been left ajar, the manor was full of back passages and hidden doors that made it quite easy for a person to move about without being discovered. She'd learned on her tour of the manor, that the grand master bedrooms once occupied by the earl and countess were connected by a discreet passage so the couple could meet privately without the entire household knowing whether they were spending the night together or not.

"Where does that door lead?" she asked Willoughby, pointing to the jib door.

"That's the little library. Gerald likes to sit there with his cigars and agricultural journals."

Winifred suggested they work in pairs, so Lucy and Sue were assigned to the hallway outside the library. Willoughby and Flora were given the job of checking the contents of the rooms along the hallway, which included a billiard room, a boot room, and several guest bedrooms. Winifred herself was doing a quick survey of the library and then planned to go on to Gerald's little hideaway.

The plan was for one member of the team to assess the various items in the assigned space and for the other to check them off on the printed inventory. Sue and Lucy were working their way down the corridor, with Lucy describing and Sue checking, when they heard a dreadful crash in the library. They rushed in and found Winifred on the floor where she'd landed after tumbling from a library ladder.

"Are you all right?" asked Lucy, bending over the fallen woman. She was on her back, and one leg was twisted beneath her in an impossible position.

"My leg . . ." she began, then fell back with a groan.

"Don't try to move," said Sue, reaching for the phone. "I'm calling for help."

"We're here and you're going to be all right," said Lucy, taking Winifred's hand and holding tight.

Winifred was obviously in quite a bit of pain, her face was white and she was pressing her lips together. "I can't believe I was so careless," she whispered.

"That's how it is with accidents," said Lucy. "One minute everything is fine and the next you're flying through the air."

"The ladder just slid out from under me when I was reaching for the Thomas Aquinas."

Lucy glanced up at the ladder, which rolled on a track attached to the top of the bookshelf just below the row of vases. Sue, she noticed, was also eyeing the same spot with a curious expression on her face and the phone in her hand.

"Help should be here any minute," said Sue.

True to her word, Quimby rushed into the room and quickly

took in the situation. "I was a medic in Afghanistan," he announced, taking over from Lucy. "I think I can make you a bit more comfortable until the ambulance gets here." He was already checking Winifred's pulse and examining her eyes. "Is there a blanket or any sort of cover around here?"

Lucy grabbed a paisley lying on the back of a sofa and he used it to cover Winifred.

"You're going to be fine," he said, looking into the stricken woman's eyes and holding her hands. "I know you're in pain, but you need to stay with me."

Winifred managed a little nod, but her eyes were closing.

"Hey, there," said Quimby in a sharp voice. "None of that. Rise and shine."

Her eyelids flew open.

"Tell me your middle name," he said.

"Guinevere," she whispered.

"So your folks liked old time names?"

"An aunt . . ." she said in a barely audible voice.

"So you were named after an aunt. I hope she was rich," said Quimby.

" 'Fraid not," said Winifred, her eyes closing again.

Fortunately, the ambulance crew arrived and quickly bundled her onto a stretcher and carried her off.

"That looked like a nasty break," said Quimby when they had gone. "She was going into shock."

"What happened?" asked Flora, who had noticed the commotion and come to see what was the matter.

"Winifred took a tumble from the ladder," explained Quimby. "She broke her leg."

"Oh, my God!" exclaimed Flora. "I have to tell Mummy!" She ran off just as Willoughby came in, looking rather put out.

"At this rate, we'll never get this inventory finished," he said, grumbling. "My time would be better spent on the guidebook. That's what I'm supposed to be doing."

"We've had an accident," said Quimby. "Winifred fell off—"

"I can't imagine what she was doing up there," said Willoughby, interrupting him. "She really had no business being there."

Lucy was surprised at Maurice's reaction and wondered if he

simply wasn't interested in his colleague's mishap or if he was defending his turf. The library, after all, was his responsibility.

Quimby was studying the ladder's operation. "The fault doesn't seem to be with the ladder. It's perfectly sound."

"Of course it is," snapped Willoughby.

"She said it slipped right out from under her," said Lucy, joining him.

"Well, it shouldn't have. See here. It has a kind of braking mechanism. When a person stands on it, puts weight on it, it doesn't slide. As I said," insisted Willoughby, "everything in here is shipshape and present and accounted for . . . except for Flora, who was supposed to be helping me."

"Flora wasn't with you?" asked Lucy.

"Winifred probably reached too far and lost her balance," said Willoughby, ignoring Lucy's question and casting an eye at the ladder. "It's easy enough to do."

"I think I'd better find her ladyship and let her know that it was an accident, nothing more," said Quimby, taking his leave. "Flora can be a bit of an alarmist."

"That girl is little more than a nuisance," said Willoughby. "Since the inventory taking appears to be indefinitely postponed, I think I will go down to the chapel and check some dates on the tablets there. I believe I've found a significant discrepancy."

He also left, leaving Lucy and Sue alone in the vast library.

"Is it me or does Willoughby protest a bit too much?" asked Lucy. "If he was alone, which he admitted before realizing it was a mistake, he could have pushed the ladder out from under Winifred."

"You do have a suspicious mind. Why would he do that?" asked Sue, who was studying the vases with a puzzled expression. "I can't help but wonder . . . those vases look a bit modern to me."

Lucy looked up at the white Chinese vases that were decorated with blue designs. "I have to admit, I've seen similar ones in the Christmas Tree Shop," she said, naming a chain of popular discount gift shops back home.

"Me, too," said Sue, climbing the ladder to get a closer look.

"Do be careful," said Lucy, anxious for her friend.

"Quimby said the ladder is perfectly sound," insisted Sue, who was halfway up.

Lucy was hovering nervously at the base of the ladder, though what she thought she could do to prevent Sue from falling wasn't clear to her.

Reaching the top, Sue reached for the nearest vase with both hands and Lucy held her breath. "As I thought!" exclaimed Sue, a note of triumph in her voice as she made a half turn, still holding the very large vase and pointing to a label on its base. "Made in China."

"What do you think you're doing?" demanded Willoughby, making them both jump.

They hadn't noticed him returning to the room.

"This vase is not an antique," said Sue, looking down at him from her lofty perch.

"Of course it is," said Willoughby, reaching for the inventory and flipping through it. "Right here it says eleven Tang dynasty vases."

"I'm no expert on dynasties, but I'm pretty sure the Tangs, whoever they were, didn't use little sticky labels that say MADE IN CHINA," declared Sue, handing the vase down to Lucy, who passed it to Willoughby.

He adjusted his glasses, looked at the label, and sat down on a sofa with a thump. "I don't know anything about this," he said indignantly.

An odd thing to say, thought Lucy, considering that nobody had asked him.

Chapter Seventeen

Armed with one of the vases, Lucy and Sue hurried off to find Poppy.

She was in her office, a large, sunny room that overlooked the parterre garden on the east side of the manor. It was a charming room with flowery chintz curtains on the windows and many gilt-framed watercolors on the pale green walls. The mantel was filled with family photos and numerous engraved invitations, many beginning with the letters *HRH*. Poppy's large desk, however, was all business with a couple of computer screens, several phones, and piles of papers. A top-of-the-line copy machine stood nearby; the control panel rivaled that of a 747 jet.

"What is it now?" she asked when they entered. Rolling her eyes, she looked heavenward as if for divine intervention.

"We were helping with the inventory—" began Sue.

"Yes?"

"And I thought these vases looked a bit, well, inauthentic . . ."

"And?"

"They were made in China," announced Sue.

"Of course. They are antique Chinese vases, part of a noted family collection," said Poppy.

"Not these. These have little gold stick-on labels," said Lucy.

"Catalog numbers, surely."

"I'm afraid not," said Sue, tipping the vase bottom up so Poppy could see the offending label for herself.

Poppy half rose from her chair to check the label and, recognizing it as one she was quite familiar with and knowing an identical label was actually affixed to many items in the manor gift shop, she sank back into her chair with an enormous groan. "Oh, dear," she said, adding a big sigh. "Are they all like this?"

"I didn't check each one," admitted Sue, "but I suspect they are."

"I'd better call Perry," said Poppy, reaching for a phone. "We have to look into this."

Fifteen minutes later, Lucy and Sue, Perry and Poppy were in the library. Perry was aloft on the ladder, checking the vases one by one and concluding that even the ones missing the tiny little gold labels were indeed fakes. "They're much lighter than the antiques. When you get a good look up close there's no question that they're modern. There's no crackling, none of those little spots that the old ones have. These are too shiny by far, though I think there's been a halfhearted effort to scuff them up and make them look antique."

"How long do you think they've been up there?" asked Poppy, biting her lip.

"There's not much dust," said Perry, rubbing his thumb against his fingers, "so I don't think the switch was made too long ago."

"If Lady Wickham took the little St. Roch figure, perhaps she's been helping herself to other things, too," said Lucy.

"She's probably had Harrison doing the dirty work," said Sue.

"I've actually seen Harrison sneak out of the kitchen with bottles of wine hidden under her sweater," said Lucy.

"I don't know who she thinks she's fooling with that caper," said Perry, smiling. "She's been doing it for years. I actually felt a bit sorry for her when she had to ask Gerald for that sherry. She couldn't snitch it because he was standing in the way, which I suspect he may have been doing quite intentionally."

"You've never challenged her?" asked Lucy, somewhat incredulous.

"Of course not. All that subterfuge is quite unnecessary, but I suppose it gives the old crow a bit of a thrill," said Poppy.

"And what about the items from the manor? The figurine and the vases?"

"Well, we can't be sure it's Aunt," said Perry.

"And even if it is, well, I don't think we want to make an issue of it," said Poppy.

"But those vases must have been enormously valuable," said Lucy. "You said they were part of a famous collection."

"Surely they belong to the nation, to everyone," said Sue.

"They belong to the family," said Perry, correcting her. "And this is a family matter, which the family will deal with."

"Of course," said Sue, chagrined. "It's really none of my business."

"Oh, no. We're grateful," said Perry.

"Absolutely," agreed Poppy. "Much better to discover something like this ourselves, so we can handle it without a lot of fuss."

"And it's about time we realized how desperate poor old Aunt Millicent really is. I certainly didn't have a clue," said Perry, seating himself in a rose-covered slipper chair.

"We don't know for sure that she's been taking things," said Poppy, sitting down in the matching chair.

"I guess we'll have to have a little talk with her," said Perry, "even though I doubt she'll admit to any wrong-doing."

"I wouldn't come right out and confront her," cautioned Poppy. "We'll explore some options. She could live here."

"Perish the thought," said Perry.

"Or perhaps an allowance of some sort," suggested Poppy.

"Maybe we can get her into a Grace and Favor apartment at Kensington or Hampton Court," said Perry. "I've always felt rather guilty, you know. Poor Wilfred had the title for only a couple weeks when he had that heart attack; he and Aunt Millicent hadn't even moved into the manor."

"Don't forget. Wilfred was shagging that call girl at the time," said Poppy.

"I suspect Dad didn't want the title any more than I do," said Perry. "I'm sure it meant more to Wilfred than to either of us."

"Certainly to Aunt Millicent," said Poppy with a chuckle.

Lucy and Sue shared a glance. It was obvious they'd been forgotten.

"We'll be off," said Sue as they began to leave the room.

"She is quite chummy with the Queen," Perry was saying as they closed the door behind them.

Climbing upstairs to their quarters, Lucy expressed her surprise at Perry and Poppy's reaction. "I certainly didn't expect them to be quite so forgiving."

"I don't know if that's what they are being," said Sue. "I think they simply want to keep yet another scandal in the family."

"I guess I can't expect them to turn her in to the police," said Lucy.

"Not hardly," said Sue. "What is that upper class mantra? Never apologize and never explain?"

"I thought it was 'mad, bad, and dangerous to know'," said Lucy, as they reached the guest level. "I never thought I'd be saying this, but I'm looking forward to returning to my simple middle-class life in Maine."

"The thing that really puzzles me"—Sue followed Lucy into her room and seated herself on a chintz-covered nursing chair—"is why Harrison is keeping up this stiff upper lip nonsense. It's her son who was found in the secret chamber, after all. Even if they were estranged, there'd have to be some sort of blood tie, wouldn't there?"

Lucy picked up an emery board and perched on the cushioned stool that sat in front of a charming dressing table, a feature that she was determined to re-create in her bedroom when she returned home. "Maybe there is no blood tie," she said as she filed her nails. "Maybe Cyril was actually Lady Wickham's love child, kept secret all these years. She's the one who's been in seclusion since his death was discovered."

Sue stared at her friend. "I think you're out of your mind. Secret love child? That phrase does not come to mind when I think of Lady Wickham."

"She must have been young once. Perry said she was quite the girl back in the swinging sixties," said Lucy, holding out her hand and examining her nails. "And maybe Cyril was killed because he would have had a claim on the earldom. Did you think of that?"

"No, Lucy, that never occurred to me. Cyril was a thug—a drug dealer from a tough part of London."

"Stranger things have happened," insisted Lucy, starting to file the nails on her other hand. "There are all sorts of rules about these titles and estates. Most are entailed but some aren't. Perry doesn't have any children and it doesn't look like he will. When the earl on *Downton Abbey* only had daughters, the title went to Cousin Matthew. Maybe Cyril was a cousin and that's why Perry and Poppy don't want to pursue the matter with Lady Wickham."

"Or maybe they simply don't want to embarrass a sad old woman," said Sue.

"Do you think they knew she was stealing all along?" asked Lucy.

"I wouldn't be surprised if somebody knew," said Sue. "That ladder was pretty steady when I was on it. I think it's entirely possible that someone pushed it out from under Winifred, fearing that she was about to discover the switch. What with all these jib doors and secret chambers, an assailant could have popped out from anywhere."

"And disappeared just as quickly," said Lucy with a shudder. "This place is starting to seem more like Wolf Hall than Downton Abbey. You don't know who you can trust."

Sue wrapped her arms across her chest and rubbed her upper arms. "I know. It's a horrible feeling, isn't it? I feel like I have to keep looking over my shoulders."

"We can't go on like this," declared Lucy. "We have to get to the bottom of this mess, and Cyril is the key. Somebody killed him for a reason."

"We have to be very careful, Lucy," warned Sue. "We're dealing with a dangerous person."

"You're right," agreed Lucy, "but there is one person who was vetted by the police and cleared . . . and that person also knew Cyril."

"Robert Goodenough, the vicar," said Sue.

"Right," said Lucy, standing up and marching over to the wardrobe where she pulled out a jacket. "Let's pay him a visit."

"Not so fast," said Sue. "He's a busy man. We can't just march in and start asking questions. We need to make an appointment."

"Right," said Lucy, watching and waiting while Sue called the vicarage.

As it happened, Robert was away at a diocesan conference but the church secretary said he'd be available the following morning and the meeting was set.

"What do we do until then?" asked Lucy. "They can't continue taking inventory without Winifred."

"Well, I'm going to stretch out on that lovely chaise longue in my room with the latest British *Vogue*," said Sue.

"I've got my jacket out, so I think I'll go for a walk," said Lucy. "I do my best thinking when I'm walking."

"Be sure to take a stick," said Sue. "Just in case."

"Good idea," said Lucy, remembering a well-stocked umbrella stand in the kitchen.

When she got there she found Harrison sitting at the scrubbed pine table enjoying a cuppa and a smoke. Seeing her, Harrison quickly stubbed out the cigarette in her saucer.

"No need for that," said Lucy. "It's none of my affair if you smoke."

"Lady Philippa doesn't like me to smoke indoors," said Harrison in a resentful tone. "Things used to be different, you know, when servants had their own place downstairs. There was up and there was down, and those that lived upstairs weren't welcome downstairs. That was for them that was in service, you see. It's all changed now."

"Back then you could smoke if you wanted to?" asked Lucy.

"Different houses had different rules, o' course, but the butler that used to be here, Chivers was his name, he enjoyed a cigarette himself and didn't mind if others did, too, so long as it didn't interfere with their work."

"I suppose that was some time ago," said Lucy. "I thought that people stopped going into service after World War I."

"Some places stuck to the old ways longer," said Harrison, lighting up a fresh cigarette. She inhaled deeply, then continued. "The old earl, Poppy and Perry's grandfather, he lived to be quite old. He didn't like change so he kept the house staffed just as it was when he was a little boy. When he died there were a lot of old folks still working here, including Chivers. The old earl's first son, that was m'lady's husband and Perry's uncle, he would've kept the old folks on. Some said it was like going back in time, coming here. They had maids laying the fires every morning and bringing tea in bed to the married ladies. There were footmen at dinner. People knew their places, that was for sure. But," she added with a sniff, "everything changed when his lordship that was died and this crew came in."

"You miss those days?" asked Lucy.

"I like being in service. I always have. I suits her ladyship and she suits me."

"It must have been hard when you had a child," suggested Lucy.

"Not so bad. Her ladyship sent me off to my sister's when she realized I was up the spout. That's what we used to call it, y'see."

"A funny term," said Lucy.

"But she kept the job for me and I came back after little Cyril was born. My sister kept him, and maybe that was a bit of a mistake. I think she was much too soft on him. If I'd raised him, I dare say he might've turned out a bit better. I sent money, o' course, but I didn't know that her husband—Alf that was—well, he had some friends that were what you call bad company. Alf himself wasn't above helping himself to anything that fell off a truck. That's what he called it. You'd see they had a nice new set of furniture or my sister'd have a mink stole. Alf would say it fell off a truck, and he'd wink."

"Some things have gone missing here," began Lucy, aware that she was treading on thin ice. "Do you think Cyril could have had anything to do with that?"

Harrison took a final draw on her cigarette and stubbed it out, then rose and carried her cup and saucer to the sink. She dumped the butts in the trash and put the crockery in the dishwasher, then turned to Lucy. "Like I told the cops, I don't know what Cyril was up to. We wasn't close and that's the truth. I don't suppose I could've expected anything else, not with Doris raising him." She straightened her shoulders. "Don't get me wrong. I don't have any regrets, not really. I suits her ladyship and she suits me. I wouldn't want it any other way."

Lucy couldn't put her conversation with Harrison out of her mind while she wandered through the garden. In this day and age, it seemed impossible that a person could have such antiquated views and be satisfied with such a limited life. She wondered if there was more to the relationship between Lady Wickham and Harrison than that of an employer and employee. Could the two be lovers? Was it some sort of dominant-submissive relationship? Perhaps even sadomasochistic? Lucy was thinking of calling her friend Rachel, the psychology major, when her ring tone went off and she pulled her cell phone out of her pocket.

It was Bill.

She took a moment to consider how amazing it was that this tiny bit of plastic and electronic circuitry could connect her to him across the vast Atlantic Ocean. "Hi!" she exclaimed, seating herself on a stone bench. "I'm glad you called. I've been missing you."

"So you haven't fallen for some duke or other?" he teased.

"No dukes, but there are some pretty hunky gardeners around here," she said, noticing Dishy Geoff bending over a flower bed. "Unfortunately, from what I've gathered, they're all married."

"Well, so are you and don't forget it."

"No chance," said Lucy, missing her husband's embrace and the way his beard tickled the back of her neck. "How's everybody? Have you heard from Toby lately?"

"I Skyped with Patrick last night. He showed me a picture he drew in school. It was a picture of you."

"I wish I'd seen it," said Lucy, practically knocked off the bench by a wave of longing for her grandson.

"Toby said he tried to call you but the satellite was down and he hadn't got the time difference right, anyway. Something like that."

"Likely story," said Lucy, somewhat doubtful of her son's supposed efforts to contact her. "How are the girls?"

"Usual stuff. Elizabeth's sick of her job at the hotel and hates all men. Sarah's been working hard preparing to defend her senior thesis paper, and Zoe's decided to follow in her sister's footsteps at Winchester."

"She's given up on Strethmore?" asked Lucy, surprised by this turn of events. "It was her top choice. She must be disappointed."

"To tell the truth, I think she doesn't understand why a college with a billion dollar endowment doesn't care enough about having her attend that they won't cough up more financial aid. She's a smart girl. She knows we just don't have the money and she doesn't want to be burdened with enormous student loans."

"She must be disappointed. What about that investment scheme of yours?" asked Lucy, fearing that Bill had gone ahead and invested the money.

"Funny thing about that," said Bill. "I took your advice and checked with Toby about this guy, and it turned out Toby never heard of him. He wasn't a friend at all. He was just posing to win my confidence and probably steal our money. Doug Fitzpatrick was not who he claimed to be."

"Wow," said Lucy. "That was a good catch. Did you press charges?"

"I did check with the police chief, but he said there was no crime because I didn't lose any money. If I'd invested and the guy had absconded, then we'd have a case." He paused. "In any case, Fitzpatrick's gone. I tried calling his so-called office and the number was no longer in service."

"That was a close one," said Lucy. "I'm glad you decided to check him out with Toby."

"I came close to being a sucker. I admit it," said Bill in a rueful tone. "I was having coffee at Jake's with some of the guys one morning and Sid mentioned getting an e-mail claiming his nephew had been arrested in Mexico and couldn't get out of jail until he sent him five hundred dollars to pay a fine. When he checked with his sister, it turned out the kid was working as a lifeguard at their health club. It got me thinking, you know?"

"Good thinking," said Lucy.

"You can't believe everything people tell you," said Bill.

"Funny thing," said Lucy, remembering DI Hennessy's claim that he suspected people didn't always tell him the truth. "I heard somebody else say that very same thing."

"Well, I'm glad you'll be home soon," said Bill. "I miss you."

"And I miss you."

Chapter Eighteen

Robert and Sarah were sitting in the vicarage garden, drinking tea from large mugs, when Lucy and Sue arrived the next morning. It was unseasonably hot and the sun was very bright, but they had set up chairs in a shady spot.

"Elevenses," said Robert with a huge grin. "I can't seem to break the habit of drinking tea even when it's so warm, like today."

"Will you join us?" asked Sarah. "The water's still hot."

"Thanks," said Lucy, who would much rather have had a tall glass of iced tea.

"I have lemonade," said Sarah, sensing her hesitation.

"That would be lovely," cooed Sue.

"Make that two," said Lucy, fanning herself with her hands.

"Make yourselves comfortable," said Sarah, "I'll be back in a minute."

Lucy and Sue seated themselves carefully in the rickety deck chairs, which were nothing more than strips of rather old, faded striped canvas slung on folding wooden frames. Lucy wasn't convinced the fabric was still strong enough to support her, and found it quite impossible to sit up straight as the chair's design required one to adopt a semi-prone position. Sue, she noticed, was having the same problem. When Sarah arrived with the tall glasses of lemonade, she discovered that she had to stretch her neck like a turtle in order to drink.

"I hope we're not keeping you from your work," said Sue.

"No problem," said Robert. "I was working on my sermon, but I wasn't getting very far."

"It must be quite a challenge coming up with something new every week," said Lucy.

"Coming up with ideas isn't the problem," said Robert. "It's trying to present them in ways that will be acceptable to the congregation."

"Folks around here are very old-fashioned," said Sarah.

"I suppose it's quite a change from your church in London," said Lucy, attempting to steer the conversation in that direction.

"The thing I don't understand," said Robert, "is why so many people around here insist on voting for the Conservative candidate when it's not in their best interest. Of course, the folks up at the manor want to keep taxes low and the Conservative line definitely benefits them. But when old Simpkins, who's worked at the ironmongers since he was ten years old and never made more than fifty pounds a week says he's going to vote Conservative, I just have to scratch my head."

"I was actually surprised to learn that Perry and Poppy are Conservatives," said Sue, pausing to attempt the neck-stretching exercise necessary for taking a sip of lemonade. "They seem so modern and progressive."

"Progressive when it benefits them, like getting government grants to fix the roof on the manor, but quite resentful when the tax bill comes," said Sarah.

"I have noticed that when the manor is in need of some repair or other, it's a valuable part of the nation's heritage that belongs to all the people," said Lucy, "but when something goes missing or a visitor wanders through the wrong door, it's suddenly their family heritage that's being threatened."

"Have there been incidents at the manor?" asked Sarah. "Has something been stolen?"

Lucy suddenly feared she might have said too much and shook

her head. "No. It was just something Poppy said . . . or maybe it was Flora. I'm not sure."

"And Lucy knows better than to gossip about her hosts," said Sue with a meaningful glance.

"I do. I'm ashamed of myself," said Lucy.

"If you are truly penitent and contrite, your sins will surely be forgiven," said Robert with a twinkle in his eye.

"I have to admit that we are terribly curious about Cyril and his mother, who doesn't seem at all distressed by her son's grisly end," said Sue. "I understand you knew them in Hoxton?"

"I never met Cyril's mother," confessed Robert, "but Hoxton was a very tough place and Cyril fit right in. It was rumored that his grandfather had links to the notorious Kray brothers. And his uncle—I understand his aunt and uncle brought him up, and, well, there's really no way to say it nicely—his uncle was a small-time crook. I'm afraid that by the time I met him, Cyril was rather fixed in his ways. He ran a couple prostitutes and sold drugs. He even tried to get one of the boys in the church youth group to sell for him."

"Robert told him to get lost and the next day Robert was attacked by a couple thugs. That's the way things were in Hoxton," said Sarah.

"Harrison told me she blamed her sister and her brother-in-law for turning Cyril to a life of crime," said Lucy.

"She definitely has a point," said Robert, "but I find people do what they need to do to survive and in Hoxton, crime was one of the few viable options available to people."

"Harrison herself isn't exactly honest," said Lucy. "We've seen her steal bottles of wine."

Sue gave her another meaningful glance and hurried to explain. "It's really kind of a joke. Everybody knows about it. She's not fooling anyone."

"Maybe larceny is in the blood," said Sarah, "and maybe she chose a life in service as a way to stay on the straight and narrow, a way to escape her criminal family."

"She is certainly very devoted to Lady Wickham," said Lucy. "We even wondered if maybe Cyril was actually her ladyship's child."

"Born on a long vacation in Switzerland and passed off to a childless couple?" suggested Sarah with a smile. "Like in a novel? And since the earl is childless, the poor outcast finds himself the lord of the manor?"

"I know it sounds silly, but I imagine these things do happen," said Lucy. "Especially when you consider how much morals have changed in recent years. When Lady Wickham was a girl an unwed mother was a social outcast."

"Don't forget. It can work the other way around, you know," said Robert after draining his mug. "We don't know who Cyril's father was. There's a long tradition in this country of the young titled gentlemen interfering with the pretty little maids."

"Robert!" chided his wife with a smile. "Such thoughts! You ought to know better!"

"You mean I ought to know my place," he said, rising from his chair. "And I'm afraid that right now, the place I ought to be is at my desk working on my sermon." He paused. "I've got to say, you ladies have given me much to think about, and I thank you."

"It's we who should thank you," said Sue, struggling to rise from the sling chair and finally getting a hand from Robert.

"It's been lovely," said Lucy, also needing a hand to extract herself from the chair.

"I keep telling Robert we need new chairs, but he says these remind him of his childhood," said Sarah.

"My da used to bring them when we went to Brighton. It was a summer ritual."

"It's nice to have happy childhood memories," said Lucy.

"Indeed," said Robert. " I don't think Cyril had a happy childhood."

"Not that an unhappy childhood excuses the bad choices he made," said Sarah.

"It doesn't excuse them, but perhaps it helps us understand," said Robert. "And to understand all is to forgive all."

"He's hopeless," said Sarah, watching as her husband walked across the lawn and back to the church. "Absolutely hopeless."

Lucy and Sue thanked Sarah for the tea and headed back to the manor, grateful for the trees that shaded the path.

"You know," began Lucy, "maybe we've got things wrong. We

keep expecting Harrison to break down in grief over her son's death, but maybe she really is a cold-blooded monster. Maybe this faithful servant act is just that, an act."

"Lucy, you really do have a mind like a sewer," said Sue, clucking her tongue.

"I'm taking that as a compliment," said Lucy. "It's what makes me a good reporter, not accepting the first thing I hear as gospel truth."

"So you think Harrison is really some sort of Mrs. Danvers character who makes life a misery for her mistress?" She chuckled. "Somehow I don't see Lady Wickham as a gullible Rebecca."

"Appearances can be deceiving," said Lucy, carefully negotiating a stile. "Don't you think it's odd that Lady Wickham has been confined to her room for days? Maybe she's a prisoner, and Harrison brings up these huge trays of food and eats them herself right in front of her. The poor old thing might be fading away, denied sustenance by her cruel servant."

"Well," said Sue, after negotiating the stile herself, "since you're writing a far-fetched romance, maybe someone in the family is trying to do away with Lady Wickham and has enlisted Harrison to help, promising her a nice pension and a seaside cottage."

"It's a lovely thought," said Lucy, plucking a long piece of grass and pulling off the seed heads one by one, "but Poppy and Perry seemed truly upset about the old woman's situation. Why would they want to get rid of her?"

"Maybe it's not either of them. Maybe it's Desi or Flora or Gerald."

"But you still haven't come up with a motive. What would any of them possibly gain by knocking off the old bird?"

"She must know something!" exclaimed Sue, seizing on the idea. "A terrible secret that will ruin everything. Like the old earl got Harrison pregnant and Cyril was his love child, who will inherit the title and the whole caboodle."

They stepped out of the shade and onto the huge lawn that surrounded the manor. It stood on a slight rise, dominating the landscape with its three pointy towers piercing the sky. As they looked, a dark cloud passed in front of the sun, casting the ancient castle in shadow, and it suddenly seemed quite a forbidding, even menacing, place.

"You know, there's supposed to be an oubliette in the basement somewhere," said Sue. "Perry told me. It's a hole in the ground where you lock up somebody you want to forget and leave them to die."

"I know what an oubliette is," said Lucy, shuddering at the idea. "I suppose there's been a lot of strife and bloodshed through the years, considering the family's long history. I took a course in English history in college and I can tell you, it wasn't pretty."

"I watched *The Tudors*," said Sue as they began the long march across the lawn.

They trudged along under the hot sun, discovering that while the lawn looked to be a smooth expanse, it actually undulated and contained a few surprises, including a hidden copse of trees.

"Let's go that way," suggested Lucy. "It will get us out of the sun for a little bit, anyway."

"I could use a bit of a rest," admitted Sue. "These are new sandals and they're not quite broken in."

Lucy glanced down at the bejeweled flip-flops Sue was wearing and contrasted them with her sensible athletic shoes. "There's nothing to them. How can they hurt?"

"It's the part that goes between my toes," said Sue.

"Well, perhaps there's a bench in among those trees and we can sit a bit," said Lucy.

When they reached the wooded area, they discovered it held an ancient walled garden. They pushed open the gate. The garden was largely given over to weeds but did contain a lichen-stained stone bench.

"It's just like *The Secret Garden*," said Lucy, sitting down beside Sue. "I loved that book when I was a girl."

"Maybe Flora will restore it," said Sue, who had removed one of the sandals and was rubbing the space between her big toe and its neighbor. "It would give her something to think about besides not eating."

"We can suggest it when we get back," said Lucy, watching as Sue began working on the other foot. "Do you have blisters?"

"Not yet, but I'm working on them," said Sue, waving away a mosquito.

"We'll be eaten alive if we stay here," said Lucy, slapping at one of the bloodsuckers that had landed on her arm. "Can you walk?"

"I'll go barefoot," said Sue, slipping her fingers through the straps of her sandals and standing up. "I don't think they have snakes here, do they?"

"Just watch where you step," advised Lucy, pulling open the gate and discovering Gerald on the other side.

"Oh!" she exclaimed. "You startled me!"

"What in damnation are you doing here?" he demanded, blocking the opening in the wall.

Looking over his shoulder, Lucy saw Vickie walking across the lawn toward the house.

"We were just resting a moment," said Sue, holding up her sandals. "My feet were killing me."

"Serves you right," declared Gerald, "wearing foolish things like that."

"We were just leaving," said Lucy, hoping that Gerald would take the hint and move aside so they could leave the walled garden.

"Leaving, that's what women are good at," said Gerald. "She's leaving, too." He cocked his head in Vickie's direction. "All your sort care about is money. No contracts, no Vickie. That's what she told me." He fumed and shook his walking stick right in front of Sue's face. "Can you believe it? After . . . well, everything I did for her. Damned ungrateful. No notion of fair play whatsoever." He humphed. "And they call yours *the fair sex*. Nothing fair about any of you!"

"It must be getting on to cocktail time," said Sue, glancing at her watch.

"Rather early, isn't it?" said Lucy, who knew it was only lunchtime.

Gerald was having none of that. "Must be five o'clock somewhere," he said, turning abruptly and marching off.

Lucy collapsed against the gateway. "Good thinking," she said, congratulating Sue. "I thought he was going to start whacking us with that stick of his."

"What do you suppose Vickie did?" mused Sue in a low voice as they followed him across the lawn.

"I think it's pretty obvious," replied Lucy. "I think he thought she was interested in him, but she was really only interested in closing some sort of sponsorship deal."

"Poppy was dead set against that, wasn't she?"

"So Poppy nixed his chances with Vickie," concluded Lucy. "I see rough waters ahead. How many more days till we go home?"

"Three, sweetie. Only three."

Lucy sighed. "Well, I've got to say, life here among the blue bloods isn't at all what I expected."

Chapter Nineteen

As Lucy and Sue drew closer to the manor, they heard the wail of a siren and quickened their pace, fearing some sort of accident or perhaps a fire. When they reached the drive, they saw an ambulance arrive with its siren blaring and lights flashing.

"Probably one of the visitors fell ill," said Sue. When the ambulance continued past the visitor's entrance where a handful of people turned to watch as it turned into the gate to the private stable yard, she changed her mind. "Do you think it's Lady Wickham? Maybe she isn't faking like we thought and is really sick. She could have had a heart attack or stroke."

"I have no idea," said Lucy, quickening her pace. "Accidents can happen to anyone. I hope it's not serious."

When they entered the private yard, however, they saw the EMTs were already carrying someone out on a stretcher and loading the blanket-covered person into the ambulance. Poppy was a step or two behind, clutching a sweater and her purse as she hurried to accompany the victim in the ambulance. In a matter of moments, the doors were slammed shut and the ambulance took off, slowly at first but picking up speed as soon as it cleared the gate in the stable yard wall.

Perry was standing in the doorway, watching anxiously as the ambulance departed. They hurried up to him.

"What happened?" asked Sue.

"Flora overdosed," he said, his face white.

Lucy was shocked, but not surprised. Realizing that Flora's addiction to drugs explained a lot about the girl's condition—and perhaps about Cyril's presence at the manor.

"How awful," said Sue.

"Will she be all right?" asked Lucy.

"I think it's really bad," said Perry. "Desi found her. He's pretty shaken up."

They followed Perry into the great room where Desi was slumped over the sink, filling a glass with water.

"Thank heaven you found her," Perry told him, wrapping his arm around his nephew's shoulders.

Desi carefully set the glass down on the counter and embraced Perry; the two men clung together for a long moment.

Desi pulled away, shaking his head. "Thank God she's into vinyl. She got this old turntable. Unearthed it from the attic, I think. She insisted the sound was better, richer. She was really into it. When the record stuck and Nina Simone was singing the same phrase over and over, I went in her room to see what was going on and there she was, lying on the floor." He paused. "I've been around drugs enough to recognize an overdose. I only hope I was in time. I shouldn't have waited so long before checking on her."

"You can't blame yourself," said Lucy. "You did the right thing."

"I was so mad at her. I kept thinking she should get off her butt and fix the damn thing. It was driving me crazy," he said, staring at the glass of water.

"How long do you think she was out?" asked Perry.

"The LP was about halfway through when it stuck," answered Desi, finally picking up the glass and taking a long drink.

"So maybe fifteen minutes at the most?" said Sue, estimating the time.

"She might have started the record and then shot up afterwards," said Lucy. "It may have been only a few minutes."

"However long it was, it was too long," said Desi.

Full of bluster, his father came into the room.

"What's this? Quimby tells me Flora's overdosed? They took her in an ambulance and Poppy went, too."

"And I'm going, too," said Desi, setting down the glass. "I can't stand waiting here."

"I'll drive," said Perry. "You're in no shape—"

"He's in no shape? What's that supposed to mean?" demanded Gerald, waving his walking stick in his son's face.

"Back off, Gerald," said Perry. "Desi found her. It's thanks to him that she's in the hospital."

"It's thanks to him that she's in this mess in the first place, you mean," thundered Gerald, practically nose to nose with Desi. "Where do you think she got the drugs? From this artsy-fartsy ballerina, that's who!" he yelled, stabbing his finger into Desi's chest. "Actors and dancers and rock and rollers, they're all dope fiends and you can't tell me any different. Anybody who reads the papers knows they're always overdosing."

Desi was shaking his head. "I knew . . . no, I suspected she was using, but I didn't know for sure. And you're right. I have seen a lot of people, some of them friends, get in trouble with drugs, but I was not getting drugs for Flora. I've seen how much damage that stuff can do and I stay clear of it."

Gerald didn't seem convinced, but he was less agitated, merely clutching the walking stick and occasionally lifting it and then thumping it on the floor. "Damned foolish girl," he declared. "You'd think she'd know better."

"Mother shouldn't be alone at the hospital," said Desi. "Are you coming?"

Gerald considered the matter for a moment. "No. You and Perry go. I'll hold the fort here."

"There's bound to be press," said Perry as he and Desi crossed the room toward the doorway. "You'd better have some sort of statement ready."

"Damned nosey bastards!" thundered Gerald. "I'm not saying anything to anybody. It's none of their business."

"Righto," said Perry, giving them a curt little wave of farewell.

As soon as they left, Lucy turned to Gerald. "Is there something we can get you? Something we can do?"

"Sorry about all this," he replied, seemingly at a loss now that there was no one to yell at. "Nothing to do but to carry on, I suppose. I know what I'd like—a stiff whiskey. How about you girls?"

"I could use a glass of wine," said Sue, sliding on to a chair.

"I could, too," admitted Lucy as Gerald took a bottle of chardonnay out of the refrigerator.

They were an awkward little group, sitting together at the big scrubbed pine table with their drinks. After a few minutes of silence, Lucy got up and opened the refrigerator, thinking she could make some sort of meal. She found some frozen pizzas in the freezer and asked if anyone would like some.

"I hate to admit it," said Sue, "but I am starving."

The phone rang and Gerald answered it, listened a moment, and then slammed it back on its hook. "Damned impertinent," he fumed, draining his drink. Then he picked up his walking stick and put on his hat. "I'll eat at the pub," he said, marching out.

The phone continued to ring frequently while Lucy and Sue ate their pizzas. They always answered it, hoping for news of Flora, but the callers were all reporters. Their answer was always the same—"no comment"—which got them some rather rude replies.

Lucy was shocked to discover that journalists in England seemed to behave quite differently from their American colleagues.

"I wish we could turn the phone off," she said after a particularly nasty exchange.

"I'll answer and give them what-for," said Harrison, who had come into the kitchen to prepare Lady Wickham's dinner. "You folks don't need to be bothered with the likes of them."

"Are you sure?" asked Lucy, surprised at this turn of events.

"Never fear, I'm used to these nosey-parkers. They're always calling m'lady, you see," said Harrison, frying up a rather large steak.

"How is Lady Wickham?" asked Lucy. "I understand she hasn't been well lately."

Harrison's eyebrows shot up and she gave Lucy a sharp look. "That's none of your affair," she snapped as the phone rang once again. "And that's exactly what I'm going to tell these Fleet Street muckrakers!"

Lucy decided it would be best not to reveal the fact that she herself was a journalist, even though her muckraking was limited to a small coastal town in Maine, and suggested to Sue that they leave the great room and let Harrison get on with her duties. Although still light outside, they had the garden to themselves since the visitors were gone for the day, so they took a stroll around the formal parterre garden, then paused by the fountain to enjoy the quiet.

It didn't take long, however, for the mosquitoes to discover them and they decided to go inside.

"You know," said Sue as they approached the big house, "I think this is the lull before the storm. I bet all hell will break loose tomorrow."

Her words hardly seemed prophetic when Perry greeted them with a big smile the next morning. "Good news!" he announced as they arrived in the great room for breakfast. "Flora's going to be fine."

"That's wonderful," said Lucy, accepting the mug of coffee he'd poured for her.

"What a relief," said Sue, taking her mug over to the table and sitting down.

"She's going to have to stay in hospital for a day or two"—he paused before delivering the bad news—"which is just as well because the police are coming back to question everyone again."

"I suppose they want to know how she got the heroin," said Sue. "Why don't they just ask her?"

"Doctors have forbidden it," said Perry with a knowing look that Lucy took to mean they had been heavily influenced by Flora's parents.

"Maybe there's a connection to Cyril," said Lucy in a speculative tone. "Maybe he was the dealer. Maybe Cyril was involved with the poor kid who overdosed in the maze . . ."

"I wouldn't be at all surprised if he was," said Perry, who was busy slicing bread and putting the pieces in the toaster. "We're all supposed to gather in the library at ten this morning, just like in an Agatha Christie mystery."

"And all will be revealed," said Lucy.

"I rather doubt it," said Perry, leaning against the counter and cradling a mug in his hands while waiting for the toast to brown. "Sergeant Izzy there isn't as sharp as Miss Marple and the inspector is certainly no Hercule Poirot."

Lucy did feel a bit like a character in a mystery novel when she and Sue went to the library at the appointed time and found everyone, including Lady Wickham, gathered there.

She was dressed in one of her usual flower-printed chiffon dresses, her dyed hair had been touched up, and if she truly had been sick, it seemed she had certainly made a quick recovery. She was scolding Inspector Hennessy, telling him in no uncertain terms that he had no business telling her what to do.

"I am the daughter of a marquess and the wife of an earl and I do not intend to allow someone like you to poke and pry into my private life."

"Lady Wickham hasn't been well," said Harrison, aware that the inspector was not sympathetic to this line of argument. "It would be best if she could rest in her room until she is needed for questioning."

"My health is not the issue," declared Lady Wickham, contrary as ever. "What I mean is that I am quite obviously above suspicion and I do not wish to waste time in pointless conversation when I have better things to do."

"You are not above the law, even if you are a countess," began Hennessy, glaring at the old woman.

"We will be happy to accommodate your ladyship," said Sgt. Matthews, interrupting her boss. "We will speak with you only if we feel it necessary after we've completed all the interviews." She paused. "Will that be agreeable?"

"I suppose it will have to do," said Lady Wickham, attempting to look down her nose at the sergeant and failing, due to the young woman's superior height.

"Now, please take a seat with the others as the inspector wishes to speak to all of you together."

"I don't imagine we'll need to keep you long," said Hennessy, placing himself in front of the fireplace and facing the assembled group, who were seated on three sofas. Gerald and Poppy, as well as Lady Wickham, were all on the center sofa, opposite the fireplace. Harrison stood protectively behind her ladyship. Willoughby, Quimby, and Vickie were on the inspector's right, and Sue, Lucy, and Perry were on the left. Winifred, wearing an ankle cast, was standing to one side, along with Sgt. Matthews. Lucy thought it might be her imagination, but she sensed an air of nervous expectation.

"I'm taking the rather unusual step of speaking with you as a group," began Hennessy, "because I believe recent events have made clear the need for you to come together as a community and to cooperate with this investigation. A young woman has nearly died and some of you had knowledge that, had you shared with us, might have prevented this terrible situation."

He studied the group, making eye contact with each member, and didn't find much encouragement, so he continued. "This young woman, a lovely young woman, seemed to have everything going for her. A loving family. A privileged life. No money worries. Acceptance at a top university. An aristocratic pedigree. But for some reason she became involved with drugs to the point of becoming addicted."

This got a reaction as Poppy gave a little gasp.

Hennessy was quick to press the point. "You can play the denial game and pretend that this was simply a one-time thing and she made a near fatal mistake, but the facts do not support that theory. Whatever the reason, this lovely young woman became entangled in the world of drugs and some of you knew what was happening and did nothing."

"I knew," said Vickie, blurting out the words. "She was getting the heroin from Cyril, the dead guy. Sometimes the kid Eric made the delivery. He worked for Cyril."

Hearing this, Lucy turned to see Harrison's reaction, but the lady's maid remained stone-faced and apparently unmoved as Vickie continued speaking.

"She even had me pawn some jewelry for her so she could pay him when she got in debt. She couldn't do without it, and when he died . . . well, she must've got some bad stuff off the street in Oxford. That's why she overdosed."

Lucy and Sue exchanged a long glance, wondering if Flora hadn't been meeting her tutor as she claimed on the day she drove them to Oxford, but had been buying drugs instead.

"What do you mean, got it in Oxford?" demanded Gerald. "She hasn't left the manor for days. You were in Oxford yesterday, though, weren't you? You were the one who got the bad drugs."

Vickie looked as if she'd been slapped in the face, and then her face crumpled and she burst into tears. "I did and I'm so sorry. I didn't know. How could I know? She was so desperate . . ."

"Finally, I think we're making some progress," said Hennessy. "In addition, it has come to my attention that a number of valuable items are missing from the manor. Isn't that so?" he continued, giving a nod to Winifred.

"Yes. I haven't had time to complete my inventory—I've had to work off an older and incomplete one—but a cursory examination reveals that numerous pieces are missing, mostly from rarely used rooms on the upper stories. These include a small Cezanne, conservatively estimated to be worth at least a million pounds at auction. A rough estimate of the total value is well over two million."

"Oh, my God," moaned Poppy. "We're ruined."

"It wasn't that stupid girl, was it?" demanded Gerald.

"No, I'm sure not," said Vickie, quick to defend Flora. "She was using her trust fund. She told me it was pretty much gone and that's why she had me pawn some jewelry for her."

"This is unbelievable," said Perry, shaking his head.

"Now I'll be speaking to each of you individually, and I want you to examine your consciences and your memories and tell me anything that you think might have any relevance at all. An operation of this scope couldn't take place without somebody noticing something . . ."

It was then that the door opened and the vicar burst in, his face alight with joy. "I have wonderful news," he began, then sensing the tense situation, switched gears. "Oh, my goodness, do forgive me. I was so happy to hear that Flora will be all right. That hasn't changed, has it?"

"No, no," said Hennessy. "The young lady will recover."

"Praise be to God," said the vicar. "And no thanks to me. I should have spoken up about Cyril. I gave him the benefit of the doubt, which I now realize was a mistake."

"Perhaps you'd like to share what you know," said Hennessy in an authoritative tone.

"Well," began the vicar with a sympathetic nod to Harrison, "Hoxton is a tough environment and Cyril did what most people do in that situation—he did what he had to in order to survive. He had a gang of sorts and they started out stealing handbags from old ladies and beating up anybody who wasn't properly British. It was all about the group, about a group being stronger than one person. As they got older, the gang became less important. Some of them had families, a few got sent to jail. Cyril, however, got involved in the drug scene, first using and then selling. I had a run-in with him when he tried to recruit boys from the church youth group and I'm sad to say he was successful with young Eric Starkey. I lost track of Cyril and I must admit it was quite a shock when I ran into him here . . . at the manor, of all places."

Hennessy nodded. "Somebody was so shocked that they killed him."

"But it wasn't me," said the vicar, stepping beside Harrison and taking her hand in his.

Much to Lucy's surprise, the lady's maid didn't snatch her hand away and tears came to her eyes, causing her to blink furiously. Robert then made the sign of the cross on her forehead and gave her a benediction. When he was finished and the amen was said, she quickly wiped her eyes and resumed her previous stone-faced expression.

"But what brought you here today?" asked Perry. "You said you had wonderful news."

"Oh, yes, I almost forgot," said Robert as the sparkle returned to his eyes. "When I was in Hoxton, I made the acquaintance of a prominent couple who became interested in my work with the young people there. I have stayed in touch with them through the years, and asked them if they would like to attend the opening of the hat show. I'm happy to say that Kate and Wills—"

"Oh, my," gasped Lady Wickham, collapsing in a dead faint.

Chapter Twenty

All attention was focused on Lady Wickham, who did not regain consciousness for some time, despite Harrison's efforts. The lady's maid rebuffed all offers of help and continued to chafe the old woman's wrists and to wave an ancient vial of smelling salts under her nose, to no avail.

"I really think we have to call for an ambulance," Poppy finally said after some moments had passed. "Perhaps she's had a stroke or something."

"Shall I put in a call?" asked Sgt. Matthews, indicating her walkie-talkie. "I can have the EMTs here in minutes."

That seemed to do the trick. Lady Wickham's eyelids fluttered and she made a great show of regaining consciousness. "Dear me," she moaned. "What happened?"

"You just took a turn. Nothing to worry about m'lady," cooed Harrison. "It was the vicar's announcement that took you by surprise."

"Yes, it was quite a shock," Lady Wickham said, nodding. "Imagine, a black man like the vicar on intimate terms with the Duke and Duchess of Cambridge. I never would have dreamt such a thing was possible."

"Really, Aunt, this is the twenty-first century," said Perry. "The royals are well aware that Britain is changing."

"It's rather more than that," said the vicar, looking somewhat amused. "The prince is committed to carrying on his mother's good works."

"Dear me," moaned Lady Wickham, sinking back on to the pillowed back of the sofa. "Don't mention that dreadful hussy Diana to me."

"Well, it's great news, Vicar, and I for one am terribly grateful, not to mention pleased and excited," said Perry. "I have a great deal to do to prepare for a royal visit." He turned to the inspector. "Do you need me? Is it all right if I get on with things in the long gallery?"

"No problem at all," said the inspector, consulting his notebook. "I think we'd like to begin this morning with Maurice Willoughby." He raised his head and looked around the library expectantly, but there was no sign of the librarian.

"I wonder where he's got to?" said Quimby. "Shall I go look for him?"

"No need," said the inspector, giving Sgt. Matthews a meaningful glance, which resulted in her leaving the library. "I'll begin with you, Mr. Quimby."

"As for the rest of us?" asked Poppy. "I have quite a few things I need to attend to."

"Just don't leave the manor. I'm sure I'll be able to find you when I need to," said the inspector.

"Good," said Perry, taking Robert's arm. "Would you like to come along with me and give me the necessary contact information? I imagine I will have to talk to Kensington Palace."

"I don't have it with me. I was so eager to share the good news that I didn't think to bring it. I'll have to go back to the vicarage and text you," said Robert, casting a questioning look at the inspector.

The inspector gave him an approving nod, then indicated to Quimby that he should follow him to the adjoining little library that had been prepared for the interviews. The group gradually dispersed, going their separate ways.

"I think I'll go along to the long gallery and help Perry," said Sue. "Do you want to come?"

Lucy, who was curious about Willoughby's disappearance, declined the invitation. She recalled Bill telling her that Doug Fitzpatrick wasn't the man he claimed to be and she had a similar suspicion about Willoughby. "I think I'll take another look at that perennial border," she said, telling a little white lie. "I want to take some photos so I don't forget how they got that fabulous look."

"Planning something similar back home?" asked Sue, raising an eyebrow.

"Not on quite the same scale," admitted Lucy with a shrug, "but I think I could borrow a few ideas."

When she got outside, however, she didn't head in the direction of the fabulous serpentine perennial border that was the envy of gardeners throughout the world, but instead followed the shady path through the woods to a cluster of cottages that housed various manor employees, including Willoughby. The cottages were joined in a row like townhouses, with walled gardens to the rear and a road in front where a few modest cars were parked. Lucy wasn't sure exactly which cottage was Willoughby's, but when she walked around back she peeked through an open gate and spotted a woman hanging wash on a clothesline.

Taking a closer look, she recognized Sally, the maid who took care of their rooms at the manor. "Hi!" she called. "It's a great day for drying."

"It is indeed," said Sally, whose hair was blowing in the breeze. "I have a machine, but I like to dry my clothes on the line. They smell so nice when I bring them in."

"Me too," said Lucy. "I like nothing better than to see my pretty sheets flapping in the breeze on a sunny day."

"It's the simple pleasures that are the best," said Sally. "Sometimes I feel sorry for them that's up at the manor. It's all very grand, but they don't get to enjoy the little things." She pointed to a flowerpot that contained a lush geranium. "When you've got millions of plants, all flowering at once, you don't really see them, do you? I've had this geranium for years and I bring it in every winter and put it out every summer. This plant and me are old friends."

"I have some like that, too," said Lucy. "I have my mother's spider plant. It must be more than twenty years old, since she's been gone for some time."

"Oh, I am sorry," said Sally.

"Thank you," said Lucy. "You know, I'm actually looking for Mr. Willoughby. He's wanted up at the manor, but I'm not sure which cottage is his."

"Mr. Willoughby hurried out some time ago. It looked like he was setting out on a hike. He had a backpack and a stick." She paused. "He gave me a big wave."

"Interesting," said Lucy. "Is this his day off?"

"Not usually. He has the weekends. A lot of folks who work at the manor are needed on the weekends because that's the busiest time with the most visitors, but he doesn't have anything to do with them, and I think they like to show the library sometimes, too. They have special behind the scenes tours on the weekends. That's what they call them, and they charge an extra ten pounds." She grinned. "That Poppy doesn't miss much. She's quite the businesswoman."

"Yes, indeed," said Lucy. "Well, I guess I'll be off. It's been nice talking to you."

"Same here," said Sally, lifting her empty laundry basket and carrying it inside.

Lucy walked along, wondering if Willoughby was going for a hike or a quick exit and wishing she could get a peek inside his cottage. She still wasn't sure which was his. She had noticed a few window curtains twitching as she passed, which she took to mean she was under observation.

The trip wasn't wasted, she decided, as she intended to tell Hennessy what Sally had told her about Willoughby's departure. The historian had always topped her list of suspects in the murder because he seemed the most likely person to know about the secret room, apart from the family. She was mindful of Bill's discovery that Doug Fitzpatrick was not the person he pretended to be, and remembered a couple incidents when Willoughby seemed to have let his mask, or rather his accent, slip. She doubted an educated librarian would ask for a *cuppa* tea, and she was pretty sure she'd heard a bit of a Cockney twang once or twice. Not that she was any expert on British accents, she admitted, thinking that perhaps she was being overly hasty in suspecting Willoughby.

There was also the fact of Flora's overdose, which rather changed the equation. She remembered Flora and Desi saying how they had enjoyed exploring the manor when they were kids, and it seemed likely that they might have discovered the secret room. She didn't think Flora could have succeeded in killing Cyril and hiding his body by herself, but she and Desi were close and he might have helped his sister. Or he might have discovered that Cyril was her supplier and decided to eliminate him.

These were the thoughts that occupied her mind as she walked along the path, intending to make good her avowed intention of studying the perennial border, when she heard angry male voices. Most probably a couple gardeners voicing some sort of disagreement, she thought, pausing to listen and recognizing Robert's deep bass voice.

Giving in to curiosity she crept closer, confident that a tall hedge would conceal her, and peered through a gap in the greenery to see who the vicar was arguing with. She wasn't all that surprised when she saw that it was Willoughby, and that her suspicions about him were correct.

"I know you, and you're no more Maurice Willoughby than I'm Saint Peter. You're Bert Winston, right? You were one of Cyril's boys back in Hoxton, weren't you? And you did time for it, too, as I recall. You were delivering a warning to a Pakistani kid, Khalid somebody, wasn't it? You beat him to a bloody pulp."

"Don't be daft," snapped Willoughby. "I don't know what you're talking about."

"You didn't go to Southampton or Reading or any university. You took some jailhouse courses and watched a few movies and you've been putting on a big act. I suppose you had plenty of time to practice a posh accent—" Robert's accusation ended rather suddenly with a series of thuds and grunts.

When Lucy rounded the hedge, she saw the two men engaged in a fistfight. She ducked back behind the hedge and reached for her cell phone, but the only number she could remember was Sue's. She began punching it in with trembling fingers but must have done something wrong because the darn thing didn't work.

The thuds and grunts had escalated and included groans. She knew she had to get help fast, before Willoughby killed Robert . . . or Robert killed Willoughby. Lucy had rarely seen men fight, except in movies and TV, and she found it terrifying. Somehow she had to stop it. The phone was hopeless so she decided the only thing to do was to intervene. She plucked up all her courage and ran around the hedge, yelling, "Stop it, stop it!" at the very moment Willoughby delivered a roundhouse punch that knocked out Robert.

She instinctively ran toward Robert, intending to help him, but Willoughby blocked her and she realized her danger. She turned to run and dashed for a gap in the hedge but soon discovered she had taken the wrong direction and was in the maze. She could hear him panting behind her as she ran, trying desperately to remember if it was three lefts and then all rights or the other way around. Finding herself completely confused, she ran blindly, taking each turn as it came and miraculously found the exit. She was almost there when she took a terrific blow to her back and fell flat on her face. Willoughby's enormous weight landed on her back. She tried to free herself, but his hands were around her neck. Struggling to breathe, she scratched at the hands in vain.

Suddenly, a dark shadow seemed to float through the air, only to land with a thud, and she was able to breathe again.

Scrambling to her feet, she saw Desi deliver a serious punch to Willoughby's jaw and he crumpled to the ground.

"What was that?" gasped Lucy, her hands at her neck.

"A grand jeté," said Desi. "I needed to cover a lot of ground, fast." He shrugged. "Nothing to it, really. I do that ballet jump all the time."

Willoughby regained consciousness just as several uniformed police officers arrived and took him into custody. Lucy, along with Robert and Desi, followed the group back to the manor where several official vehicles were parked. Inspector Hennessy informed Willoughby of the charges against him, namely theft and murder, and he was bundled into one of the vehicles and taken away. They were watching the car disappear down the drive when Harrison was brought out of the house in the custody of Sgt. Matthews and a uniformed police woman, followed by Poppy and

Gerald, who both looked quite solemn. Hennessy had his charges ready—conspiracy to commit theft and interference with police.

"What's this all about?" demanded Desi.

"It seems that Harrison and Willoughby were in cahoots, stealing bits and pieces from the manor," said Poppy. "One of the dealers who'd been buying the pieces identified them."

"What about Aunt Millicent?" asked Desi. "Flora rather suspected she was part of the ring, perhaps even the head of it."

"If so, we do not have a case against Lady Wickham," said the inspector, getting into his car and giving the driver a nod.

"Interesting morning," said Gerald, adding a *humph* before marching off.

"Where's he going?" asked Lucy.

"To the barns," said Desi with a smile. "Whenever things get tough, Dad goes to check on the livestock."

Poppy wasn't about to seek solace with the livestock, however, and turned to Robert. "You knew Cyril was engaged in selling drugs and never thought to warn us?" she demanded. "How could you do that in good conscience? And you a vicar, too?"

"I saw him only briefly. He told me his mother worked here and convinced me he'd changed his ways." Robert gave a rueful smile. "Being a man of faith, I took him at his word."

"Well, it would have saved us a lot of grief and sadness," said Poppy.

"I know, and I regret it," said Robert. "I have to confess I am more ashamed of my failure to recognize your librarian, Willoughby. I knew him before as Bert Winston . . . when he was in the same gang as Cyril and Eric, but I didn't make the connection. I think I was dazzled by the grand setting and never tumbled to the fact that he wasn't who he pretended to be."

"When did you figure it out?" asked Lucy.

"It was when I came here. I ran into him in the hallway, and something he said when he greeted me got me thinking."

"What was it?" asked Poppy.

"He called me 'Rev' and it took me right back to Hoxton. That's what they called me there." He paused. "Nobody here has ever called me that."

"It certainly wouldn't occur to me," said Poppy. "But why did he kill Cyril? They were old pals, no?"

"They were, and that was a big problem for Willoughby. He'd created a new persona and would have been terrified that Cyril would expose him, revealing his true identity. In fact, knowing Cyril as I do, I imagine he threatened to do exactly that. He might have demanded a cut of the antiques operation or even tried to blackmail him, which would have pushed Willoughby into a corner. He may have felt that killing Cyril was his only option."

"I feel a bit sorry for Willoughby," said Desi. "He worked so hard trying to be upper class, when we're trying not to be."

"What do you mean trying?" asked Poppy. "I'm a worker bee these days and, as you can imagine, I have quite a lot to do."

"C'mon, Mum," said Desi, wrapping an arm around his mother's shoulders. "Call it a day. I'll take you into town and give you lunch at the Ritz. What do you say?"

"I'd be delighted, that's what I say," she replied, giving him a fond pat on the cheek.

"What about you?" Robert asked Lucy as they watched mother and son walk off together. "Are you all right?"

"I am. What about you? I think you better get some ice on that jaw of yours."

"I will. Good thing Sarah's out today. She'd be furious with me."

"Where is she?" asked Lucy.

"Shopping for a dress to wear to the gala opening," said Robert, before striding off in the direction of the vicarage.

Dressed in a gold silk sheath that left one shoulder bare, Sarah did her husband proud at the opening, but it was Lady Wickham who drew the most admiring glances. She was dressed in a black chiffon evening gown topped with a white fur stole and numerous pieces of diamond jewelry, including a magnificent necklace and an enormous tiara.

"It's the Mucklemore Jewel," said Perry in a waspish tone. "She refused to lend it to me for the show and now I know why."

But even Lady Wickham's glory dimmed when Dishy Geoff,

dressed once again as a footman, rapped his stick on the floor and announced, "The Duke and Duchess of Cambridge."

The crowd parted as the Red Sea did for Moses, and everyone, including Lucy and Sue, bowed or curtsied. Even if protocol didn't require bows from Americans, they had discussed the matter in advance and decided that they should adopt the custom of the country they were visiting and had practiced curtseying in front of the mirror in Lucy's room.

Lady Wickham took it upon herself to welcome the royal couple, neatly cutting off Poppy and Gerald, as well as Perry, who were the proper hosts. She rushed forward, coming to an abrupt halt in front of Kate and Wills, plucked up the sides of her voluminous skirt and attempted a deep curtsey that went wrong, and tumbled down onto her knees.

The prince reached down politely and gave her a hand, helping her rise to her feet. "The hat show is called Heads Up! not bottoms up!"

Everyone laughed, even her ladyship.

Epilogue

"The captain has informed me," began the flight attendant's announcement, "that we are preparing for landing. At this time we ask you to turn off all electronic devices. Please return your seats to the upright position, replace the tray tables against the seat backs, and fasten your seatbelts."

"Already," said Sue with a smile, checking her cell phone for texts before turning it off. "The flight home always seems so much quicker."

"In this direction the clock is our friend," said Lucy. "It's only a little bit past six and we left at four, right?"

"Crazy," said Sue, peering out the window as they flew over Boston Harbor.

Lucy leaned back in her seat, mentally reviewing the purchases she'd made in the shops at Heathrow: a bottle of single malt scotch for Bill, Cath Kidston tote bags for her friends Pam and Rachel, Burberry cologne for Elizabeth and Zoe, and a Paddington bear for Patrick. It was that last thought of Patrick, far away in Alaska, that prompted a deep sigh.

"Didn't you have a good time in jolly old?" asked Sue, a note of concern in her voice as she gave Lucy's hand a squeeze.

Lucy was suddenly overcome with gratitude and affection for

her best friend. "Oh, Sue, I can't thank you enough. This trip was wonderful. I feel so much better. It was just what I needed."

"I'm really glad you came," said Sue. "It was good to have a friend, considering everything that happened. I wouldn't have liked to be there on my own, what with the murder and everything."

"It was quite an adventure," said Lucy as the plane began to descend. "But now it's back to reality."

"It's good to be home, right?" prompted Sue.

"Oh, yeah, but I'm kind of nervous about it, too. I don't want to sink back into depression, you know?"

"I'm sure you won't," said Sue when the wheels of the jet hit the tarmac with a thud.

"I wish I could be as confident as you," admitted Lucy as the plane taxied to the gate.

It seemed to take a long time for the plane to empty, and there was some sort of problem with the baggage carousel that delayed the arrival of their bags, but Sue used the time to check her messages. She didn't seem to notice that the friendly beagle making the rounds of the baggage area with a Customs officer was taking an awful lot of interest in her bags. That meant a nervous delay at Customs as her case was x-rayed and her stash of Cadbury chocolate bars was discovered.

"The ones in the UK are better tasting. Everyone says so," she told the officer. "Would you like one?"

"Now that would be against regulations," he said with a smile as he handed her the suitcase with the chocolate bars inside. "Have a nice day."

"That was close," muttered Sue as they headed for the big double doors that opened to the ARRIVALS area. "I was afraid that they'd confiscate my Cadburys or maybe even arrest me for smuggling."

"I don't think you should have tried to bribe him," said Lucy as the doors slid open and revealed a crowd of people—lovers and families and friends waiting to greet their dear ones.

"Makes you wish someone was here for us," said Lucy, who knew they had a long drive ahead back to Tinker's Cove.

"Hold on," said Sue, "I think I see—"

"Patrick!" screamed Lucy, spotting her grandson waiting for her along with his father, Toby, and grandfather, Bill. People stood aside as she ran to embrace Patrick, who had grown so much and was quite the handsome five-year-old.

"I c-can't b-believe it!" she stammered. "What are you doing here?"

"We spent the day in Boston," explained Bill. "We went to the Aquarium and the Children's Museum, all the time following the plane's progress on the British Air website, and then Sue texted us about Customs and gave us the green light so we skedaddled over here. I gotta tell you the traffic was brutal."

"No," she said, turning to Toby. "Why aren't you in Alaska?"

"The agency sent me to take a course at the university. It's eight weeks so I brought the family. The house is rented so we'll have to stay with you. In fact, Molly's there now. That's okay, right?"

Bill scratched his beard. "It's going to be awfully crowded. . . ."

Sue looked doubtful. "There'll be so much laundry, and think of the meals and the grocery bills. . . ."

Lucy, who was holding Patrick's hand, stared at them in disbelief. Then seeing their suppressed smiles, she realized they were teasing. "Oh, you guys!" she exclaimed, rolling her eyes. "It's going to be wonderful. A full house! I can't wait to get home. Let's go!"

With family tensions intensifying in Tinker's Cove, part-time reporter Lucy Stone could really use some time off the grid. But after she RSVPs to an unconventional celebration on remote Holiday Island, Lucy realizes that disconnecting from reality comes at a deadly price . . .

Lucy doesn't know what to expect as she arrives on a private Maine island owned by eccentric billionaire Scott Newman, only that the exclusive experience should make for a very intriguing feature story. An avid environmentalist, Scott has stripped the isolated property of modern conveniences in favor of an extreme eco-friendly lifestyle. A trip to Holiday Island is like traveling back to the nineteenth century, and it turns out other residents aren't exactly enthusiastic about living without cell service and electricity . . .

Before Lucy can get the full scoop on Scott, she is horrified to find one of his daughters dead at the bottom of a seaside cliff. The young woman's tragic end gets pinned as an accident, but a sinister plot unfolds when there's a sudden disappearance . . .

Stuck on a clammy island with murder suspects aplenty, the simple life isn't so idyllic after all. Now Lucy must tap into the limited resources around her to outwit a cold-blooded killer—before it's lights out for her next!

Please turn the page for an exciting sneak peek of

Leslie Meier's next Lucy Stone mystery

INVITATION ONLY MURDER

now on sale wherever print and e-books are sold!

Chapter One

The little bell on the door to the *Pennysaver* newspaper office in Tinker's Cove, Maine, jangled and Lucy Stone looked up from the story she was writing about the new recycling regulations—paper, glass, and plastic would not be accepted unless clean and separate, no more single stream—to see who had come in, and smiled broadly. It was her oldest and best friend, Sue Finch, looking every bit as stylish and put-together as usual with her dark hair cut in a neat bob, and dressed in her usual summer uniform: striped French fisherman's jersey, black Bermudas, espadrilles, and straw sun hat. Skipping a greeting, Sue pulled an envelope from her straw carry-all with a perfectly manicured hand and declared, "Guess what came in today's mail? It's an invitation to die for!"

Lucy, who was used to playing second fiddle to Sue, raised an inquisitive eyebrow. She was also dressed in her usual summer uniform: a freebie T-shirt from the lumber yard, a pair of cut-off jeans, and neon orange running shoes. She hadn't bothered to style her hair this sunny June morning, thinking that it looked fine, and had missed a stubborn lock in back that curled up like a drake's tail feather. "Do tell," she said, leaning back in her desk chair.

"Just look at the paper," cooed Sue, pulling a square of sturdy card stock out of the velvet-smooth lined envelope. "Hand made. And the lettering is hand-pressed. And, oh, the address on the envelope was done by a calligrapher," she continued, handing the envelope to Lucy. "Trust me, something like this doesn't come cheap."

"Is it a wedding invitation?" asked Lucy, admiring the elaborate, swirling script on the front of the envelope. Turning the envelope over and studying the back she recognized the formally identified senders: Mr. and Mrs. Scott Newman. Everybody in town had heard of the Newmans, who had recently bought an island off the coast and proceeded to hire every contractor in the county to restore the property's long-abandoned buildings, including the magnificent barn that was considered an architectural masterpiece.

"No. It's for a 'night to remember,' that's what they're calling it," replied Sue, handing Lucy the invitation. "It's to celebrate the Newman family's donation of the island to the Coastal Maine Land Trust and to thank all the people who worked on the restoration."

"I bet we're invited, too," said Lucy, whose husband, Bill, a restoration carpenter, had been the lead contractor for the project. "The invitation's probably in the mailbox at home."

"It's going to be fabulous, if this invitation is any indication," said Sue. "No expense spared and believe me, the Newmans have plenty of expense to spare."

Lucy knew all about Scott Newman; she'd written a profile of the billionaire venture capitalist when rumors started floating that he was interested in acquiring Fletcher's Island for his family's summer vacations. When she interviewed him, she'd been somewhat surprised to learn that he was a keen preservationist who was interested in keeping the island completely off the grid and was refusing to install modern innovations, allowing only the original nineteenth-century technology. He planned to collect rainwater in a cistern, use a primitive electric generation system, and to cook on an enormous wood stove, all of which were considered wonderfully advanced when the island was developed by wood tycoon Edward T. Fletcher. When Lucy asked if this wasn't rather impractical, Newman had replied that it was modern life that was impractical, citing scientific studies linking climate change to human activity. "The old ways were much kinder to the environment, and face it, we've only got one planet, there's no Planet B," he declared. "We've got to take care of Earth or we're all doomed."

Some of the locals hired to work on the restoration project had a good laugh over Newman's proclaimed environmental stewardship, as restoring the nineteenth-century structures required using thousands of kilowatts of electricity, provided by gas-greedy portable generators. His insistence on using authentic materials such as lath and horsehair plaster rather than sheetrock, and searching out recycled flooring, windows, and doors, not to mention hardware, had required lots of workers who had to be ferried to and from the island on power boats that burned gallons of fossil fuel. "It's like the cloth versus disposable diapers thing," Bill had told her. "Sure the disposables fill up the landfill, but washing the cloth diapers uses water and energy. It's kind of six of one and half a dozen of the other when it comes to the environment."

Most controversial was the restoration of the immense barn, which alone was estimated to cost at least two million dollars. The huge number of cedar shingles required for the roof and siding had created an industry shortage that sent the price skyrocketing and shook the commodities market. The *Pennysaver* had received numerous letters to the editor protesting the shingle shortage and arguing that there were better ways to spend two million dollars. One writer proposed restoring the sprawling local elementary school, for example, which he claimed was a prime example of nineteen-sixties architecture.

Locals had also refused to be bamboozled by Newman's supposed generosity in donating the island to the land trust, while reserving his right to retain it for his own use, during his lifetime. It was true that he'd also preserved the rights of the Hopkins family, long-term residents of the island, to remain there, but again, only during his lifetime. But while the agreement set limits on how the island could be used and was intended to preserve the island's environment in perpetuity, the gift had come with plenty of strings attached and had garnered a large tax deduction for the Newmans, a fact that many writers of letters to the editor had also pointed out.

Despite the controversy, however, the party was eagerly anticipated by everyone who received an invitation, and that included land trust board members, contractors, local officials, and media, which was pretty much a Who's Who of the entire town. The question that was on everyone's lips, as the big day drew closer, was how were the Newmans going to pull off such a big party while preserving their nineteenth-century lifestyle? Sue Finch wasn't the only one to wonder, "Are we going to have to swim there? And are we all going to be sitting in the dark, huddled around a campfire, toasting wienies on sticks?"

Lucy was pondering that very question when she drove home from work a week or so later and found a rusting and dented old Subaru parked in her driveway. The car was missing a couple of hubcaps, had a crumpled front fender, and the glass on a rear window had been replaced with duct tape and a plastic grocery bag. Continuing her examination with the keen eye of an investigative reporter she noticed the registration was out of date, and so was the required state inspection sticker.

Climbing the porch steps of the antique farmhouse that she and Bill had renovated and entering the kitchen, she was greeted by her aging black Lab, Libby. Arthritis didn't stop Libby from rising stiffly from her comfy dog bed and wagging her tail in welcome, earning her a treat and a pat on the head from Lucy.

Voices could be heard in the adjacent family room and Lucy stuck her head in, curious to learn who owned the Subaru. "Oh, hi, Mom," said her daughter Zoe, quickly disentangling herself from the arms of a shabby-looking fellow with a stubbly three-day beard. "Mom, this is Mike Snider."

Mike didn't bother to get up from the comfy sectional where he was reclining, or even to lift his head from the throw pillow it was resting on. "Hiya," he said, raising one hand and giving a little flap.

Lucy glared at him, taking in his shaved head, tattooed neck, and torn jeans that clearly needed a wash. Worst of all was the T-shirt with a message that was clearly unprintable for a family newspaper like the *Pennysaver.* "Hiya, yourself," said Lucy, turning on her heel and marching out of the room, leaving no doubt that this was a situation that did not meet with her approval.

Back in the kitchen, she got busy on dinner, noisily pulling pots out of cabinets and slamming them down on the stove. She was filling a pasta pot with water when the couple appeared, holding hands, and were met with a low growl from Libby, who watched them through narrowed eyes and flattened ears from her doggy bed. She was clearly considering getting to her feet, painful though it would be, when Mike reached for the knob and pulled the door open. "Catch ya later," he said, before stepping through the doorway. Moments later Lucy heard the roar of the Subaru's unmuffled engine, which sputtered out a few times before catching, and carrying Mike away.

"Who is he? And where did you meet him?" she demanded, turning to face Zoe. Zoe was her youngest, at twenty, and every bit as pretty as her older sisters, Elizabeth and Sara. She shared Elizabeth's dark hair and petite build, but had Sara's peachy skin and pouty lips. Today she was glowing, no doubt the result of her aborted activities on the sectional.

"At school, Mom," she answered, referring to Winchester College, a local liberal arts university where she was a junior currently majoring in French after trying political science, psychology, and art history. She had hopes of joining Elizabeth in Paris, where her older sister was working as an assistant concierge at the toney Cavendish Hotel. "Mike's a TA in the computer science department. He's really smart. Even Sara says so," she added, bolstering her case with a reference to the family's doubting Thomas, who was a grad student at Winchester.

"He might be smart," admitted Lucy, "but he's certainly not socialized. Libby has better manners, and she's a dog."

"He's a little rough around the edges," said Zoe, beaming, "but Libby only gets up to greet you because she knows you'll give her a treat."

"That was unkind," retorted Lucy, bending over the dog and scratching her behind her ears. "You love me, you really, really love me, don't you."

The dog yawned, and settled her chin on her front paws.

"And that car," said Lucy, reverting to the subject at hand. "The registration's elapsed and so has the inspection, which is understandable since I doubt it would pass. It definitely needs a new muffler."

"Mike's got better things to think about than bother with stuff like that, he's working on a computer game that's going to be revolutionary, that's going to change everything."

"Well, if you ask me, he'd be better off taking a shower and changing into clean clothes."

"Oh, you don't understand anything!" declared Zoe, storming up the stairs to her room, where she slammed the door.

"What was that all about?" asked Bill, stepping into the kitchen and kissing his wife on the cheek, before depositing his empty lunch cooler on the counter. Lucy smiled, noticing that Libby didn't get up for him but did manage to thump her tail a few times.

"Zoe's got a new boyfriend," explained Lucy. "A real loser."

"She'll learn," said Bill, opening the refrigerator door and extracting a can of beer. "She's got to figure these things out for herself."

"Just you wait until you meet him," said Lucy, tearing up lettuce for salad. "I bet you'll change your tune then."

Bill sat down at the round golden oak table and popped the tab on his beer. "Whaddya think about this island shindig?" he asked. "I'm not gonna have to wear a jacket and tie, am I?"

"No jackets, no ties," said Lucy, repeating the verdict Sue had handed down when Lucy called for advice. "It's resort casual."